COLD BLOODED

He shook her. "Take me to Dr. Slade."

"I won't."

"I'll kill you too, then I'll find him anyway." He put the hot muzzle of his gun to her head. It burned her skin.

"You want to die unnecessarily?"

"I don't give a damn."

"If you stay with me, I'll let you live."

She hesitated. Looked at Tedescu's body on the floor. Then nodded. She led him to an office with the sign CLINICAL DIRECTOR. He jiggled the locked handle. Fired into the keyhole. Then kicked the door open.

Her father, standing behind his desk, held a gun in one hand and a phone in the other. "Raven knows," he shouted into the mouthpiece, "about Tedescu's plan but his comrades are here—"

"Hang up the phone, Dr. Slade, or I'll kill your daughter."

"She doesn't know anything."

"But you do. Tell us, or watch her die."

Other books by Daniel Keyes:

Novels:

FLOWERS FOR ALGERNON
THE TOUCH
THE FIFTH SALLY

Nonfiction:

THE MINDS OF BILLY MILLIGAN
UNVEILING CLAUDIA: A TRUE STORY OF
   SERIAL MURDER
ALGERNON, CHARLIE AND I: A WRITER'S
   JOURNEY

DANIEL KEYES

THE ASYLUM PROPHECIES

LEISURE BOOKS   NEW YORK CITY

For my wife Aurea and my daughters, Hillary Ann and Leslie Joan, without whose constant encouragement and care this novel would never have been written.

A LEISURE BOOK®

October 2009

Dorchester Publishing Co., Inc.
200 Madison Avenue
New York, NY 10016

ISBN 10: 0-8439-6271-2
ISBN 13: 978-0-8439-6271-0

Visit us online at www.dorchesterpub.com.

"It is a riddle wrapped in a mystery inside an enigma."

—Winston Churchill
Radio Broadcast: 1939

AUTHOR'S NOTE

This is a work of fiction. Although creative license has been taken, the two little-known terrorist organizations portrayed in this novel do exist.

Both Marxist-Leninist groups, one Greek, the other Iranian, were spawned by government-led attacks on university students who were protesting what they considered to be CIA-backed tyrannical regimes.

THE ASYLUM
PROPHECIES

PREFACE

Revolutionary Organization 17 November

On the night of November 17, 1973, Greek students gathered on the grounds of the Athens Polytechnic University, protesting against what they perceived to be the CIA-backed seven-year military dictatorship of Colonel Papadopoulos. Riot police attacked. Army tanks crashed through the gate. Thirty-four students were killed, 800 wounded.

Two years later, Athens CIA station chief Richard Welch was assassinated in front of his wife and driver. The terrorists identified themselves as "Revolutionary Organization 17 November," known as 17N. This was their first retaliation for the attack on November 17.

During the twenty-eight years between 1975 and 2003, 17N committed more than sixty additional deadly attacks against Europeans and Americans, including the assassination in June 2000 of the Athens British military attaché. Unlike Germany's Red Army Faction (RAF), Italy's Red Brigades (BR), and France's Action Direct (AD), not a single 17N member was identified or captured. The counterterrorism agency of the U.S. State Department listed it among the world's most dangerous urban terror groups.

17N, once called the last of Europe's Marxist-Leninist terrorists, still exists.

Mujihadeen-e Kalq

("Holy Jihadists of the People")

On November 4, 1979, a group of Iranian Marxist university students who objected to U.S. influence in Iran, especially the CIA support of the deposed Shah Pahlavi, attacked and helped occupy the American embassy in Teheran. They held sixty-three U.S. diplomats and three other citizens hostage.

At first, the militant students—once estimated to have a following of 500,000—had the support of the postrevolutionary Iranian leadership. But the students opposed Ayatollah Khomeini's theocracy. They demanded a Marxist secular democracy which would grant women equality with men. As a consequence, most—including their leaders—were hunted down, tortured and executed by Iran's Revolutionary Guards. Those who escaped went into hiding. In 1993, Maryam Rajavi was chosen president-elect of the *Mujihadeen-e Kalq*. She helped create a fighting force composed mostly of women.

MEK joined Saddam Hussein in the war against Iran. After the war, they helped Chemical Ali gas thousands of Kurds and Marsh Arabs to death. As a reward, Saddam Hussein granted them sanctuary close to the Iraq-Iran border in a compound called Ashraf. Reduced to a cadre of 3,800, they are now a mostly female-led militia.

When Maryam Rajavi went into exile in France, several

of her devoted women followers immolated themselves in protest.

The State Department named MEK a terrorist organization because of their attacks on American interests. However, the Pentagon—hoping to use them as spies and insurgents in the event of a future war against Iran—have demanded, with the support of several senators, that MEK be removed from the terrorist list. MEK still exists.

In *The Asylum Prophecies* these two terrorist groups form an alliance for a catastrophic attack on our soil.

CHAPTER ONE

Athens, Greece

Raven Slade opened her eyes and blinked at the light filtering through the chicken-wire window. She jumped off her cot and rolled the mattress against the wall. Stood on it tiptoe, craning her neck to catch a glimpse of the outside world. When she saw the Acropolis and Parthenon silhouetted against the setting sun, she slid down and sat cross-legged on the damp mattress. Which asylum was she in this time?

. . . sis, like, i guess we're not in ohio anymore . . .

She hadn't heard that high-pitched voice in her head for a long time. Better to ignore her.

She stared at the bandages on her wrists and gingerly lifted the right one. She stuck her fingernail under the scar and peeled away a crust. Yes, the scab was real. That meant *she* was real. She leaned back against the padded wall and listened for her sister's voice. Nothing. She touched her breasts, waist, thighs, legs. She was herself again. Good to be back.

A female said through the observation slot, "I am coming in, Raven. I must talk to you." The slot closed and the door opened. Nurse Faye Sawyer stepped inside.

She glanced up at the attractive middle-aged woman with

olive-smooth face, dark eyes, hair crowned with a glistening black braid.

"I have come to take you out now, Raven."

"Did my father, like, call off the suicide watch?"

"Attendant on duty reports you are cooperative for past three days."

"So can I do my candy striper bit again?"

"Mr. Jason Tedescu, new patient in infirmary, wants speak with you. Says you was his best drama student at Waybridge University."

"Sure I'll see him."

"First come clean yourself and dress." In the shower room, nurse Sawyer helped her bathe and put fresh bandages on her wrists. When Sawyer held out her candy-cane outfit, she smiled. "I think of Christmas when I wear this."

"You bring smiles to wounded soldiers and sick people. You always center of attention. Before you go visit Mr. Tedescu, I fix you hair to look nice."

Her scalp tingled as Sawyer brushed hard. After Mother killed herself, no one else ever brushed her hair. She closed her eyes. When Sawyer put the brush down, she whispered, "Don't stop."

"You look pretty, Raven."

She opened her eyes and saw blonde hairs on her skirt. "You pulled out my hair, bitch!"

"Little bit came out. Is normal."

She squeezed her right hand into a fist and swung around to punch, but Sawyer caught it in midair and twisted her arm. "Control you self, Raven, or I write in your chart you still talk with your dead sister."

"No! I don't want my father to lock me up again."

"You be calm?"

"I promise."

"You promise many times. Show both hands."

She uncrossed her fingers and brought her hands around in front. "See?"

"All right. We go to infirmary."

She followed Sawyer down the corridor, then stopped.

"What is problem, Raven?"

"I changed my mind."

"You must go visit Mr. Tedescu."

"I don't *must* do anything."

Sawyer pulled a cigarette lighter out of her pocket and flicked it until the wick flamed.

"Take it away!"

"So is you. Not the other one. Now, do what I say."

"Okay. Just put out the fire."

Sawyer closed the lighter and slipped it back into her pocket. "Come, cheer up Mr. Tedescu."

In the first bed, a young man wearing an oxygen mask waved. "I missed you, Raven."

She patted his hand. "Get well."

She passed between beds and wheelchairs waving to the patients on both sides. She was a queen inspecting the troops. The men who were awake blew kisses.

From the far end of the infirmary, she heard someone shout, "You on the wheelchair, shut up and let us sleep!" Someone else called out, "Damn it, you're not only one here!"

As she approached the half-open privacy curtain, she heard her former drama coach's pompous lecture.

"Remember, students, this is Aristophanes' antiwar comedy. The character's name *Lysistrata* means 'she who disbands armies.' She stops the war between Athens and Sparta by making the love-starved women refrain from having sex with their men."

She recalled the last role she had rehearsed.

Parting the half-open curtain, she delivered her lines:

"You know how to work. Play him, lead him on.
Seduce him to the cozening-point—kiss him, kiss him.
Then slip your mouth aside just as he is sure of it.
Ungirdle every caress his mouth feels at . . ."

Potbellied little Mr. Tedescu spun around in his wheelchair. "Raven?"

Nurse Sawyer pushed her close to him. "Raven Slade come visit like you ask, Professor Tedescu."

"Not *professor!* They never . . . made me *professor.* And where are my 17N comrades?"

"They not arrive yet, Mr. Tedescu, but candy striper Raven here to cheer you."

His glare softened. "My favorite drama student memorized roles quicker and with more feeling than any other student actor. I have something to ask you." He frowned at Sawyer. "Go away. This is between me and my protégé."

Sawyer stepped around the curtain, but Raven saw her shadow linger on the other side.

"Come closer, Raven," Tedescu said.

She leaned over, trying not to gag at the odor of his sweat-drenched body.

"Do you remember our last conference in my office, after the rehearsal, before your breakdown?"

How could she ever forget?

That afternoon, sitting in the chair beside his desk, she felt the horny bastard slide his fat fingers up her skirt. Good thing she crossed her legs. That's what Lysistrata would have done. He stumbled to his lavatory.

She noticed a stack of papers on his desk, cover sheet titled *Operation Dragon's Teeth.* Notes for a new play? She read them quickly. Three rhyming quatrains like the prophecies of Nostradamus. She started to put them back, but when he came out, wiping his hands, he saw her.

"How dare you read things on my desk."

"Sorry, Mr. Tedescu. I thought they were acting notes."

He raised his fist. She jumped off the chair and he chased her around his desk.

"Don't hit me."

A knock at his door stopped him. A student stuck his head in. "Sorry to be late for our meeting."

She pushed Tedescu aside and ran out of the office.

That was the last time she saw him until now.

"Mr. Tedescu, how could I ever forget that last day?"

She saw him glance at Sawyer's silhouette behind the curtain. "Go away, Nurse! This is private!"

Shoes squished as Sawyer moved.

"You always had an incredible memory for your roles. Do you recall what was on those pages?

. . . raven, your shmuck drama coach is asking you to perform a scene from his three-act dragon's teeth play . . .

She ignored the voice in her head and recited the lines, for him. "I understand some of the images and references from your lectures, but they still don't make sense."

"They are prophecies only for my 17N and MEK comrades."

. . . what the hell is 17n or a mek . . . ?

The nagging high-pitched voice in her head prevented her from hearing what he said after that, but he suddenly leaned forward in the wheelchair and grabbed her throat with both hands. Choking her. "I can't let you live, you bitch."

She tried to pull away, but his grip was strong. Fingers tightened around her neck.

The privacy curtain swished open and Nurse Sawyer dashed in. She punched Tedescu in the face. He let go. Her second punch knocked him unconscious.

"Jesus, just in time. He tried to kill me."

Sawyer checked his pulse and called a passing attendant. "This patient fainted. When he revive, he restricted to infirmary. No visitors absolutely."

Outside the infirmary, she asked, "Raven, what you say to him that make him attack you?"

She was about to recite the three quatrains, but she remembered he said they were only for *17N* and *MEK*. "Nothing. He just, like, freaked out."

Sawyer twisted her wrist. "I heard part about *17 November* and the *Mujihadeen-e Kalq*."

"Muja-Dino-*what?*"

"Tell me, or I write in your chart you have hallucination and talk to your dead sister. Your father lock you up again."

She pulled free. "Write whatever the hell you want."

"What's going on here?"

She turned at the sound of her father's voice. "She saved my life. Mr. Tedescu was going to kill me. But now she says she's going to write that I'm still crazy."

He turned to Sawyer. "I'll take care of this, Nurse. You can go back to the nurse's station on the military ward."

Sawyer hesitated, then stalked off.

"Are you all right, Raven?"

"Before Mr. Tedescu attacked me, he asked if I remembered something I once read on his desk in his office. I thought they were acting notes. But he said they were his prophecies, and he made me recite them for him. Then he said he had to kill me because the plans of *Operation Dragon's Teeth* was only for his comrades of 17N and MEK."

Her father grabbed her arm. "Quick, come with me!"

"What he was talking about, Dad. What's a MEK?"

Her father rushed her into his office and locked the door. "No time to explain, Raven."

"He made me recite three stanzas to see if I remembered them. The first one began—"

"Don't tell me, Raven."

"Why not?"

"If I'm captured and interrogated, I don't think I could hold out."

"You're scaring me."

"Sorry, but we have to act fast. Thousands of lives may be at risk. Listen to my voice. You've heard me give you this command before. *Raven, roost.*"

. . . he's hypnotizing you, raven, don't listen . . .

She heard her sister's warning voice, but she couldn't stop her eyes from closing.

"Repeat my command, Raven."

She whispered, *"Raven, roost."* Then went limp.

She felt his hand on her forehead. "Raven, you're going to sleep again, as you have many times before. Deep sleep. You see willows weeping. You smell sweet roses in a garden. You feel wind breathing on your face. Look at the yellow and orange butterflies. Ignore the inner voice of your twin who is jealous that you were the one born alive. Now, sleep. Deep sleep until I tell you to awake."

. . . careful, raven, in the past he always explained why he's hypnotizing you, don't give in . . .

Too late. She was already in the garden, lying on the grass. His voice echoed through the silence. "You won't remember Jason Tedescu's prophecies. They will remain buried in your subconscious, guarded by your fear of fire and your sister's fear of heights. Only when you hear the phrases, '*17N is defeated. MEK is defeated.*' will you be able to recall the prophecies and tell them to the CIA or FBI. Now, repeat the words about 17N and MEK that will unblock the prophecies."

"*17N is defeated. MEK is defeated.*"

"I'm going to count to five and say '*Raven fly.*' You'll awaken. One. Two. Three. Four. Five. *Raven fly.*"

She opened her eyes.

"Raven, what do you recall?"

"Getting dressed after Nurse Sawyer brushed my hair."

"Excellent. Now come with me to the dayroom and bring cookies and juice to the soldiers."

Still trembling, she followed him out of his office. "Remember, Raven, it's good for therapy—theirs and yours—to have our American and Greek wounded soldiers talk out their war horrors." He nudged her gently into the dayroom. "But don't flirt."

Raven paused at the entrance. Men, some with legs or arms in casts, turned their wheelchairs and smiled at her. Others playing dominoes looked up and waved.

Through the glass partition, she saw Sawyer at the nurses' station, watching.

She sashayed into the dayroom. Was this a stage, or a movie set? As she moved among the patients, she knew they wanted to touch her. Most were being treated for *shell shock.* Or was it *battle fatigue?* What was it called now? Oh, yes. *Post-traumatic stress disorder.* The way they looked at her, she knew they were damned stressed.

Sawyer once said it was better for them to talk out their memories of the Persian Gulf War to a candy striper, rather than to the clinical director or even a psychiatric nurse. But Sawyer always questioned her afterward about what they said.

She waved to soldiers. One blew her a kiss. A Greek corporal made a jerking motion with his fist between his legs. She looked away.

She saw someone in a wheelchair with his back to the nurses' station, face swathed in bandages, left arm in a sling. Must be a new admission. He waved at her with his free hand.

She walked over and stroked his brow. "How are you?"

In a deep mellow voice with a slight Greek accent, he whispered, "Better with your soft fingers on my forehead."

"You speak excellent English."

"I was an exchange student in America."

"What's your name?"

"Zorba."

She laughed. "Zorba the Greek? You're toying with me."

"I would like to."

She winked. "I'm going to call you *'the man in the white gauze mask.'*"

• She glanced around for her favorite attendant. There was young Platon Eliade, dealing cards at a table near the window. She knew he and the American G.I.'s gambled with matchsticks but settled up afterward with money. She headed toward the card table.

Suddenly, a cracking sound, like a car backfiring. Platon jumped to his feet knocking over the table. "Clear the dayroom! Back to your wards!" He pulled an automatic from under his smock and headed for the corridor.

. . . raven, what the hell is an attendant in this crazy house doing with a gun . . . ?

CHAPTER TWO

Doors smashed open. Glass shattered. Four men in black ski masks burst in shouting curses. A fat man fired at the American patients.

Raven froze. This can't really be happening. Must be another nightmare. But when she saw a red stain spread across Platon's white smock, she ran to hide behind the Greek soldier with the bandaged face.

He shook off his sling and put his arm around her. "Stay with me, beautiful. No one will harm you."

A fat intruder tossed him a ski mask. Zorba turned his back, unraveled the bandages and pulled down the mask, revealing only dark eyes through the slits.

He pointed at Sawyer staring through the nurses' station window. "She saw my face! Get her!"

The one-armed invader and another with a toothpick sticking through his mask ran out into the corridor. A third on a crutch limped toward Zorba and handed him an automatic.

She stared. "Zorba, you're one of *them!*"

"Take me to clinical director's office."

"Why?"

"I must see your father. He is a CIA informant."

She screamed, "You're crazy."

He pointed the gun at her. "Be silent if you want to live! Take me to Dr. Slade."

She led him from one corridor to another away from her father's office. As they passed the infirmary, she heard patients groaning. An orderly pushing a man in a wheelchair into the corridor froze, then fled. The wheelchair tipped over. The occupant freed himself and jumped off.

It was Mr. Tedescu, running toward her. Hands out to grab her. "Die, Raven! You must die!"

Zorba said, "Back away, old man. Don't interfere."

But Tedescu kept running toward them.

Zorba fired twice. Blood spurted from the hospital gown. Tedescu collapsed.

The one with the crutch turned a corner and limped to the body on the floor. A gravel-sounding voice, said, "You fool! It is *him!* He call from hospital to meet him here."

Zorba bent over and studied the face. "I didn't know. I never met Tedescu. What is he doing in the Athens Asylum?"

"He say, because girl remembers plan, he must kill her."

A gurgling sound came from the dying man's lips.

The man with the crutch bent over the body. "Jason, forgive my idiot son's mistake. What you want us to do?"

"*Operation Dragon's Teeth,* launch it without me."

"We do not have the plan."

Tedescu pointed at her. "Raven knows." Then his eyes went blank and his head flopped to one side.

The one who called himself Zorba looked at her. "What does he mean? What do you know?"

. . . *think fast, raven* . . .

"Probably means I *know* him. In college, he was my drama coach at the Greek Theater Club. I didn't even know he was coming here."

He shook her. "Take me to Dr. Slade."

"I won't."

"I'll kill you too, then I'll find him anyway." He put the hot muzzle of his gun to her head. It burned her skin. "You want to die unnecessarily?"

"I don't give a damn."

"If you stay with me, I'll let you live."

She hesitated. Looked at Tedescu's body on the floor. Then nodded. She led him to an office with the sign CLINICAL DIRECTOR. He jiggled the locked handle. Fired into the keyhole. Then kicked the door open.

Her father, standing behind his desk, held a gun in one hand and a phone in the other. "Raven knows," he shouted into the mouthpiece, "about Tedescu's plan for a terrorist attack in the States, but his comrades are here—"

"Hang up and put the gun down, Dr. Slade, or I'll kill your daughter."

"She doesn't know anything."

"But you do. Tell us, or watch her die."

Her father, still holding the receiver against his left ear, looked at him, then at her. "Forgive me, Raven." He fired the gun at his own forehead. The bloody phone fell to the floor. He slumped across his desk.

"No, Daddy! No!" she screamed. Tried to run to him but Zorba held her tight.

"It's too late. He left you to face the music alone."

Two other masked gunmen rushed in. A fat one shouted, "Are you all right, Alexi?"

The one with the toothpick punched the fat one in the shoulder. "No names!"

. . . *so his name isn't zorba, it's alexi* . . .

"No matter," the one-armed man said. "17N leaves no survivors."

The fat one shouted, "Shoot the girl too."

"No," the man with the crutch said. "Maybe Tedescu's last words means she knows prophecies. Take her with us."

The one called Alexi turned to the one man. "Did you stop the nurse?"

The toothpick jiggled through the mask. "She run out back door before we get there. Her car was park in alley. She drive away fast."

The one-armed man said, "What we do with this one?"

The limping man said, "Use her as shield until we find out what she knows about *Operation Dragon's Teeth*. Then kill her as Tedescu wanted. Son, leave our message!"

Alexi went to the desk and crumpled a sheet of paper. He dipped it into her father's blood and, using it as a brush, he smeared on the wall: *Death to Enemies of the People*. With a flourish, he signed it *17N*.

What did her father say about remembering *17N* and *MEK*? What did those names mean?

Alexi dragged her across the corridor, around a corner, down a flight of stairs through the exit toward a black car. The man with the toothpick slid behind the wheel. "Why are you bringing the girl?"

"To learn what she knows about Tedescu's prophecies."

The limping man pointed his crutch at the trunk. "Lock her in there."

"No room, Father," Alexi said. "It's full of weapons." He blindfolded her and shoved her into the backseat. She felt the fat man's body against hers. Then Alexi got in, squeezing her between them.

The car lurched and sped away.

She closed her eyes and breathed. In. Out. In. Out. Help me, Sis. No answer. Where are you when I need you?

Alexi shouted to the driver, "Take an indirect route to the safe house."

She felt the car turn, lurch, turn again.

The driver said, "Minivan behind us."

"Cut through the alley."

"Is gone now."

She felt the car hit trash cans. It jolted to a stop. The one Alexi had called Father jabbed her with his crutch and pulled her out of the car. "If you want to live, do not resist." He tested her blindfold. She heard the car door slam, then felt a gust as it pulled away.

He dragged her onto a curb. Into a building. Crutch hitting up twenty-seven steps. Sound of a key in a lock. A door creaked open, then closed behind them. He dragged her across carpeting to another door and started to push her inside. She pulled away, but he punched her stomach. She fell back and he slammed the door.

What was she was leaning against? Clothing on hangers. A closet. No room to move. She pulled off the blindfold. No window. No light. No air. Can't breathe. Can't think. Falling apart. Mustn't faint. Hang on.

She shouted, "I can't stand it in here!"

A fist banged on the closet door. "Then sit."

"You bastard!"

"Careful how you talk to Greek patriot."

Sis, she thought, I need you now.

. . . *breathe slowly, raven. one breath. another. in and out like dad taught you. stay calm. they can't keep you locked up forever. play along until you find out what they plan to do, you're good at making men do what you want* . . .

She heard an outside door open, then close. The voice of Alexi said, "Vasili thinks we were followed."

A thump of the crutch. "Then better to kill her now."

"First, I'll work on her to find out what she knows."

"Do not cross me now, Alexi. Why you think you can control this woman?"

"Remember in America when the heiress Patty Hearst joined her kidnappers?"

"You mean Stockholm syndrome? Think you can make this one fall in love with you?"

"It's worth a try."

"What if you cannot, Alexi?"

"Then I'll dispose of her as Tedescu intended."

"If only Tedescu lived long enough to give us his plan."

She banged on the closet door. "Let me out!"

"Ignore her. Concentrate on our Piraeus bombing."

"I'm still worried about that, Father. Women and children are sure to be at the terminal."

"Is always collateral damage in fog of war. Go now."

Footsteps. The outside door opening. Then closing. Which one stayed behind? She jiggled the knob. Threw herself against the closet door. "Let me out!"

No answer.

She started wheezing and lay back against the clothing. Then the thump-thump of a crutch coming closer.

Sis, what if he tries to rape me?

. . . *i'll kick him in the balls for you* . . .

What if he tortures me?

. . . *pain always makes you feel real. the worst he can do is kill you and save you the trouble. every time you tried to commit suicide like mom did, you failed. so let him do it for you. then we'll be together again inseparable* . . .

Sound of a key turning in the closet lock. Blinding light as the door creaked open. A hand grabbed her leg.

. . . *fly, sister raven, fly* . . .

CHAPTER THREE

Cincinnati, Ohio

A signal beeped in the Intelligence Analysis section of the FBI Cincinnati field office. Frank Dugan put down his cheeseburger and swiveled from his desk to the console. He turned on the closed-circuit unit and read the message on the monitor:

> FROM: *Athens Interpol secure site*
> TO: *All International Field Offices*
> RE: *17 November Terrorists*

The picture focused on a white-haired man with a thick mustache, adjusting a black patch over his right eye. The wall behind him bore the inscription:

HELLENIC REPUBLIC
MINISTRY OF PUBLIC ORDER
HEADQUARTERS OF THE HELLENIC POLICE
INTERNATIONAL POLICE COOPERATION DIVISION

An echolike voice reverberated. "This is Captain Hector Eliade, head of the Hellenic Police Counterterrorism Task Force in Athens. Two days ago the elusive Marxist-Leninist terror cult *17 November* attacked the Athens Asylum. Two Americans dead, one wounded. Clinical Director Roger Slade took his own life. His daughter, Raven Slade, a patient at the facility, taken hostage.

"Ohio's Waybridge University classics instructor, Jason Tedescu, being treated in the infirmary was one of those killed during the assault. Our antiterrorism task force has intel that—during his years as an expatriate in America—he planted homegrown terrorist sleeper cells.

"New chatter indicates that Tedescu was attempting to create an alliance between 17N and an unidentified Mideast terrorist group. A joint assault against targets in the United States. Code name: *Operation Dragon's Teeth.*

"Other patients in the Athens Asylum overheard Tedescu speaking to Raven Slade, then attacking her. His dying words to his killers were: *'Raven knows.'*

"Top priority is to extract the hostage for our own interrogation. We must learn *what* Raven Slade knows about plans of the intended attack before 17N tortures it out of her. If that is not possible, she must be silenced to prevent her from passing message to the terrorists."

The screen went black.

He studied the world map on the wall above the console. When he first transferred from New York to Cincinnati, he'd outlined his Balkans area with a yellow marker. Now, he reached over and pulled the red pushpin out of Slovenia's capital Ljubljana, and jabbed it into Athens, Greece.

His intercom buzzed. Assistant Director Mason wanted to know if he'd picked up the message from Interpol.

"I did."

"Up to my office ASAP."

Moments later, he stepped out of the elevator onto the blue plush carpeting and knocked at Mason's door.

"Come!"

He opened it partway and looked at the chief's gray hair, as always swept across his forehead in an exaggerated pompadour.

Mason had his fingers clasped on the huge mahogany desk. "What do you think, Dugan?"

"Captain Eliade is suggesting that if the Greek police can rescue Raven Slade they intend to aggressively interrogate her. Since she's an American outside the States. That's CIA business."

As Mason nodded, his gray pompadour flipped forward. He smoothed it back into place. "Since FBI embassy legats are now permitted to investigate crimes against Americans anywhere in the world, it becomes our business as well as the CIA's."

"So we're getting involved in 17N's kidnapping of Raven Slade?"

"It's more than just that. You're the Balkans analyst. Tell me about 17N."

"It's a Greek Marxist-Leninist terror group. This attack on the Athens Asylum is their most recent of more than sixty attacks on Europeans, Turks and American targets."

"How are they different from other European terrorists?"

"Big difference. Not a single first- or second-generation 17N terrorist has ever been captured or even identified during the twenty-eight years of their existence."

"So they're middle-aged by now. How is it they still haven't been caught?"

"They've melded into Greek society as doctors, professors, mechanics, sculptors, all ordinary citizens. In their clandestine lives, they still avenge their dead and wounded comrades with ingeniously planned acts of terror."

"Do I sense a touch of respect in your voice?"

He shrugged. "When students of Athens Technicon University were demonstrating against the brutal regime of Colonel George Papadopoulos, the police and military brutally attacked them on *17 November 1973*."

"So why the aggression against us?"

"As I said, they're Marxist-Leninist. During the Communist resistance against King Constantine's tyrannical monarchy, it was widely believed the CIA was behind defeat of the left wing. A coup brought Papadopoulos into power. The students—now middle-aged as you say—never forgave Americans, Europeans and the present Greek government. Ergo, the long-lived underground of two generations of 17N."

Mason cracked his knuckles. "This communique about 17N's possible alliance with fundamentalist Islamists for another major attack on us has raised hackles in D.C. The director called. He wants you back in the New York field office to confer with their top Mideast section analyst."

He felt his legs jiggle. He pressed his hands against his knees to stop it. "Back to New York?"

"Sorry, Dugan. I know you requested a transfer out of Manhattan after 9/11. But this is for just one or two days."

"Why me?"

"The Balkans is your bailiwick. You've spent time in Greece and you've studied the 17N attacks. We've got to find out what Raven Slade knows before they torture it out of her. The Mideast analyst in New York may be able to help you identify the fanatic Islamists involved with them."

"For Greek Orthodox Christians like 17N," he said, "an alliance with Muslims makes strange bedfellows."

"Then it's up to you to bone up on this terrorist group they're getting into bed with."

CHAPTER FOUR

Athens

Faye Sawyer had been startled by the gunshots as she was watching Raven through the nurses' station window. When the new patient pulled off his face bandages, she suspected he was 17N. Not yet time to reveal her own true identity.

She slipped out of her nurse's uniform and into her skirt and blouse. Raven's medical file was open on her desk. She grabbed it and ran out the rear exit. Her maroon minivan was parked in the alley. Easy enough to escape, but first she would follow to see where 17N was taking Raven.

Headlights off, she drove around the rear of the asylum and parked close to the main entrance. Unlocked the glove compartment. Pulled out her gun.

She tailed the black sedan as it it made several turns, doubled back, then finally stopped in front of a nondescript building with a street-level used-clothing store. She parked with headlights off. Two men dragged Raven through a doorway, then drove off. Minutes later, lights flashed on in a second-floor window. At least, she knew the safe house where they would hold Raven hostage.

* * *

She drove to a deserted area on the outskirts of Athens and pulled off the road. Using one of her disposable cell phones, she dialed long distance to Iraq.

A pickup. "Who is calling?"

She recognized the voice of Nabila, General Rihana Hassan's aide-de-camp. "This is Major Fatima Sayid."

"*Allahu akbar,*" Nabila said.

"Yes. Praise Allah. Connect me to General Hassan."

"She is supervising tank maneuvers. I will patch you through to her secure cell phone."

Moments later, a woman's strident voice came on. "*Salaam alaikum,* Major."

She visualized the leader's pink face framed by an olive-drab head scarf that barely hid tufts of white hair, her muscular body stretching the buttons of her uniform.

"*Alaikum salaam,* General."

"Good to hear from you, Fatima. I am pleased you are safe. *Allahu akbar.*"

Yes, God is great, she thought, and responded quickly, "*Nam. Allahu akbar.*"

"Have you confirmed our alliance with 17 November?"

"Not yet, General." She described what happened at the asylum. "Before Jason Tedescu was shot, he had his protégé Raven recite something. Then he tried to strangle her. I do not think we should approach 17N until we know what they learn from her."

"You sound concerned. You think Tedescu informed 17N that he planned *Dragon's Teeth* as our joint operation?"

"I heard a few lines that Raven recited. If I can get to her before they kill her, I can learn the rest of what she knows."

"How can you be sure?"

"Remember, I was her psychiatric nurse. Her father diagnosed her disorder as borderline personality combined with histrionic personality."

"Westerners have all kinds of personality disorders. What do those tell us?"

"As a borderline, she presents with symptoms of seeing the world around her as unreal. Feeling she, herself, is unreal. At times, seeing and hearing herself as another person."

"Like an out-of-body experience?"

"Yes, and similar to multiple personality disorder, but without amnesia."

"Those appear to be inner experiences, Fatima. How are they manifested?"

"Self-mutilation and suicidal behavior. Terror of being left alone often leads frantic efforts to avoid abandonment. They are committed, usually for less than six months, as schizophrenics. Their well-known mantra is, '*I hate you. Don't leave me.*'"

"And how does borderline fit in with—what did you call it?—histrionic personality?"

"As a histrionic, she is lively and dramatic. Must always be the center of attention. Highly suggestible and seductive."

"Sounds like a handful. How do you intend to proceed?"

"Often, in the past, Raven's father hypnotized her. I believe that is what he did after Tedescu spoke to her. I suggest we let 17N try to extract his prophetic details of the operation. If they do not succeed, I will get her away from them and try my hand at controlling her."

"Excellent, Fatima. Stay in Athens until then."

"Before I contact 17N, do we really need them?"

"After Tedescu approached us, our intelligence sources reported that he planted Greek sleeper cells in three major American cities. Most are middle-aged by now. If, as you say, Tedescu's protégé memorized his prophecies of the targets, as well as our weapon and how to use it, we must find out what she knows."

"I agree, General."

"Now that you have found the safe house, make contact. If 17N refuses, or if they are unable to extract the secret from her, use whatever force is necessary to bring her here to Ashraf. With your training, I have no doubt you will break through."

"It shall be done."

"*Inshallah.*"

"Yes, General. 'If God wills.'"

"*Salaam alaikum,* Fatima."

"*Alaikum salaam.*"

CHAPTER FIVE

Athens

A flashing bright light awakened Raven. All night. Every night. On and off. On and off. How many days was it? Had to keep track. The light didn't stay on long enough for her to get her bearings. Dark again. Weak and groggy. Mouth dry.

How to keep track of the days—or nights? Nothing to use for scratching marks on the wall. She fingered the six old scars on her stomach that she'd cut to record the number of times her father committed her to asylums.

A thin ray of light blinded her. A hand threw in a flask. Just in time. She gulped tepid water.

All right. Starting now, she'd tattoo a daily calendar on her flesh. Four or five days since they kidnapped her. She pulled up the right sleeve of her blouse and clawed five lines on her arm. The smell of blood assured her she wasn't dreaming. The pain brought her back to the real world.

The day after she drank the water, she banged on the door. "Let me out! I gotta pee!" No answer. She pounded. "I'll do it in here!"

No answer. Well, the hell with you. She pulled her slacks and panties down and squatted. Relieving herself on the pile of clothing. Wiped herself with something like a scarf. If

Alexi's limping father was going to kill her, he was taking his sweet time. If he wanted to rape her, what was he waiting for? She had to stay focused to survive. She'd fight him until she was ready to take her own life.

The closet door opened. Light blinded her. He lurched into the closet with his crutch. He spread her legs. She kicked, but he was too strong. He fumbled with his zipper.

The smell of her own urine. Ecchhh. The gorge rising in her throat. She puked in his face.

He slapped her. "Bitch! Next time I will rape you with my crutch."

"Which end?"

"Maybe I will kill you first and have your body."

"Might as well send your son to do a man's job."

He punched her and backed out of the closet. The taste of vomit stayed in her mouth until she fell asleep.

Now how long? She felt her arm. Time for a sixth cut. She had to shit. As she bent over and squatted, the door swung open.

"God, what a stink!" Alexi's voice.

"It's your father's fault for not letting me go to the toilet."

He struck the back of her head. "Speak when you are told!" He blindfolded her and led her by the hand. "Go now. After you finish, I'll give you a shower."

"Why do I need a blindfold?"

"I told you not to talk."

"Good cop, bad cop? I guess you're the good cop."

He pushed her down on the toilet. No seat. Cold porcelain. When she was done, he pulled her up by her shoulders and pushed her through a shower curtain. He turned on the water. Cold! He washed her.

"Enjoying yourself?"

"Not yet," he said.

"Better get to it before your old man does."

He shoved her back into the closet and locked the door. Someone had cleaned it.

"Put on dry clothes from hangers."

"They're men's clothes."

"In the dark no one will know the difference."

"That's what my father used to say. If I dressed like a boy, I'd be safe from men like your father pawing me."

He slammed the door. "Your own stupid father blew his brains out instead of protecting you."

"Don't leave me alone."

Silence.

Fumbling in the dark, she found a sweatshirt and trousers and put them on.

How much time passing? A memory flash. The gunshot. Standing outside herself watching herself watching blood dripping from her father's forehead. Alexi scrawling *17N* on the wall in Daddy's blood.

"What's 17N?" she asked.

"You'll learn when I can trust you."

"You can trust me now."

Another day? Another night? She banged on the door. "I'm hungry!"

No answer.

She marked the passage of days. But time? An hour? Two? The closet door opened, and someone shoved a plate into her hands. She dipped her finger into it. "Cold moussaka? I hate even hot moussaka. I won't eat this crap."

He shoved the plate at her, smearing greasy food against her face. "Eat or not," Alexi said. "This is all you get for the next few days." He slammed the closet door and locked it again.

She cursed him silently, but wiped the moussaka into her mouth. Forced herself to swallow. At least she wouldn't starve. A long time to be locked away. But he was a man, and he'd want to see her naked when he was ready to take her.

She needed to stay alive until she could make him want sex like the men in *Lysistrata*. She could play the role. There'd be a standing ovation.

Then she heard the high-pitched voice.

. . . better seduce him soon, sis. or else find a way to kill yourself . . .

CHAPTER SIX

New York City

Dugan asked the cabdriver to take an indirect route to the Jacob K. Javits Federal Building. "Pass by where the Twin Towers once stood."

"In this traffic? It'll take forever."

"It'll mean an extra tip. I want to see the place."

Twenty-five minutes later, the cab pulled up close to the reconstruction area once called the World Trade Center.

Dugan reached into his briefcase, through the plastic bag until he felt the baseball. He ran his fingers along the stitches and squeezed them. "Okay, that's enough."

The driver turned. "You made me buck all that traffic for a couple of seconds look?"

"That's right. Let's go."

Forty minutes later the cab pulled up to the twenty-eight-story federal building. He paid the driver and handed him an extra ten dollars.

Inside, the guards examined his FBI badge and ID, then let him through the turnstiles to the elevators leading to the FBI field office. He got off on the twenty-sixth floor to the Operations and Command Center.

He made his way to Foreign Counterintelligence and told the white-haired secretary he had an appointment to meet the new Mideast intelligence analyst. She pressed the intercom. "Agent Frank Dugan is here." Then, she gestured. "Third office on the left. Ms. Herrick is expecting you."

As he approached the door, a buzzer unlocked it. A delicate, almost childlike voice said, "Come in, Agent Dugan." Elizabeth Herrick stood up behind her desk. Attractive, delicate features, with shoulder-length auburn hair. She extended her hand and shook his with a firm grip, then waited for him to lead the conversation.

He asked, "How do you like New York, Ms. Herrick?"

"Most people call me Liz. This is my first assignment. I'm just out of Quantico."

"Did you enjoy shooting cardboard people in Hogan's Alley?"

"I qualified."

"Quantico's not the Mideast. Where'd you study?"

"In Teheran."

That set him back. This lovely young analyst from Iran? Not a trace of accent. "I guess you speak Farsi."

"And Arabic. Look, let's cut the bullshit, Dugan. We're both after the same terrorists. I have humint about MEK considering a possible alliance with 17N for *Operation Dragon's Teeth.*"

"Okay, but you don't have to bite."

Her laugh was like a bubbling stream. She turned on her computer and entered the password *Tentmaker.* Then she rotated the monitor toward him.

He saw a face hidden behind a kaffiyeh.

"Code name *Tentmaker,*" she said, "was army intelligence in Iran, serving with the ayatollah's Revolutionary Guard. He's now being handled by a CIA case officer."

"How did you make contact with him?"

"My mother was a secretary with the American embassy at the time of the Iranian revolution. *Tentmaker* got us out of the country before the embassy was invaded and the staff taken hostage."

"What made you trust him?"

She closed her eyes as if remembering. "I woke up in the middle of the night when I heard what I thought was a Revolutionary Guard soldier. He whispered the first verse of the *Rubáiyát*.

'Awake! for Morning in the Bowl of Night
Has flung the Stone that puts the Stars to Flight:
And Lo! The Hunter of the East has caught
The Sultan's Turret in a Noose of Light.'

Omar Khyyám, the Persian tentmaker, was Sunni. Ayatollah's Revolutionary Guard is Shia. This Sunni guard, code name *Tentmaker*, drove us to Turkey."

The picture cut to a landscape of scrubs and dunes, obviously filmed by a shaky handheld camera. A voice whispered, "This is *Mujihadeen-e Kalq*'s Camp Ashraf in the northeast area of Iraq."

The camera zoomed in on a barbed-wire barricade. Behind it, women in olive-drab uniforms stood at attention in a formation of tank turrets. Instead of the traditional female hijab, they wore the male kaffiyeh, tied around the head and shoulders.

Dugan smirked. "Obviously, these *'Islamic Holy Warriors of the People'* are flaunting their equality with Muslim men."

Her nostrils flared. Probably repressing a wisecrack for his sexist remark. He asked, "So who are these women?"

"Formerly, the radical Muslim student group that helped overthrow Shah Pahlevi, who they considered a CIA puppet. After the shah fled Iran to the United States, they led the takeover of the American embassy in Teheran and kept the hostages for 444 days. Tentmaker got us out of the country."

"But that was ages ago during the Carter administration. What do they have to do with us now?"

"After the Iranian revolution, they demonstrated for the cause they believed in—a liberal Marxist-Islamist Iran. Ayatollah Kohmeini betrayed them. The mullahs who took power transformed Iran into a theocracy under the Islamic religious legal code of sharia. The student *Mujihadeen-e Kalq* rebelled against the mullahs. At that time their supporters numbered 500,000 strong, but the ayatollah's Revolutionary Guard arrested, tortured and executed most of them. The remaining 4,000, now in Ashraf, are the only Iranian opposition against the mullahs."

"Yet, during the Iraq-Iran war, they sided with Saddam. Helped his cousin Chemical Ali use poison gas against the Kurds and the Marsh Arabs. Men, women and children."

She shrugged. "They're dangerous, but interesting."

The scene cut from inspection of troops, past underbrush, to a tunnel opening. The voice said, "This is one of several Ashraf tunnels MEK uses to penetrate the border between Iraq and Iran during their hit-and-run attacks. It's also where Saddam hid many of his bioterror weapons."

The picture suddenly cut off, but *Tentmaker*'s voice continued. "MEK now holds all of Saddam's biological weapons. Their original plan was to deliver one of them to Hezbollah cells in America. But, since their break with the mullahs, they have been seeking other allies. If the alliance between them and 17N succeeds, *Operation Dragon's Teeth* will make the Twin Towers look like a minor toothache."

She turned off the monitor. "Sorry, that must have hit a nerve. I know what happened to your family."

"I'm getting over it. Wouldn't the U.N. inspectors have found those weapons of mass destruction?"

"Sure, if MEK had allowed them to search inside their compound," she said. "But, according to an earlier report from Tentmaker, MEK prevented them from entering Ashraf."

"When I'm in Greece, how do I contact *Tentmaker*?"

"Through his CIA handler, code name *Charon*."

"Just what I need. The mythical old Greek ferryman who rows the dead across the river Styx to hell."

"Before that, what's your next port of call?"

"I'll fly back to Cincinnati and visit Tedescu's office. I want to see what I can learn about his past behavior in the Classics Department and with Raven Slade."

"After that, what?"

"Off to Greece. So who's my contact here?"

She hesitated. "As far as the FBI is concerned—other than your position as legat to the embassy in Greece—you won't exist."

"If I decode Tedescu's message, am I supposed to swallow it along with a cyanide pill?"

"In that event—and only then—contact me."

"Your code name?"

"*Cymbal*."

"An unusual one. What made you choose it?"

"*Liz* spelled backward is *Zil*—Turkish for *cymbals*. What's yours?"

"As a homebound analyst, I never needed a code name. I guess as an overseas agent, I'd better choose one." He thought about it. Then he smiled. "For *Operation Dragon's Teeth*, call me *Dentist*."

"Even though—as far as the FBI is concerned—you no longer exist, think of me as your umbilical cord here."

He looked into her blue eyes. "*Cymbal*, I hope you won't cut me off and throw away my afterbirth."

"Of course not, *Dentist*. At least, not while you're still alive."

Chapter Seven

Athens

When the closet door opened, Raven saw a plate of fish and potatoes on the table. Her stomach growled.

The man the others called Alexi, still wearing his ski mask, pulled out a chair for her. "Sit. Eat."

"How come now you're being nice to me? My last meal?"

"That depends on you."

. . . figure out what he's up to, raven . . . you're the one who can wrap men around your finger . . .

"Whatever your reasons for holding me, I want you to know I admire strong men who fight against tyranny."

"That's what I want to hear."

She chewed the fish, spitting out the bones. "What other things do you want to hear?"

"What would you do if I raped you?"

"On a full stomach? Probably throw up all over you like I did to your father."

His laugh was deep.

She had to keep playing him. "You have a sexy laugh, but you won't have to rape me. I'm yours to command."

"How do you feel about that?"

"I won't know until I see your face."

"I'll take off the mask when I can trust you."

"I'm your hostage. How can I harm you?"

"Don't think of yourself as a hostage, but as someone who can help the underprivileged who suffer because American capitalists are sucking money from our country like vampires suck blood from their poor victims."

She thought a moment. "So you're a Communist."

"Marxist-Leninist. We believe people should have the power. Not parasite children of the rich. America is the evil empire."

She saw him studying her closely.

. . . don't contradict him . . .

"At present," he said, "even our own government officials are dominated by the American CIA. There is much your newspapers don't publish because they're influenced by mind-control advertisers."

"Mind control? I want to learn more."

"Your CIA backed the fascist junta of tyrant Colonel Papadopoulos. Worse than the Nazis. He ruled our people with an iron fist. He would not tolerate dissent. On 17 November 1973, his tanks attacked peaceful protesting students at the Athens Polytechnic University. They murdered thirty of my father's classmates—including his sweetheart. My father and his closest friend were among the eight hundred wounded."

"Your father? The one who limps?"

"He has an artificial leg. Before that, he used to run the marathon. Your country is to blame."

"I don't really understand."

"You'll learn the truth here."

Her life depended on understanding his hatred of Americans. "I'm listening."

"When the colonel's junta was toppled the following year, my father and his close friend Jason Tedescu formed 17N—in memory of the seventeenth of November massacre."

Those words. *17 November, 17N.* Something Mr. Tedescu said were only for them and MEK. Was that a hallucination? "What did any of that have to do with my father? He wasn't political. He was a psychiatrist."

"He treated American sympathizers and Greeks. Your father was really a CIA mole."

"A spy? Impossible. He'd have told me. He loved me."

"You think so? Then why did he lock you away in an insane asylum?"

She opened her mouth, but no answer came out. She stared at him through blurred eyes.

"I'll tell you why," he said, stroking her hair. "Because America turns people like him against their own children, sending sons and daughters to die in wars against workers of the world. When you see through the capitalist lies you will be reborn."

. . . *play along with him* . . .

"Teach me."

His voice softened. "You're not only beautiful, Raven, you're also intelligent." He pulled off his ski mask. She saw a handsome, craggy face with thick black brows, dark penetrating eyes. Did letting her see him unmasked mean he no longer cared if she could identify him? A reprieve or a death sentence?

"Are you going to kill me?"

"No."

Could he hear her heart pounding? "Are you going to rape me?"

"No. I'm going to tear away your mental blindfold so you can see you've been living a lie."

"Show me."

"That's enough for today."

She got up and headed toward the closet.

He stopped her. "There's an empty room with a small

window where you may sleep. I'll get a mattress so you'll be comfortable."

She stroked his hand. "I appreciate your kindness."

As he stepped out of the kitchen, she thought of trying the front door. Better not. He'd surely hear her turn the knob. She had to make him want her. To please him, she cleaned off the table and washed the dishes.

Returning with the mattress, he smiled when he saw her at the sink.

"Do you have a regular job?" she asked.

"I'm a tour guide. I lead groups of stupid tourists through ruins and tell them stories of our golden age."

"You said you learned English in America. How come?"

"I was an exchange student in Detroit for three years."

"Well, then America can't be all that bad if young people from different countries want to go there to study."

He threw the mattress on the floor. "Fool! America does that to deceive the rest of the world about their real intentions—dominating by spreading their decadent ideas." He grabbed her shoulders and pushed her back into the closet.

"You said I could sleep in the room with a window."

"When you are ready to see the light."

That didn't make sense, but she'd better not provoke him again. "I'm sorry. I didn't mean anything by that. Give me another chance."

He slammed the door and locked it. "We shall see."

To live she had to make him think about her more than politics. She had to make him want her. She would start again in the morning. Inscribe tomorrow on her skin. As she cut a seventh line on her arm, she bit her tongue to keep from crying out. Thank God for the pain.

CHAPTER EIGHT

Waybridge, Ohio

Frank Dugan restrained his Maserati to the lousy speed limit of thirty-five. Crummy two-lane. Couldn't believe it would take an hour and forty-five minutes from the Cincinnati airport to Waybridge.

From the overpass, he saw the tower of a high-Victorian Gothic mansion on a cliff. According to records, that's where Raven Slade had once been committed. Maybe he should explore the place before continuing to the university. Turning left onto a steeply rising gravel path, he drove through a rusty gate off its hinges. But the windows and doors were boarded up. He didn't know the asylum had been shut down.

Why stop at this madhouse on the mountain anyway? Maybe because his gut told him he might find answers in its corridors and padded cells. Well, first check Tedescu's files for possible clues to his encrypted prophecy.

As he backed down the path, his secure cell phone rang. "Yeah?"

"*Dentist*, this is *Cymbal*."

"Already? I haven't even left Ohio."

"Signal from *Charon* in Crete. He reports that before Slade shot himself, he phoned from the Athens Asylum. The last thing he said was, 'My daughter knows.'"

"Knows what?"

"*Charon* heard a gunshot, then a gurgling sound and Slade's phone went dead. According to Greek police, that's when 17N took his daughter hostage."

"I'm headed to the university to check out Tedescu's files. Maybe I can find out what Raven knew."

"Good luck." Then the phone went dead.

He drove to the campus and circled until he found the College of Liberal Arts. Lucky to find a parking space close to Lordon Hall. The directory listed Tedescu's office as 132-A. Inside, he saw a note taped on the door.

Mr. Tedescu is in Greece presenting a paper at the annual Convention of Classical Scholars. Lectures and conferences canceled for two weeks. Leave term papers and research reports with his assistant Ms. Salinas.

Just then, the adjacent door opened and what looked like a coed with a pigtail and cheerleader's skirt brushed by him. She took down the notice and replaced it with another.

Lectures in CLASSICAL HISTORY AND MYTHO-LOGY are cancelled for the rest of the semester. Contact his assistant Ms. Salinas for information.

So news of Tedescu's death had finally reached the department.

"I'm looking for Mr. Tedescu's assistant," he said.

She turned, but instead of a teenage student, he stared at a middle-aged woman. Facial skin tight, as if from plastic surgery, made her triangular skull look like the warning on a bottle of poison. Eyes red. Arms folded like crossbones across where her bosom should have been. "I'm Ms. Salinas. What do you want?"

"I'm FBI, Ms. Salinas. I need a minute of your time."

"Oh my! The dean just told me that Jason passed away in Athens. Do you know what happened?"

"I'd like to see his office."

She glanced around, as if unsure it was all right, then took a key ring from her pocket, fumbling until she found the right one. She unlocked the door to 132-A and waved him in.

He glanced around the room. Nothing on the desk but a bronze bust of Zeus. A large portrait of an elderly man in convocation cap and gown hung on the right wall.

"Is that Jason Tedescu?"

She took a handkerchief out of her pocket and wiped dust from the gilt frame. "Yes."

He moved to the legal-size file cabinet against the wall and pulled a drawer. It was locked.

He pointed to the key ring in her hand. "Unlock the files, please."

"There's nothing inside."

"Why is that?"

"Before he left for Greece, Jason donated all his papers and personal manuscripts to the library."

"I'd like to see for myself."

She flipped the keys until she found the right one. She inserted it into the lock and pulled all the drawers open. She was right. They were empty.

"They didn't tell us how he died," she said.

"How well did you know him?"

"I transferred with Jason from the University of Chicago when he got the appointment here."

"And your duties?"

"As his assistant, I covered his classes. Helped with research, typed exams, arranged student conferences."

"Did he have any favorite students?"

She stared past him. "The only one he got really close to was Dr. Slade's daughter, Raven."

"How close?"

"She was in his classics courses. He was also faculty advisor and director of the Theater Department's drama program. I saw all of her performances." There was an edge in her voice. "She's an incredible actress."

"Incredible how?"

"When she took the stage, other actors faded into the scenery. She sank herself into every role and actually *seemed* to become the character she was portraying. You forgot she was acting."

"Sounds impressive."

"Even offstage, during readings and rehearsals she was always the center of attention. You could say she lit up a room." Then she spat out the word, "*Seductive.*"

"And when she wasn't the center?"

"Withdrew, appeared depressed."

"And you say Jason Tedescu coached her?"

Skull-face looked away. "More like guided her. Until she had her breakdown, and her father withdrew her from the college."

"Did you witness it?"

"Oh, yes. I realized something was wrong during the first rehearsal of *Lysistrata*. After Raven mounted the second tier and called down to the sex-starved women to withhold their bodies from their men, she turned pale and collapsed. Jason—I mean Mr. Tedescu—took her into his office for a conference. That was the last time Jason or I saw her before her father was transferred to Athens."

"Did Mr. Tedescu ever mention why he left Greece in the first place?"

"When he was young, he'd been a senior at the Athens Polytechnic before the junta's army massacred his classmates.

He received a scalp wound and came to America for medical treatment. While he was here he got a student visa to continue his studies."

"Did he travel much?"

"Oh, yes. All across the country, lecturing, visiting Greek communities. He was researching the book he was writing, *Greeks in America*."

And, no doubt, establishing his homegrown sleeper cells.

He decided to take a shot. "It might comfort you to know Raven was with him before he died in Athens."

Her hollow eyes showed no sign. "How was that possible?"

"She was in the Athens Asylum when he collapsed during a lecture and a colleague brought him in. He tried to strangle her. He was shot during a terrorist attack."

Her face remained frozen, but she crossed her bony arms again. "He was like the Delphic oracle. Always treating her as if *she* was his high priestess."

No doubting the jealousy in her voice.

"Thanks for your time, Ms. Salinas. I'll head over to the library to glance through his papers."

"That's not possible, Agent Dugan."

"Why not?"

"He made me executrix of his professional papers. As per his wishes, to ensure the cryptic integrity of his prophecies, I sent them to the archives of the National Library of Greece in Athens."

"Well, I'm headed there myself. I'll have a look-see."

She stiffened. "As per his wishes, I included a codicil that his papers be sealed for ten years. Then to be viewed only by scholars and historians."

Thinking about that, he leaned against one of the empty file cabinets. As it tilted, he saw the edge of a paper slip out. He picked it up and smoothed the creased page. A title, *OPERATION DRAGON'S TEETH*, and a caption, *WHAT*, above two hand-lettered lines. Words crossed out, revised several times. He read them aloud.

> " *'Seeds of Slow Death wait in our Tunnels far . . .*
> *To punish all Crusaders. Inshallah . . .'*

"Any idea *what* this—?"

Her sudden movement made him look up. The bronze bust of Zeus upraised in both her hands. Her skull's eyes glared. He turned to deflect the blow.

Too late.

Exploding pain. Everything blurred. Fading. Then darkness . . .

CHAPTER NINE

Athens

Dr. Martin Kyle waved to the convention audience as they stood and applauded his lecture at the academy of the Greek National Library. Stroking his Vandyke beard, he stepped from behind the podium to a table and autographed his most recent book, *A Jungian Analysis of Cults that Kill.*

When the hall was almost empty, he sat back and loosened his tie. Two Greek officers approached, flanking an elderly man who had a black patch covering his right eye.

"Dr. Kyle, I am Captain Hector Eliade of Hellenic Police Counterterrorism Task Force." His deep voice echoed in the near-empty auditorium. "I enjoyed your lecture. Now, I would appreciate if you could answer a few questions."

"About what?"

"How well did you know Jason Tedescu?"

"We both teach at Waybridge University, in Ohio. I drove him to the hospital last week. What is this about?"

"I ask the questions here, Dr. Kyle. Why did you take him to the Athens Asylum Hospital?"

"He asked me to. It's closest to the academy center. Right after his presentation on ancient Greek and Roman riddles, he had a seizure. How is he doing?"

"What Greek riddles was he discussing?"

"Ancient ones, especially the story of Homer dying after he was unable to solve the fisher-boys' riddle."

"What did Tedescu say about it?"

"That Homer went to the oracle in Apollo's temple at Delphi to find out where he had been born. The oracle's prophetess told him his mother's home had been on the island of Ios. Then she added, 'Beware of young children bringing you riddles.'"

"Yes, Dr. Kyle, go on."

"Aged Homer journeyed to Ios. There on the beach two boys who had been fishing approached him. He asked what they caught. One boy answered, *'What we caught we threw away, and what we didn't catch, we kept.'*

"Then Homer remembered the oracle's warning about children bringing him riddles. Unable to solve the fisher-boys' riddle, he had a heart attack and died."

"Did he give his audience the solution to the riddle?"

"Strangely, not. That's when he had his own sudden seizure and collapsed at the lectern."

"What can you tell us about his association with the Greek Marxist terrorist cult 17 November?"

He retightened his tie. "I don't know that he is associated with them."

"You lecture about cults that kill, and he lectures about riddles of death. Did he ever mention 17N? Or MEK?"

"Why do you keep speaking about him in the past tense?"

"He was shot to death in the asylum."

"Oh, my God! I don't understand. What does he have to do with 17N?"

"That is what we are trying to determine. We have reason to believe he tried to strangle the clinical director's daughter before she was abducted."

"Why would I know anything about that?"

"According to the biographical note in your book, you

specialize in secret societies. Your Web page states that you studied not only Greek mythology and folklore, but Arab and Persian secret religious practices."

"I use those as background material, but it's not my primary profession. I'm a Jungian analytical therapist."

"How long are you planning to stay in Greece?"

"My schedule will allow me to visit a few Greek islands and Cyprus for another three weeks. Then I return to Athens to join the tour group for the return flight to Ohio."

"Have you ever visited Teheran or Baghdad?"

He ran the back of his hand across his lips. What could his current Greek studies have to do with Iran or Iraq? "In the past, I studied Islamic cults, but I don't see—"

"Are you familiar with the Iranian Islamic-Marxist *Mujihadeen-e Kalq*, commonly known as MEK?"

"Their student leaders helped take over the American embassy in Teheran."

"What about now? Are they, or are they not, a cult? Do they follow leaders blindly, to the death?"

"According to defectors from the group, they are led mostly by women. Those married are forced to divorce. Their children are sent away. The MEK rule is absolute celibacy. When their leader, Maryam Rajavi, was taken prisoner during her self-imposed exile in Paris, several of her followers set themselves on fire. They are Islamic-Marxist, anti-American terrorists. Many who have defected call them a cult. Why the interest in that group now?"

"We have received intelligence that they may be forming an alliance with the Greek 17N Marxist terrorists. The assault on the Athens Asylum, we believe, was a prelude."

"What did Jason Tedescu have to do with them?"

Eliade tapped a finger against his cheek. "Long ago, he was among the students protesting at the Polytechnic and was maimed during the junta attack. We believe he planted 17N terrorist sleeper cells in America."

"It's hard for me to imagine an alliance between Greek Orthodox 17N and Muslim MEK." Kyle picked up his lecture notes, dropped several pages on the floor. Swooped them up and crammed them into his briefcase. "Muslims and the Greek Orthodox have hated and fought each other, even before the Crusades. Why would MEK make an alliance with an ancient enemy?"

Eliade shrugged. "These days, many TV pundits quote the old cliché. *'My enemy's enemy is my friend.'* "

"But not many know it's an ancient Arab proverb."

"Considering your expertise on these matters, may we seek your further assistance before you leave Greece?"

"Of course. Feel free to call on me any—"

Captain Eliade walked away with his officers. "While you're visiting here, have a pleasant and peaceful vacation. But I suggest you too beware of Greek riddles. Many Greeks have solved the answer to the fisher-boys' riddle: *'What we caught we threw away, and what we didn't catch, we kept.'* "

"And that is . . . ?"

Without turning back to face him, Eliade's answer echoed in the vacant assembly hall. *"Lice."*

CHAPTER TEN

On what she calculated was the ninth day, Raven kicked the closet door. "I have to pee." She heard movement, a key unlocking. Morning light blinding her.

Alexi smiled. "You know your way to the toilet."

His smile made her feel better. She was pleased he let her go alone. Before she left the bathroom, she checked the window. Nailed down.

When she came out and headed back to the closet, he stopped her. "Sit. Join me for a coffee and pita." He brought two steaming cups and a plate of warm bread to the table. He tore off a piece and dipped it into his coffee. She followed his example.

"Now, we continue our discussion from the other day."

She clasped her hands on the table like a child in school. "Yes, Alexi. Whatever you say."

"Good girl."

. . . *maybe he'll give you a gold star for obedience* . . .

He asked, "What nation is the evil empire?"

What did he want her to say? To believe? "America."

"Why did your father lock you in the Athens Asylum?"

. . . *what answer will please him* . . . ?

He asked, "Do you want me to tell you?"

"Yes."

"Because he abused you when you were a little girl, and you were probably starting to remember."

She nodded. "He—"

. . . keep your mouth shut, raven . . .

"And no one cares what is happening to you."

"How do you know?"

"I will prove it." He left the kitchen and returned minutes later with a notebook computer. He moved the mouse. "I'm loading the search engine."

"What's that?" She knew, of course, but she agreed with Sis to keep playing dumb blonde.

"It allows me to search newspaper stories from anywhere on any particular day."

. . . make him want to teach you. men like that . . .

"Amazing! What are you going to search for?"

"Newspaper stories from the day we liberated the asylum. Let's see if anyone cared enough to mention you being taken away."

A chill came over her. "Of course, there'll be some mention. It's news."

He typed *Raven Slade*. "How long have you been with us?"

Beneath the table she ran her fingers across the scratches on her arm. "Today makes nine days."

"Next to your name, I'll add the dates since you joined us. Here are the newspapers. *New York Times, Daily News, International Herald Tribune.* See? Not a word. If they cared, there would be news about you."

She suddenly felt frightened. "Check the local papers."

He added names of Greek newspapers. Nothing about her being kidnapped. He was right. No one cared.

"That's why you're better off here with us. Do you understand, Raven?"

"I'm beginning to."

"After I accidentally shot Jason Tedescu, I heard him say, 'Raven Knows.' What did you talk about? What do you know?"

She shook her head. "I don't know what I know."

Alexi got up from the table and went to the cupboard over the stove. She didn't see what he was doing. "One of our members always keeps a supply for himself." He handed her a piece of dark chocolate.

She nibbled. Then took a large bite, then another, feeling her cheeks fill with sweet saliva.

. . . better than a gold star . . .

She jumped up and hugged him.

He stared at her left arm. "How did you get those scratches?"

"I do it to keep track of the days. My personal calendar." She counted off each line. "Nine scratches for nine days."

He twisted it. "No more of that. I'll let you know what day it is. How to spend your time. When to eat. When to sleep. When to go to the toilet. No more scratches."

"You're hurting me."

He released her and stroked her cheek. "If you come to see things clearly, you can become one of us."

"I'll do whatever you ask."

"Good. I have to go out for a while. I'll be back in about ten minutes."

She felt panic. "Don't leave me alone."

"I'll be gone just a short while."

"Take me with you."

"I can't. You have to stay here."

She clung to him. "Don't leave me."

"I thought you were ready to do what I say."

She felt faint. Mustn't get him angry. "Yes, of course." She cleared the table. "I'll wash the cups and plates while you're gone. Hurry back."

He kissed her forehead. "That's a good girl."

As he went out the door, she noticed he'd left it ajar. She ran to the window and saw him cross the street. This was her chance to get away. Out of this prison, down the steps to freedom. She reached to open the door.

. . . hold off, raven. he's probably watching from across the street . . .

She pulled her hand away as if the doorknob were red-hot. She wove her fingers through a tuft of her hair so tight she almost pulled it out. If he'd wanted to kill her he'd have done it at the asylum. Well, if they needed her, they'd let her survive. She slammed the door shut and went back to the sink. She opened the drawers. No knives or forks. Only spoons.

. . . break a plate. to cut your throat . . .

"Why are you telling me to kill myself?"

. . . do it now . . .

"No!"

. . . coward . . .

"You're the coward. I'll choose the time and place to die—like Mom did. What do you think of that?"

No answer. Sister was gone.

Footsteps on the staircase. He was coming back. She forced herself back inside the closet and pulled the door closed. Sobbing, she raked her nail across her arm for the end of the tenth day.

Oh, Jesus! Alexi forbade her to scratch herself again. Mustn't make him angry. She spat on her hand and rubbed the fresh scar. If he asks, she'll say she forgot. Or it was an accident. She had to make him believe she was his—body and soul. She had to make him want her.

In the dark, she fingered her scars as if they were braille. The tenth day was raw and hurt most of all.

CHAPTER ELEVEN

Alexi Costa battled American soldiers, heard their screams as he beheaded them. Then they all turned into women and babies. He sat up in bed sweating. Swallowed the phlegm rising in his throat. Stupid nightmare! He looked at his watch. Nearly seven. Raven must still be asleep in the spare room. He didn't wake her when he came in last night, pleased she hadn't tried to escape.

A soft knock at the front door surprised him. Who would come to the safe house without calling first? He opened the night table drawer and pulled out his Beretta .22.

"Who's there?" No answer. Holding the gun behind his back, he reached for the doorknob. A folded sheet of paper slid under the door. He yanked the door open. A small boy turned to run downstairs, but he grabbed the kid's arm. "What are you doing here?"

"Lady give me ten drachmae to bring paper this address," the boy whined. "No one answer. I push under door."

"What did she look like?"

"Tall. Eyes like coal. Black hair on head like crown. Olive skin. Middle-age but beautiful."

"Stay where you are." He unfolded the paper.
CALL NUMBER 210–722 09 53—URGENT.
He dug into his pocket and fished out a euro. "Forget you ever came here."

The boy grabbed the coin and dashed down the staircase.

He stepped back inside, locked the door and stared at the message. No one but 17N knew the location of the safe house. If the police had discovered it, they'd have raided long ago. He stared at his phone. Calls could be traced. Well, the note-writer already knew where he was.

He reached into his desk drawer and pulled out one of his disposable cell phones. He dialed. After four rings, he was about to shut it off, but a soft voice hissed, "I am glad you call, Alexi."

"Who are you?"

"We do not talk on phone. We meet."

"Meet a stranger? Maybe you want to kill me."

A chuckle. "If that is what I want, you would already be dead. I knew where to send the boy."

"Where do you want to meet?"

"Half hour, in Plaka near the taverna."

She was no fool. The best place for privacy was an outdoor café crowded with tourists. "How will I find you?"

"I find you. We recognize each other. Do not call this number again. Is prepaid cell I destroy after we hang up."

Dazed, he tried to visualize the women he had slept with. Too many. Narrow it down. The boy said she was beautiful and tall. Black eyes and black hair like a crown. Well, he'd find out soon enough. He wedged the Beretta under the belt in the small of his back. Not that he'd be able to use it in a crowd. But why take chances?

He went to the spare room and knocked.

"Let me out."

"Not yet, Raven. I have an errand."

"Don't leave me alone!"

"I'll let you out when I return."

He stepped out into the hallway, locked the door. Then down to the basement and out of the building by the rear cellar exit. Glancing around to be sure no one was watching, he mounted his black cycle and roared out of the alley.

It took fifteen minutes to reach the Plaka. Crowded as usual. Waiters moved with their trays between tables. He headed for a table close to the taverna as instructed.

The waiter removed a pile of saucers. "You want menu?"

"A coffee and cognac."

At that moment, two strong hands gripped his shoulders from behind. The phone voice said, "Coffee for two."

"Yes, madame."

She released her grip and he turned in his chair. With the morning sun behind her, he saw the silhouette of a tall, slender woman.

"You have me at a disadvantage," he said. "Come sit, so I can see who arranged this tête-à-tête."

Her laugh was throaty. She stepped around and faced him. As the boy described her, hair braided in a crown, dark eyes and olive skin. But no lipstick or rouge—no makeup at all. About forty, but still lovely. The sun reflected off a gold crescent, dangling from a gold necklace.

She quickly tucked it inside between her breasts and dropped her purse on the table. A loud clank. A gun? She'd chosen this crowded place. She wouldn't use it here. As she clasped her hands, he noticed the nails on her long fingers weren't manicured. Thumb and forefinger of her right hand were callused.

"So we meet again," she said.

"Again? I don't recall—"

The waiter brought coffee and a bottle of cognac. "Shall I pour cognac for madame?"

She placed a palm over the cup. "No alcohol for me."

"Well," he said after the waiter left, "are you going to tell me how you found me, how you were able to pick me out in this crowd? Or do you intend to remain a mystery woman?"

She sipped her coffee, then looked at him over the rim of her cup. "No problem. I see your face in Athens Asylum, when you remove head bandages and put on mask before you kidnap Raven."

He caught his breath. That's where he'd seen her face. Through the window of the nurses' station. "Nurse Faye Sawyer?"

"Actually, Major Fatima Sayid."

"Major?"

"Of *Mujihadeen-e Kalq. People's Holy Army of Liberation.* Some call us MEK."

"I know about MEK. The U.S. State Department declared your organization terrorist in . . . when . . . ?"

"Nineteen ninety-seven. Long after they put 17N on same list. Our groups have much in common."

"But you're Islamic. We are Christian Orthodox."

"Both honor our ancestor Abraham. We are both Marxist-Leninist."

He slumped in his seat. "How did you find me?"

"Maybe you forget. Your people not catch me after the shooting. I escape but instead of drive away, I follow."

"I thought you were a nurse."

"We knew, as you did, that Dr. Slade was CIA informant."

"What is your purpose here?"

"Same as your people. Together we do as Osama's martyrs did on 9/11." Leaning closer, she said, "Your comrade Jason Tedescu communicated with my leader to arrange alliance of MEK and 17N for *Operation Dragon's Teeth.*"

"I don't understand. We are a small group. You have a well-armed military. Four thousand? Five thousand?"

"Is no difference. We all know President Bush will not be restrained by United Nations. If America invades Iraq, their air force is sure to bomb our Ashraf base. We must strike first."

She was sure as hell fascinating. Unblinking cobra's eyes and hypnotic voice. Probably could get anyone to do whatever she wanted. He visualized holding her in his arms but, remembering the pressure of her fingers gripping his shoulders from behind, he shook off the thought.

"What do you want with us?"

"Jason Tedescu passed to us information that many years ago he planted 17N sleeper cells in American cities. He shared with us about *Operation Dragon's Teeth*."

He lifted the cup to his lips and mumbled over the rim. "How is that possible?"

"At the convention, before you shot him, Tedescu sent our general Hassan a second e-mail proposing an alliance."

"Why do we need MEK? As you say, we have the sleeper cells he planted in America."

"The problem is," she whispered, "his sleepers are *old* men, maybe senile. Pity if they die without fulfilling their mission."

"What do your people propose?"

"You know the cities but not the targets. We have the weapon but our Hezbollah cells in America are under constant surveillance. With our weapon and your sleepers we can strike a massive blow."

She was damned serious. "So you're suggesting—?"

"Détente. After U.S. State Department named us terrorists, they cut off all money from our 'Canadian Homeland Charity for Starving Muslim Children.' We have weapon hidden in Ashraf."

"What is the weapon?"

"First you pay us fifty thousand dollars."

"We don't have that kind of money. Our group is small."

"But daring. Steal from bank that does business with Americans. When you have money, bring it with you to our courier who then gives you the package."

"Where do we make the exchange?"

"At the Kent State University memorial to students killed by the Ohio National Guard."

"Very symbolic, but how will I contact the courier?"

"Go to Daffodil Hill and place glass with unlit candle upside down on one marker. Then put pebble on it. Our courier will approach and say 'teeth' and you will answer, 'dragon's.'"

Stupid to use the operation name. He shrugged.

"You give her the money. She gives you the package."

"I'll place your proposal before my people. How can I reach you?"

"I call you. I must have your answer before America invades Iraq. After that, it will be difficult. One thing more. Have you tamed Raven?"

"I am bringing her around to our way of thinking."

"Stockholm mind control?"

He smiled. "Raven now hates America as much as we do."

"With her, it is not possible to be sure. In asylum, I cared for her during schizophrenic relapses. Cuts herself. Afraid to be alone. Suicidal. Phobias of heights and fire. You may think you can brainwash her, but Dr. Slade's posthypnotic suggestion is surely blocking Tedescu's message."

"You were there. What did you learn?"

"Tedescu made her recite it from memory. It was in riddles."

"My father said comrade Tedescu always thought of himself as a prophet like Nostradamus."

"Except Tedescu was not predicting future," she said. "He was creating it."

Almost made sense. "But Nostradamus wrote his prophecies in obscure quatrains because he feared the Inquisition. Why would Tedescu do that now?"

"He distrusted the CIA. Before he died, I heard only two lines Raven read aloud.

"'*Unfaced Goddess guards future from the windswept tower. And in serious hate she butchers flesh of all.*'"

"Do those images mean anything to you?"

"No."

"Then they are riddles to be solved. Try to extract the rest from her. If you do not succeed, I will take her to Ashraf. As nurse who worked with Dr. Slade, I learned to deal with minds like hers. Leave her with us for a while, and you will know if she has really joined your cause."

"I'll discuss this with my comrades and call you."

As Fatima stood, the crescent necklace slipped out from between bold breasts. She threaded her way through the crowded tables and hailed a taxi.

Follow her? No point. She'd reached out to him. One thing bothered him. He'd heard that MEK was not only an Islamic-Marxist terrorist militia, it was a cult led by megalomaniac females. He would let Major Fatima deal the cards, but he'd watch closely how she held the deck in those callused hands.

He paid the bill and went around the alley to where his Harley was parked. As he pulled out, he looked around carefully. Why bother? She already knew the location of the safe house.

Fatima said patients like Raven couldn't tolerate being alone. Self-mutilating and suicidal. What if she wasn't completely under his control? What if he wasn't skilled enough to get the rest of Tedescu's prophecies from her?

In that case, he would send her to Ashraf as Fatima suggested. Let MEK deal with her the way Hezbollah and Hamas and Al Qaeda brainwashed their own mindless suicide martyrs.

CHAPTER TWELVE

Waybridge, Ohio

Dugan swam up through the throbbing pain in his head. He rocked back and forth. What the hell! The bitch Salinas tried to kill him. Why? He struggled upright and leaned against the office wall. He looked for the scrap of paper. She must have taken it. What about it set her off?

He closed his eyes. Thank God the blow hadn't knocked it out of his memory.

Seeds of Slow Death wait in our Tunnel~~s~~far . . .
To punish all Crusaders, Inshallah . . .

Probably from one of Tedescu's lectures. The second line was clear enough, an Islamic jihad slogan against Christians. *Inshallah* was a Muslim call to Allah.

Something was dripping down his cheek. He knew damned well what it was and he struggled to his feet, rocking back and forth.

His STU-III cell phone rang. He picked it up with his bloody hand. "Yeah?"

"Go secure, *Dentist.*"

He was still groggy. "What?"

"Use your CIK. First go secure."

He fished around in his pocket among his car keys until he found his crypto-ignition key. He pressed the secure button. "Go ahead."

"This is *Cymbal*."

"At least you haven't cut me off. What's up?"

"*Charon* got a signal from *Tentmaker*. One of the *Mujihedeen-e Kalq*'s officers is now in Athens to finalize an alliance with 17N."

"Any clue to the time frame?"

"Intel from State indicates President Bush will order a preemptive strike against Iraq. *Tentmaker* says if MEK can't come to an understanding with 17N, they'll launch their own preemptive terror attack—against us."

"When do I leave for Greece?"

"Now."

"I'll drive back to Cincinnati and pack."

"There's not enough time. Waybridge University has a flying school and airport."

"Probably a small one."

"Large enough for JPATS."

He shook his head to clear it. Throbbing nearly floored him. *Justice Prisoner & Alien Transportation System*'s air fleet was used by the marshal service to transport prisoners and criminal aliens between judicial districts, correctional institutions and foreign countries. More recently, the Justice Department of International Affairs used them for extraordinary extradition of suspects from foreign countries.

"Why JPATS?"

Liz was quiet longer than usual.

He sensed wheels turning within wheels.

"There's been a change of plan. The director wants you inserted into Greece covertly without going through their customs or immigration. You're not to go to our embassy as a legal attaché. Captain Eliade suspects that one reason no

17N terrorist has ever been caught—even identified—is because many Greek professors, powerful politicians, even judges, are sympathetic to them."

That explained Ms. Salinas.

"He already has one of his own undercover agents living among the students," she said. "The director is having me wire euro funds to the Olympia Bank in Athens under the cover name *Spiros Diodorus*. I'll send accreditation papers to you at the American Express office in Syntagma Square."

"Accreditation for what?"

"Graduate student at the Polytechnic Institute where 17N began."

"What about—?"

But the phone went dead. He waited the required two seconds before he extracted his CIK. At least skull-face Salinas hadn't taken his briefcase. He grabbed it off the floor and stumbled out of Tedescu's office. Down the hallway to the parking lot. He tossed his briefcase into the passenger seat and slid gingerly behind the Maserati's wheel. He screeched from the curb, weaving back and forth across the two lanes. Amazed that he made it to the university airport in one piece.

He pulled up to a Learjet on the tarmac. As he got out of his car, someone wearing a U.S. Marshal jacket came up to him, grabbed his arms around back and snapped on handcuffs.

"What the hell—!"

"Don't struggle. This is necessary."

"What's going on?"

"An ICE flight."

"Meaning what?"

"*Immigration Customs and Enforcement.* SOP to throw off anyone who might be surveilling you. Sorry for the discomfort. I'll uncuff you on the plane."

"Standard operating procedure, shit!"

"Force of habit. We usually strip a terror suspect and put a hood over his or her head."

"Well, don't. I've got a head wound and I'd probably pass out. You didn't have to make the cuffs so tight."

"Too suspicious to loosen them now."

He noticed another marshal getting into his Maserati and driving away. "Where the hell is he taking my car?"

"Into storage in Cincinnati until you get back." His escort helped him up the steps of the jet and shoved him through the hatch. "That is—*if* you get back."

"Hey, take it easy!"

Inside, the marshal unlocked the cuffs. "Sorry, but this is a university town. 17N and MEK may have informants among foreign exchange students. I had to make it look convincing."

"I didn't eat anything today," Dugan said.

"I'll get you some food when we reach cruising altitude. Want something to drink in the meantime?"

"You got bourbon?"

"Jack Daniel's okay?"

"A double will do fine."

Seconds later the marshal came out of the galley with a bottle and two glasses. "Mind if I join you? I don't like drinking alone."

"You're not flying this crate, are you?"

"Nope. I'm your guard."

"Okay then."

They clinked glasses. "Good luck in Greece, whatever your assignment is."

"Thanks." He looked out the window as the plane roared off. The airport shrank. They nosed through the clouds.

When the jet reached cruising level, the marshal said, "Give me your wallet and everything you're carrying."

He emptied his pockets.

"Keep your secure cell and the CIK." The marshal handed him a knapsack. "Change clothes in the head."

He glanced down at his jacket, tie and slacks. "What's wrong with what I'm wearing?"

"In Greece, it's safer not to look like an American."

Made sense. He grabbed the knapsack and squeezed into the head. He changed into a pair of worn jeans, black cotton T-shirt, oil-stained sandals, a threadbare sweater and a leather jacket with holes in the elbows. When he saw himself in the mirror, he figured with a two-day growth of beard he'd pass for a student. He rolled his civvies and stuffed them into the knapsack.

When he came out, the marshal nodded. "Now, you can probably pass for a non-American."

"What about a passport? ID?"

The marshal tore open a manila envelope. *Cymbal* had prepared a passport with his own photograph under the name Spiros Diodorus. The envelope contained a roll of euros and Greek drachmae.

"I can use another bourbon."

"I'm ahead of you. It's at your seat."

He downed it and unzipped his briefcase. He rummaged through it until he found his son's baseball wrapped in crumpled paper. He rolled the ball between his hands. Visualized the framed photograph on his office desk. Frank Junior holding the ball aloft. His own gray-haired mother beside his son, both smiling proudly into the camera.

He smoothed the paper. Junior had written a puzzle for him to solve, confirming where they were to meet for breakfast to celebrate the trophy for his no-hitter. Capital letters, *"THROUGH A GLASS DARKLY, SEE THE GLOBE TURN."*

He and his son had played at solving riddles since the boy was seven. Junior was fascinated when he told him that in college he'd avoided fraternities and formed *The Chinese Gordon Semantic Society*.

In grade school, Junior tried to follow in his footsteps. When he took his son to see the movie *Batman Forever*, Junior was so fascinated by the spooky Riddler, Edward Nygma, that he formed his own elementary school club. *The Nygma Riddling Society*. Taking after his old man.

He glanced again at his son's riddle on the wrinkled paper. "*THROUGH A GLASS DARKLY, SEE THE GLOBE TURN.*" It had been easy enough to solve. Junior and his grandmother had expected him to join them for brunch at Windows on the World atop the Twin Towers. That was 9/11. But he didn't make it in time.

He rewrapped the baseball and tucked Junior's last riddle back into his bag. The next attack in America would be *Operation Dragon's Teeth*. He downed the bourbon. Now it was up to him to get to Raven Slade and find out what she'd learned of the prophetic riddles giving Tedescu's comrades directions to awaken the sleeper cells in the U.S.

He rubbed the swelling on his head where Salinas had bashed him. At least, he'd found the scrap with two lines.

Seeds of Slow Death wait in our Tunnels far . . .
To punish all Crusaders, Inshallah . . .

If he could find and decode the rest, it might thwart a catastrophe. He'd have to find a way to get into the Athens Library archives. No way was he going to wait ten years.

CHAPTER THIRTEEN

Athens

Alexi circled the block around Theodor's Auto Repair twice. He parked in the alley and locked his motorcycle. At the street-level doorway, he pressed the buzzer. *Three. Pause. Two.* He heard the peephole slot click open, then the sound of the door being unlocked.

His father let him in, double-bolted the door behind him, and lurched on his crutch across the corridor. Inside, the back room air was clouded in a haze of cigar smoke.

Myron filled a glass of ouzo. "Drink, my son."

"I had a strange meeting today." As he sipped ouzo, he glanced at the original leaders of 17N around the table.

He looked at each comrade. Still hard to believe these middle-aged men had once been peacefully protesting Technicon University students. Twenty-nine years since the massacre wounded their classmates, minds and bodies, but not their passion to avenge the slaughter of 17 November.

Potbellied Theodor, cheeks bulging like a squirrel, was munching on his favorite chocolates. Hard to imagine him as a nineteen-year-old political science student who agitated against the junta before he faced tanks crashing the gate.

Tall, one-armed Vasili, a former star basketball player, who retrained himself to play outstanding soccer, opened the palm of his good right hand. "Does the meeting concern us?"

"It does."

Soft-spoken Yorgo looked up and smoothed his handlebar mustache as he waited for an answer. Hard to belive this gentle poet-singer fired the gun that assassinated the CIA station chief. 17N's first revenge against the Americans.

Dimitri, the oldest, wrinkled but still boyish-looking, wiggled the toothpick, as always, from one side of his mouth to the other.

Vasili rubbed his pinned-up left sleeve. "Are you going to keep us in suspense, Alexi?"

"Remember Faye Sawyer from the asylum?"

"She saw your face," Yorgo said, "but escaped before we could catch her."

"She has contacted me."

His father leaned forward on his crutch. "How is that possible?"

"She didn't try to escape. She followed us to the safe house. She knows where we have Raven."

No one spoke. Each looked at the man next to him as if deciding who was to blame.

Yorgo said, almost in a whisper, "She contacted you?"

"Her real name is Fatima Sayid," he said, refilling his glass with ouzo, "a major in the *Mujihadeen-e Kalq*."

His father said, "The Iranian terrorist student group that helped the mullahs overthrow Shah Pahlavi."

Vasili leaned his long frame forward. "If they're Iranian, why did they side with Saddam Hussein and fight against their own country?"

Wiping chocolate from his lips, Theodor said, "And if they switch sides whenever it suits them, who can trust them?"

Dimitri wriggled the toothpick to the other side of his mouth. "What did this major have to say?"

"She was in the asylum infirmary when Tedescu made Raven recite his prophecies in the form of riddles."

"My old riddling comrade," his father said, "always made them up, then forgot the solutions. What did this Nurse Fatima overhear?"

"Only two lines." He mimicked Fatima's voice.

*"Unfaced Goddess guards future from the windswept tower.
And in serious hate she butchers flesh of all."*

Yorgo cracked his knuckles. "Guarding the future must mean she is an oracle prophesizing what is foretold. Like Apollo's Sybil at Delphi."

Vasili shook his head. "The Delphic oracle is not on a windswept tower. Its fumes drift up from a dark grotto."

"If she butchers the flesh," Theodor said, "she may be the oracle's high priestess sacrificing a goat to the gods."

Dimitri chewed his toothpick. "A sacrifice to the gods 'in serious hate'? Not likely."

Theodor bit off another piece of chocolate. "Yet Tedescu planted our sleepers in America and planned *Dragon's Teeth*. So what does this mean, Alexi?"

"MEK wishes to make an alliance with us for the operation."

"Absurd," his father shouted. "It is *our* plan, *our* revenge."

"True," he said, "but the major pointed out that our sleepers in America are middle-aged."

His father jabbed the air with his crutch like a sword. "MEK women also now growing old. Maybe fat."

"Fatima's point is that the first generation of 17N is an effective force here in Greece. In America, our aging sleepers, without MEK's weapon, will be a wasted resource."

Dimitri chewed on his toothpick. "I do not trust terrorists

who change sides whenever it suits them. They will betray us when it is to their benefit."

"They want revenge against the CIA as much as we do."

Yorgo said, "What weapon does MEK intend to give us?"

"Not give. Sell."

Theodor mumbled through his full mouth, "So these Islamic-Marxists want to *capitalize* on our causes."

"Look, Saddam used Iraq's Oil-for-Food money to provide MEK with tanks and mortars and old AK-47s. It also paid for bioterror weapons from the Chechen mafia. She says MEK still has some, but we must pay to cover their expenses."

"How much?" Myron asked.

"Fifty thousand U.S. dollars."

Yorgo lit a cigar and puffed out a circle. "And where do we get that kind of money?"

"She suggests we rob a bank that does business with American companies."

Dimitri said, "Like the Athens Bank?"

"Why not? We've robbed other ones."

"Each time was more dangerous than the last." Vasili lifted his arm-stump. "I am against risking our lives for the Muslims."

Alexi sensed the caution of old men who had survived in the shadows for so long. "I'll take the risk."

Myron snorted. "Alone?"

He visualized the TV image of Patty Hearst, converted to the cause of the Symbionese Liberation Army, aiming her rifle at a bank employee. "I will use Raven to help me."

His father swatted the air with the back of his crutch. "I am opposed."

Yorgo said, "I agree with Myron. She may put us all in danger."

"I've been working on her for two weeks, gaining her trust

with methods the North Koreans used many years ago to program enemies into agents."

Myron asked, "And you think you can do that with her?"

"I do. And without touching her."

Dimitri tongued his toothpick back and forth. "A waste of that lovely young body."

Vasili chuckled. "Alexi, are you sure *she* did not brainwash *you?*"

He turned to his father. "I ask your permission."

Myron's brow furrowed. "All right. Let her help you rob the bank, but if she resists or tries to escape, shoot her. Make it look like a bank guard did it."

"But, if she dies, Tedescu's prophecies die with her."

"I did not say *kill* her. Shoot her in leg or arm. Then bring her here, and we will get message out of her the same way Captain Eliade's counterterror people torture some of our sympathizers to get information about us."

"And if that fails?"

Myron tapped his crutch against his leg. "Then, she is no use to us. Dispose of her."

Saliva dripped from Dimitri's toothpick. "But, Alexi, before you kill that sexy young thing, let me borrow her body for an hour or two."

CHAPTER FOURTEEN

Crete, Greece

JPAT's Learjet landed. Dugan climbed out and glanced around at a small airport. "Where the hell is this?"

"Crete," the marshal said.

"I thought I was being flown to Athens."

"Last minute orders to insert you indirectly. Your handler will make contact. Code greeting is *River Crossing*." The marshal pulled up the steps and waved good-bye. The plane took off.

He looked around at the bleak surroundings. How the hell was he supposed to liaison with a CIA case officer based in Cyprus from this deserted hellhole in Crete?

Minutes later, a banged-up yellow Mercedes pulled to a stop. A grizzled old man opened the rear door. "Taxi."

He shook his head.

The driver spread his hands. "I told come here for you from plane to *cross river*. This your taxi."

It figured. He got into the cab and settled back. Apparently, from here on, his actions would be controlled—or should he say, handled—by handler *Charon*.

The driver headed toward a cluster of low buildings.

"What's the name of this city?"

"Herakleion."

A long way from Athens.

The driver pulled up to a mud-colored apartment building. "Second floor. Room 204."

All right. A CIA safe house. He climbed the rickety stairs and knocked. No response. He knocked again. The door opened as far as the chain would allow. "Passport."

Dugan handed it through the opening. Seconds later, the door opened and a bald man peered at him through black-rimmed eyeglasses.

"Welcome to Herakleion, Spiros Diodorus."

"I thought we were going to rendezvous in Cyprus."

"Often, it's best to do these things indirectly. Come in. Sit. Your flight must have been tiring. Join me for a drink? Strong Greek vodka dulls my toothache."

"You should really see a dentist."

"Of course, that's why you're here."

"I thought I was going to open my practice in Athens."

"You will take the night ferry from Crete to Piraeus."

So Charon—who ferried the dead across the river Styx—would be guiding him. Grim touch. "Okay, fill me in."

"Dr. Slade phoned me and said his daughter had memorized Tedescu's three quatrain enigmas. Most likely coded plans for a terrorist attack on the U.S. Slade said he hypnotized Raven and gave her a posthypnotic suggestion to block it until someone said the phrase to unlock memory."

"What's the phrase?"

"I couldn't make it out over the shouting. Then a gunshot. I learned later that Slade killed himself."

"So, where does that leave us?"

"We assume 17N will try to get Tedescu's prophecies out of her. If they can't, or can't solve the riddles, they'll attempt to brainwash her into joining them."

"Stockholm syndrome? Patty Hearst style?"

"I know from Slade's earlier reports that his daughter is

mentally unstable. If they succeed with mind control, your job is to free and deprogram her."

"Then, I suppose, JPATS extradites her to the States?"

"That's not the plan. We don't want her back home."

"What then?"

"Turn her over to the Greeks for aggressive interrogation."

The thought sickened him, but he understood where *Charon* was going. "I speak Greek pretty well, but I never mastered the Athenian accent."

"There are dozens of dialects from more than 160 populated Greek Islands. Just act confident. Students at the Polytechnic will assume you're from one of them."

"What's my base of operations?"

"Student quarter."

"I'll have to find a place to live."

"Our Greek contact already arranged for one of their undercover agents to rent a room for you in a boardinghouse known to be occupied by many of the radicals."

"17N sympathizers?"

"As well as fascists, anti-Turkish racists and anarchists. All dyed-in-the-wool America haters."

"I get the picture. *Cymbal* tells me you're handling agent *Tentmaker* in Iran's Revolutionary Guard."

"He's no longer there. He was compromised when he helped Elizabeth and her mother escape from Iran before the embassy takeover."

"Where is he now?"

"He slipped out of Teheran along with the survivors of the dissidents. He's now with the male cadre among the *Mujihadeen-e Kalq* in Ashraf."

"How do I contact either of you?"

"You don't communicate with him. You deal only with me. I'll program my number into your SIU-III secure phone under the name *Charon*."

"So, are you going to ferry me across the river to the netherworld in Athens?"

"Not yet, *Dentist.* But just in case I'm wrong, if you know you're going to die in Greece, remember to slip a coin under your tongue."

"What for?"

"*Charon's* fare to ferry you across the river Styx, to hell."

CHAPTER FIFTEEN

Athens

During her first practice run to the bank, Raven steered too hard. The Harley bucked out from under her, nearly throwing her in front of an oncoming car. The driver honked and shook his fist. Her body was shaking, but she managed to stick up the middle finger of her leather glove and gave him the bird.

When was the last time she felt her heart thump so hard? She swerved, circled and tried again. Better.

She straddled the cycle across from the Athens Bank waiting for Alexi to come out. Engine idling, dry tongue licking her dry mouth, she kept her eyes fixed on the armored car.

Checked her watch. Twenty minutes. What was taking him so long? Her face and neck were sweating. She was becoming nauseated. She pulled off her left glove and started to rake her right forearm with her fingernails. But she stopped. She promised him she wouldn't cut herself again.

. . . *stop thinking* . . .

The sound of a child crying made her turn. A woman with a swollen belly approached, pushing a baby carriage on the sidewalk with one hand and pulling a screaming toddler with the other.

She caught sight of Alexi coming out of the bank through the revolving door. Where were the armored car guards?

The woman came abreast of her, struggling to push the baby carriage while restraining the little one. At the corner, the child pulled free.

The mother screamed. "Tino! No! No!"

The boy ran into the street.

Oh, my God! Speeding drivers won't see the kid. She jumped off the cycle and ran after the boy. Dodging oncoming traffic, she caught him. Swept the struggling child into her arms and held him against her body. His flailing hand hit her face shield, nearly knocking off her helmet, but she quickly pulled the face guard back into place.

She carried him to the curb and handed him to his mother. "A fine-looking boy. I wish I had a—"

The woman slapped her son's face. "Bad boy!" She pulled him along twisting his arm.

. . . *see? that's the thanks you get, sis, stupid mother doesn't deserve children. concentrate on why you're here. your life depends on it* . . .

Remounting the cycle, she checked the handlebar rearview mirror and adjusted her black wig under the helmet.

At that moment, Alexi pulled down his ski cap into a mask. A guard—hand on holster—came through the revolving door. Another guard followed, carrying the money bag.

She tapped the gas pedal, raced the engine.

Alexi pulled out his gun. As the first guard turned, Alexi shot him. The other guard dropped the money bag. Alexi shot him as he lay facedown on the sidewalk.

The bank alarm startled her.

Alexi grabbed the bag and sprinted across the street. He leaped onto the seat behind her, clutching the money bag in one hand and circling her waist with the other. She felt his gun pressing against her side. She slammed the gas pedal and the souped-up Harley roared.

She shouted into the wind, "I was surprised when you killed the guards. I didn't think you would."

"It was necessary!"

Down one street. Turned at the first intersection. Changed direction at the next block, again at the next. Her vision blurred as she stopped behind a white van. Alexi jumped off and opened the rear doors. He tossed the money bag inside and pulled down the ramp. She rode the Harley up into the rear of the van and leaped out. Alexi shoved the ramp in and locked the rear doors. He ran back to the van and took the wheel.

She chanced a second look behind. No one following. Feeling light-headed, she slid beside him into the passenger seat, she pulled off her helmet and leaned her head against his shoulder. "Thank God!"

Alexi slipped the gun into his jacket pocket and put his free arm around her. She sighed as he drove the van cautiously back into the center of Athens, past the crowded Plaka where tourists lounged at outdoor tables reading newspapers and sipping drinks.

He drove past the safe house and circled the block to Theodor's Auto Repair.

He honked his horn and the shop door opened. The fat masked man looked around, then signaled for them to pull in. Alexi raised the money bag trophy. "Here's the cash for MEK. She's wonderful. Boy, can she drive a cycle."

When they were inside, the fat man lowered the garage door. He opened the money bag and lifted out packets of hundred-dollar bills in Athens Bank wrappings. Turning toward the adjacent office, he said, "Wait here."

The oil fumes made her dizzy. She slipped on the grease-slick floor, but Alexi caught her and pulled her to him.

She looked down. "Is that your gun against my body?"

He raised her head and slid his tongue between her lips. She closed her eyes. She'd been kissed before, but never like this. As he started to let go, she clung to him.

"Now is not the time," he whispered. "When we're alone." He took her hand and led her through the door to where the fat man had taken the money.

Several men, still wearing their ski masks, shouted, "Happy Name Day!"

In the center of a desk she saw a white cake inscribed in chocolate, TO NIKKI—OUR FIRST WOMAN COMRADE. In the center, a single candle.

She asked, "Who's Nikki?"

The tall, one-armed man said, "You are."

The man who had tried to rape her in the closet on the first day pushed through the others with his crutch.

Alexi said, "This is my father."

She forced herself to say, "Pleased to meet you."

He said, "This is your name day." His gravely voice set her teeth on edge. "Your nom de guerre from now on is *Nikki*."

"But it's not my birthday."

Alexi said, "We Greeks don't pay much attention to the day of one's birth. You are celebrated on the ascension day of the saint for whom you are being named."

"Who's my saint?"

"Saint Nicholas."

She visualized a Christmas tree in the Waybridge University quad. Heard "Jingle Bells" in her mind. She bit her tongue.

Each one came up and handed her a gift. Sunglasses, sweater, kerchief, walking shoes. A short man with one of those funny-looking Greek guitars that looked like a bowl at one end, strummed, and sang softly:

"Oh beautiful Nikki
With sun-drenched hair
And eyes blue as the Ionian sea.
I, Yorgo, welcome you among us
On your Name Day."

She applauded. Through his mask he kissed her on both cheeks. So did the others. When one with a toothpick protruding through his mask approached, she pulled back.

Alexi said, "We call him *Toothpick* because he always has one in his mouth."

"Is he going to jab it in my face?"

Toothpick said, "Never, Comrade Nikki." He took it out, kissed both her cheeks through his mask, then put the toothpick back and bowed as he retreated.

"You should feel honored," Alexi said. "That is the first time I have ever seen him without a toothpick."

The others laughed.

Alexi's cell phone rang. The smile vanished. He nodded several times. "Yes, of course." He turned off the phone. "I have to leave now."

She clutched his arm. "Where are we going?"

"You will stay here."

"Take me with you."

"I'll be back later. I have to meet someone."

"A woman?"

"You're the only woman for me. Toothpick will drive you to the safe house. I'll be back tonight."

As he walked out the door, she put her hand over her mouth. The door closed behind him. The others were watching. Don't let them see how the darkness closed in on her whenever he left.

Alexi's father limped forward and lit the single candle on the cake.

She recoiled.

"What is wrong?"

"Fire terrifies me."

His strong fingers grabbed her neck. "We cure you. Make wish and blow."

She fought the urge to kick him as he pushed her toward the flaming wick. She closed her eyes. She wished for Alexi to save her from the fire.

When she finally looked up and saw the swirling smoke, she was sure she hadn't blown out the flame.

She thought, How come you blew out my candle, Sis?

. . . *it's my candle, stupid. after all these goddamn years, i finally have a name of my own. forget the sis shit from now on call me nikki . . .*

CHAPTER SIXTEEN

Dugan stepped off the tram in Omonia Square and glanced around. Not the trash-filled plaza he remembered from when he was here with his ex-wife and son. Bustling street sweepers rounded the corner. Oh, sure. Athens was sprucing up for the 2004 Olympics, but what would the place look like after international visitors left?

He walked to the American Express office and paused outside to watch two workmen in coveralls scrubbing red graffiti from the marble wall. He could make out only the letters—*go . . . hom . . . Amer and Turk . . . bast . . .* and he mused over the renowned Greek reputation for hospitality to strangers. Probably a holdover from ancient Greece, when people feared that any stranger might be a god come down from Olympus in human form.

Gimme that old-time religion.

He passed between two police officers flanking the American Express entrance. Were security precautions for all foreigners or just Turks, non-Greek Cypriots and Americans?

Inside, at the counter, a frozen-faced clerk asked, "How I may help you?"

"Mail for Spiros Diodorus."

"Passport."

The clerk studied it. "You do not sound Greek to me."

"Neither do you," he said in Greek.

The clerk stomped away from the counter. Moments later, he returned and handed over a bulky envelope addressed to *Spiros Diodorus*. Return address *University of Cincinnati School of Dentistry*. *Cymbal*'s idea of a joke.

He strolled to an outdoor café on Oikonomon Street and ordered an ouzo. Waiting for his drink, he opened the envelope and pulled out a bankbook. A hundred thousand euros deposited into the Olympia Bank for the account of Spiros Diodorus. Also documents accepting him as a doctoral candidate at Athens Polytechnic University.

Ten minutes later, the waiter finally brought the ouzo.

"The service here is very slow," he said.

The waiter turned away muttering, *"Filese to kolo mou."*

"Is that where you're used to being kissed?"

The man's eyes widened. "You know Greek?"

"I am from Sparta, but I was taught how to deal with foul-mouthed Athenian waiters."

It took two bus changes to get to the Olympia Bank. He withdrew 300 euros. The sun had set, and streetlights came on, so he splurged for a taxi to the house in the student quarter where a room had been rented for him.

Inside, the dark hallway smelled of feta cheese and hashish. Searching for a wall switch, he stubbed his toe against the first step and yelped. The single bulb dangling from its wire suddenly illuminated the staircase.

A young woman headed down the stairs toward him. "Why didn't you turn on the light?"

As she approached, he saw her slender body, short black hair. Delicate mouth curled in her oval-shaped face.

"I'm moving in. Didn't know where the switch was."

Then she was directly under the bulb, and her face darkened into a black mask. As she passed him, her breasts brushed his left arm. The light went out.

"Here, against the wall," she said, "before the first and after the last step of every landing."

He heard a click, then the ratcheting of a timer.

As the light came on, her mask vanished. "Just moving in? Where are you from?"

"Samos." He'd prepared an explanation for the dialect. "Although my parents lived in many of the islands."

"Have you been here before?"

"My first time in Athens."

The light went out again. He reached across, twisted the timer and the bulb glowed. He paused and looked into her black-rimmed eyes. Some women used a dark-colored pencil to achieve the effect. Her's suggested too much alcohol or dope. Or both. As she smiled, the corners of her lips turned up delicately to the right.

"You'd better get up to the next landing," she said, "before you're trapped again midway in the dark."

He made it to the third landing. "Thank you."

She called up to him, "We'll probably run into each other again. I live on the third floor too." Then she was out the front door, silhouetted against streetlights.

He made it across the hall to his room, and switched on the light. Hardly enough space to turn around. It smelled of cigarette smoke. He frowned at the piss yellow peeling walls and the narrow bed. Beside it, a desk with a lamp faced the window. He pulled the chain, but no bulb. He took his suit and shirt out of the knapsack, unrolled them and hung everything on the single hook inside the door.

He went to the window to survey lights of the square below. His window faced a brick wall. The hell with it. He'd go down and stroll through the student neighborhood to reacquaint himself with the city he'd last visited with his ex-wife and son.

Carefully working the light timers on his way down, he

came out of the rooming house and turned onto Panipisti-miou Street. A few blocks from the Polytechnic.

During their last trip here for Helena's father's funeral, she told him how her mother had spent nearly two weeks barricaded inside the student union building, broadcasting on clandestine radio for the citizens of Greece to rise up and overthrow the dictatorship.

Years later, she said her mother told her the revolution worked, until Colonel Papadopoulos called in the army. Some of the survivors, as well as parents of the dead and wounded, blamed her mother's *rabble-rousing* broadcasts for the attack.

He walked to the street where army tanks had broken through the gate. He was surprised to find it locked.

A female voice behind him, said, "Since 17 November 1973, this gate has never been unlocked."

He turned and saw the young woman he'd encountered on the stairway. "Meeting twice in an hour is what I call coincidence or fate."

"Neither," she said. "I followed you to see if you're sympathetic to student dissent or a government spy."

"What do you think?"

"I will have to get to know you before I judge."

"Are we going to get to know each other?"

"Since your room is next to mine on the third floor, we'd better."

"How do you know my room is next to yours?"

She smiled. "It is the only vacant room in the house."

Where had he seen that provocative upturned smile before? He pointed to the gate. "Why has it been locked since 1973?"

"As a symbol of continuing resistance."

"Against whom? Isn't Greece now a constitutional democracy?"

"Some think it is. Others believe it's a puppet regime of the United States."

He tried to gauge her attitude. Was she a 17N sympathizer? "How about you? What do you think?"

"It is a long story. Buy me a retsina and I will educate you."

"You've got a deal."

"Your name?" she asked.

"Spiros Diodorus. Yours?"

"Artemis."

"Apollo's sister, the virgin huntress."

"Let us just say, huntress."

He stared at that saucy smile. *Artemis? Real or code name?*

She took his hand and led him the long way around the Polytechnic. "This is Exarchia Square where students usually hang out. I like the Parnassus Café."

"Home of your brother Apollo, as well as Dionysus and the Muses."

"So you know your mythology," she said. "Do not spout it too freely. Makes it obvious you learned it in a classics course. And that—although you speak the language well enough—you are probably not Greek."

"Thanks for the advice."

"The Parnassus is like an old *cafe aman,* where some students play *rembetika* with their *bouzoukis.*"

He knew *bouzoukis* were the long-necked guitars shaped at the bottom like bowls, but his face must have betrayed his ignorance of the other words.

"In the old days," she said, "*cafe aman* were neighborhood speakeasies. *Rembetika* are the Greek blues."

"I knew that."

Her lips curled again. "Of course you did."

Inside, a waiter led them to a table and lit the candle. "You wish now to order?"

"Retsina for the lady, ouzo for me." Looking at her by the flickering light, he realized where he'd seen that off-center mouth before. Ellen Barkin in the movie *Sea of Love*. He remembered the haunting melody.

The waiter brought their drinks and handed him the bill.

"We'll want more," he said. "I'll pay when we're done."

"Pay now," the waiter said.

Before he could protest, Artemis said, "They never know when there will be a violent demonstration and police round up students. The café owner does not want to go to the jail to collect for drinks."

He paid and added a tip. The waiter threw the extra euros back on the table.

"He doesn't like tips?"

"He suspects you are not really a sympathizer."

The bouzouki players reminded him of the last time he was here. With Helena. He glanced around at the tables.

"You are looking for someone?"

"My ex-wife."

"Why do you think she might be here?"

"She ran off with a bouzouki player. Maybe one of these."

"What is her name?"

"Helena. A Greek beauty, with a face that turned on a thousand men."

Artemis touched his palm. "Yes, but you are so handsome, I cannot imagine why any woman would leave you."

He raised his glass. "Here's to getting to know each other."

She blinked before touching her glass against his, lips curled in that sardonic smile. "To dissent!" she said loudly. "Down with Turks, imperialist Brits and government lackeys of the capitalist Americans!"

Students at nearby tables raised their glasses. "*Hopa!*"

As he'd suspected, she identified with the terrorists. Had

to be careful, but he might learn something from her. He raised his glass and joined in, "*Hopa!*"

The waiter came back and picked up his tip.

Three students on the small platform tuned their bouzoukis. The sound jarred his eardrums, but he lifted his glass in their direction.

A middle-aged man with a gray handlebar mustache got up and sang softly to the *rembetika*.

". . . *Arms tattooed with Morpheus needles,*
Soul scarred with hate . . . Let me die again . . .
For the thousandth time, The sleep of death . . ."

Artemis sighed. "So sad, so romantic." She touched his hand again. Her look suggested they would use only one of their third-floor rooms that night. He thought of the hostage he'd come here to rescue and pulled his hand away.

Her dark eyes opened wide in surprise and she shrugged.

Several young men, arms entwined, took the older man's place in the center of the floor and danced in a semicircle. The audience clinked glasses to the beat.

Suddenly, the music was drowned out by shouting in the street. Odor of burning rubber filtered into the café. Students rushed to the entrance.

"Demonstrating anarchists are burning tires again. Come, let us watch the police break it up."

"Is it safe?"

"If we do not take sides," she said, leading him to Exarchia Square. "It is more performance art than riot."

Protesters marched carrying homemade banners. Police appeared from around the corner, stomping in formation, batons extended.

One woman threw a rock. It bounced off a shield. When she turned to lose herself in the crowd, he froze. He'd seen her before. She moved beside a tall, one-armed protester and handed him something. He slipped it into his pinned-up sleeve. An officer approached with raised baton.

The woman jumped at the officer, clawing his face. He smashed his baton over her head. She didn't let go. He hit her again and again until she fell to the ground.

Memory of the knockout blow to his own head. The fury in Ms. Salinas's face before she bashed him unconscious in Tedescu's office. If she didn't survive this beating to her head, Tedescu's message would be buried with her.

Unless . . . What was the paper she gave the one-armed man? Where was he? Gone. Merged into the taunting crowd.

From the police side, tear gas canisters bounced along the ground leaving smoke trails. Demonstrators wrapped handkerchiefs around their heads and surged forward.

The gas made him choke.

Artemis tore her kerchief, put half to her face and handed him the other half. "Here. It will soon blow away and the police will back off."

One student tripped, then another. The police cuffed them and surged forward.

He shouted above the din, "They're not backing off!"

"These are not anarchists! They are 17N supporters! The police will round them up. We must leave quickly!"

She led him down the street, around the corner, away from the confrontation, into the rooming house. He reached to turn the switch.

She stopped him. "No light. The police will search student apartments for supporters of 17N."

"Third floor in the dark? We'll break our necks."

"I have evaded them before. I will lead you." She took his hand. Halfway up the first flight, she stopped and leaned back against the wall.

"What are you—?"

"Shhhh. We do not want anyone to hear us." She pulled

his body against her, breasts pressing into his shirt. He tried to back away but she grabbed his buttocks with both hands and pulled him closer.

"Are you crazy?"

"Yes."

He managed one step up, but as he lifted his leg she pulled down his zipper. Another step up, almost tripping in the dark. She reached for his soft penis and slid it under her skirt. No underwear. She rubbed him against her pubic hair.

He felt himself hardening. "I can't believe this."

"You do not have to believe. I will take you as you are."

Then she slid him inside her. At each upward step, it was thrust after thrust. Too dark to see her face. He tripped on the first landing, but she caught him and drew him in deeper.

The hallway light illuminated. He saw that half smile of her lips. He started to pull out, but she swung him around the corner into the darkness of the second landing and forced him back in. Her movements kept in rhythm with the clicking light timer.

Halfway up the third flight of stairs, the light went off and plunged them again into darkness. He felt her vibrating. She released him and started to fall. He caught her limp body.

"Don't stop," she whispered.

The light from below went on again. "Someone's coming."

"Me."

"I mean the light," he said.

"It's from the second floor."

"How do you know?"

"You and I have the only rooms on the third."

By the time they reached the third landing, the second-floor light went out. He was limp, but she was still throbbing. Talk about esprit de l'escalier! He loved that great French expression, realizing what you should have said or done after you left someplace, and were headed for the stairs.

At his door, he dug into his pocket for his room key.

"Not your room," she said. "The police will search the building for new occupants. They know me. They will not search my room."

He hesitated, but she pulled him to her door, unlocked it and led him inside. Her window faced the sky. Her eyes glistened in the moonlight. "That was interesting, Artemis."

She pulled him into her bed. "I am not finished."

He drew back. She slid her hand into his trousers, along his wet thigh and clutched his balls in her fingers. "Tell me, handsome, how do you like fucking on the stairs?"

"I'll have to think about it."

She squeezed.

CHAPTER SEVENTEEN

When Alexi's father released his grip on her neck, Raven straightened up. No candle smoke. The black wick shriveled. She looked around at her masked captors. Were they ever going to trust her enough to reveal their faces? Only Alexi could protect her, but he was off somewhere.

"Come, Nikki," Alexi's father said, "I take you back to safe house."

Remembering how he had nearly raped her in the closet, she backed away.

"I do not harm you, Nikki."

She glanced from one mask to the next. Which one would protect her from their leader?

"You will go with someone else?"

She nodded.

He looked around. "Take her, Toothpick, but no touch until my son is finished with her."

Relieved, she put her hand on Toothpick's shoulder. "I'll go with you."

Toothpick drove silently, dark eyes glancing at her through the slits in his mask.

"Watch where you're driving."

"I prefer watch you."

He pulled up in front of the safe house, walked around the car and opened the door for her. She hesitated.

"Do not be afraid, Nikki. I would never touch you against your will." He led her upstairs, stopping only to check the doorjamb for hairs. Inside, he asked, "Do you still sleep in the closet?"

"I've been a good girl, so Alexi promoted me." She pointed to the spare room.

"All right. But I must lock you in."

She smiled. "I wouldn't have it any other way."

That night she tossed and turned. Would Alexi be back before morning as he promised? Should she tell him how his father had treated her?

. . . better not . . .

It might help to turn them against each other.

. . . and it might backfire. choose the right time . . .

She couldn't bear the thought of spending nights alone. She tried to sleep but tossed and turned until the morning light filtered through the small window.

She heard the outside door open. Had Toothpick changed his mind? Was it Myron? Alexi? She got off the cot and shoved it against the door. It wouldn't hold out for long against a determined attacker. She looked around. Nothing to defend herself.

The key clicked in the spare room lock. She grabbed the pillow and held it against her body like a shield.

. . . are you kidding, stupid? think that'll work like a chastity belt . . . ?

Shut up unless you've got a better idea.

The door opened overturning the cot. Light flooded the room. "Good morning, Nikki. What's with the barricade?"

"I'm always scared when I'm alone, Alexi. Don't leave me again."

He took her into his arms and held her close. "I can't promise that. But I'll tell you what. You deserve a break. As your reward, I'm going to take you on one of my deluxe tours of the Athens landmarks."

"Which ones?"

"You'll know when we get there."

She followed him downstairs, out of the safe house, and around the corner to the Harley. When he got on the saddle, she pouted. "Let me drive. I need to stay in practice."

"From the way you handled it at the bank, I'd say you don't have to rehearse anymore. Climb on."

She mounted behind him and hugged his waist. A long straightaway then, after a few turns, he pulled up to a taverna. "We'll get a couple of sandwiches and a bottle of wine to drink at our destination."

He bought gyros, a bottle of retsina and put them into one of the saddlebags. As he circled past the shopping district he pointed up. "Look."

"The Parthenon!" She nearly fell off the bike. "Oh, my God! I've never seen it this close."

"The Acropolis is the best place to start your tour."

"I can't!"

"What do you mean?"

"I'm afraid of heights!"

He locked the bike and slung the saddlebag over his shoulder. "If tourists can do it, so can you."

He gripped her arm and pulled her forward.

"No!"

"First fire? Now this? If you are to be one of us, you must overcome your fears." He dragged her to the first level. Up one diagonal, then across to another. Up. Up.

"Stop! I'll pass out!"

"I won't let you."

. . . close your eyes. let him lead you. i'll try not to panic . . .

Finally, he stopped. "Here we are at the top. Now that wasn't so bad, was it?"

. . . don't make me look down . . .

Out of breath, she gazed across at the Parthenon.

"That was a temple to Athena," he said. "It used to have a forty-foot-high statue of the goddess holding Winged Nike in her right hand."

"I know Athena was the goddess of war. Who's Winged Nike?"

"*Nike* means victory. Most famous for her flying speed. "He pointed to a smaller structure on the promontory overlooking the cliff." That's the temple to the other *Nike. Nike Apteros.* 'Wingless Victory.' "

"Why *Wingless?*"

She felt his strong hands grip her shoulders. "The ancient Athenians cut off her wings to prevent her—their Victory—from ever departing from Athens."

"They kept her hostage—like me?"

"And, like you, she came to love this mountain."

"Well, she had no choice since they cut off her wings. That's probably why your father named me after her?"

. . . he looks really upset. stupid to anger him . . .

"Sorry I said that. Don't mean to sound ungrateful. I meant it as a joke. Forgive me."

They sat on a boulder and ate their gyros and drank retsina. She looked at the sun filtering through the Parthenon. She knew it was terrifying for Sis to be up so high, but for her it was exciting to be with him. Not in the present but in the mythic past.

He kissed her and bit her lower lip. She took a deep breath and listened to the wind through the columns. *Fly and tell Zeus you are in love with Alexi.* Why was the heat rising her face? She was sure he would see her blush. She tried to act calm. "Did you hear that?"

"Hear what?"

"Never mind. It was probably the wind."

. . . it was just in your stupid head . . .

But does that mean it's true? Am I really falling in love with him? And if I am, should I let him know?

. . . better play it cool until you figure out what his feelings are. if it helps or makes things more dangerous . . .

Affection can't hurt. It might make him want me.

. . . just don't lose control of your heart . . .

"Raven, you're blushing. What's going on?"

She took a deep breath. "You didn't hear the voice."

He touched her cheek. "You have beauty that makes Aphrodite look ordinary, and imagination of the poet Sappho."

"You really didn't hear the voice?"

He ran his fingers across her lips. "Only those blessed by the gods can hear it."

She smiled. He pulled her close. The beat of his heart flooded her with strange heat. She started to pull away.

. . . careful. he holds your life in his hands. don't fall in love with him . . .

"We'd better go back down before dark," he said.

She picked up the remnants of their picnic. Eyes closed, she clung to him and stumbled one step below another.

When they reached street level, he led her back to the motorcycle. "You can drive back if you like."

She shook her head. "I've had enough excitement today."

"All right, you handled her well during the bank robbery. In fact you drove as if you were born to it."

"Well, you said Nike was the goddess of speed."

As they entered the safe house, Alexi said, "Collect your things. You're moving."

"I'm being evicted?"

"Only from this place. We're going to my private apartment where we can be alone."

She looked into his dark eyes. Despite the part of her that feared heights, she'd wanted him to carry her down from the Acropolis in his arms.

Now, standing outside herself, Raven saw her sister.

. . . will it be you or me, raven? or a ménage à trois for two . . . ?

Cool it, Sis. He's mine.

. . . cut the sis crap. i've got a name of my own . . . from now on call me nikki apteros . . .

Since Wingless Victory means you can't stand heights, how'd you fly down from the Acropolis?

. . . fly? shit, i didn't even look down . . .

CHAPTER EIGHTEEN

Alexi watched Nikki walk ahead of him up the steps of the safe house. Slender body. Trim hips. Undulating tight ass. She was his for now. He unlocked the door, but as she reached for the knob he grabbed her wrist.

She looked up at him. "Sorry, just wanted to help."

"Watch what I do, and remember." He put his hand to the top of the doorjamb and removed a hair, then another at the bottom. He held them out for her to see. "These hairs are white. My father was here and left."

"A warning signal?"

"Exactly." He opened the door. Inside, she dropped her backpack and embraced him. He pushed her away gently.

"What's wrong?"

"Not among the terrible memories you must have of this place. We'll go to my apartment where you can be happy."

"I don't remember happiness."

He'd never seen anyone so unpredictable. One minute a young girl, then, without warning, a gutsy tomboy. "I'll help you remember happiness. Gather your things. We'll leave this safe house now, but you'll be safe. Trust me."

"I trust you." She stood on tiptoe and kissed his cheek. He reached for her breasts, but she pulled away. "You said not here."

She ran to the closet and stuffed things he'd bought her into a pillowcase. "Thank you for everything."

Her trusting look made him want to sweep her into his arms. Restrain yourself. Be gentle. She's strong enough to endure brainwashing. Still, his pearl was embedded in the softness within a hard shell. Hearing her hum softly pleased him. He enjoyed making her happy. But be careful. Don't fall in love. She might not have long to live.

"Was it terrible," he asked, "being locked in the closet?"

"I used pain on my body to distract my mind, but my voice spoke to me of hope."

"Voice?"

"Telling me it would be over soon. Assuring me that, if not, I could leap into the darkness."

"I don't understand."

"My voice told me I could take my own life and fly to freedom like my mother did."

"Would you really kill yourself?"

"I've thought of it often."

"Promise never to do it again. I can't imagine being without you."

"You've cut off my wings. As long as I have you, I don't need to die."

Not only was she a visionary, she could tolerate pain and face death. It wouldn't be easy to get Tedescu's prophecies from her.

He said, "I bought you another gift." When they returned to the Harley, he reached into a compartment and pulled out a black handbag.

"Wow. I need a purse. But it's huge, like a tote bag."

"It's large because it has a false bottom. Look." He pulled a hidden zipper. The bottom opened to reveal a secret compartment.

"Why would I need to hide anything from you?"

"Not from me, but one must always plan ahead."

"Yes. A good idea." She pulled her red and black wigs out of the pillowcase and slipped them into the false bottom.

"That's my girl."

She kissed him and whispered, "Thank you."

"Now we go to my place. I drive."

She climbed onto the Harley behind him and clung tight. They roared out of the alley down the street, weaving between student bicycles and scooters. He scratched a parked car's fender. She thought of the scratches on her arm. She'd stopped at eleven, but more days had passed since her father killed himself. She could still hear the shot, see blood dripping down his face, watch him fall. No matter how she tried to erase the memory, it left traces like red chalk smudged on the blackboard of her mind.

. . . to live, you'll have to make alexi need you. do whatever he wants. keep him happy . . .

The muscles on his back vibrated against her breasts. She closed her eyes as their bodies moved, rising and falling. His swooping turns were smoother than hers had been at the bank. Finally, he pulled into Exarchia Square and turned off the engine.

Street cleaners were sweeping away debris of torn protest signs and tear gas canisters. He said, "Looks as if there was a recent confrontation."

She followed him into the building, up to his second-floor apartment. Not what she'd expected. The large living room was almost bare. She studied unframed cubist paintings covering the walls.

He dropped the packages he was carrying and took her into his arms. "Let me show you our bedroom."

Unlike the neat living room, the bedroom was cluttered. King-size bed, sheets and blankets tangled as if he'd jumped up in a hurry. Clothing, books and newspapers scattered on the floor. A wastebasket overflowing.

"You need someone to pick up after you."

"Then I'd never find anything," he said. "This looks like disorder, but I know where everything is."

"You're kidding."

He set her down on the bed and pulled away the blanket. Would he use protection? Should she ask?

. . . better not. your life is on the edge anyway . . .

He unbuttoned his shirt. As she reached to help him pull it off, she saw crisscrossed welts on his back. She touched the raised flesh. "What caused these?"

"My father," he said.

"Myron was that cruel to you?"

"Not cruel, strict. He whipped me to teach me."

"Right from wrong?"

"That came later. When I was a boy, I used to walk and talk in my sleep. At first, he put bells on my feet to wake me when I got out of bed. That didn't work, so he tied my feet together. Somehow I always managed to get free, kept walking and talking in my sleep."

"What did he do?"

"That's when he started whipping me. Until I was thirteen or fourteen."

She stroked his hair, his hands, his back. "We've both suffered so much. Hold me."

He turned away from her. "I want you to kiss them."

She hesitated, then ran her dry lips slowly down the welt on his left shoulder. His back tensed. She opened her lips and slid her tongue against the raised flesh, licking it down his back.

He quivered and rolled away. She turned her hip toward him. "Kiss my scars too." She closed her eyes and waited.

His cell phone rang.

She clung to him. "Don't answer."

He hesitated. It rang again and again. He pushed her aside and picked up. Caller ID showed it was Myron.

"It's my father. I can't ignore his call."

"Why? Will he whip you if you do?"

He looked at her, then at the phone, then back at her. "You don't understand."

"I think I do. As well as you understand me."

He pressed the ON button. "Yes?"

She heard Myron's rough voice through the phone. *"What took so long?"*

"I was in the bathroom."

"You should keep the phone with you at all times."

"I didn't think of it."

"Not thinking ahead is one of your weaknesses. We are ready to bomb Piraeus. We do it tomorrow afternoon. Come to the garage right away."

"But—"

The line went dead.

She opened her arms and waited. He slipped into his shirt. "I must go."

"What's so important that we can't—?"

"I don't have time."

"Don't leave me alone again."

"I'll be back. My father needs me at the shop now." He threw her a kiss and locked the door behind him.

She lay back on the pillow and thought of what she heard Myron say audibly over the phone. *Piraeus bombing tomorrow.* She remembered the day Alexi first locked her in the closet, Myron telling him about bombing the Piraeus International

Passenger Terminal. When Alexi had complained that innocent people would die, Myron lectured him about *collateral damage* during the fog of war.

She knew that meant women and children were going to die. She thought about it long and hard. Not children.

. . . damn his father for coitus interruptus. let's pay him back with firebombing interruptus . . .

I can't.

. . . you're so weak. if i'd come out of mom's womb first, i'd be strong enough not to need your voice to keep me from going schizo. i'll do it myself . . .

She watched herself pick up the second phone from the night table and dial for the operator.

A metallic voice said, "Your call?"

Out loud, she said, ". . . *athens police* . . ."

It rang several times before a man answered. "Hellenic Police Department. How may I help you?"

". . . *i have information about a 17N bombing* . . ."

"One moment. I will transfer you."

She started to hang up, but Nikki wouldn't let her. After several clicks a voice came on. Probably taping her.

"Captain Hector Eliade, Hellenic Police Counterterrorism Task Force speaking. You have information?"

She hesitated. Nikki was silent. Always starting things and leaving the dirty work for her to clean up. What the hell! Alexi would damn her if he found out, but she would damn herself if she didn't. She put her handkerchief over the mouthpiece. "This is a warning. Passenger terminal in Piraeus will be bombed. Children will die."

"When?"

"Tomorrow or the day after. I-I'm not sure."

"Who is this?"

She hung up. She believed Alexi's argument that America and its dominated Greek government were evil. But that didn't justify firebombing mothers and their babies. If preventing the deaths of the innocent was a betrayal of 17N, so be it.

   . . . *glad you finally agree with me, raven* . . .

   You shouldn't have made me. What if Alexi finds out?

   . . . *tell your lousy lover to go fuck himself* . . .

CHAPTER NINETEEN

Dugan awoke to the muffled beeping of his secure cell phone. After a few seconds, he found it in his jeans pocket. The timer said 4:00 A.M. He looked at Tia's curved body under the sheet and took the phone into the bathroom.

"Who's calling at this ungodly hour?"

"Dentist?"

"Who is this?"

"I decided it's best that you know the code name of the Greek agent who arranged for your room." He recognized Charon's voice.

"What's his name?"

"It's not a him it's a her. Same house you're in. Code name *Artemis.*"

He almost dropped the phone. "You sure?"

"Info direct from Captain Hector Eliade of the antiterrorism task force."

"Thanks for the warning."

"I felt you should know, in case you run into her." He clicked off.

So she wasn't a student radical. He wished he'd known. What was the penalty for screwing a Greek agent? Correction. *Being screwed by* a Greek agent. Maybe she was a double agent, sent to catch him in a honey trap, like the KGB did during the Cold War. Well, if she was a double, he was doubly screwed.

He went back into the bedroom and looked down at her. The problem was he had a sweet tooth. He thought of the British expression: "In for a penny, in for a pound."

As he slipped back into bed beside her, she woke. He kissed her shoulder and slid his hand across her breasts.

Her eyes opened wide. "What are you doing?"

"Picking up where we left off on the stairs."

She pulled away and got out of bed. "Why are men always horny first thing in the morning?"

"Unfinished business."

"Well, I need a coffee and pastry. Go wash. I will meet you at the sidewalk café."

Grumbling, he rolled out of bed and pulled on his T-shirt and jeans. He turned to face her. "You're sure?"

She pushed him toward the bathroom. "Save that thought for another time, another staircase." She turned on the TV. "First we check morning news. Maybe there is something about the riot."

He went to the sink and turned on the hot water. It came out cold. As he soaped his hands and face, he heard the announcement from the TV.

"Early this morning, police released the following tape segment of criminals' escape recorded by the Athens Bank's outside surveillance camera. It is believed members of Second Generation 17N were responsible for the robbery."

Dugan stepped out of the bathroom and glanced at the screen. At first, he saw what looked like a man on a black motorcycle. A child's swinging arms knocked the helmet aside. The picture froze on a face no longer hidden by the face guard. The same face as the one in the photo Interpol faxed to FBI headquarters. Raven Slade drove the getaway cycle. She was no longer a goddamned hostage.

Artemis said, "I didn't know 17N had a woman among them. I thought they were all middle-aged men."

"Things change." He went back into the bathroom and dried his hands and face. He closed the door and pressed *Charon's* number on the secure phone.

A cautious, "Who's calling?"

"*Dentist* again."

Charon said, "I guess you saw the TV news."

"It complicates things. If Raven Slade's pulled a Patty Hearst, she won't come with me willingly."

"We can't assume that," Charon said. "I just got curious intel. A woman phoned the Greek antiterrorism task force yesterday and warned that 17N was planning a bombing today or tomorrow in Piraeus."

"You think it was Raven?"

"Not sure, but who else would know about their plan and warn us?"

"Maybe they didn't succeed in brainwashing her. What do you think I should do?"

"Get your ass down to Piraeus."

"To the passenger terminal they're going to bomb!"

"Just to the dock where you can get a clear view of a black motorcycle pulling into one of the parking lots. Since she warned the antiterrorist task force, the police are surely on the alert."

"What if I see her?"

"Use your judgment." *Charon* clicked off.

Dugan came out of the bathroom, but Artemis was gone. He dressed, grabbed his backpack and went out into the hallway. When he turned on the light, he saw her waiting on the landing.

"Kind of early to pick up where we left off," he said. "Besides, I don't think I'm ready for another relationship."

She frowned. "*Relationship?* Do not kid yourself. I just wanted to get laid."

"Thanks for telling me. I've got to leave now."

"I am going with you to Piraeus."

"What makes you think that's where I'm headed?"

"A Raven shot off her mouth."

The light went out as they reached the second landing. She pressed herself against him in the dark. "There are decent hotels in Piraeus. We might be able to spend another night together."

He reached for the switch on the wall and turned it on. He looked into her eyes. Suspicious? Questioning? If she was a double agent, she was damned good.

"Are you still interested?" she said.

"I thought you had enough of me."

The corner of her mouth curled. "I will let you know when I have enough."

"Why are women turned on in times of danger?"

"Men think they are the hunters, but women often have to point out the directions. If you are ready, my car is parked around the corner."

"Okay, huntress Artemis, let's stalk our bird of prey."

CHAPTER TWENTY

When Alexi entered the back room of the auto repair shop, only Toothpick and Fat Theodor were missing. The others were hunched over the table, looking at something.

"What's going on?" he asked.

Myron waved him over.

He joined them. Myron smoothed out a folded sheet of paper. "See what Vasili brought us."

He read the lines:

> ### WHAT
> *Seeds of Slow Death wait in our tunnels far*
> *To punish all Crusaders. Inshallah.*
> *And Holy Fighters join our comrades now,*
> *To spread the shearers' dander I avow.*

"A damned riddle. Where did it come from?"

Vasili held up his pinned sleeve. "During protest a wild woman dressed like a schoolgirl slipped it to me. Before the police beat her, she say Tedescu intended for us to have this prophecy."

Yorgo said, "I agree with Alexi it is a riddle. But how do we solve it?"

"We put our heads together," Myron said. "Jason Tedescu

was my comrade. I always knew his thinking. The passage about punishing crusaders, and *Inshallah*—Arabic for God willing—must refer to the alliance with MEK that Major Fatima Sayid told Alexi that Tedescu was arranging."

"I agree," Yorgo said, "but what are *seeds of slow death in tunnels far? And what's this about shearers' dander?*"

Vasili said, "Major Fatima told Alexi they have weapons in their tunnels between Iraq and Iran."

"So the WHAT of the title," Alexi said, "must refer to the weapon for *Operation Dragon's Teeth.*"

His father, tapping his crutch against his shoe, nodded. "Jason knew I would understand. Before World War II, both our grandfathers were shepherds. Many who sheared fleece became sick. That is the weapon of slow death."

Vasili frowned. "The sheep?"

Myron shook his head. "*Dander* that spreads from sheared fleece contains small amounts of anthrax."

Alexi slammed his fist into his palm. "Weaponized anthrax can kill hundreds of thousands."

"We know the cities where Tedescu's sleeper cells have been dormant for many years," Vasili said. "Now, we provide them with *Mujihadeen-e Kalq*'s weapon of mass destruction."

"But we do not know the targets," Yorgo said, "or the method of delivering the anthrax."

Myron said, "There is surely more to the message. It is your job to get it from her, my son. Can you do it?"

Before he could answer, heavy footsteps approaching made them turn. Theodor, breathless and perspiring, shouted, "It is too late!"

Yorgo said, "You look like the devil is chasing you."

"The she-devil Nikki has put us in danger. Alexi, you must terminate her at once."

"What are you talking about?"

Theodor waved a video disk. "Your precious Nikki has compromised us."

"I don't understand. She helped me rob the bank. We celebrated her name day. I'm sure she's loyal to our cause."

"She may be loyal," Theodor said, chewing on a piece of chocolate, "but she has revealed herself."

"I don't understand. The robbery and our escape were flawless."

"Your brainwashed woman made her debut on television!"

"How is that possible?"

Myron waved his crutch at Theodor. "Play it."

Theodor went to the counter, moved aside the tools and slipped the disk into the DVR. "The bank surveillance camera caught Raven's face."

"Impossible. Her helmet has a dark visor."

"You were so preoccupied with the money bag you did not see her play heroine. Watch."

Then he saw Nikki leap off the Harley and rush to save the child. The boy's flailing hand against her helmet forced the dark guard off her face.

"By tomorrow," Vasili said, "her photograph will be circulated by Interpol around the world—connecting her to the bank robbery, and to us."

Myron tossed his crutch to the floor and dropped into his chair. "Alexi, I know you consider her your woman. She knows too much. She must not fall into the hands of Eliade."

"I need time to get the rest of Tedescu's prophecies from her."

"It is too late for that." Myron stomped his good foot on the floor. "You saw the video. We cannot risk her leading them to us."

"What do you want me to do?"

"How have you arranged the Piraeus firebombing?"

"I set the bomb trigger. She drives the van to the international passenger pavilion. After the explosion, we discard the van and escape on the Harley."

"Change of plan," Myron said. "Toothpick carries and detonates the bomb."

"Why Dimitri?"

"This is Nikki's last mission. I will reset the timer to shorten the fuse."

"But that will also endanger Toothpick," Yorgo said. "Ever since November 17, you two have been like brothers."

Alexi asked, "Why should he die now?"

"He too has come under Nikki's spell. That makes him undependable. He will be happy to die a martyr's death."

"Perhaps," Yorgo muttered, "if he is given the choice."

"Are you questioning my decision? Maybe you prefer to be leader."

Yorgo shook his head. "I find it ironic that he will die at the hands of his comrades."

"Father, can't we find another way? She has pyrophobia."

"There are no good ways to die," Myron said. "If she is captured, Eliade's police will torture her into betraying us. Perhaps they will even extract from her the rest of Tedescu's prophecies. My way is merciful. I will reset the timer to three o'clock in the afternoon."

Myron made a clenched-fist salute. The others followed.

He joined in the salute, but a moment later than the others. His father's expression showed that he noticed. Myron wouldn't say anything, but there would be consequences. Even when he was a boy, waiting to learn his punishment was always worse than the punishment itself.

Myron's expression was icy. "Take your woman passionately tonight, son. Tomorrow will be her last day on earth."

Over the years, he had come to accept his father's double-edged weapon of domination. One side, passion cooked hot. The other, temper served cold.

He struggled for words to reveal his feelings. But all he could say was, "Yes, Father."

But instead of going directly to the apartment, Alexi drove to a taverna. Drink would help him build up the courage to take the woman he had fallen in love with—for the last time.

CHAPTER TWENTY-ONE

Raven stirred awake when she felt Alexi crawl into bed. Her body warmed when he kissed her eyes, but when she opened them, she saw his sad expression.

"Is Myron going to harm me?"

He pulled away. "That's a terrible thing to say. My father would never do such a thing. Are you trying to turn me against him?"

"Ask him. See if he denies it."

Alexi kissed her throat. "I don't want to hear more."

She said, "At times I have a strong survival instinct. Other times I want to die."

"There's something you must tell me. Someone heard you recite prophetic riddles before Tedescu died."

"I think you shot him, but I don't remember."

"You must try."

She struggled to recall that day. Nurse Sawyer taking her to the asylum infirmary to see her old teacher. All she remembered after that was her father saying, *"Raven fly"* and telling her to cheer up the other patients in the dayroom.

"I'm trying, but there's nothing."

"If you love me, you'll try harder."

"Sorry, Alexi, but it's blank. I'd probably need a psychiatrist to help me remember, but that would take time."

Alexi lay silent. "There is so little time."

She turned away from him, raised her hips and guided his hand along the raised flesh of her scars that commemorated each imprisonment in an asylum. She wanted him to kiss them as she'd done for him.

Sensing his hesitation, she drew away. "Forget it."

He turned her body and looked down at her. She knew he was going to do what he wanted. She blanked her mind, trying to block out the present.

. . . think of the future. only the future . . .

Maybe if she told him what he wanted to know. *Raven fly*, she thought, hoping it would help. But without her father's voice, it didn't work.

Alexi slipped the pillow beneath her back. She was dry. She couldn't believe he would. But he did. It hurt. She fought against crying out at each thrust.

Finally, he turned away, breathing hard and drifted off.

It's not his fault, she thought. It's his father.

. . . to hell with both father and son . . .

He loves me. He was eager to have me.

. . . well. you can have the self-centered bastard . . .

Guarded by the man she loved, she slept in his arms.

Weird dream . . . Her mother made her wear slacks and a shirt and tie when she went to school. Everyone called her a tomboy. She soon figured out it was to please her father who always wanted a son. In secret, she used her mother's powder, rouge and lipstick. Not good at it. One day, when her father wasn't around, her mother let her put on girls' clothing and taught her how to apply makeup.

As she grew up, she prayed there'd be a second child, a brother, so she could be her father's girl. After Mother's suicide she knew it would never happen. That's when she started hearing the voice of her dead twin who now took the name Nikki Apteros.

Tonight, safe in Alexi's arms, she started counting backward to block the unpleasant thoughts. By fourteen she lost track.

She awoke early, alone. Alexi must have gone to Theodor's shop to help repaint and dry the van before placing the bomb inside. Today they would drive to Piraeus. She heated coffee on the hot plate. It would be an unsuccessful firebombing because she'd warned the police, and they'd guard the terminal. As she sipped coffee at the kitchen window, she watched the sun rise above Mount Acropolis, illuminating the Parthenon. She looked away.

Bad luck to be fearful in the morning.

She pulled her blonde hair into a bun and slipped on the black wig. She bound her breasts tight. In jeans and a black sweater, no one would know she was a woman. When she looked into the mirror, she liked what she saw. Today she'd give an Academy Award performance.

She locked the door behind her, yanked two hairs from her black wig, spit on both ends and stuck one high, the other one low across the doorjamb.

Out through the rear of the building, she crossed the street and went around the corner to the auto repair shop. As she'd expected, two of the men—still masked—were blow-drying light blue paint on the white van. Toothpick was filling the motorcycle gas tank. Alexi's father, crutch propped against the workbench, was working on the bomb.

She asked Alexi, "What is he doing?"

"Fine-tuning the fuse to give you and Toothpick two extra minutes to get away."

"Toothpick? I thought I was going with you."

"Change of plan. I have to be somewhere else."

"You're leaving me?"

"Just to Cyprus overnight, my love. I'll be back before you

know it. Toothpick was overjoyed when I told him he'd have to take my place."

Something was wrong. She touched the side of the van. Although the blue paint hadn't completely dried, fat Theodor and one-armed Vasili lifted the Harley into the back, facing the rear doors. Myron slipped the bomb into a backpack and handed it to his son.

Alexi placed it on the passenger seat. "Toothpick, don't forget. Cradle it carefully until you reach Piraeus. When Nikki sees you returning after you set the bomb, she'll open the rear doors and mount the cycle. You drive the van away seconds before the bomb explodes. All eyes will be turned toward the blast. You'll both escape before anyone knows what's happened. Drive to a deserted street, abandon the van and return on the cycle."

After the Harley was loaded into the van, one-armed Vasili shut the rear doors. She slid behind the wheel. Toothpick climbed into the passenger seat beside her and held the backpack on his lap. Theodor raised the garage door.

Alexi lingered at her window and whispered, "I'm eager for your safe return, Nikki."

She knew that meant they would make love again when he got back from Cyprus. Maybe this time they would conceive a baby. They'd name it Achilles if it was a boy. It had to be a boy. She felt his fingers tremble as he touched her lips. Tears misting in his eyes. Why?

She oversteered and scraped the wall as she drove out.

Alexi had to jump out of the way. "What's the matter?"

"Nothing. The sad look in your eyes distracted me."

She pulled out of the repair shop, and the door clanged shut behind the van.

She cursed herself for having looked up at the Acropolis this morning. Now she was sure it was a bad omen.

* * *

Sun reflecting on the sea blinded her momentarily as she drove on the winding road toward Port Piraeus, but she didn't slow down. Out of the corner of her eye, she noticed Toothpick's sidelong glances. "Why are you looking at me?"

He put his hand on her leg. "I have never been this close to a woman as beautiful as you."

She slapped his hand away. "You horny goat. You know I belong to Alexi."

"Could there not be a taste for me?"

She winked. "Sticking me with that toothpick?"

He took it out and pulled off his mask. His wrinkled face was surprisingly youthful. "If I could have an hour with you, I would never need this in my mouth again."

She laughed and pushed his hand away from her thigh. "And don't play with yourself. You'll need to keep your hand steady when you switch on the timer."

"Be careful, Nikki. I feel things are not right."

"Let me focus on driving," she said. "Keep your mind on the bomb. Look, both international terminals just ahead."

"Park between them, Nikki."

"I can get you closer."

"This is near enough. I saw how you reacted to the candle on the cake. I know fire frightens you."

She looked around. The terminal plaza was deserted. Where the hell were the police? Did they assume her warning about the bombing was a prank call?

Toothpick said, "There's a space between the passenger terminal and the Salamina-Perama commuting dock."

She backed in. Toothpick pulled his mask back on and got out with the backpack over his shoulder. He walked slowly toward the terminal.

What was that beside her on the passenger seat? In his excitement, he'd dropped his toothpick and left it behind. She pulled a tissue out of the glove compartment and picked

it up. She slipped it into her pocket. *He'll be surprised that
she saved it for him.*

She watched through the rearview mirror as he lifted the
backpack flap and reached in to hit the switch.

Suddenly, he turned toward her. *"Go, Nikki! Forget me!
Save yourself!"* He ran *away* from her, *toward* the international
passenger terminal.

The bomb exploded. Tongues of flame enveloped him. She
swallowed a scream.

Through the flames, she saw his left arm where it was
torn from his body. His severed hand that stroked her thigh,
still clutched the backpack. She fought panic, pulled away,
and swerved onto the sidewalk, scattering pedestrians.

Around one corner, then another. A kilometer away, she
jumped out of the driver's seat, ran around and unlocked
the rear doors. She felt the scream still trying to get out.
She mounted the Harley, and roared out of the van.

As she sped away from Piraeus, she dug into her pocket
and pulled out the toothpick. *She should have let him touch
her. All he wanted was to feel her.* She jabbed the toothpick
into her wrist again and again, until it drew blood. And the
scream finally burst from her lips.

CHAPTER TWENTY-TWO

Artemis didn't slow down as she pulled into the international passenger terminal. "I'll park here, Dugan. We'll walk the rest of the way to the ferry slip."

He heard an explosion and saw the fire. Sirens blared. People gathered outside the terminal, but police herded them back. A crowd surged away from the terminal toward the dock.

Artemis pressed through them toward the terminal.

He shouted, "Where the hell are you going?"

"The bombing is finished."

He saw a light blue van careen past them, onto the sidewalk, then back into the road. Someone involved in the bombing? Or a frightened gawker?

At the terminal plaza, he saw a man on fire sprawled on the dock, clothing burned off. Skin covered with what looked like tar.

A black sedan swerved close. A huge man, wearing a black patch covering his right eye, stepped out and gestured for an officer to let him pass. He recognized Captain Hector Eliade who broadcast the news about 17N.

Officers separated the barricades to make way for him. As the captain approached the body, an ambulance—siren wailing, lights whirling—backed up. Medics pulled a gurney from the rear and ran with it toward the body.

Captain Eliade shouted, "Do not touch him! I must find out if he can speak!" He knelt beside the body. "If you can hear me, move your leg."

A gurgling sound from the man's lips. One leg thrashed.

As Dugan watched, his own skin tingled. Hell of a time to empathize with a terrorist bomber.

Finally, Eliade waved for the medics to remove the burned man. They lifted him onto the gurney and wheeled it to the rear of the ambulance. Sliding the gurney in, they slammed the doors and drove away, siren wailing.

Had to get in touch with *Charon*. Maybe he knew what was going on. Turning away from the crowd, he pulled out his cell phone and punched in the number.

A hesitant voice came on. "Yes?"

"Charon?"

"Who's calling?"

"Dentist." He described what was happening.

Charon said, "We don't want our blackbird to fly out of Greece. If she makes it back to the States, it may be almost impossible to extradite her to Athens."

"Extraordinary rendition?"

"Don't know what you're talking about. But it would take a long time to go through channels with an asylum judge. Find her. Stop her. If you can't get Tedescu's message out of her, turn her over to Eliade. He's an expert interrogator. Do whatever it takes to keep her in Athens."

Charon clicked off.

As he turned, he saw Eliade watching him with his good left eye, then pointing him out to one of the officers.

The officer waved his baton. "Halt!"

"I was just passing by," he said.

The officer jabbed the baton into his belly. "Hands behind back now!"

He looked around for Artemis. Nowhere. She'd managed

to slip away to avoid being taken into custody. Maybe she *was* a double agent. The officer cuffed him and shoved him into a police van.

Eliade got back into the black sedan and waved for his chauffeur to drive. The police van followed.

What the hell was he supposed to do now? Resist? Obey? Identify himself? Don't panic. Clear your mind. He'd never faced torture. Hell, he was an analyst, not an agent.

He should have prepared for this with a cyanide pill.

CHAPTER TWENTY-THREE

Piraeus to Athens

Raven careened on the Harley down one street, up another. Finally, she swerved into an alley a few blocks from the safe house, parked and pulled out her cell phone.

She let it ring three times. Cut off. Two more rings. Then another three.

Alexi's cautious voice answered, "Yes?"

"This is Nikki. There was an accident."

"We heard about it on the radio. Were you followed?"

"I don't think so."

"Drive around a while. When you are sure no one is tailing you, go to the apartment."

"Shouldn't I go to the safe house?"

"First, go home and change clothes. It's time for you to become a woman again. Stay in the apartment until I arrive. Keep calm."

Easy for him to say. She drove for another ten minutes, then parked the cycle in an alley and walked casually down the street. Passersby mustn't see her trembling.

At the apartment house, she used the outside key, and forced herself to climb to the second floor. Don't look down. She removed the black hairs she'd pasted across the doorjamb and went inside. She dashed into the bathroom, turned on the shower and scrubbed until her body felt raw.

Did Myron make a mistake when he reset the bomb's timer switch? Or did he purposely set it to detonate sooner, with no time for Toothpick to get away? Why would Myron want to kill his comrade?

She could still recall seconds before the firebomb exploded. Heard Toothpick shout, *"Go, Nikki! Forget me! Save yourself!"*

He'd been more concerned about her than himself. She wished she hadn't stopped him from touching her. He'd have had a few moments of pleasure before that horrible death.

An insistent knock on the door cut off her thoughts. Expecting Alexi, she threw the door open but faced a tall woman, braids crowning her forehead.

"Nurse Sawyer, I don't understand. How did you escape? What happened?"

"I watched dangerous people take you hostage."

"Where were you? You were never supposed to leave me alone."

"I am sorry, Raven." Sawyer's voice was soft, but her eyes were hard. "I have come to take care of you." She pushed the tote bag at her. "Pack your things quickly. Take only what you need. We must leave at once."

"I don't understand."

She heard footsteps climbing the stairs up to the apartment. The door swung open. Sawyer pulled a gun from her purse. "Who is there? Step out where I can see you or I will fire."

A hand appeared in the doorway, also holding a gun. Alexi's voice. "Put *your* weapon down, or I'll shoot."

"It is me, Fatima. Hold fire and I will hold mine."

. . . *fatima* . . . ?

Alexi stepped into view, aiming at the nurse. She stood her ground, her gun still pointed at him.

"Put your weapon down, Fatima."

"You first, Alexi."

. . . *what the hell's going on? gunfight at the o.k. corral? who's directing this goddamned cowboy movie anyway* . . . ?

CHAPTER TWENTY-FOUR

To Dugan, the ride in the police paddy wagon felt like twenty or twenty-five minutes. It pulled up in front of a garage with the sign THEODOR'S AUTO REPAIR. Moments later, the back door opened. Without warning, someone pulled a black hood over his head. Obviously, the Hellas police didn't want him to see the other prisoners.

Another long, bumpy ride. Then a stop, and they hustled him out along with the newcomers. Would they all be thrown into the same cell?

A baton prodded him forward into a building. When someone yanked off his hood, he saw that he and three others were in a long room with a mirror covering one wall. A two-way mirror? So they were going to be watched while being interrogated. He studied his fellow prisoners.

The fat one's mouth had a rim smear of chocolate. The other two looked familiar. The handlebar-mustached *rembetika* singer of sad lyrics in the Parnassas Café. The third was the tall, one-armed man Tedescu's assistant had passed an envelope to before she attacked the police and was battered unconscious. Had Ms. Salinas gotten away? Was she lying somewhere in a coma? Or dead?

The overhead light went off, and the wall in front of them vanished. He'd been right about the two-way mirror,

but he and the other three weren't going to be observed.
They would do the observing.

Through the glass, he saw a room with a hospital bed, an
intravenous unit and a heart monitor. A cart held surgical
instruments. Two attendants wheeled in a gurney and transferred a charred body onto the bed.

Someone in a hospital gown, wearing a surgical mask,
entered and picked up a scalpel. "Dimitri, we found your
name in your wallet. Before I cut burned tissue away, tell me
what you know about *Operation Dragon's Teeth*."

He'd heard that hollow, echolike voice before. When the
interrogator turned, he saw the black eye patch above
the surgeon's mask. This wasn't medical treatment. He and
his three fellow prisoners were being forced to watch Captain Hector Eliade conduct an *aggressive interrogation*.

The scalpel glinted in the fluorescent light as Eliade sliced
away a strip of charred flesh. He held it up to the light.
"Who in 17N leads *Operation Dragon's Teeth?*"

The burned body twisted.

"Where are 17N's terrorist sleeper cells in America?"

Screams reverberated through the loudspeaker.

"What are the cities and targets of the attack?"

It nauseated him. Exactly what the Human Rights Watch
meant when they accused governments of ignoring the Geneva conventions against torture.

The fart smell from the fat chocolate-eater beside him
made it obvious he shit his pants. The one-armed man tee-
tered forward and back but caught himself. The *rembetika*
singer with the handlebar mustache sang softly, *"Let me die
again . . . For the thousandth time, the sleep of death . . ."*

Eliade sliced off another strip of blackened flesh and held
it to the light as if studying it for answers. To avoid such
pain, he knew he'd confess to anything. So much for the
value of torture interrogation.

The body on the bed thrashed.

His own throat filled with phlegm.

More screams echoing from Dante's hell.

Eliade leaned close to his victim as if listening. "What? The 17N safe house? Is that what this key we found in your trouser pocket is for? Thank you for your voluntary assistance. That will be enough for today. I am sure we will get the rest of the information from your comrades now that they see how you cooperated."

The body writhed against the restraints.

"Dimitri, tell me, who is the woman who drove you to Piraeus? Is she the hostage from the Athens Asylum? The same woman who drove the motorcycle during the bank robbery?"

Another scream, then sound from the other side of the observation room was cut off.

Bright lights flashed on. He had to cover his eyes. Eliade, still in his surgical mask, left the interrogation room and joined them. "Your comrade has told me everything, but I must confirm information. Who is next?"

The fat prisoner—whose farts stank up the observation cell—bleated, "I know nothing. I only own the auto repair shop."

The one-armed man held his nose with his free hand and mumbled, "We are innocent bystanders."

The *rembetika* player sang softly, "I am ready to die for the cause."

Eliade turned to the guards. "Take those three into the corridor and let them choose who is to be interrogated first. I will deal with the younger one myself."

How long would he be able to hold out before revealing his identity? He was no hero. When the other three were gone, Eliade switched off the overhead light and reilluminated the two-way mirror. So the sadist was going to try to soften him up by making him watch the other three prisoners being tortured.

Unlike CIA spooks, he didn't have a cyanide-filled false tooth to bite.

"Observe the bed," Eliade said.

He stared through the two-way mirror. The empty bed twisted and turned like a bucking horse. Screams echoed in the vacant room.

He gasped. "An adjustable bed and recorded screams?"

"By an actor."

"And the burned man . . . ?"

"Died in the ambulance on the way here."

"Then why this charade?"

"Welcome to the virtual theater of Greek tragedy, Agent Frank Dugan. Or should I call you *Dentist?*"

"What the hell—?"

"I was alerted by our contact at Interpol."

"How can you justify what I just witnessed?"

"Call it *Theater of Torture.* We Greeks have always been emotionally involved while witnessing psychologically painful dramas. It is *catharsis* that cleanses the spirit."

"So the whole show was just an act to soften up the other three prisoners."

"Your own performance was impressive, Agent Dugan. It is a good thing *Cymbal* in New York notified me about you ahead of time."

"What if she hadn't?"

"Theatrical Illusion might have become Performance Art."

"Forgive me if I don't applaud."

"As they say in Western theater, 'Break a leg.' Now, let us see how our three 17N terrorists react to what they believe they saw and heard."

Eliade called for the guards to bring the prisoners back

into the observation room. As they stumbled in, he said, "One of you will tell us what we need to know. The other two will die painful deaths. Choose your fates."

The *rembetika* singer-poet smoothed his handlebar mustache. "I will never betray 17N. I am ready to die."

"Even if it is very slowly?"

"I sang at the barricades when the police and tanks attacked us. I have not feared death since then."

What was going to be the next act? How would Eliade follow his skin-slicing performance?

He motioned to the guards. "Take this one into the interrogation room and prepare him. The rest of you may observe your comrade's bravado."

Though he knew Eliade would merely pretend to torture the man, still it would be disturbing to watch.

The guards tore off Yorgo's clothes and strapped him naked into a chair bolted to the floor. Eliade signaled one of his aides to bring something alongside. A table with wires, levers and clamps. How the hell was he going to break the singer-poet by pretending to use electric shock?

"Before I begin this procedure, I give you one final opportunity to identify the other terrorists."

The poet strummed an imaginary *rembetika* and sang:

"Gods on Parnassus, protect your humble servants,
Who kill to bring power to the people.
Lord of the thunderbolt, spare me pain,
Dispatch this mortal flesh quickly to the netherworld."

Eliade untangled the wires and tested the clamps. He signaled one of his guards to hit the switch.

Probably just low voltage to give Yorgo the impression pain would soon follow. Strong scene. Greek theatergoers would find this really cathartic.

"Terrorist," Eliade commanded, "name your 17N comrades!"

"Zeus, lord of lightning,
Split me swiftly,
Dispatch your servant
To dwell among the dead in Hades."

He was surprised as Eliade fastened a clamp to both nipples on Yorgo's chest, and two more to the testicles. Even low-level voltage would be agonizing. Mustn't be squeamish. This might save thousands of American lives.

"Last warning. Stop singing and talk."

"Hermes, guide my soul.
To Hades, where—"

Eliade threw the switch.

"Aaaaggghhh!"

"Answer my questions, terrorist-poet."

Yorgo's body quivered, but he shook his head.

Eliade turned up the voltage. "Now?"

"Our Father who are in heaven,
Hallowed be thy name, thy kingdom come
Thy will be—Ahhhh . . . !"

This was no performance. Eliade was really torturing the poor bastard. The singer's shaking stopped. His head flopped to one side, eyes wide-open.

Eliade came back into the observation room.

What to say to the son of a bitch? This was more than aggressive interrogation. It was murder. What they would do to Raven Slade if—as assigned—he brought her here for questioning?

"I can't belive what I just saw. How do you justify killing a man that way."

Eliade removed the gauze cover, leaving his face still a one-eyed mask. He switched a speaker and called, "Artemis, come into the observation room."

Artemis?

Seconds later, the door opened. He started to speak, but her look signaled him not to.

Eliade pointed to the stinking fat man and toward the one-armed scarecrow. "These two terrorists would rather die than give us information about 17N. The Dentist is offended that I tortured a man in an effort to save thousands of men, women and children from horrible deaths. You may proceed without torture."

She reached between her breasts and drew out a dagger.

Eliade turned to the other two. "Are you both also willing to die for 17N?"

The trembling fat one said, "Not me. I will tell you."

Eliade pulled out a recorder. "Your names."

"I am Theodor Pavli." He pointed to the one-armed prisoner. "This is Vasili Sorostos."

"And the names of the other members of 17N."

Between the two, they rattled off fifteen more names.

"No others? Who are the leaders?"

Pavli hesitated.

Artemis aimed her throwing knife.

The fat man choked out, "Since Jason Tedescu is dead, Myron Costa alone rules 17N!"

One-arm shouted, "His son, Alexi, is the leader of Second Generation 17N!"

"And what of the female, Raven Slade?"

"I do not know that name," the fat man said.

"The young woman you took hostage from the asylum."

"Oh, she is Nikki, Alexi's woman."

"Where are they?"

"Myron has fled."

Eliade turned to the one-armed man. "Your turn. Where has he gone?"

"To one of the islands."

"Which one?"

"I do not know. There are more than fourteen hundred."

Eliade looked at Artemis. She drew her hand back to throw the knife. The man clutched his empty sleeve. "I swear. He never told us. It is his secret retreat."

Eliade pressed him. "Where is the safe house?"

"Omonia Square. Across from the archaeological museum. A few streets from Alexi Costa's apartment." He stuttered out Alexi's address, the safe house and the repair shop.

Artemis slipped the dagger back into her cleavage.

Eliade took off his surgeon's gown and ordered his guards to remove both men. After they were gone, he dangled the key. "Dentist, you may go with her to examine the safe house."

"The business about the key was real?"

"Before he died at the terminal, Dimitri told me that Myron Costa and his son, Alexi, had betrayed both him and the woman. He realized the plan had been for both of them to die in the premature bombing."

"Did he tell you her name?"

"Only her code name. Nikki."

"Captain Eliade, you said you were alerted to my presence here, but I went immediately undercover. How did you know where I'd be?"

"At first, I was not sure if you were the undercover FBI agent or a 17N terrorist, so I had you watched."

"By whom?"

"My eyes and ears among radical student groups. Meet Agent Tia—code name *Artemis*—who works undercover."

She sure does. "We've met."

"It was prearranged. She selected your room so she could observe you. She knew when you'd be coming."

That she did.

Her lovely lips restrained that turned-up smile.

"Agent Dugan, if you have any lustful ideas," Eliade said, "keep one thing in mind if you do not want to return to America as a eunuch."

"What's that?"

"Tia is my daughter."

CHAPTER TWENTY-FIVE

Fatima saw the gun in Alexi's hand. "Lower your weapon," she said, "and I will do the same."

"Major Sayid, what right do you have to enter my home?"

"It concerns the alliance of which we spoke."

"In what way?"

"I have been ordered to take Raven to Ashraf."

"Like hell you will."

Do not upset him, she told herself. Let the arrogant Greek settle down. "Put your gun away and let us discuss this calmly."

"You first, Fatima."

". . . *fatima? she's lying, alexi. she's faye . . .*"

"That was a cover name," he said. "Her real name is Major Fatima Sayid."

Fatima recognized the *other* voice that came from Raven at times in the asylum. The one Raven called *Sister.* "Do not listen to her, Alexi. She is in her schizophrenic phase. Do not let her interfere with our alliance." She saw his gun barrel waver. "Both our groups need each other to achieve our objective."

". . . *she's using you, alexi. shoot her before she kills us both . . .*"

The little fool had indeed dissociated. That made her a

serious threat. "Look, Alexi." She slipped the Makarov back into her purse. "I have put my gun away."

He hesitated, then lowered his.

She took out a cigarette, lit it and waved the lighter flame. She expected Raven to recoil, but instead she controlled herself.

"What happened to your fear of fire?"

"*. . . you're thinking of raven. i'm not afraid of fire or you . . .*"

"And who are you?"

"*. . . nikki apteros . . .*"

"You and I have crossed paths before."

"*. . . i'll be happy if it never happens again . . .*"

She rubbed her forefinger against the barrel of her gun and turned back to Alexi. "I saw the surveillance tape on television. Her likeness has already been circulated by Interpol around the world, connecting her to 17N."

"I'm aware of that."

"Have you gotten Tedescu's prophecies from her?"

"Not from her, but we've learned the weapon is anthrax."

"That is already known to us. It is the one weapon Jason Tedescu chose from our armory. What else have you learned? The targets? The method of delivering it?"

"I need more time."

"My general thinks the sands are running out. Decide. If Raven had died in the premature bombing at Piraeus before we solved the prophecies, both our groups would have lost the advantage. That was a stupid mistake. I helped her father keep her under control whenever she acted crazy like this until he hypnotized her. I know borderline and histrionic patients. If anyone can break through and retrieve the prophecies I can."

"*. . . alexi, don't let her fuck with my mind . . .*"

"You are having one of Raven's temporary breakdowns, Raven," she said. "I can help you."

"Cut it out, both of you," Alexi said. "Let me think."

She insisted, "I believe Dr. Slade hypnotized her and blocked her memory with a posthypnotic suggestion before he killed himself. You had her for about three weeks without success. Give her to me and I will break her down."

"Can't you do it here?"

"It needs a change of location. I need to work on her somewhere else to be certain your father does not interfere."

"I'll need his approval."

She saw the girl's expression change from fear to anger.

". . . i can't believe what you're saying, alexi. if you let her take me away, i'll kill myself . . ."

"Do not pay attention to her raving, Alexi. Borderline patients often mutilate themselves and threaten suicide, but they rarely die."

"She cut herself at first," he said, "but she stopped."

"Because now she deludes herself into believing you will never abandon her."

". . . i hate you, alexi. you'll miss me when I'm dead. don't leave me . . ."

"You see? Classic borderline. But also histrionic."

". . . don't listen to her, alexi . . ."

"You'll be safe with her, Nikki. I can't protect you."

". . . both of you can go to hell . . . !"

"All right, Fatima," he said. "Take her."

When Raven threw herself on the floor, she removed a small bottle from her purse and filled a syringe.

". . . not a needle! alexi, stop her . . . !"

"Hold her, Alexi. We must get her out of here." She slipped the needle under the girl's skin.

"What did you give her?" he asked.

"A combination of morphine and scopolamine. Used to be given to women during childbirth. Creates twilight sleep. She will remember nothing afterwards."

". . . *asshole, i'm not having a baby! don't . . .*"

Her movements slowed. Eyes rolled, then closed.

"The sleep will last for a few hours. Give me the fifty thousand dollars."

"When I get the anthrax." She reached for her gun. He did the same. "You think I am a fool, Fatima? Do you think I brought it here?"

She studied his expression. He was not bluffing. "All right. An exchange. You give the money to the courier at Kent State. Now, help me get this one into my minivan out front."

Alexi picked Raven up and slung her across his shoulder. With his free hand, he grabbed the tote bag he'd bought her.

"She will not need it."

"A woman feels comfortable with her personal things."

"We will cure her of that."

When they reached the first landing, she opened the door and glanced around. "I do not see anyone. We carry her between us pretending she is drunk." Downstairs, she helped him drag Raven to her maroon minivan. She unlocked the doors and he slid her in the back.

"How are you going to break the posthypnotic command?"

"Do not worry. I have much experience with hypnotized subjects. I believe Raven was in control at the time. Not Nikki. I'll use the same weapon borderlines use to turn hospital staffs against each other. Divide and conquer."

"You won't harm her?"

"Of course not. I will bypass Dr. Slade's posthypnotic suggestion to Raven and use Nikki to help me unlock her memory of Tedescu's prophecies."

"Where are you taking her?"

"First to my place. Then to Camp Ashraf."

"What if you can't break through the hypnotic block?"

"Then MEK will save you the trouble of killing her."

An hour later, as she pulled up to her five-story tenement, she saw Raven stir and look out the window.

". . . *jesus, what a crummy neighborhood . . .*"

"All I could afford on my salary, Nikki." No point letting her know this was temporary living quarters, or that General Hassan did not authorize supplementary funds.

After a few seconds, she heard the lower-pitched voice. "I'm Raven."

"All right, Raven. Here is your bag."

"How long are we staying here?"

"For the night. Tomorrow we take a train to our destination."

"You didn't tell me where we're going."

"I will tell you, when you need to know."

As she pushed Raven through the doorway, into the building, the girl resisted. She pulled out her cigarette lighter and waved it in her face. Raven fell back against the wall and screamed.

"Go upstairs, Raven."

"How far?"

"The fifth floor."

"Jesus! Doesn't this joint have an elevator?"

"It is out of order."

". . . *i'm not walking up five lousy flights . . .*"

So she had switched back to Nikki. She pulled her. When Nikki fought, she pulled out the Makarov. "I have a silencer on this gun. I'll use if you don't control yourself."

". . . *then you'll never solve tedescu's riddles . . .*"

She dragged her by the hair. "All right, Nikki or Raven— whoever you are now—this is my temporary abode. In a few days, we will visit my real home."

No point revealing too much until she discovered if Dr. Slade had been able to hypnotize both sides of the borderline dissociation coin. As she unlocked the door, the softer voice said, "Small room. Only one bed."

"Queen-size. Big enough for both of us."

"I'm not gay."

"Neither am I. It is against my religion. I will sleep nearest to the window." She looked at her watch. "Time for evening prayers. I must wash."

"Me too."

Through the window, she saw the sun almost setting. "You will have to wait until I am finished, Raven." She went into the bathroom and removed her blouse, shoes and stockings. Scrubbed her feet and legs, then arms and face. Appropriately clean for evening prayers, she put on her nightgown and stepped out. "You may use the sink now."

With the girl out of sight, she took her worn prayer rug out of the closet, unrolled it and spread it on the floor facing east toward Mecca.

"What are you doing?"

"Is it Raven or Nikki who is asking?"

"Raven."

"This is *Salat al-Maghrib*, sunset prayer."

"May I watch?"

"If you do not interrupt."

She stood erect, legs evenly spaced apart, cupped her hands, thumbs behind her ears, palms facing *gibla*. She whispered the first prayer. Then, placing her right palm over her left she put her hands to her chest and whispered the second prayer. She bowed, knelt, with her legs beneath her, the soles of her feet facing away from *gibla*. Finally, she lay prostrate, arm and fingers extended as she finished the sunset prayer. All as the mullah taught her in the madrassa when she was a child. Then she rolled up the rug and put it back into the closet.

"May I ask something now?"

"Go ahead, Raven."

"You're a psychiatric nurse. My mind is all messed up. Did I really see what I think I saw, or am I dreaming?"

"Prayers to Allah are not dreams."

"Then why does everything seem unreal? This strange neighborhood. What I watched you doing. It's like a movie. Have I gone nuts again?"

"You have occasional schizophrenic episodes."

"What do you mean 'occasional'? Isn't crazy, crazy?"

"Borderline patients like yourself at times experience psychotic breakdowns. Feeling the world is not real. That you are unreal. Also you have phobias. You for fire. Your other self for heights."

"Is that why my father committed me to the asylum?"

"Yes. Now let us sleep. We have an early train to catch."

"Where to? You said you'd tell me."

"First to the north of Greece, then Turkey."

"Why Turkey?"

"That will be a surprise. Now get into bed."

"I'm not sleepy."

She opened her purse and pulled out a container of pills. "These will help. You need rest for our trip."

"I don't take sleeping pills."

"Well then . . ." She pulled the medical case out of her purse and showed the syringe. "You prefer an injection?"

". . . i'll take the stinking pills . . ."

So it was Nikki who swallowed them, put her head on the pillow and soon began to snore.

When she was sure her prisoner was asleep, she went to the closet and removed two chadors. They would have to change garments before they crossed the border into Turkey. This light-skinned, blue-eyed blonde would attract too much attention. Wearing black from head to toe with faces veiled, they would board the train to Istanbul and then travel unimpeded into Iraq.

Since she was taller than her prisoner, it took more than an hour to shorten one chador. She examined the tote bag. Nothing more dangerous than a small nail file. She rolled up the shortened chador and put it inside.

In the folder she'd taken during the attack on the asylum, she found Raven's passport. Using the photograph, she arranged for the Islamic counterfeiting network in Athens to forge a passport with a Persian name. She kept the same initials. *Rima Sohrab.* That would enable Raven to pass with her through checkpoints between Greece and Turkey and then into Iraq. She put the forged passport into Raven's handbag alongside the shortened chador.

From Istanbul, they would depart for Ashraf where she would convert Raven to Islam and retrieve Tedescu's message. Whether or not she succeeded, Raven or Nikki—whoever it was at the time—would never leave Iraq alive.

Chapter Twenty-six

Dugan wondered why Tia was driving past an auto repair shop, then twice around a construction site. "I thought we were going to investigate the safe house. How come you drive in circles to get someplace?"

"Precautions, Dugan. 17N has many sympathizers here."

"So that's why it took twenty-seven years for the Hellenic police to catch any of them."

"I do not appreciate a negative attitude."

Careful. Don't irritate her. "Sorry, Tia. I'm on edge. No offense meant."

She huffed. "None taken. But I do not understand why they sent an intelligence analyst to do a field agent's job."

He felt like saying, "For the same reason they sent a woman to do a man's job." But a sexist crack like that would surely provoke another confrontation. He said, "I guess I was most expendable."

She pulled up to a building with a street-level secondhand clothing store. A placard in the window read, CLOSED FOR LUNCH AND SIESTA. The upper level, with window shades drawn, looked like an apartment.

He asked, "Do we wait until they come back?"

"We go in now."

"You have keys to the store?"

"I have a lock pick," she said.

"I'm crossing my fingers."

"Uncross them, Dugan. You may need them to fire your gun. We separate. I unlock the front. You go to the rear delivery entrance and I will let you in."

He went around back. Moments later, the delivery door opened. He entered the store and joined her.

"No one here," he said.

She put her finger to her lips and pointed to the second landing. She led the way.

Thank heavens the stairs didn't creak. The smell of stale coffee. No sound of movement.

She drew her knife. "I go ahead."

He pushed her aside. "Hold it."

"What?"

"We have to be careful."

"I am always care—"

"Shhhh!" He flashed his light up and down the doorjamb. Near the top, he saw a gray hair across the crack. Shone the light to the bottom. Another gray hair.

She pouted. "You're damned good for a computer jockey."

He removed both hairs and laid them carefully in front of the door. "Remind me to replace them on our way out."

"I doubt you will forget." She cracked the door open slowly. No one inside. She put her knife away. "Try not to move anything. If they return, I don't want them to know we were here."

"Give me a break, Tia. I'm no rookie cop."

"Forgive me, *Dentist*."

"All right, Tia. Truce?"

She nodded. But he knew that, among the ancient Greeks, truces were made to be broken.

In the kitchen, she touched a coffee cup. "Warm."

"I guess one of our terrorists was here not long ago."

They moved from the kitchen into a living room cluttered with cut-up newspapers. He reached for one.

"Don't touch!"

He pulled back as if from a hot stove.

"We'll analyze them later to see articles they clipped."

He moved to the bookshelves and read titles aloud. "*Terrorism and the Media; The Red Brigades and Left Wing Terrorism in Italy; Hezbollah and Political Violence in Lebanon: The Future of Islamic Jihad.*"

He pointed to a door alongside the stairs. "We'd better check the basement." He took the lead and reached for the light switch.

She pulled his hand. "It might be wired."

"You don't think—"

"They have always been on guard. Do not take chances."

Using his flashlight, he led the way down the basement steps to the stone floor. On one door, his light illuminated a red flag with a central yellow star enclosing red letters *17N.* "I guess this is the right place."

He pushed the door open and stared. Rifles and rockets stacked against the wall in rows up to the ceiling. "Jeez, look at this armory."

"Those were reported stolen from the Greek army depot." She flashed her light on two open metal drums. One labeled NAPTHENE. The second marked PALMITATE. "This gray-white material looks like soap powder. That one has thick liquid."

"Back off! Don't touch those canisters!"

She looked startled. "Why?"

"After World War II, the American Chemical Corps combined *napthene* and *palmitate* to make *napalm!*"

She stared at him. "You think this was in the firebomb they used in Piraeus?"

"It's possible. When napalm strikes humans, the burns

don't look like ordinary searing. They go deep, and the skin turns to a sticky tarlike magma."

"Like the dead skin my father stripped from the corpse."

"Had me going there for a while. I had no idea the guy was dead by the time your father got him to headquarters."

"Neither did the man's 17N comrades."

"Still, your father tortured one of them to death."

"Sometimes, the illusion of torture doesn't work," she said. "The poet-singer didn't break. Besides, you said a bouzouki player stole your wife. Maybe he was the one."

"I find it hard to believe you approve of torture."

"I don't."

That made him feel better. "Back home, we'd never be permitted to do those things."

"Of course not. That is why your government outsources aggressive interrogation to secret prisons in countries like Egypt, Jordan, Saudi Arabia and—"

"Greece?"

"Only because of *Operation Dragon's Teeth*."

"What now?" he asked.

"We better check Alexi Costa's private apartment."

"You know where it is?"

"The fat man gave the address. Exarchia Square."

"Near our place?"

"Of course. Student quarter. Where else?"

He followed her out the rear door and replaced the gray hairs. "I don't know the way there."

She opened the car door for him. "Not to worry. I am driving."

Was the smile in the turned-up corner of those lips mocking him? He slid into the passenger seat and fastened his seat belt. Tires screeched from the curb. She turned into the plaza and—seconds later—jammed the brakes in front of a two-story building. "We are here."

He looked around. "Damn! Just a couple of blocks away from our rooming house."

"Terrorists often hide in plain sight." She walked around to the passenger's side and opened the door for him.

"That's not necessary, you know."

"I know. But the expression on your face amuses me."

He followed her into the building, up to the second-floor apartment. She checked the doorjamb and held up two red hairs. "Obviously, our bird has different colored feathers."

Inside the apartment, he paused at the unframed cubist paintings covering the walls of the otherwise bare living room.

She nudged him. "No time to contemplate a terrorist's taste in art."

He went into the bedroom. Two open suitcases. Empty hangers. Women's clothing strewn on the bed, on chairs on the floor. "Someone tore out of here in a hell of a hurry."

Tia examined the dresser top. "She could not have been here very long. Very little makeup and only one bottle of perfume." She touched the stopper to her wrist and sniffed. "But she has good taste."

He picked up a folder. "A train timetable."

"They may have dropped it."

"Look at the marked route. Athens to Thessaloniki to Alexandroupolis. Why would they be going to Thrace?"

"There's a change of trains at Thessaloniki. The marked route leads to the Greek-Turkey border at Pithion."

"I doubt their destination is Turkey. What would be the point of that?"

"Who knows? I will call my father and suggest he dispatch officers to watch for a man and a woman at those train stops and alert the guards to detain them before they cross the Uzunköprü Turkish frontier."

"You really think they're headed for Istanbul?"

"Perhaps en route to somewhere else. If we are lucky, we may find Raven before Alexi takes her out of the country."

"Then what? Theater of Torture, or the real thing?"

"If Alexi has brainwashed her into joining 17N, there will be no time for rehearsal. Just whatever is necessary to get Tedescu's plans about the targets in your country."

"All right. You made your point."

She slipped her hand into his. "So where can we go to be together?"

"Thirty-two Panepistimou Street," he said.

"The National Library of Greece?" She pulled her hand away. "Why in the world—?"

"Before Salinas bashed my skull, she said she donated Tedescu's papers to the Athens library. They're probably still being cataloged for the archives."

"What has that to do with finding Raven?"

"His papers might reveal his involvement in 17N's conspiracy. He was egotistical enough to leave his secret for posterity. Must have considered himself a modern-day Nostradamus. I don't intend to wait ten years to find out what Raven learned about *Operation Dragon's Teeth.*"

"You are really fixated on pulling those teeth."

"Sure, call me *Dentist.*"

CHAPTER TWENTY-SEVEN

Athens to Istanbul

Fatima looked at her prisoner curled up in the bed. Just as well the girl was disoriented. Easier to handle borderlines during their dissociative episodes. At those times Raven would not know if she was herself or the dead twin who became Nikki.

After sunrise prayers, she reached under her bed for the knapsack she packed the night before. She had carefully rolled her brown uniform and head scarf and slipped her loaded Makarov between them and the two black chadors. Another reason for not flying. Her backpack would not be inspected on trains in Alexandroupolis, or from Istanbul to Tatvan near the Iraqi border.

She shook her prisoner. "Wake up. We're leaving."

Raven yawned and turned over. "I need more sleep."

A quick shove knocked her off the bed.

"What the hell!"

"Your life depends on obeying my commands. Go wash and brush your teeth. We have to catch our train."

". . . all right. don't get all bent outta shape . . ."

So she was Nikki again. A last look around the room where she spent the last months on this mission. She would never return, God willing. God is great. Then in Arabic. *Inshallah. Allahu akbar.*

Outside, she hailed a taxi. "To the railway office. Karolou 1, Omonia Square."

She opened the door but it was Raven who hesitated. "I want to sit up front with the driver. Not in the back."

"Aboard the train you will have a seat by the window."

"Why the hell are we taking a train?"

"We are going on a trip."

"This isn't real, Nurse Sawyer. Am I in another world?"

"My name is Major Fatima Sayid, and you will soon enter the real world. Islam."

When the taxi pulled up to the ticket office, she paid the driver and got out. Annoyed when her prisoner pulled back, she grabbed a fistful of long blonde hair. "I have no patience with a spoiled brat."

"I'll tell Alexi when I get back to Athens."

"Alexi intends to kill you. I am saving your life."

"You're crazy. He loves me."

"Are you sure it is not Nikki he loves?"

"What are you're talking about?"

"Your dead twin has come back from the grave into your mind. I suspect Alexi loves her more than he cares for you."

"You're trying to turn me against myself."

"Allah may be able to save you by merging you with the being who possesses your mind at times. If you do not resist, Islam will help you find your true self. But you must follow my instructions. Remember, it is for your sake."

"All right. Whatever you say."

Raven stayed close behind her at the ticket window. "Two for two-berth sleeping car to Thessaloniki. And from there to Pithion."

The ticket clerk said, "Why you go to Turkish frontier?"

"For sightseeing in Istanbul."

"There is much to see here in Greece."

"I have seen enough in Greece. The tickets, please."

No mistaking the sneer on his face. "Flilia-Dostluk Express leaves in ten minutes."

Raven hung back. "Why are we going to Turkey?"

"Only passing through on the way to Iraq."

"That's gonna take forever. Why don't we fly?"

"You know very well, Raven, that the Nikki part of you is afraid of flying."

"But heights don't bother *me*."

"Anyway, flying is too complicated with the new security searches. A long train trip will let you view the scenery and give us the opportunity to become better acquainted."

They boarded. The last sleeper car ahead of the dining car was more pleasant than the coach she had taken when she first traveled from Baghdad to Athens.

"Settle in, Raven. I must say *salat al-zuhr*, the noon prayer." She used the sink in their compartment to wash before praying. Since they were headed north, she turned right toward *gibla*.

"Why are you facing that way?"

"It is the direction of the sacred mosque in Mecca. Muslims pray in that direction."

"I thought you needed a prayer rug."

"An exception is made when one travels."

She saw Raven studying her. "Am I allowed to ask what kind of prayers they are?"

"Chapters of the Quran called *surahs*."

"Can anyone say those prayers?"

"Only those who convert to Islam and make a *shahadah*— a declaration of faith. Are you interested?"

"I'm not sure. I'd have to know more about it."

"When we get to our destination, I will advise you."

She was pleased to see that Raven had become subdued during the prayer session. It would be a blessing if she could convert this suggestible girl to Islam. A blue-eyed, blonde-haired jihadist would be useful in MEK's coming attack against the West. But first she would have to deal with the dissociation. Raven or Nikki? Divide and conquer.

"Islam is the faith spreading through the Middle East. Soon we will conquer the rest of the world."

"But aren't Islamic woman treated like cattle? The burka, the face covering, and stuff like that?"

"In Ashraf, you will learn that we are different. We are Muslim, but we fight against the mullahs with their medieval beliefs in the laws of sharia. We have high regard for women. True we are Shia, but we joined Iraq's Sunni military in the war against Iran. We are flexible."

"Some of your terrorists killed innocent children."

"The children of our enemies grow up to kill Muslims. Infidel children are fighters-in-the-making. Why wait until they are old enough to carry guns?"

"What about the suicide bombers?"

"You have often spoken of suicide, Raven."

"Sure, to put myself out of my misery the way my mother did. But not for the same reason your people do."

"Those who choose to give themselves up to the will of Allah are blessed martyrs."

"I heard that guy martyrs get seventy-two virgins in heaven. What do women martyrs get?"

"You ask too many questions."

"And what if heaven runs out of virgins?"

"Do not blaspheme, or you will end up in the fiery pits of hell. And you're afraid of fire, aren't you?"

"You know I am. But since Nikki is terrified of heights, she could never go to heaven."

"When we get to Ashraf, you will convert to Islam."

"What if I don't want to?"

"I know you are confused. We will deal with that when the time comes. Let us talk of other things."

"Like what?"

"When you were with Tedescu, I heard you recite lines about an unfaced goddess? Did he ever refer to her in his lectures?"

"I don't remember."

Raven's memory was obviously blocked. Too risky to use the twilight-sleep sedative to try to reach Nikki. She needed Raven alert when they reached checkpoints at both frontiers. Better to let her doze until after they crossed into Turkey.

She watched Raven stir whenever the loudspeaker called out the cities at each major transit stop. Finally: "Pithion! Last stop in Greece! Have passports ready for inspection. Passengers for Istanbul must cross border and purchase visas at Uzunköprü Turkish frontier!"

She opened the storage closet, took her chador from her knapsack and slipped it on.

". . . *why the hell are you wearing that witches' costume? we going to a masquerade . . . ?*"

"Modest Muslim women wear the chador." She opened Raven's bag, took out the one she had shortened, and handed it to her.

". . . *i'm not going to wear that crummy shroud . . .*"

So she had changed again. "Nikki, we cannot pass through Turkey into Iran and then into Iraq dressed in Western women's revealing clothes. These will protect us from the prying eyes of men."

". . . *i don't mind men eyeing me . . .*"

She grabbed Nikki by the neck and squeezed. "You are going to become a Muslim woman. Start behaving like one."

". . . *what the hell are you talking about . . . ?*"

"If you want to live, Nikki, you must do as I say."

". . . *okay, just to satisfy your weird ideas . . .*"

She helped Nikki into the chador. When the train pulled to a stop, she pushed her out the door. The foolish girl caught her foot in the hem and stumbled.

". . . *i'll break my neck wearing this damned thing* . . ."

The station at Pithion looked like frontier towns she had seen in American Western movies during her stay in Athens. A few ramshackle buildings alongside the tracks. People sitting outside the taverna. Several women in chadors. Student travelers asleep on benches and on the ground. All waiting for the train to the Uzunköprü frontier. A uniformed officer checked their passports.

Finally, the three-car shuttle rolled in from Turkey, and Greek border guards checked Greece-bound passengers. After the train emptied, the guards signaled for those heading for Turkey to board. Everyone shoved to get on. Fortunately, the men avoided crowding them. The train chugged slowly back over desolate land, across a bridge and over a river. It stopped at the other side of the frontier.

There, Turkish officials came aboard and checked passports. As she anticipated, getting the visa at Uzunköprü was cursory. Two women in black from head to toe aroused no suspicion. The Turkish guard took both passports.

"You are Fatima Sayid?"

She nodded.

"And you are Rima Sohrab?"

Nikki didn't respond.

"Are you Rima Sohrab?"

A sharp elbow jab in the spine made her glance around dazed. "I-I guess so."

Apparently, the Raven persona had returned.

The guard frowned.

She motioned with her index finger to her forehead, as if turning a screw.

"Ah, crazy," the guard said. "I understand."

He stamped both passports and waved them back onto the train. "Have a good trip to Istanbul. Do not forget to visit Topkapi Palace Museum. They made a film there."

"Thank you," she said. "I did not see the film, but we will be sure to visit the museum."

Back aboard, Raven said, "May I ask a question?"

"Yes."

"What if Nikki converts to Islam, but I don't want to?"

"Whether your body converts to Islam as Raven or as Nikki there is no going back."

"What's to stop me?"

"Sharia law requires that the body of an apostate be flogged, stoned and then beheaded."

Raven pressed her fist against her mouth. "Sorry I asked."

Chapter Twenty-eight

Athens

Although it was late at night, Dugan saw the CLOSED signs blocking both curved staircases leading up to the Vallianios National Library.

"That is that," Tia said. "Let us leave." She nestled her head against his shoulder. "Your room or mine?"

"Pull around to the parking area in back."

"Do you not see the sign?"

"I didn't think we'd be so lucky," he said.

"Lucky? *Closed* means *locked*."

He put two fingers to her lips. "No lock ever stopped me from getting through a door. Let's go."

She drove to the rear of the three-building complex. "That is the university. The other is the academy. The library reading room is in the center." She pulled into the parking lot behind the library. "This is the back entrance."

"How do you know?"

"I have done research here."

He shouldered his bag. "Use your flashlight."

She reached into the glove compartment and fished around until she found it, clicked it on and off.

He took a small plastic case out of his bag.

"What is that?"

"A burglar's pick." He slipped two metal rods into the lock and jimmied back and forth several times. "This is a goddamned tough one."

"Here, let me try."

He smiled and held out the pick.

She pushed it aside and dug into her purse. He heard the jingling sound of a key ring. She selected one and slipped it into the lock. It clicked open. She waved her flashlight. "After you, *Dentist*."

"How in hell did you get a key?"

"Simple. As I said, I do research here for the counterterrorism division. My father made it for me."

"You could have said so."

"You did not ask."

"Do you happen to know the location of the cataloging office?"

She put the flashlight under her chin, turning her smile into the mask of comedy. "Follow me." She opened the door to an office and turned on the overhead fluorescent.

He said, "Better not. Someone might see the light."

"No windows in here. Sunlight would damage the manuscripts."

"I didn't think of that," he said. He pointed to files from floor to ceiling. "It'll take forever to find Tedescu's archives on those shelves."

"We do not have to search there."

"Then where?"

"Salinas told you she shipped the manuscript to arrive while Tedescu was here at the convention. I doubt the archives librarian had time to open it. Let us go through that pile of recent deliveries." She held up a thin package. "Return address: Jason Tedescu; Waybridge University; Waybridge, Ohio."

He blew her a kiss. "Now, where the hell can we get it copied? It's late, and I'd hate to keep it out overnight."

"No problem. There's a copying machine I use often. Follow me."

In the reading room, she pulled the plastic cover off the copier. "Since there are windows here, we must do it by flashlight. Hand me the pages. I will copy them."

Five minutes later, he resealed the manuscript in its wrapping. "I sure hate 17N getting their hands on it."

"I have an idea," she said, taking the manuscript. Back in the archives, she tossed it behind stacked shelves. "The librarian probably carelessly let the package drop there after it was delivered."

He kissed her cheek. "Okay, now let's see his goddamned prophecies."

MANIFESTO

I, Jason Tedescu, hereby confess, postmortem, that I conceived of Operation Dragon's Teeth. On the 17th of November 1973, I was wounded at Athens Polytechnic Institute during the student uprising against Colonel Papadopoulos and his fascist junta.

On that day, many Greek students were killed because of the CIA's attempt at regime change. I was sent to the United States for treatment, but stayed on to study for my PhD in Classical Literature. During that time, I devoted leaves of absence from the university to plant Greek sleeper cells across America.

I coordinated the creation of 17N with my comrade, Myron Costa. I take full responsibility for ordering the execution of the CIA station chief in 1975 and subsequent attacks on American and Greek government officials.

I pray that I will live to see the awakening of sleeper cells I planted throughout the Capitalist States of America. Attacks on three of its major centers will most likely result in collateral damage to hundreds of thousands of citizens. In the fog of war, this is unavoidable.

The first part of my ENIGMA: WHERE, reveals the cities and targets. The second part: WHAT, alludes to the weapon and its source. The third part: HOW, describes my own ingenious method of its disbursement.

I hereby authorize my executrix to use her own judgment in donating this encoded prophecy to the Greek archives so that after my death future classical scholars will discover the brilliant strategy of the genius Jason Tedescu they neglected to promote to full professor.

She took the next page of the manuscript. "Let me read it aloud. Hearing it might help.

"WHERE
*Unfaced goddess sees future from a Windswept Tower
In serious hate she butchers flesh of all.
Escaped Bull-man stops 'neath the sunken wall.*
DEATH PENALTY EXPLODES FIVE-PETALED
FLOWER."

"Oh, shit!" he said. "The son of a bitch buried his prophecy—the targets, the weapon and how to use it—in riddles."

She looked at him. "What do you think these riddles—as you call them—mean?"

"How the hell do I know?"

"Aren't intelligence analysts expert at dealing with puzzles?"

"Decrypting and analyzing international chatter is different from solving riddles. Go on, read the rest."

She turned the page. "The others are blank."

"But the manifesto mentions three quatrains: *where, what* and *how.*"

She looked closer. "The other two are missing. Someone must have separated them."

"Probably Salinas who beaned me with the bust of Zeus. And gotten herself beaten maybe to death in that protest riot. Tedescu trusted her to use her judgment about sending the donation here."

"But why send only the first part?"

"She worshipped him," he said. "Called him an oracle. Probably thought of herself as his high priestess, protecting his legacy by interpreting them herself. She must have distributed them as she saw fit."

"All right let's deal with the four lines we've got."

He glanced at the page. "Tedescu was a lousy poet, but he seems to have considered himself an oracle. The first lines refer to Greek myths. During his lectures, he likely planted allusions for students to memorize for his quizzes. Looks like he adapted them as prophetic clues."

Tia flicked her finger on the page. "So both 17N and MEK are aware that Raven may know the meanings. But *she* does not know that she knows. If she's being taken to Ashraf, they'll torture it out of her."

He picked up the manuscript. "They have her, but we've got this. Only one problem. The lines don't make sense."

Tia ran her finger down the page. "First, we have to identify and understand the significance of each image and classical reference. Let's give the classical scholar credit. There are probably layers of meaning. Dig beneath the gums, Dentist."

"You must have learned your Greek history and mythology. So that's your bailiwick."

"All right." She pointed to the first two lines.

Unfaced goddess sees future from the Windswept Tower.
In serious hate she butchers flesh of all.

She frowned. "I never heard of an unfaced goddess."

"What about the *Windswept Tower?*"

"Doesn't ring a bell."

"It doesn't say bell tower."

"All right, analyst. Let's get on with the rest of it. '*Escaped Bull-man stops 'neath the sunken wall.*' Head of a bull, body of a man—*the Minotaur.*"

"But what does it signify?"s

"Listen and learn, Mr. Analyst. Poseidon presented Minos a white bull as a gift. His queen made love with it and gave birth to a man with a bull's head."

"That's probably where we get the expression, 'She's full of bull.'"

She whacked him. "The king hid the Minotaur in a labyrinth. So, what could be the location of the labyrinth in America?"

"I know a few. The Olcott Center labyrinth in Wheaton, Illinois. The Labyrinth Society in Connecticut. The Grace Cathedral labyrinth in San Francisco. But there are hundreds of others. The riddle could refer to any of those. Where does that lead us?"

She shook her head. "Those real labyrinths would be on the surface. This probably refers to something deeper."

"Deeper . . . A maze below ground . . . Buried power lines? Cables? Sewers? Animal burrows? Snake holes? Underground streams?" He slapped his forehead. "Wait a goddamned minute! *Underground!* Just like the British underground, New York's subway is a labyrinth of tracks."

"I think you're on the right track, but how do we pinpoint the actual target?"

"In some areas, where the train comes out from underground, there are embankments."

She shook her head. "They would be *beside* the walls. Not 'neath them."

He chewed his lip. "Subway . . . Subway . . . Wait. One New York subway station has the word *wall* in its name. *Wall Street*. And, come to think of it, there's a statue of a bull in front of the New York Stock Exchange. Second target—the capitalist power base."

"So Bull-man's labyrinth is target number two," she said, "the New York Stock Exchange. But we still have to get targets one and three, and find out who the sleepers are and the weapon."

"And how he planned for his sleepers to use it."

"The library cleaning staff will be coming in soon," she said. "Let's work on this at home."

He collected the pages, and they moved out quickly to the parking lot. On the way back to the housing complex, he asked, "Your place or mine?"

"Mine has better lighting."

As they entered the apartment hallway, he studied her face until the light went out, hiding that off-center smile. "In the dark, you're a goddess with no face."

"I don't take that as a compliment."

"And since you're Artemis the huntress, I can attest to the fact that after your kill you'd '*butcher flesh of all.*' "

She reached past him and switched on the light. "You bastard. Tonight you can sleep in your own room. Alone."

Chapter Twenty-nine

Istanbul to Tatvan, Turkey

"Fatima, why can't we visit the Topkapi Palace Museum?"

"We do not have time. We must get our tickets at the train station."

"Another train? I'm sick of trains."

"This is the last one."

"Where are we going?"

"To the border between Turkey and Iraq."

"I don't want to go to Iraq!"

How much longer could she put up with this spoiled girl? "We are expected. I notified them we are coming."

"I saw on a TV program that America won a war in Iraq."

"The capitalist crusaders won Desert Storm, the first battle, but there will be others. We will win the war."

"Who's we?"

"Islamic jihad, *Inshallah!*"

"That means, 'If God wills,' doesn't it?"

"You have an excellent memory, Raven. Once we are aboard the train, on our way, you will use it to recall Tedescu's quatrains."

"I don't understand."

"You will, in time."

"Tell me now."

She twisted Raven's arm through the chador and pulled her close. "You do not give me orders. I, Major Fatima Sayid, tell you what to do and what not to do."

"You're hurting me."

"This is nothing compared to what you will feel if you give me more trouble." She could not see Raven's expression through the head-and-face covering. She eased her grip. No sense antagonizing her further. There was much work to do.

She led her to the ticket office window inside the Haydarpasa station. "Two sleepers on the Dogu Express from Istanbul to Tatvan."

"Two *yatakli vagon* on Dogu Express," he said. "You save 20 percent if you buy round-trip."

"We will not return."

She paid in euros and he handed her the tickets. She took Raven's arm again. "Come, troublemaker, we get on the train right now."

On the way to their sleeper car, a conductor reached out to help her up the steps. She drew away. "You must not touch me."

"I beg your pardon, madame. I forget. It is not the same in Turkey as in your country."

"*. . . i don't mind if you touch me . . .*"

The conductor looked confused.

It was Nikki again. She pushed her ahead up the steps. Then she turned to the conductor and, once again, with her finger to her forehead, made the screwing motion.

"*. . . screw you. i'm not the one with the loose screw. I'm not the one who's crazy . . .*"

Fatima shrugged and said to the conductor, "You see?"

He turned away to help another traveler.

Once they were in their compartment, she slid her head covering back and Raven's as well. She stared hard into the girl's eyes. "I warn you for the last time, Raven or Nikki, if you give me any more trouble, I will keep you sedated for the entire trip."

"Sorry. I'll try to be good."

That sounded like Raven. "You will do more than try."

"I'll *try* to do more than try."

She slapped the girl.

Raven slapped back and pulled off her chador. Standing in her underwear, she crossed her arms.

". . . *what the hell are you gonna do about it . . . ?*"

"So you have changed again. I see there is only one way to deal with you." She reached into her backpack and lifted out a small black case. She took out a hypodermic syringe and slid in a needle.

"No! Please! I'll be good!" Raven ran to the compartment door and started to open it.

She caught her with one arm, threw her down on the settee and jabbed in the needle.

"I'm afraid! I'm afraid!"

"There is nothing to be afraid of. You will be in twilight sleep until we reach Tatvan. When you awaken, you will remember nothing of what happened to you."

"W-wha you gonna do t-to m-me?"

"I will ask questions and you will answer. I have often seen your father hypnotize you. After you awake, you will not remember."

Raven's eyes rolled. Then closed. Head drooped.

Now to transform the twilight sleep into hypnotic sleep. She sat beside her and whispered, "You are asleep, but both of you hear my voice. You will both obey my voice. Listen to the train wheels turning . . . softer . . . softer . . . Hear leaves rustling in the breeze. Even in sleep you can speak. Do you understand?"

A groan. A nod.

Good. She had planned this ever since Tedescu dismissed her from his wheelchair in the infirmary, when Raven spoke to him. Now she had the opportunity to find out what Raven had memorized and recited to him.

"We will travel back in time, to the Athens Asylum. We are going to the hospital to visit your former teacher Jason Tedescu. Can you see Mr. Tedescu?"

A whispered, "Yes . . ."

"What is he doing?"

"Telling me to recite the lines I read in his office."

"Repeat them for me."

Then she shuddered. "Fire! I don't want to burn! Oh, God, no more fire!"

"Sleep, Raven, sleep. Calm now. The fire is out. Try again. What were the lines?"

"I don't remember."

"In the name of Allah, you must remember."

"*. . . we're up too high! too high! i'll fall and break my neck! don't look down . . .*"

"All right, Nikki. I'm sure your father's posthypnotic suggestion did not block *your* memory of Tedescu's prophecy. Recite the first quatrain: *WHAT.*"

Nikki rocked back and forth, then mumbled:

"*. . . unfaced goddess guards future from the wind-swept tower. in serious hate she butchers flesh of all . . . escaped bull-man stops 'neath the sunken wall, death penalty explodes five-petaled flower . . .*"

"Go on."

"*. . . that's the only part I heard . . .*"

"There must be more."

Her head drooped into a somnambulistic sleep.

Dr. Slade must have buried the prophecies behind Raven's

borderline/histrionic personalities. To penetrate the shield of his posthypnotic command, she must find a way to bypass Raven's pyrophobia and Nikki's acrophobia.

They got off the train at Tatvan, and traveled by bus to the Iraq border. If she failed to interpret the enigmas by then, her hostage would be of no use. The Red Wednesday fire celebration would wreak havoc with Raven's mind. Prayers from atop the minaret would panic Nikki. Perhaps by using each of their phobias, she would divide them.

But she must do it carefully, to avoid changing a borderline's periodic schizophrenia into an irreversible catatonic withdrawal.

CHAPTER THIRTY

Dugan's secure cell phone rang. He looked at the caller ID signal. Scrambled letters. "Tia, it's *Charon*." He inserted the unscrambler key. "Yeah?"

"*Dentist?*"

"Hey, man, it's good to hear your voice. What's up?"

"An emergency contact with *Tentmaker* from the Ashraf compound in Iraq."

He tilted the phone so Tia could hear. "Go ahead."

"Have to make this quick. *Tentmaker* intercepted a call to MEK's leader, General Hassan. Nurse Fatima Sayid is on her way to Ashraf with Raven Slade. She informed the general that she plans to decondition the phobias and break through the hypnotic barrier."

"How'd he find all this out?"

"MEK uses him as their service technician for computers and electronic equipment. He managed to slip bugs into the officers' quarters."

"Did he learn their plan for Raven?"

"He says General Hassan told Fatima their top priority is to extract Tedescu's prophecies."

"We've figured out only the first line of WHERE. The New York Stock Exchange."

"If Fatima succeeds in dehypnotizing Raven," *Charon* said, "we're lost."

"They'd still have to solve the rest of the riddles."

"According to *Tentmaker,* there are some pretty smart women in that group."

"Can you keep me updated on their progress?"

"I'll try. Over and out."

Dugan turned off his key. "Tia, what do you think?"

"I'd say we're in a psychological race against two terrorist groups. We can only hope that if Fatima is skillful enough to pry the rest of the enigmas out of Raven, *Tentmaker* can get it to us in time for us to solve them."

"Then they'd have no further use for her," he said. "They'd probably make sure she doesn't fall into the hands of Greek intelligence."

"You think they'll kill her?"

"Isn't what your father would do?"

She turned away to avoid looking into his eyes.

CHAPTER THIRTY-ONE

Tatvan, Turkey to Ashraf, Iraq

The screech of metal on metal and a jolting stop awoke Raven from a deep sleep. She rolled over but a bed railing stopped her from falling. An upper sleeping berth? On a train? Why was she on a train? She looked down and saw her body still asleep. Was she crazy again?

She heard whispered prayers from below and remembered that Fatima was taking her somewhere.

A loudspeaker: *"Tatvan! Last stop before Iraq border!"*

Iraq? What's going on?

A black tent loomed over her. "Get up, Rima Sohrab."

A talking tent? Then she remembered the chador and the woman inside it. "You got me, like, mixed up with someone else. I'm not Rima what's-her-name."

"All right, then. Put on your chador and get down from that berth. Now. Quickly."

". . . okay. okay. don't blow a gasket . . ."

She turned and looked back at the rumpled blanket. Where was her sleeping self?

. . . *oh, no. not this out-of-body shit again* . . .

She reached for the rolled-up shroud on the shelf behind her and slipped into it. Now she too was a black tent.

"Come down."

"Aye! Aye, sir!" She started to salute, but her arm caught in the chador. Oh, to hell with it! She climbed down and looked up at the tall tent. At least she didn't have to see Fatima's angry face.

"We have to get off the train, Raven." Throaty voice softer now. "Take your tote bag and let us leave."

They followed departing passengers to the steps. She hesitated, expecting the conductor to help her down. But he backed away. Oh, yeah. Muslims don't touch strange Muslim women. Guess the chador does work like a chastity belt. She made her way to the ground. "Where to now, Major Fatima?"

"Shhhh! Do not call my name until we reach Ashraf."

"There it's okay?"

"There it is required."

When they boarded the bus, instead of sitting in two empty seats up front, Fatima pushed her toward the rear.

"What's wrong with these seats up front?"

"That is where men sit. We sit in back of bus."

Well, I'll be damned! Segregation. *Where was Rosa Parks when you needed her?*

She hesitated. A nudge in her back guided her into a window seat. "So, Muslim women are subservient to men?"

"When we get to Ashraf, you will see who dominates."

It was a bumpy ride on lousy roads until they reached Baghdad. Then, wide avenues and modern buildings. They were the last ones off the bus.

"Are we staying here?"

"Quiet," Fatima whispered. "Do not speak English. Spies are everywhere."

At a taxi stand, Fatima bargained for a ride to Ashraf. A few minutes of haggling. Then they drove off. The countryside was flat—sand and scrub grass. Monotonous. Dreary. She started to nod, but Fatima shook her.

"We are here."

The taxi pulled up to a gate, and a woman wearing military olive-drab stepped out of the sentry box. "Identify yourselves."

Fatima pulled back the headpiece of her chador and showed her face.

The sentry saluted. "Major Sayid. Welcome back. May I ask who is your companion?"

"Rima Sohrab, a new recruit."

. . . what the hell is she talking about . . . ?

"Welcome to Camp Ashraf, Comrade Rima Sohrab."

. . . better keep my mouth shut until i figure out what's going on . . .

The sentry picked up the phone. "Please send a jeep for returning Major Sayid."

A few minutes later, a jeep pulled up. A uniformed woman driver jumped out and saluted. "Your destination, Major?"

"A brief tour of the grounds for our new recruit Comrade Rima Sohrab. Then to my quarters in unit three."

Fatima pushed her into the jeep. "What you are about to see will impress you."

Fatima was right. The streets were paved. They passed a fountain splashing water over rocks. A pool with several women swimming laps. A mosque in the center, surrounded by sculptures.

Pointing to a modern building, Fatima said, "Our hospital. And there, is our library. Beyond it, our museum. Saddam Hussein granted us these thirty-five square kilometers of desert, and we turned it into an oasis."

"You said you're Iranians. Why would he do that?"

"As reward for joining the Iraqi army in the war against Iran's mullah tyrants."

"You have an army?"

"Nearly four thousand. Well trained, most commanded by *female mujihadeen*." Fatima pointed. "Look for yourself."

On the plain ahead, she saw hundreds of women wearing military olive-drab uniforms with identical matching headscarves—standing at attention in battle tank hatches. Others held machine guns and rocket launchers at the ready. Fatima pointed to a tall woman in an armored personnel carrier. "That is our leader, General Hassan."

She shrugged. "So what?"

"Enough sightseeing for now. Driver, to the residential units."

They drove past blocks of buildings with well-tended lawns and gardens blooming with purple, white and yellow flowers.

The driver pulled up to unit three. Fatima led the way inside her austere room, everything neatly arranged. She went to a closet and pulled out an olive-drab military uniform like the ones worn on the parade grounds.

"Put this on, Rima. A chador is not appropriate here. If it doesn't fit properly, we will have one of the men tailor it for you."

"Thank God! I thought I'd never get out of this tent."

"No longer say, 'Thank God,' Raven. Say, '*Allahu akbar.*' God is great."

"One thing I don't see are playgrounds. Where are the children?"

Fatima cleared her throat. "There are no children."

"How come?"

"Our leaders ordered that children be sent away to relatives. Those of us who were married were required to divorce our husbands. Celibacy rules here. Therefore, no more children."

She was tempted to say, "If you don't have children here,

Ashraf will end up being an old ladies' home." Instead, she whispered, *"Inshallah."*

"Jason Tedescu was right. I did hear him say you learn quickly. Tell me the lines you recited to him in the hospital."

"It was nothing."

"I was there. I heard you"

She took a deep breath. "I don't remember."

"You repressed it, Raven. I was trained in depth hypnosis. I will help you retrieve your memory."

"I don't want to remember."

"That is for me to decide. I choose what you remember and what you forget. When you convert to Islam, it will no longer be up to you."

She started to say, I don't want to become a Muslim, but the voice in her mind intruded.

. . . don't be stupid enough to fight her now . . .

"You're absolutely right, Major Fatima. I will follow wherever you lead."

A pat on the head and a smile. "Good. We put off memory exercises until after New Year's Day."

"But January 1 is seven months away."

"Nowrooz, our Persian New Year, is March 20. We begin *Chahar Shanbeh Suri* tomorrow."

"What's that?"

"Tomorrow, six days before New Year's Monday, we celebrate Red Wednesday Festival, a custom that predates the Christian and Islamic era to the time when the people of this country worshipped Zoroaster. The mullahs do not approve. But they tolerate it just as your Christian churches accept the pagan Santa Claus."

"Sounds like fun. I always loved Christmastime. What do you do here?"

"On that day, some soldiers put on white sheets or costumes instead of uniforms. They paint their faces and run through the streets banging pots and pans, making deafening noise to drive out last year's evil spirits. The highlights of Red Wednesday are the fires."

She felt her chest tighten. "Fires?"

"That is why it is called Red Wednesday. We burn effigies of the ayatollah and the president of Iran and some of the mullahs. I will arrange for you, as newcomer to MEK and Islam, to have honor of lighting the first one."

. . . raven, don't let her see your fear . . .

"We build horseshoe-shaped fires all around the camp and jump over the flames—"

"I couldn't—"

"—to purify ourselves from last year's bad times."

"—go near the fire."

"You will conquer your pyrophobia here."

"I want to go home."

"You have no other home. You must swear allegiance to Allah and Muhammed—peace and blessings be upon him."

"You can't force me to become a Muslim."

"Making allegiance to Allah must be voluntary. It is for you to decide."

"If I decide not to?"

"Then you will be killed as an infidel."

". . . to hell with you and your female army. i don't give a damn if I live or die . . ."

CHAPTER THIRTY-TWO

As Fatima left the mosque after evening prayers, an aide approached with an order for her to attend an emergency meeting of senior officers.

She joined the three other officers already in the library drinking coffee. General Hassan entered, and they snapped to attention.

"The New Year's celebration is upon us," she said, "and Fatima has completed her mission to Greece. We must now consider our strategy for the coming year.

"Our sources have convinced me that the United States will soon invade Iraq for the second time. Since our own sleeper cells in America were exposed to the FBI by a traitor, it is imperative we cement an alliance with another group that has sleepers in place. Major Fatima has been negotiating with 17N. I call on her to give her estimate of the situation."

She sipped her sweet coffee and glanced at her three comrades. "I was nearby in the asylum infirmary when the 17N Greek scholar Tedescu had Raven Slade recite his prophetic enigmas. I overheard just a few lines. His plan encoded *Operation Dragon's Teeth*, as well as the unique method he devised for delivering our weapon."

Colonel Samira Abdelaziz asked, "What about 17N?"

"Alexi Costa, leader of their Second Generation, assures me his people are as loyal to Marxist-Leninism as we are. If we can firm up arrangements as Tedescu intended, 17N agrees to an alliance."

The general nodded. "Excellent, Fatima. Although we missed your presence, your stay in Athens was worthwhile." She turned to Major Kalila Sahadi. "You have already made your position known to me. Please share it with the rest of us so we may consider the alternatives."

Kalila looked at her sternly. "It is common knowledge, Fatima, that 17N is composed of about only twenty elderly men in Athens. I admit their attacks in Greece have been successful, but time is against them. On the other hand, Hezbollah also has homegrown sleeper cells in America. Like us, they are Shia. I believe it best to make our alliance with Hezbollah."

"Major Fatima," the general said, "you look upset."

Not looking at Kalila, she forced herself to keep her voice calm. "Hezbollah may be Shia, but they support the Iranian theocracy that betrayed our cause. The Revolutionary Guard and their Kuds commando force are being used by the ayatollah to create a Middle East ruled by Iranian mullahs. The Guards continue to subjugate women under the imam's interpretation of sharia laws. How can we make alliance with them and the Kud's puppet Hezbollah?"

Kalila answered defiantly, "Perhaps you have come to identify with the Greeks' Christian-Orthodox religion. I feel we should trust only Shia."

She struggled to control her anger. Settle down. A display of hostility would put her at a disadvantage. She glanced at Colonel Samira Abdelaziz. Samira's expression never revealed her feelings. Although cold and stern, she was a brilliant military leader. She would surely agree that it would be a mistake to give the weapon to Hezbollah.

The colonel's voice was flat. "I respect Fatima's and Kalila's positions, but I disagree with both."

Kalila pushed her cup aside, not bothering to wipe the spilled coffee.

Samira said, "Like all *mujihadeen*. I resent America's State Department adding us to their terrorist list and freezing our assets. On the other hand, I have recently received intelligence from our charity supporters in the United States that may provide a third alternative."

She must have already informed General Hassan of this, because the general did not appear surprised.

Samira glanced at each listener in turn. "There is dispute in the top echelons of American decision makers. The State Department is coming under increased pressure by several senators and another powerful group of leaders."

Oh, she was a great speaker. Another dramatic pause to hold everyone's attention.

"The Pentagon is attempting to persuade the State Department to remove us from the terrorist list because some of their chiefs of staff foresee a different strategy. One of their scenarios is to use us as spearhead of a second-front invasion of Iran. The mullahs will fall. With the aid of the American military, we will replace the ayatollah's fascist tyranny with a true Islamic-Marxist society."

It was the first she'd heard of this. She had her own arguments against making common cause with their capitalist enemy. But after all, one's enemy's enemy . . .

"We have three points of view to consider," General Hassan said. "Red Wednesday's fires will drive out the evils of the past year and ensure success in our future endeavors. Whichever path we choose, we will succeed. *Inshallah*."

All echoed, *"Inshallah."*

Time to blunt the positions of her own comrades. "I beg your pardon, General," Fatima said, "but I believe it important to prepare for the eventuality that the Pentagon might not prevail over the State Department soon enough. I have been working to acquire Tedescu's battle plan by breaking through the posthypnotic commands set by Raven's father."

Hassan was studying her closely. "How do you propose to do that, Major Sayid?"

"The ancient strategy: divide and conquer."

"Explain."

"Borderlines are divisive. When Dr. Slade induced hypnotism, it was with Raven, not her dissociated self. I intend to circumvent his posthypnotic suggestion by concentrating on the suggestible, histrionic Nikki. If I can extract the quatrains, we can solve them and use Tedescu's sleeper cells to implement *Operation Dragon's Teeth*."

The general was silent for a few moments, then said, "You have my permission to proceed."

After she left the meeting, she walked in the cool night air turning things over in her mind. Rather than face political infighting with the other officers, after she broke Nikki's resistance, she would take it on herself to complete shipment of the weapon to her courier in America.

In bed that night, she planned how to use the fire ceremony to overwhelm Raven's pyrophobia. Then, she would use Nikki's acrophobia to make an end-run around Raven's posthypnotic barrier. Satisfied with her plans, she slept soundly.

At the call of the muezzin, she awakened Raven for sunrise prayers.

"Where is everybody?"

"Out early, setting up for Red Wednesday."

She saw Raven's eyes cloud, then widen. "I won't jump over fire!"

"It will help you overcome your fear. Let us join the celebration. No uniform today. On this holiday most of our holy warriors dress up in white sheets or costumes."

She reached into her footlocker and pulled out a loose cotton outfit she had the men tailor for Raven. Red, white and blue stripes, a top hat, and a white beard. Across the jacket, sewn flaming letters spelled, AMERICANS BURN IN HELL.

"You're making me dress up like Uncle Sam?"

"For a little while. Part of the ceremony."

"Then what?"

"After we cast out last year's misfortunes and fears, you will don the white sheet of hope for the new year."

She led the girl outside the barracks and waved at masked women arranging meat pies and sweets on makeshift tables. She had really missed Ashraf during her stay in Athens. "See, Raven? Everyone is happy to celebrate Nowrooz."

When the others saw Raven's costume, they danced around her and shouted, "Down with capitalism! Power to the people!" One waved a torch at her. "Burn in hell, *Am'riki!*"

Raven fell back, but Fatima caught her. "Come see Haji Firuz." She pointed to a man in blackface dressed in red satin, with a cone-shaped red hat, dancing down the street singing as he banged a tambourine.

"So you use the men here not only as tailors but also as buffoons," Raven said. "In old minstrel shows, comedians wore blackface to make people laugh. In America, we now know it's racist."

"You misjudge us. Haji Firuz is an ancient symbolic bearer of good news that winter is gone and spring has come."

Cheers and pot-banging echoed from behind one building. A parade of masked revelers turned the corner carrying effigies of Ayatollah Khomeini, Shah Pahlevi and Uncle Sam. They set the figures afire.

Two masked revelers ran to Raven, tore off her Uncle Sam costume and torched it. Raven fainted.

Fatima knelt beside Raven and draped a white sheet on her. She signaled for two masked revelers to carry her back to the barracks. Had she miscalculated? Had she pushed the girl too far, too soon? No. She must not fail. She would keep at it.

"Listen, Raven," she whispered into her ear. "I have taken the fire away. You are safe now. Repeat, '*Fatima kept me safe from the fire.*'"

A gurgling, then, "Fatima kept me safe from the fire."

"Excellent, Raven. Now, you will sleep, but you will be able to hear my voice. Say, '*I will hear Fatima's voice.*'"

"I will hear Fatima's voice."

"I will trust whatever Fatima says." She repeated the mantra three times, then, "You remember the lines you recited to Jason Tedescu. Repeat them now."

No response.

"You must repeat them."

Still no response.

She leaned back. Her final tactic would be to take Raven to the top of the minaret tower. Work on Nikki's acrophobia to breach the posthypnotic block. If fear of heights didn't work, she might as well save face and pretend Raven had fallen to her death from the minaret tower.

CHAPTER THIRTY-THREE

Athens

Dugan told himself not to let impatience block his thinking. Deal with this damned riddle one line at a time. One image at a time. "Okay," he said to Tia. "Any ideas? Look at line four again."

DEATH PENALTY EXPLODES FIVE-PETALED FLOWER.

"*Death penalty* means execution," she said. "Where do they execute murderers in America?"

"Many states have death row."

"How about the methods?"

"Most commonly electric chair, or injection. In some rare cases, hanging, firing squad."

"I do not see any of those locations as a target," she said. "*Five-petaled flower.* What about weed-killer in a garden?"

"Blooming targets?" he said. "Roses? Violets? Chrysanthemums? I don't think he was *that* subtle."

"Also too subtle for me."

He picked up the page and stared at it. "Wait. Look at the second line again."

She read: *DEATH PENALTY EXPLODES FIVE-PETALED FLOWER.*

"Notice anything unusual about the lettering?"

"The only line in capital letters."

"And the death penalty is *capital* punishment."

Her eyes widened. "Capit-*al*. Capit-*ol*. Oh, my God. Washington, D. C., is your country's capital."

"Let's not get carried away until we figure out *where* in the capital," he said. "The target could be any place in D.C. The capitol building? The White House? The Supreme Court?"

She mused. "*Five-petaled flower* . . . doesn't the Pentagon have five sides?"

He slammed his fist on the rickety table. "They didn't get all five sides in 9/11. They're going after it again."

He tried to restrain his excitement. "Okay, the stock exchange in New York and the Pentagon in D.C. Before we congratulate ourselves, let's solve the first two lines of the quatrain."

Unfaced Goddess guards future from the Windswept Tower.
In serious hate she butchers flesh of all.

"You're handling the mythology," he said. "What goddess has no face?"

"Never heard of one in Greek or Roman mythology."

He said, "Maybe a goddess statue whose face was smashed by invaders opposed to her worship."

"There are hundreds of defaced statues across Greece. Many without noses."

"Okay, forget *who* she is. *Where* is she?"

"She '*guards future.*' Prophetesses—originally maidens associated with one of the gods—foretold the future with obscure metaphorical enigmas. Later, middle-aged women dressed as young girls did the same thing in honor of the past high priestesses."

The image of Salina dressed as a coed made sense. Knuckles to his forehead. "But where? Where?"

"One of the most famous oracles was Apollo's in Delphi."

"Delphi . . . Delphi . . . There's a Delphi in Ohio, but it's a small city. Hardly the location for a terror attack like the other two."

She stared at the page. "It has to be a major city."

"I'm remembering lines from a poem we studied in school," he said. " '. . . *proud to be Hog Butcher, Tool Maker, Stacker of Wheat . . .*' Something, something . . . '*City of the Big Shoulders.*' *Windswept Tower.* Hold everything. The *butcher* is from Carl Sandburg's 'Chicago.' Otherwise known as *the Windy City.*"

"You've got it. New York, Washington D.C., Chicago."

"We've got the stock exchange and the Pentagon," he said, "but not the Chicago target."

"What are you going to do?"

"Call *Charon* to pass this on to Homeland Security. They've got to set up security at the stock exchange and the Pentagon, and raise the disaster alert level to red in Chicago."

He dialed his secure cell phone. Got his key ready. Nothing. Dialed again. Still nothing. "Damn. Never had trouble getting through to him before."

It would be risky to make direct contact with New York. They said use *Cymbal* only in a dire emergency. Well this qualified. If he couldn't contact *Charon* in Cyprus, he was alone and adrift. He punched in the letters and numbers to New York.

After what seemed like forever, someone picked up. He inserted his key, and heard the corresponding click on the other end. Elizabeth Herrick's voice whispered, "Why are you calling here?"

"Dire emergency, *Cymbal.* I have urgent news for Homeland Security, but I can't reach *Tentmaker*'s handler."

"We just got the info from the CIA," she said. "*Charon* was assassinated in Cyprus two days ago."

"Oh, my God! Any idea who—?"

"17N. Watch your back, but don't call here again. You no longer exist."

The phone clicked off.

He tried it again. Nothing.

Tia stared at him. "Your face is dead white. What's happening?"

He shook his head. "I've been terminated by the FBI. I'm an agent without a country. Now, what the hell do I do?"

CHAPTER THIRTY-FOUR

Ashraf

Fatima glared at Raven snoring through the muezzin's call to morning prayer. She shook her roughly. "Wake up. It is time for you to convert to Islam."

"What are you talking about?"

"The Quran foretold that you are destined to be saved, Raven."

"How do you know?"

"From the fifth *surah* called 'The Table Spread' in the Holy Quran revealed at Al-Madinah. It refers to Adam's sons. The Lord accepted gifts from Abel, but not from Cain. Cain killed his brother. As it says, 'Then Allah sent a *raven* scratching upon the ground to show him how to hide his brother's naked corpse. He said: Woe unto me! Am I not able to be as this *raven* and so hide my brother's naked corpse? And he became repentant.'"

"The Quran mentions my name twice?"

"See, *you* were chosen to convert to Islam."

"I'm already a Christian."

Her teachers in the madrassa had prepared for that argument. "Muslims accept Abraham and Jesus as prophets. But Muhammed—peace and blessings be upon him—was proclaimed the last prophet. So you see, you are not abandoning your faith, you are merely carrying it logically forward."

"What does a Muslim have to do?"

"Pray five times a day."

"You already told me. That takes up a lot of time."

"Time well spent in preparing to meet Allah in heaven."

"I need to think about it."

"What is there to think about? Islam is spreading. We are the *ummah*, unified as one Muslim community throughout the world. I know you have always feared being left alone. Accept Islam, become part of the *ummah*, and you will never again be alone."

"I don't know . . ."

"Time is running out. You must decide if you are willing to convert, or spend the rest of your days alone."

Raven grasped a strand of her hair and twisted it.

"Hear me, Raven. Open your mind and listen to me. Your father often put you into trances with words. Now listen to my words and sleep. Come out of the darkness into the light of Allah. Sleep. Sleep. See the whipped sandstorm's golden dunes, spiraling desert sands into whirling dervishes."

She saw Raven's body stiffen, jaws clenched.

"Do not resist, Raven, or Nikki, whoever is hearing my voice. You are trying to keep your eyes open, but they are closing of their own accord. Close. Close. Your eyes are now closed."

Body language showed she was resisting. Not for long. If she couldn't break through Raven's posthypnotic block, she would go around it. Since histrionics were highly suggestible, she would work on Nikki.

"Sleep, Nikki. I know you are afraid of heights, so you will go around the muezzin tower and convert to Islam."

She coughed. ". . . *how do i do it . . . ?*"

"Say to yourself, 'I freely wish to embrace Islam.'"

Nikki's lips moved. ". . . *all right* . . ."

The girl had pulled that one before. "Show me your hands, Nikki."

She extended her open palms.

"Good, now tell yourself, 'I freely wish to embrace Islam.'"

Her eyes closed. ". . . *okay. did that. what next* . . . ?"

"Say, in Arabic, 'Ash-hadu an la ilaha illAllah,' which translates as, 'I bear witness and attest that there is no God worthy of worship but the One God Allah.'"

". . . *okay, ash-hadu an la ilaha illallah* . . ."

"Excellent. Now repeat, 'Wa ash-hadu anna Muhammed-ar-rasool ullah,' which means, 'I bear witness and attest that Muhammed—peace and blessings be upon him—is the messenger of Allah.'"

". . . *wa ash-hadu anna muhammed-ar-rasool ullah* . . ."

"Welcome to the faith."

". . . *whew. thanks* . . ."

"Just one more thing."

". . . *i knew there was a catch* . . ."

"Go to the sink and wash yourself from head to the bottoms of your feet, cleansing yourself of your past life. Then dress. I have a driver waiting. We will say morning prayers at the mosque."

As she listened to the water running, she adjusted the scimitar in the belt below her jacket. If hypnotized Nikki couldn't give her Tedescu's prophecies she was useless as a hostage. Too dangerous to let her live.

She didn't speak during the drive until they approached the mosque. A long shadow crossed their path. Her new convert looked up at the minaret spire, then quickly covered her eyes. Still Nikki. A good sign.

After morning prayers, she took her by the hand. "The

minaret is decorated with an amazing design of blue and white tiles. Come, we will look inside."

"*. . . just on ground level . . .*"

"Of course. I know you are afraid of heights." She pulled her to the passageway leading up the spiral staircase.

Nikki's hand clenched hers. "*. . . too narrow . . .*"

"You and I are slender enough to pass through. Come."

"*. . . you're crazy. i'm not going up there . . .*"

"You will obey my commands."

"*. . . like hell I will . . .*"

She pulled the scimitar from the belt beneath her jacket and held it against Nikki's throat. "Then both you and Raven will have a long fall to a fiery hell sooner than either of you expected."

With her free hand, she grabbed the long blonde tresses and pulled her up the spiral stairway step by step. The hollow minaret echoed Nikki's screams. She forced her out of the tower exit onto the parapet. She released her, and the wind whipped blonde hair around the girl's face.

"You are Nikki, correct?"

She nodded.

"Now tell me what you overheard Raven recite to Mr. Tedescu."

"*. . . drop dead . . .*"

She pulled her to the edge of the parapet. "See how high up we are? You will suffer the fall. Then Raven will suffer the fire."

She held fast. Nikki struggled to look away. "Are you going to cooperate?"

She nodded.

"Listen carefully. Before you were named Nikki, Raven knew you only as *Sis*. You were present when Raven recited the prophetic riddles she had memorized. But by the time your father hypnotized her, you had dissociated. You, Nikki, were neither hypnotized nor given a posthypnotic suggestion of amnesia."

"*. . . that's partly right . . .*"

"Explain."

"*. . . got only the second four-line poem. the what. not the where or the how . . .*"

"Why not the first and third?"

"*. . . because i was distracted when your shoes squished behind the hospital curtain . . .*"

"So you know the second prophecy, but only Raven knows all three."

"*. . . right . . .*"

"Can you penetrate Raven's subconscious and retrieve the first and last quatrains?"

Moments of silence. Then, "*. . . nope. like, there's a brick wall blocking them . . .*"

"Tell me what you heard."

She closed her eyes and spoke with a trembling voice:

"WHAT

. . . the seeds of slow death await in tunnels far to punish all crusaders, inshallah and holy fighters join our comrades now, to spread the shearer's dander I avow . . ."

"That is of no use to us. Tedescu's assistant already e-mailed it to us. We—the *Mujihadeen-e Kalq*—are the holy fighters, and the seeds of death are hidden in our tunnels."

"*. . . don't blame me . . .*"

"You must tell me the first and third quatrains."

"*. . . if i had them, i'd tell you. you'll have to get them from raven. but if you kill me, it's all gone . . .*"

Nikki was right. "Did you hear anything else?"

"*. . . just a line. doesn't make sense . . .*"

"Tell me."

"... *okay. his labor five sweeps dirt from dung-filled stall* ..."

"Do you know what that means?"

"... *no. maybe raven does* ..."

"Let me talk to Raven."

"... *i'll try* ..."

Nikki closed her eyes. When she opened them, she looked around confused.

"Why are we in the minaret tower?"

"Raven?"

"Of course. Were you expecting someone else?"

"Has Tedescu ever mentioned in one of his lectures, that '*His labor five sweeps dirt from dung-filled stall*'?"

"Sure."

"What does it mean?"

"Heracles' fifth labor was to sweep cow shit out of the Aegean stables."

"What's the connection with the other prophecies?"

"I haven't the slightest idea."

She tried to hide her frustration. If she failed to get the answers during one last attempt, she would turn Raven over to the men.

Knowing how years of MEK's rule of chastity must have frustrated their male lust, they would most likely force themselves on her. Then, according to the sharia law regarding raped Muslim women, they would stone her as an adulteress and bury her broken body in the desert.

Would it be Nikki or Raven the men raped? And which of the two would be stoned and buried alive?

CHAPTER THIRTY-FIVE

Athens

The secure phone woke Dugan. He stared at it. *Charon* was dead and the FBI had cut him off. Who could be calling?

Tia stirred beside him. "Don't answer it."

He picked up and inserted his key. "Who is this?"

"This is *Tentmaker*. Am I talking to the *Dentist?*"

He shook his head to make sure he was awake. "Good to hear from you, but how come you're contacting me?"

"With our ferryman no longer crossing the river, and the banks overflowing, I had to take the oar."

"You've got my attention."

"The situation here has become critical. MEK now has Tedescu's second quatrain. Fatima told General Hassan she'd work on dehypnotizing Raven to get the first and third, but if she's unsuccessful, she intends to dispose of the girl."

"We're running out of time. Did you learn the second quatrain?"

"Take it down quickly. Then I've got to sign off."

He waved for Tia to get him a pen. "Okay."

> "WHAT
> Seeds of Slow Death await in tunnels far
> To punish all Crusaders, Inshallah.

> And Holy Fighters join our comrades now,
> To spread the Shearer's Dander I avow."

"For your information, MEK has a network of tunnels on the northeast border between Iraq and Iran. But they never allowed the U.N. inspectors into Ashraf to search for WMD."

"So that's the *tunnels far*. Any clue to the *seeds of death* or *the shearer's dander?*"

"Not yet. Someone is coming. Good-bye. Good luck."

The phone went silent. He slumped back in the chair.

"Let me see," Tia said. She glanced at what he had taken down. "This one is obvious. *Holy fighters* are the *Mujihadeen-e Kalq*. In 1988, they joined Saddam's cousin, Chemical Ali—the Butcher of Kurdistan—and helped him kill thousands of Kurds in the town of Halabja. I'm thinking it's either mustard gas or nerve gas."

He pyramided his fingers. "The word *seeds* suggests a biological rather than chemical weapon."

"I wish I'd paid more attention in biology class."

"I did. One of my areas of analyzing international traffic was tracking biological weapons of mass destruction. After 9/11."

"You surprise me more every day. What about the seeds?"

No matter how he turned it over in his mind, one thought kept surfacing. "If my analysis is right, the sleepers are planning to spread *seeds* that the second quatrain calls the *shearer's dander*."

"I don't understand. What seeds?"

"Those who shear sheeps' fleece are often sickened by it. *Shearer's dander* refers to anthrax."

"God! Didn't Tedescu stop to think about the hundreds of thousands of innocent people his sleepers will kill?"

"Terrorists don't think," he said. "They start out as fanatics and become psychotics."

"Then if they are insane they cannot win."

"Another of your ancient Greek beliefs?"

She closed her eyes. "Euripides wrote, '*Whom the gods would destroy, they first make mad.*'"

CHAPTER THIRTY-SIX

Ashraf

Raven opened her eyes. Either it was dark or she'd gone blind. She felt a blanket beneath her on the floor, her purse beside her. Was this really happening? Or was it a dream? A door opened. Someone pulled her out of the dark into the blinding light.

"What's happening? Where am I? Who are you?"

"Camp Ashraf. And I am your friend Fatima."

She shook her head to clear it. "I remember now. The fires. They jumped over the bonfire and started burning me."

"Not you, Raven. The effigy of Uncle Sam. I would never allow anything to happen to you."

"And the tower with the gold balls and the crescent?"

"You wanted to see the inside of the minaret. We explored it."

"I don't remember."

"That is not important. Now, you must listen carefully to my words. You are very tired and you want to sleep."

"In Alexi's arms."

"He is not here. He deserted you."

"I don't believe that. He'll protect me."

"Foolish girl. Do you not know men tell us that to take

advantage of us. All they want is to get into our bodies. Use us, then discard us like empty shells."

"Did a man use you like that?"

Her answer was a slap in the face. "Men are weak. They think only with their penises. Women are strong. We rule in Ashraf and we will punish America."

"How do you expect to do that?"

"With your assistance."

". . . *i'm sure as hell not gonna help you hurt my people . . .*"

"Your people are now Muslims, Nikki. You will provide me with the rest of Tedescu's prophecies. It is essential to our survival."

". . . *drop dead . . .*"

Another slap. And another. And a third.

". . . *haven't you figured out that pain doesn't bother me, bitch? hit all you want. i won't feel a thing . . .*"

She watched Fatima reach into her bag and take out a syringe. Was that it? Get her so drugged, so addicted she'd do anything they asked to get more dope.

"Don't stick that needle into me!"

"It will calm you. Help you sleep."

She started up from the floor, but Fatima straddled her and plunged the hypo into her arm.

"Can't move! Can't breathe!"

"If you calm down, you will feel better."

"Why are you doing this to me?"

"To help you, of course. I am your friend. Now, you will relax. Feel light and airy. You are drifting into a twilight sleep. When you awaken, you will feel better. Very happy. And you will praise Allah for allowing you to become one of us. You will be a beautiful martyr in heaven with the angels, Raven."

"I can't be one of the seventy-two virgins anymore."

Another slap, and she was out of her body again.

. . . why is this weird-looking woman in military uniform slapping me? is this another horror movie . . . ?

"Raven, listen to me."

". . . who the hell are you . . . ?"

"Your teacher in Islam."

". . . teacher? if eyes could kill. i'd be ready for embalming . . ."

"Calm down. I do not intend to harm you."

". . . then what . . . ?"

"You heard Raven recite the three quatrains in the infirmary. I need you to tell me the first and third."

". . . why . . . ?"

"So we can warn the United States. It is urgent."

". . . i don't believe you . . ."

"Think of fire."

". . . doesn't bother me. you have me confused with my pyrophobic sister . . ."

"Think of standing on a high mountain."

". . . i don't do mountain climbing . . ."

Another slap made her face sting.

Then, outside herself, "Bitch! Why'd you do that?"

"You are trying my patience."

Who is that wrapped in a blanket? Burning in the fires of purgatory? Screaming in a padded cell? "Stop it! I'll do anything you say. What do you want?"

"Names of the targets in three cities are hidden behind your fear of fire. Recite them and I will stop."

"Daddy says open only with the key. Who has the key?"

"Your clever father used a posthypnotic command."

"What's that?"

"Never mind. If you don't help us solve the prophecies, you are no longer of use to us."

"Thank God!"

"You mean Allah. You converted to Islam."

"I'm changing my mind."

"In that case, any Muslim anywhere in the world is required to fulfill the fatwa."

"What's that?"

"For you, first rape. Then, beheading."

She forced herself not to show her trembling. Sure, there were times she'd planned suicide. Usually something painless, like an overdose of sleeping pills. Scratching and cutting herself made her feel alive. But the thought of a sword splitting her head made her want to gag.

She swallowed the choking as Fatima headed for the door. What the hell, one last shot. "Hey, after all those years of forced chastity, sure you wouldn't rather take my place with the guys? You could say it wasn't your fault you were raped. Oh, I forgot. Militant Muslims consider a raped woman an adulteress and stone them before they bury them alive."

"You are amusing, Raven. But this will be your last stage performance." As Fatima shut the door, the room went dark again. She heard the outside lock click shut.

Waiting to be raped and have her head cut off, she curled up alongside her twin in their mother's womb.

CHAPTER THIRTY-SEVEN

Athens

Dugan heard the banging. Not on Tia's door but on his own next door. He glanced at the clock. 6:00 A.M.

"Someone is looking for you," she whispered.

He jumped out of bed and pulled the curtain aside. A police car in the street.

A voice from the corridor called out, "Mr. Diodorus! You are wanted in headquarters!"

"They're probably from my father," she said. "You'd better get out of here."

"How?"

She pointed to the window.

"From the third floor?"

"Remember my father's warning."

He pulled on his briefs, opened the window and stepped onto the ledge. Crumbling brick. He clung to the wall. Don't look down. If he fell three flights, would it kill him? Even if he didn't land on his head, there'd be lots of broken bones. Side-stepping carefully, he reached the ledge outside his room.

"Spiros Diodorus, you must to come with us!"

He made it through his window. "Just a minute. Let me put something on." He grabbed his robe and cracked the door open. "What's this about?"

An elderly officer said, "Sorry to disturb, but you are needed urgent at headquarters."

"So early?"

"Many arrived in Athens before dawn for conference. Captain Eliade requires your attendance."

At least the officer would report he'd been awakened in his own room. He slipped into his shirt and tugged on his trousers. "Have to brush my teeth. And I'll need a coffee."

The officer thought a moment, then nodded. "Brush quick. I have thermos in patrol car."

He drank it black during the ride to headquarters, grateful it was strong. Over the rim of the plastic cup, he glimpsed schoolchildren with their backpacks, newsstand workers putting out the morning papers, café owners rolling down awnings against the morning sun. An ordinary, peaceful morning in Athens.

His escort led him through the station to the far end of the staff room. An armed guard opened it and ushered him in. He hadn't expected what he saw. A mahogany conference table with Captain Hector Eliade at the far end. Seated around the table were half a dozen men in civilian clothes.

"Good morning, Mr. Spiros Diodorus." Eliade pointed at an empty chair. "These men have traveled a long way to—as you say in America—pick your brain."

No one in uniform. He suspected some were Pentagon officers in mufti. Others, probably from the State Department. If they weren't actually members of the joint counterterrorism task force, they were surrogates assigned to report on what he had to tell them.

A young, deeply tanned man scowled at him. He noticed the tan ended in a line on his forehead, so he likely wore an officer's cap. Probably army. "Mr. Diodorus, what evidence do you have that a weapon of mass destruction is about to be smuggled into the United States?"

"My analysis makes me think the weapon may already be en route."

A gray-haired man twiddled his pen. "And you believe the threat is to targets in New York, D.C. and Chicago?"

"The stock exchange in New York, the Pentagon in D.C. I haven't yet solved the Chicago target."

"Are you 100 percent certain?"

"Eighty-nine percent."

"Do you have any idea of the panic that would erupt across the nation if Homeland Security went to red alert?"

He didn't like the way the guy was now pointing the pen at him. "Probably the same as if we'd alerted the country to our intel *before* 9/11 that airplane suicide bombers were taking one-way flying lessons in the States."

The guy tossed his pen on the table and shoved back in his chair. Probably State Department.

A little man with a wispy beard leaned forward. "Your report says it is a bioterror weapon. There are so many. E. coli? Botulinum? Gas gangrene bacteria?"

He recognized Professor Sorger from the Anston Institute and answered slowly. "Before the Gulf War, Iraq was researching all those. The problem, at that time, was that biological warfare microbes had to be used as aerosols to cause the kind of mass casualties Tedescu's prophecy threatens. As you know, few microbes are robust enough to be successfully processed into today's biological weapons. Unless they've found a way to put them into microtubes."

Sorger asked, "In that case, what is your conclusion?"

"I've already solved that part of the riddle. Anthrax."

A sharp intake of breath across the room.

The Pentagon delegate frowned. "Don't tell me small, aging terrorist groups like 17N and MEK have the expertise to weaponize anthrax spores."

"No," he said, "but we know the Russians developed anthrax 836, a highly virulent strain. The KGB called it their 'battle strain' and mass produced it. It's ideal for freeze-drying into fine powder, making it the perfect biological weapon, most likely resistant to penicillin. We won't have time to develop new antibiotics."

The pen-twiddler tapped it on the table. "Isn't it true that the apocalyptic cult Aum Shinrikyo tried to use anthrax several times in subways in Japan, but failed."

"Sure. Because they tried to use fans to spread it. I feel strongly that Tedescu learned from their mistakes and has found a unique way to release it."

"How do we know MEK has it?"

"We know Iraq had large quantities. They planned to spread it over coalition lines and across Israel."

Twiddler was doodling on the pad in front of him. "Where could Saddam have gotten the stuff?"

"We know that dozens of unemployed high-level Russian scientists trafficked in biological agents of mass destruction. But, you want to know what's most ironic? In 1986, before America's break with Iraq, all their scientists needed to do to get anthrax spore samples from us was to order it by phone. We supplied seed cultures from the American Type Culture Collection in Rockville, Maryland, through the mail."

"That's all in the past," the military officer said. "What evidence do you have of current danger?"

"Head of the medical counterterrorism group pointed out that a domestic anthrax attack is our number-one national security threat. Your own military experts have predicted a 90 percent probability of such an attack in a U.S. city in two to five years, killing hundreds of thousands and costing the country more than a trillion dollars."

"How can we find out the method they plan to use for spreading the anthrax?" the professor asked.

"That's my problem. Tedescu's third quatrain is labeled HOW. If I could get that and solve it, there might be a way to block the attack."

Twiddler pointed his pen at Captain Eliade. "He tells us only Raven Slade knows it. And she's in the hands of the *Mujihadeen-e Kalq*. That seems to make it hopeless, and—"

"Not quite hopeless," the military man said. "Since MEK is the strongest opposition group to the ayatollah, one of our contingency plans is to use them as an advance force if we invade Iran. We're waiting for the State Department to remove them from the terrorist list."

Pen jabbed the desk. "They're terrorists. We're unalterably opposed to dealing with them."

Eliade said, "It looks like a standoff between the Pentagon and State."

This was making him sick to his stomach. "What the hell. It's an election year, right?"

"That has nothing to do with it," twiddler said. "The question is, since the mentally ill young woman is in enemy hands, how do we get it from her?"

Eliade said, "If you can get her out of Ashraf alive, and turn her over to me, I would know how to make her talk."

"Another Theater of Torture performance," Dugan said, "or this time the real thing?"

"We don't speak of torture," twiddler said.

"Aggressive interrogation," the professor said.

The Pentagon spokesman shook his head. "This is a waste of all our time. According to our deep-cover agent in Ashraf, Raven may be dead by morning."

* * *

He waited until the others left. "Captain Eliade, I have a request. I would like to borrow one of your officers. Perhaps the one who drove me here."

"For what purpose?"

"To follow leads on my own, incognito."

"How will you identify yourself?"

"As a student reporter for a Greek-American newspaper. The biweekly *Greek Press*.

Eliade stared at him with his good eye. He pressed the key on the intercom. "Markos Kostavros, to the conference room at once." Seconds later the officer appeared in the doorway. Eliade said, "You will accompany reporter Diodoros wherever he requires to gather news for *Hellenikos Typos*."

Kostavros touched the visor of his cap. "My honor, Mr. Diodoros. I read *Hellenikos Typos* often."

After they left the station, the officer asked the destination.

"Athens Asylum."

"You are going to write an article about the recent attack by 17N?"

"Before I write, I have to do investigative reporting."

"What part of the asylum, sir?"

"The infirmary, where the American girl spoke to Jason Tedescu before he was shot to death."

CHAPTER THIRTY-EIGHT

Ashraf

From backstage, Raven watched the young woman curled up in the corner of the room. She was waiting for her entrance cue. Before or after the ingénue was raped? Everyone wanted her to perform the play Mr. Tedescu wrote. In the script she'd read on his desk that day, she could still see Act One was *"WHERE?"* Act Two *"WHAT?"* Act Three . . . oh, yes . . . *"HOW?"* Her role was to enter stage right and face the special audience that had been invited to preview the play.

She was to recite the soliloquy only to them. Odd, she rarely forgot her part, but she couldn't remember now. Where was the prompter?

And what was her next scene?

Then she remembered the director saying that at curtain-rise the audience would watch her being raped. Not a Greek tragedy, but Pope's *Rape of the Lock*. A comedy.

Suddenly, everything went dark. She was no longer outside herself, looking at herself from backstage. Now, she was huddled against the wall, waiting. What could she use to defend herself? She felt around in her bag. Only a small nail file. Should have been carrying a knife. Wouldn't have helped. Fatima would have confiscated it.

She heard a noise. Someone working the lock. Screaming would do no good, but she could slow him down by stabbing his balls with the nail file.

The door creaked open.

She braced herself.

A voice spoke in Farsi, the language she'd heard from the women in the compound. But this was the harsh voice of a man coming at her. Heavy on top of her. Forcing her legs apart. She struggled, but he locked her hips with his knees and began to rape her.

As the curtain descended, she heard enthusiastic applause.

CHAPTER THIRTY-NINE

Athens

Dugan told Kostavros to park the police cruiser at the asylum emergency entrance and come inside with him. "Some people don't like to talk to reporters, so I'll need you to take the lead. Ask directions to the infirmary."

"I know where it is. I was with Captain Eliade when he came to investigate the shootings." He led the way. Some patients were strapped down in their beds.

"Do you know which one Tedescu was in?"

Kostavros pointed to an empty wheelchair against the wall. An orderly was mopping nearby.

"Ask if he was here that day."

As Kostavros approached, the orderly dropped the mop. He bent to pick it up and nearly knocked over his suds-filled bucket. "I swear I have done nothing illegal."

"Relax. This reporter from *Hellenikos Typos* is doing an article about the attack by 17N."

"I know nothing, Mr. Reporter. I saw nothing."

He decided to take over. "Perhaps," he said, holding out a twenty-euro note, "you *overheard* something."

The orderly looked frightened. Kostavros nodded.

"It was strange," the orderly said. "Nurse Sawyer was

there, but Mr. Tedescu shouted for her to go away and not listen. It made me curious. The director's daughter was reciting something like a poem or lines from a play. I heard only a few words."

"Go on," he said, holding out another twenty-euro note. "What words?"

"An escaped bull. The death penalty. Something about a goddess. And seeds in tunnels."

"And . . . ?"

The orderly tapped his forehead. "A dog. That's all I heard. I swear it."

He handed the man another ten-euro note and gripped his shoulder. "Do not mention this to anyone else. I do not want my article in the paper to be scooped."

The orderly nodded and slopped suds onto the passageway.

Outside, Kostavros asked, "Did you learn what you need?"

"Not enough for an article."

"How unfortunate. Where do you wish me to take you?"

He gave instructions to his apartment house.

He was in his room for less than a minute when he heard tapping at the door. He opened it and Tia threw herself onto the bed. "Tell me everything."

He described the conference session in detail.

"So what do you think?"

"It's depressing. The Pentagon wants State to remove MEK from the terrorist list. State refuses."

"Where does that leave us?"

He paced, took the bottle of Jack Daniel's from the dresser and poured two drinks. He handed her one, and raised it in a toast. "To solving the rest of Tedescu's riddles."

"The goddess without a face is still a mystery to me," she said.

"Let's put the rest of WHERE aside for now. Since we're pretty sure WHAT is weaponized anthrax, we've got to figure out how they plan to disperse it."

"We have nothing from the HOW quatrain."

"We do now." He told her about the visit to the asylum. "One clue. *Dog.*"

She raised her drink. "Hair of the dog for a hangover?"

"How about dog days?" he said. "Or Dog star?"

"Dog in the manger?" she said.

He groaned. "That's just doggerel. God, I feel we're so close it's tantalizing."

"Tantalizing comes from Tantalus," she said, "who was punished for stealing the golden dog."

"How about going to bed and letting sleeping dogs lie?"

She put her arms around him. "A dogged analyst with a one-track mind."

CHAPTER FORTY

Ashraf

Shortly after midnight, *Tentmaker* rolled off his bunk fully dressed and slipped out of the men's barracks. He'd made preparations as soon as he monitored the conversation between Fatima and the general. If he was going to get Raven back to Athens to be interrogated, he had to move fast.

He slipped through the shadows to the lockup where Fatima had put her. As he reached for the door and turned the knob, he heard Raven scream. He ran inside and flashed his light. A man on top of her was howling in pain. She was jabbing something into the would-be rapist's eye. He let go. She stabbed whatever she had into his neck. Again. Again. He gurgled and fell off her body.

She looked into the flashlight's beam. "Come on, you bastard. You want the same?"

He whispered, "Don't be alarmed."

"Stay back. If you touch me, I'll stab you and kick you in the balls. Or maybe only MEK women have balls."

"Be quiet."

"Try to rape me and you'll end up blind like this one."

"I am here to release you. If you come with me, you have a chance to live." He kicked her assailant in the head and shoved him aside. "What do you have to lose?" He took her hand and pulled her to her feet. "We move quick, quiet. If anyone stops us, I will say I am taking you out to stone you and bury you in the desert."

"You're not?"

"I told you, I am here to help you escape."

She followed him into the deserted streets littered with tattered paper uniforms and glowing embers. "Where'd everyone go?"

"Most Red Wednesday revelers are asleep now." He led her to the outskirts of the compound and helped her into a jeep parked in front of a building. But instead of starting the engine, he released the brake.

"What are you doing?"

"Shhhh!" He ran to the rear and pushed. The jeep moved slowly at first. Then faster downhill until they passed the barrack units. He jumped in, started the engine. He braked at a barbed-wire fence and jumped out. He rolled back the barbed wire into an opening wide enough to drive through, then got back into the jeep and sped into the darkness.

"You cut that wire ahead of time?"

"I told you, I planned."

"What did you plan for me?"

"You will soon find out. Settle back and close your eyes, the drive will take about an hour."

"Can you tell me where we're going?"

"Kurd area in northern Iraq, where MEK once helped Saddam by gassing thousands of their people. *Peshmerga* territory."

"What's *Peshmerga?*"

"It means, *those who face death.*"

She sucked in her breath. "I'll be at home among them."

"Sleep. We have a long trip ahead."

She closed her eyes and dozed. He saw she was gripping her weapon. A small nail file.

He stopped the jeep and she stirred awake.

". . . *where are we . . . ?*"

He was surprised how her voice changed from alto to soprano. "A small airfield."

". . . *i'm not flying anywhere . . .*"

"There is no other way."

". . . *then take me back . . .*"

"Impossible."

She braced herself to prevent him from forcing her out of the jeep. She scratched his hand with the nail file. A JPAT's marshal came up behind her and pulled a hood over her head. She struggled as he dragged her out of the jeep and tied her hands with plastic strips.

". . . *i thought you were going to help me . . .*"

Tentmaker pushed her up the ladder through the hatch and threw her onto a seat. He buckled her in. Then he removed her hood.

She screamed. ". . . *i can't fly . . .*"

"You don't have to. The plane will do it for you."

". . . *untie my hands . . .*"

"If you promise to control yourself."

". . . *i promise . . .*"

He removed the plastic cuffs.

She rubbed her wrists. ". . . *was that necessary . . . ?*"

"The way you fought coming aboard, I'd say yes."

". . . *okay. sorry. where are you taking me . . . ?*"

"Not me. The marshals will return you to Athens."

". . . *no. i want to go home to ohio . . .*"

"Not just yet. The Greek counterterrorism task force has a few questions to ask you first."

". . . *not sure i'm the one who has the answers* . . ."

"Care for a drink before takeoff?"

She looked confused, then sat back. "Sure, a rum and Coke would be nice." She drank it quickly and he gave her another. And then a third. Her voice change took him by surprise. Deeper now, more like the alto he'd heard before.

He moved near the hatch and used his secure phone. "*Dentist . . . Dentist . . .* This is *Tentmaker*. JPATS is about to take off. Favorable headwind. Should arrive early. They can stay on the tarmac in Athens's Hellenikon Airport only ten minutes. Arrange for security to pick up the package and deliver to Captain Eliade."

He looked back at her. "I've got to leave you now. Good luck."

"Okay," she said. "I guess I'm the package, but I don't have a toothache. So why the hell are you sending for a dentist?"

He turned away and climbed down the ladder. As he watched the plane take off, he felt sorry for her. She was a scrappy young woman. But Captain Eliade was well-known throughout the intelligence community as an aggressive interrogator who believed in the power of pain.

CHAPTER FORTY-ONE

Athens

Alexi's cell phone rang. He kicked off the blanket and picked up. "Yes?"

"This is *Nurse*. Raven has escaped from Ashraf."

He moved to the edge of the bed. "How?"

"A mole in our cadre helped her."

"What about Tedescu's message?"

"I thought I had more time."

What to say? He'd often berated himself for letting her take Raven from him. "Where do you think she's headed?"

"On a plane back to Athens. Intercept her at Hellenikon Airport before security picks her up. If you cannot prevent her from falling into Eliade's hands, find a way to silence her."

"What about the shipment?"

"After you deal with the Slade girl, fly to Ohio. The courier will be waiting for you at the student memorial of Kent State University. After you give her the money, she will give you the package."

After she hung up, he started to dial. Stopped. Began again. Slammed down the phone. He had to tell his father in person.

His hands were sweaty on the Harley's grips as he sped to

the garage. Two blocks away, he jammed the brakes. Stupid! Stupid! The safe house location was already compromised. He spun the bike around and headed to his father's apartment.

Ten minutes later, he pulled into the alley behind the building and looked around before he slipped into the rear doorway. On the fourth floor, he examined the doorjamb for hairs. None. He used the secret knock. One—two—one. Repeated twice.

Myron, uncombed white hair standing in tufts, let him in. "What are you doing here? Are you sure you have not been followed."

"What do you think I am?"

"You do not want to hear my answer."

He told Myron about Fatima's call.

"Nikki must not be allowed to fall into Eliade's hands. Go to airport. Get help from our sympathizers. Use element of surprise to get her away from any guard."

"If I succeed, what then?"

"Tell her it was all arranged so she help you in America. Promise to marry her after return to Greece."

"She believes in me. I hate lying to her."

"I always hated to lie to your mother, may she rest in peace. But sometimes is necessary."

He cleared security at Hellenikon Airport and stationed himself where he could scrutinize the passenger terminal. Locals, tourists, students with backpacks and nuns, all crushed together. Sleeping dogs curled against peeling walls. No wonder the Greek government was rushing to close down this place before the Olympics and replace it with the new Eleftherios Venizelos Airport.

He checked the arrival-departure board. Pointless. It wouldn't announce the gate and time of an incoming JPATS rendition flight returning Raven to Greece. The plane would most likely land at a rarely used runway.

He caught sight of a cart driver whose job it was to transport invalids and the elderly to their departure gates. He recognized him as a sympathizer. He waved for the driver to approach. The man spun the cart around and almost struck him. It gave him an idea.

"Comrade," he whispered. "The patriots need your help."

"At your service, comrade."

"I want you to wait near the airport-employees-only entrance. A guard will be escorting a young blonde woman. Watch for my signal. When I take out my comb and run it through my hair, you are to ram into the guard, take the woman aboard the cart and drive her through the main exit. I will slip outside and wait for you on my cycle."

"As you wish, comrade." The cart driver sped away.

Pleased with himself at his clever plan, he took out his comb and waited.

CHAPTER FORTY-TWO

The Learjet made a smooth landing. The marshal led Raven down the steps and pushed her into a baggage cart.

"Watch this one," he said to the old driver. "She's a wild-cat. If she starts to scream, you'll need earplugs."

She didn't resist as the driver led her out of the cart, up the steps to a door marked: AIRPORT EMPLOYEES ONLY. He pushed her into the departure lounge. Hellenikon Airport was crowded and stank of unwashed bodies.

. . . okay, move fast, raven. we can't let this old prick take us to security for questioning . . .

What am I supposed to do?

. . . use your brains and your body . . .

She felt the old guard's veined hand on her arm. She backed up against him and slapped his face. "Get your hands off me, you horny bastard! How dare you grope me!" She turned to the crowd. "He put his hand up my skirt. Help me! Stop him!"

People surrounded the startled guard. Men punched him. Women struck him with purses and umbrellas. A man in a wheelchair hit him with a cane. The guard put up his hands to defend himself.

Sobbing into a handkerchief, she pulled free and merged into the waiting passengers in the departure area. No idea what she was going to do next.

A passenger transport cart driver motioned for her to get in. He looked too eager. She ran away from him toward a group heading for the ticketing section. Okay, think fast. Where to? She moved past ticket counters. Flights to Atlanta, Newark, Philadelphia. Where did she want to go?

. . . *home to waybridge, stupid* . . .

Halfway down the ticketing area she saw a young man holding up a sign: CLASSICAL TOUR GROUP RETURNING TO COLUMBUS OHIO. MEET HERE. A group of people, dragging luggage, clustered around him. One of them looked familiar. She'd seen that salt-and-pepper Vandyke at the Waybridge campus.

The counter display blinked: FLIGHT 241. ATHENS TO COLUMBUS, OHIO. ON TIME.

That would take her closer to home than any of the others, and she could hitchhike to Waybridge. She moved to the end of a long line.

Suddenly, a blonde with bloodred lipstick—garment bag over one arm and pulling a wheeled carry-on with the other—broke through the line.

"Hey," a man shouted, "get to the end."

A woman screamed, "Be careful of my baby!"

The man with the Vandyke beard tried to block her, but she elbowed him aside and pushed to the first open booth. She slammed her passport and credit card on the counter. "Coach to Columbus, Ohio."

The clerk glanced at the angry passengers in the line, then shrugged. He made entries in the computer and handed her the ticket. "Are you checking luggage?"

"And have it get lost in this goddamned Greek airport? Hell, no. I'll carry them on." She shoved the documents into her purse.

"Lady," a man shouted, "you've got a hell of a nerve."

Ignoring him, she slung her purse over the carry-on handle

and stuck out her middle finger. She dragged the garment bag and carry-on toward the security line.

. . . get to the metal detectors ahead of her . . .

She hesitated, then understood. Passing the bitch, she went through a detector quickly. The woman laid her garment bag, and her carry-on with the purse dangling from the handle, onto the moving belt. The alarm sounded. The guard wanded her. She took off a gold necklace and placed it in the plastic container. She went through the detector again but the alarm sounded a second time. She cursed the guard, the detector and Greece, as she waited for another pass of the wand. Everyone was looking at her.

. . . grab her damned purse . . .

She hesitated, snatched the purse off the chrome carry-on handle, and dropped it into her own tote bag. No one seemed to notice. Nonchalantly, she strolled to the ladies' lavatory and entered a stall.

The expensive-looking Birkin purse must have cost at least ten thousand dollars. Alexi was right about rich American women squandering money while Third World poor scrounged for food. She scooped the passport, traveler's checks and credit cards out of the handbag and slipped them into her own. She wedged the Birkin behind the toilet seat and left the lavatory slowly. As she strode casually through the passenger lounge, she thumbed through her tote bag to discover her new identity.

Driver's license *Marsha Woods. 3740 State Street. Columbus, Ohio.* The airline ticket was for Hellas Airlines flight 241 gate C-4. She looked up at the Arrival and Departure display. DEPARTING IN TEN MINUTES.

As she headed for the departure gate, she thought she caught a glimpse of Alexi. Was it really him? Did he see her? Should she go to him?

. . . remember toothpick's last words in piraeus . . .

She turned away and joined the line at the gate. The attendant looked at her ticket. "Welcome aboard Ms. Woods. No carry-on?"

"I checked everything but this handbag."

As she entered the passageway, she glanced back. Alexi stared at her, then at the gate departure sign. Oh, God. He knew her destination.

He waved, but there was no smile on his face.

CHAPTER FORTY-THREE

Athens to Columbus, Ohio

Alexi saw the flashing sign. The flight for Columbus, Ohio, was boarding. Not one of the targets, but a major city. How to track her down?

As his father reminded him, many of the younger airport employees were Second Generation 17N or sympathizers. He went back to the ticketing area and waited until the line cleared. At the counter, he pointed to the man's name tag. "Comrade Postanaffrios, a comrade requires your help."

The attendant nodded. "How may I serve, comrade?"

"I need the name of the obnoxious American blonde woman who crashed the line, the one flying to Columbus, Ohio."

The agent glanced around, then checked his computer. He whispered, "Marsha Woods."

"Thank you, comrade."

He heard the boarding call for his own flight. He grabbed his carry-on and headed for the gate. After he finished his business at Kent State, he would find Marsha Woods's address in the Columbus, Ohio, phone book.

As he passed a newsstand, he saw the *Eleftherotypia* banner headline: 17N GREEK TERROR NETWORK MEMBERS CAPTURED.

A picture showed fat Theodor handcuffed to Vasili's right hand. The red and yellow 17N star symbol was clear in the background. He bought the paper and scanned the article as he moved along the check-in line.

"*Most members of the elusive Greek 17N terrorist group were arrested earlier today. After a failed explosion in the port city of Piraeus last month, two terrorists—Theodor Pavli and Vasili Sorostos—under interrogation by the Hellenic Antiterrorist Task Force, identified the others. All are now in custody except for the leader Myron Costa and Alexi Costa, head of the Second Generation 17N. Authorities believe they, and an American woman, former hostage Raven Slade, are planning an attack in the United States.*

"*One of the captives shouted, 'Some of us have been taken into custody, but we are still alive! New freedom fighters will continue our battle against American capitalist imperialists.*'"

He felt like vomiting. How were they caught? Had they broken under Eliade's torture and compromised the Second Generation? Were the FBI and Homeland Security alerted and already tracking him? If they took Raven into custody, she might identify him and betray the mission.

Stay calm. First, pick up the weapon MEK should already have shipped to Kent State. Then, to Columbus and find Marsha Woods's address. If he could find a way to extract the rest of Tedescu's prophetic riddles from Raven, he might—just might—let Nikki live a while longer.

CHAPTER FORTY-FOUR

One of the flight attendants checked Raven's boarding pass and waved her through to coach. An elderly man occupying the window seat smiled. She ignored him. She wished she had the aisle seat.

A teenager with an Ohio State baseball cap on backward jammed his duffle bag into the overhead compartment. He looked her up and down as he took out a blanket and pillow, sat alongside her and fastened his seat belt.

She asked, "Would you mind changing seats with me?"

He shook his head. "I need the aisle because I gotta use the toilet a lot."

Liar. Crammed alongside her, rubbing against her, she knew what he'd be doing under his blanket after the lights dimmed.

She watched the rest of the passengers move along the aisle. When they were all seated, the attendant closed the hatch. The announcement came, first in Greek, then in English, "*Please fasten seat belts, put out cigarettes and turn off cell phones.*"

The plane taxied. She clenched her fists. The wait felt like forever. Then engines screeched onto the takeoff runway. The jet roared, lifted and soared into the clouds. She closed her eyes. Don't panic, Nikki. It won't be so bad when we reach cruising altitude.

Finally, the speaker announcement, "*You may walk in the aisle, but keep seat belts on while seated. Flight attendants will take orders for drinks.*"

She opened her eyes slowly. Sighed. Unclenched her fists. Okay. Nikki wasn't the one flying.

When the cart reached her, she ordered a rum and Coke. Glass in hand, she glanced around. Alexi once said air marshals didn't drink alcohol.

The man with the salt-and-pepper Vandyke seated across from her looked to be in his early thirties. She had the vague recollection of seeing him on the quad at Waybridge. He bought a double vodka.

The man behind him didn't buy a drink but made eye contact with her. She smiled. He looked away. Unusual. Had she betrayed herself? Was he waiting until they landed in Columbus before taking her into custody?

Lights dimmed for the in-flight movie, but TV news came on first. She saw her captors for the first time without their masks. Theodor, the chocolate-eating garage owner, was not only fat but shiny bald. One-armed Vasili stood beside him. She guessed the short, mustached one, hair slicked back in what looked like a greasy toupee, was poet-singer Yorgo.

They were being led by Greek police through a crowd of onlookers. Some shouted, "Death to terrorists!" Others waved and called out, "Power to the people!"

Her palms felt clammy. She saw her bracelet scars of flesh on her left arm. How many days had she been held captive? She lost track after Alexi made her stop.

On the screen, a newscaster said, ". . . *twenty-seven-year reign of the 17N terrorist gang has been broken. In the aftermath of a botched firebombing in Piraeus, a search led to the capture of nineteen—*"

She scrunched down in her seat. The boy on the aisle, breathing hard, was staring at her with a glazed expression,

"—According to a police spokesman, three 17N members are believed to be still at large. The leader, Myron Costa. His son, Alexi Costa, head of Second Generation 17N. And the American hostage Raven Slade, alleged to have been brainwashed into joining the terrorists. Police have released a surveillance photograph taken during her participation as getaway motorcyclist during the Athens Bank robbery. It will now be shown on the screen."

At first, the face beneath the helmet was blurred, but she saw herself. She let out an ear-shattering scream. All heads turned away from the monitor toward her. The boy beside her, still clutching his blanket, fell into the aisle.

She kept screaming.

"Hey, you crazy, lady?"

The cabin lights came on.

An attendant shouted, "Is there a doctor on board?"

The man with the Vandyke raised his hand.

"This woman is hysterical," the attendant said. "Can you do something?"

Raven couldn't hear what he said, but she saw him get out of his seat and open the overhead compartment. He pulled down a black bag and came to her row. "What's wrong?"

"I didn't touch her," the old man said.

"Me neither," the boy said. "She's a wacko."

The doctor asked, "Son, will you change seats with me?"

The boy scrambled across the aisle.

She heard a voice from far away. "I'm Dr. Kyle, a psychiatrist. I may be able to help you. What's your name?"

"M-Marsha W-Woods."

"Ms. Woods, would you like me to sedate you?"

"No needles."

His forehead wrinkled. "Have you ever been hypnotized?"

"A few times."

"Was it easy or difficult to put you under?"

"Easy."

He touched the back of her hand and stroked it. "Sleep. You will soon be calm and sleep. Deep . . . deep . . . sleep. You will fall asleep by the time I reach the count of ten. One. Two. Three. Four."

. . . don't let this shrink play with your mind . . .

He smiled at her, a kind smile. Now she was sure she had seen him on campus. "You're relaxed now. When you hear me say, *'The plane has landed'* you will awaken refreshed and remember everything."

Floating back. Father hypnotizing her before he committed her to the Waybridge Asylum the first time. Again in the Athens Asylum. Kidnapped. Locked in a closet. Alexi says I mustn't scratch my arm . . . Firebomb in Piraeus. Leaping flames. Toothpick's dying words . . . *Save yourself.*

Who am I? What's happening to me?

Then she saw herself looking at herself being filmed as she boarded a plane like Ingrid Bergman giving an Academy Award performance.

She couldn't remember if *Casablanca* had a happy or tragic ending.

CHAPTER FORTY-FIVE

Kent State, Ohio

Alexi joined in the applause as his plane bounced to a landing at Columbus International Airport. He went through Customs and Immigration with no problem.

He stopped at Best Auto Rental. Since he had no idea how large the package would be, he selected a gray van and picked up an Ohio visitor's guide.

Perhaps he should confront Raven first. No. Better not risk missing the weapon delivery. He'd deal with Raven on the way back.

Following the road map, he drove north to Kent, Ohio. It was twilight when he arrived at the place where the Ohio National Guard had fired on Kent State's students who had been protesting the Vietnam War.

Three years before the massacre of students at Athens Polytechnic.

He followed signs past Taylor Hall, and pulled into the Prentice Hall parking lot where the four had been slain. Fatima had said there was a small marker stone in the wooded area around Daffodil Hill.

When the sun went down, he saw a few students stop at four marker lights. They placed flickering candles and flowers at each of the sites. A thin, pinch-faced girl wearing a head scarf, and a heavy backpack topped with a sleeping roll, was observing them.

He asked her, "What are these pedestals with lights?"

"They surround a grave plaque where each of the four fell and died."

"And why are those stones on the markers?"

"To show people stopped by and remembered."

Like the stones ancient Greeks placed at crossroads to pay homage to Hermes, he thought. "Could you direct me to Daffodil Hill?"

She pointed north. "That's where I'm going. I'll wait until you're done here and show you the way."

Several candles in the glass cups had been extinguished by the breeze. He went to each of the four marker sites and relit them with his lighter. Then he picked up a wax-filled glass in which the flame had died and turned it upside down.

The girl stared at him. "Follow me."

He walked with her up the hill. By flickering candlelight, he studied the small monument near granite slabs. Four names: *Allison Krause, Jeffrey Miller, Sandra Scheuer, Bill Schroeder.* He stopped to pick up four stones and placed one on each memorial.

"You're a thoughtful person," she said. "And you have *such pearly white teeth.*"

He studied her. So small. So young. "I've been told I have *teeth like a dragon.*"

It started to rain. She led him to a nearby oak tree and asked, "You have something for me?"

He handed her the briefcase. She opened it and checked the bundles of money. Then she unzipped her backpack and handed him a package wrapped in brown paper. "The shipment is labeled *Dental Powder*, but it sure is heavy.

Glad this is over with." She started to unroll her sleeping bag. "Gotta get some sleep."

"Out here? But it's raining."

She wiped her wet face. "I don't have a choice. It's what I have to do when my roommate's boyfriend visits."

He felt sorry for her. "I hope you don't think I'm making a pass, but I plan to sleep in the back of my van. There's room up front where you may sleep. Nothing else."

She tightened her head scarf. "You sure nothing else?"

"Absolutely. I'm so exhausted I'll collapse the minute I lie down."

"Okay," she said, picking up her backpack and sleeping roll. "I'm a good judge of character. I can tell you're a nice person dedicated to the cause of the people."

"What's your name?"

"Nahid."

"I'm Harold. Nahid is a pretty name."

"It's Persian."

"Is your family here in Ohio?"

"My grandparents."

"What about your parents?"

"My mother is a Holy Fighter for Islam. When I was a baby, she was required to divorce my father and send me to live here with his parents. We keep in touch by e-mail. She instructed me to collect the money and give you the package."

They sloshed through the wet grass back to the van.

"Security won't let us spend the night in the Prentice Hall parking lot," she said as she slid into the passenger seat, "but there's a rest stop about a mile ahead."

He drove slowly on the rain-slicked road. "I have to be careful not to fall asleep at the wheel."

She pointed to the rest area. He pulled in and parked near the lavatories. "Too bad I can't take you to dinner."

She dug into her backpack and pulled out a plastic bag. "If you don't mind dining on half a peanut butter and jelly sandwich, it's my treat."

He laughed. She was sweet. He was glad he had no intention of taking advantage of her. "Nahid, spread your blanket roll on the front seat. My sleeping bag is in back."

He went around to the rear of the van and carefully inserted the package into the storage compartment. Then he unrolled his sleeping bag alongside it and slid open the cab window. "Good night, Nahid."

"G'night, Harold. Pleasant dreams, and thanks."

He zipped himself into his sleeping bag, tossing and turning until he fell asleep.

He dreamed of his mission.

Awaken, sleepers! Prepare the attack. Let the Dragon's Teeth spring from the earth and destroy our enemy.

Dawn light seeping through the van's rear windows woke him. When he climbed out of the van, he saw the rest area was empty. Nahid, already rolling the sleeping bag on her backpack, smiled at him. "Thanks for putting me up, Harold, and for being a perfect gentleman."

"Were you able to sleep okay?"

"On and off."

"You were worried I might take advantage of you?"

"Oh, it wasn't that, Harold. You must have been having a nightmare. You were shouting odd things in your sleep."

His throat tightened. "In my sleep? What did I say? I mean what could you make out?"

"Something, like, about reaping the whirlwind. And sleeper cells in Chicago and Washington and New York. And, like, dragon's teeth. That reminds me. I'm having trouble with my gums. If it's not too expensive, I'll buy some of your dental powder."

He stared at her. How could he have been so stupid? No loose ends. No witnesses.

"I wouldn't think of letting you pay for it," he said. "Come, I have it back here."

She followed him to the rear of the van. He pushed her inside and closed the door behind them.

"What are you doing, Harold? You said you wouldn't!"

He grabbed her around the waist.

"Don't rape me! I'm a virgin."

He gripped her throat with his left hand. She clawed at his fingers. He reached his right hand around her head. Twisted. Her neck cracked and she went limp.

"I won't rape you," he muttered. "I'm sorry."

He jumped out and closed the back doors. A car pulled into the rest stop. He got behind the wheel and drove out the exit.

Where to dump her body? He didn't know the area. He checked the road map. Several lakes and streams. No one in sight. He swerved off the road close to a pond. Dragged her body out of the van and unstrapped her backpack. He took out the money package. No point drowning fifty thousand dollars. He slipped the empty knapsack back on her shoulders and carefully replaced her head scarf.

"Sorry, Nahid, but in times like these you should be careful about accepting help from strangers. At least, in heaven you'll be one of the seventy-two virgins to service your Muslim martyrs."

He rolled her gently down the hillside into the pond. It would look as if she slipped and drowned.

Crucial that he get back to Columbus right away. If Nahid heard his nightmare about cells in the three cities, Raven might also have heard it when they slept together.

He checked the map for directions to I-77. Not far from the town of *Raven*-na. Tracing I-77 South, he'd pass an exit at the city of *Ravens*-wood. Two places with her name. Signs that she had to be silenced before she was sent back to Greece for interrogation.

He stopped by the side of the road and pulled off onto the berm. He opened the package and lifted out an aluminum attaché case, its combination lock still set to all zeroes. He opened it carefully and lifted several layers of cotton padding. Dozens of thin glass tubes, each filled with white powder lay nested in the cotton. Oddly, each tube was wrapped with a studded leather strip. He felt around for instructions. Nothing. He slipped the fifty thousand dollars beneath the padding and rewrapped the case. He would have to solve the mystery of the delivery system.

He felt sorry about killing Nahid. And if he hadn't talked when he slept with Nikki, maybe he wouldn't need to carry out Myron's orders. To find her, he would check the Columbus phone book for Marsha Woods's residence.

He had hoped that after the mission, they could go to some hideaway in South America. With fifty thousand dollars they could start a new life together.

Now, it would depend on whether or not she had ever heard him talk in his sleep.

CHAPTER FORTY-SIX

Columbus, Ohio

Dr. Martin Kyle glanced at the sleeping young woman beside him, her blonde head nestled on his shoulder. Her hand on his thigh.

He reminded himself that they were now in a temporary patient-physician relationship. He'd always been able to block erotic thoughts of female students and patients. Not that he was celibate, but a mental switch always turned him off. He visualized the maxim he'd known, but had actually seen for the first time the other day on the portal of Apollo's temple. *Physician, know thyself.* As a Jungian analyst, he took it to heart.

After a few minutes, she turned and moved off his shoulder. So innocent-looking. So lovely. He covered her with a blanket. Watching over her as she slept, it made him think of his wife and how she'd betrayed him . . .

When he first met Lucy, she said they were soul mates. He considered her his anima and was faithful during their marriage. Then he learned she was having affairs with some of his patients. Male and female. The sweet wife he idolized had sought them out and seduced them.

He couldn't imagine a darker Lilith-*shadow* archetype.

The night he confronted her, she grabbed a kitchen knife, and came at him. She slashed his chest and fled. He was still haunted by the memory of struggling to reach the phone. His call to 911. Siren-wailing ambulance. Stitches to close the gash. It was grounds for divorce, but he was ashamed to testify about her affairs with his patients.

Now, he visualized holding the beautiful Marsha Woods in his arms.

An announcement startled him out of reverie. *"Ladies and gentlemen, return to your seats. Lock tray tables, and restore all seat backs to upright positions. Attendants, prepare the cabin for descent. We land at Port Columbus Airport in about three minutes."*

He looked at her, still fast asleep, lips parted. He visualized kissing her, but his oath surfaced. *Physician, do no harm.*

As the wheels touched down, he whispered in her ear, *"The plane has landed."*

No response.

He repeated the wake-up command twice. Was she so far under he couldn't reach her? It had happened with other patients, but in time he could always restore them. He pressed the ATTENDANT button.

"May I help you?"

"Better call for a wheelchair. Ms. Woods is unable to walk."

"We can take her from here."

"I treated her, I'm responsible for her well-being. I'll see her home safely."

After all other passengers deplaned, the attendant helped him support her to the ramp and into the wheelchair.

The porter asked, "She got carry-on?"

"Must have checked it through. All she had on the plane was this large handbag."

At the baggage claim carousel, he pointed to his own suitcase. The porter pulled it off. "What do hers look like?"

"I don't know."

Finally, the carousel was empty. "Coulda been put on a wrong flight," the porter said. "When it shows up, the airline'll deliver it to her address."

At Customs, the officer asked, "Anything to declare?"

"A garment bag and my medical kit. I'm a physician."

"The lady in the wheelchair. Where's 'er luggage?"

"Lost, I guess. This handbag is all she had with her."

"Open it." He fished around inside the purse, examined every item carefully and dumped them all back. "Okay, open your suitcase, Doc." He rummaged through shirts and underwear, then marked his bag and waved him through.

At Passport Control, he dug into her handbag and pulled out Marsha Woods's passport and driver's license. The agent studied them, glanced at the visas, stamped her reentry date and handed it back.

"I'll wheel her to the taxi line," the porter said, "then I gotta take the chair back inside."

"I'm in short-term parking. If you wait until I pull up and help me get her into the car, there'll be a good tip."

"Awright."

He found his white Lexus and drove behind the taxi line. The porter helped ease her into the rear passenger seat. He smiled at the twenty-dollar bill and slipped away.

"Okay, Marsha Woods. Let's get you home."

Her driver's license listed her address in the Bexley section of Columbus where several of his wealthy clients lived. Well, if you don't have a husband or a roommate, I'll put you to bed, tuck you in, and wash my hands of you.

After the twenty-five-minute drive to Bexley, he pulled up to the address on her driver's license.

The doorman approached. "You can't park here."

"I'm Dr. Kyle, from Waybridge University Medical School. Ms. Woods isn't well. Help me get her up to her apartment."

"Sure, Doc." The doorman opened the rear door and leaned in. Then he backed off. "What's this all about?"

"What do you mean?"

"What are you tryin' to pull?"

"I provided emergency treatment to Ms. Woods during the flight. I just want to see her home safely."

"Get the hell outta here before I call 911."

"I don't understand."

"If your game is burglary, this is the wrong place."

"Are you crazy?"

"No, maybe you are, *Doctor!* I've known Ms. Woods the four years she's lived here."

"So what's the problem?"

"I don't know who this broad is, but she sure as hell ain't Marsha Woods."

CHAPTER FORTY-SEVEN

Athens, Greece

Dugan's cell rang three times before he picked up. The caller said, "Go secure."

He didn't recognize the voice but he keyed the encoder. "Who is this?"

"Am I talking to *Dentist?*"

"Who wants to know?"

"*Tentmaker.*"

"Just a minute." He motioned for Tia to listen with him. "Go ahead. What's happening?"

"Your package was shipped to Athens two days ago via JPATS. She should have arrived by now."

"Two days? What took you so long to let me know?"

"I was prevented from communicating with you earlier."

"Are you all right?"

"The JPATS flight returned me safely to Kurd territory, but before I could leave the area a battle broke out between the Kurdish Democratic Party and the Patriotic Union of Kurdistan. I was finally captured by Talabani's PUK."

"That shouldn't have been a problem," he said. "Both KDP and PUK are allied with us against Saddam."

"But I was still in MEK uniform. It took me a long time to

convince them I wasn't *Mujihadeen-e Kalq* but American army intelligence."

"That puts you at risk."

"Risk is my middle name. One other thing complicates matters. In Ashraf, Fatima converted Raven to Islam."

"Religion doesn't bother me."

"But it bothers Muslims," *Tentmaker* said. "Raven pretended to convert to Islam, or changed her mind. That makes her an apostate subject to a fatwa. Any Muslim, anywhere in the world, is obliged to kill her on sight. Some may be working at the Hellenikon. Find out where security has taken her, and get her to Eliade for interrogation before the anthrax is delivered to the sleepers."

"Hellas Antiterrorist Task Force captured most 17N terrorists," Dugan said. "That should block the operation."

"I wish it were so, *Dentist*. But I've learned that one MEK group wants to bypass 17N and use their own homegrown Islamic sleepers."

"What's to stop them?"

"They haven't been able to decipher Tedescu's third quatrain riddle, so they don't know *how* to spread the anthrax. The issue boils down to whether or not Homeland Security is able to intercept the stuff before Alexi Costa gets his hands on it."

"And whether or not he's solved the third clue."

"Dugan, you'd better notify American Homeland Security to raise the warning level to code red."

"You think those politicians will listen to me? Let's face it, *Tentmaker*. You're in danger. What are your plans?"

"Something I prefer not to reveal at this time."

The phone went dead. He turned to Tia. "Two days ago? I'm afraid we missed her."

"If I know my father, he's arranged for a guard to meet the

Learjet and take her into custody. Let's move ass." She dashed out of the apartment.

He jumped into her car just as she pulled from the curb. Tires screeching, siren wailing, they cut in and out between vans and trucks on the highway. He saw her body lean forward, as if trying to force the car to move faster by pressing her breasts into the steering wheel.

"Are you trying to kill us both?"

She settled back without slowing down. "Before that happens, I feel you have a right to know about my father. He was among the Technicon students demonstrating against Colonel Papadopoulos. Along with Tedescu and Myron Costa, he was one of eight hundred wounded. Lost his right eye and hearing in his right ear."

"That's how come you're his eyes and ears?"

"My father was tempted to turn terrorist the way Jason Tedescu and Myron Costa did, but he refused to join 17N."

"What made him join the police and organize the anti-terrorism task force instead?"

"He believes in justice, not revenge. And he raised me to believe in the same thing."

Traffic at the entrance to Hellenikon Airport was bumper to bumper, all drivers honking horns at the same time. By the time she pulled into the parking section, police were waiting for them. One officer saluted her.

She said, "We're looking for a young American woman with blue eyes and blonde hair. Identity, Raven Slade."

Officers surged into the overcrowded passenger lounge.

"In the meantime," she said, "we should examine the surveillance monitor."

He followed her past Air Traffic Control to the security office. As she pushed the door open without knocking, a middle-aged pilot let go of a dark-haired woman. She slid off his lap.

"Not to worry," Tia told her. "We want to review the passenger lounge surveillance tapes for the past two days."

The pilot retrieved his cap and dashed out the door.

The blushing surveillance operator pulled down her skirt and punched keys on the computer. "This covers the last two days."

Both he and Tia hunched over the counter to study passengers coming and going.

"Slower," Tia said.

The operator pressed a button, and people moved in dreamlike motion.

"Stop!" he said. "Back up."

She rewound. He pointed to a crowd attacking an elderly security guard. A young blonde woman slipped away from the angry crowd and walked casually to the ticketing line. But instead of buying a ticket she turned and followed another blonde woman loaded with luggage.

"That's Raven Slade in the departure lounge," he said, "passing through one of the metal detectors."

They watched Raven boost the woman's purse and drop it into her own tote bag.

"She's going into the ladies' lavatory," he said.

The camera swept the lounge slowly, then panned back to the lavatory entrance. "There she goes," Tia said, "strolling out casually. What a cool customer. Let's get her."

"Hold it." He turned to the surveillance operator. "When was that taped?"

"Earlier this morning."

"Then our bird has already flown the coop."

Tia nodded. "That's possible. Let us find out if the blonde victim registered a theft complaint with security."

On the way out, she turned to the surveillance operator. "Sorry to have spoiled your romantic interlude."

At the glass-enclosed security office, he pointed to a disheveled blonde woman banging her fist on the counter. "There's the victim! Let's check her out."

Tia moved so quickly he could hardly keep up. She barged in and showed her shield. "I am with the Ministry of Order. Who is this woman and what does she want?"

"She claims her purse, with passport, credit cards and airline ticket, was stolen this morning. She demands we report it to the American embassy."

"Your name?" Tia asked the woman.

"Marsha Woods," she screeched. "I'm an American citizen, and I demand you do something about it!"

He saw Tia doing a slow burn. "Sorry, not much I can do about you being an American citizen."

He forced himself to keep a straight face. "Can you prove who you are?"

"My identification was in my purse."

"Anything else with your name on it?" he asked.

"If I'd known I was going to be robbed in a damned Greek airport, I'd have had it tattooed on my ass."

Tia said, "I will forward this matter to official channels."

"Tell your goddamned official channels this is the last time I come to this lousy country."

Tia's lips pressed to a tight line. She pointed to one of the policemen. "He will drive you to your embassy where you may complain."

"What about my flight to Columbus, Ohio?"

"There are other flights," Tia said. "You have my personal assurance I will handle things myself, *immediately*."

He turned and followed Tia out into the passenger lounge. He knew *immediately* meant she would put this unpleasant woman's case on *Greek Maybe Time*. Marsha Woods might get home just in time for Christmas.

Tia snapped her fingers. "Now let us see what flight Raven took. Perhaps we can interdict her. I suggest you call to have U.S. Customs and Immigration hold her when her plane lands in Columbus."

"I'll check." He punched Elizabeth's New York office number on his secure cell phone.

Her voice. "Who is calling?"

"*Cymbal*, this is *Dentist*. Send a bulletin ASAP for Customs or Immigration to intercept a young American woman arriving on a flight from Athens, Greece, to Columbus, Ohio. She's using the stolen identity of Ms. Marsha Woods."

Moments later, Elizabeth called back. "Marsha Woods cleared Customs and Immigration three hours ago in a wheelchair accompanied by a doctor."

"Can you get me his name?"

"I'll check. Yes, Dr. Martin Kyle, of Waybridge, Ohio."

"Thanks, *Cymbal*. I owe you one."

"Just don't call this number again. Remember, as far as the FBI is concerned, you don't exist."

When he told Tia what he'd learned, she said, "Now, *Dentist*, we have to go find her in America and extract her."

"Not very funny. You'll never be allowed to forcefully take an American citizen out of the country."

"Your government turns a blind eye to our methods when they wish to outsource interrogation."

"It'll take a long time to cut red tape."

"Like Alexander, my father will cut the Gordian knot."

"And just how do you expect to extradite her from Columbus to Athens?"

"Remember JPATS that brought you to Greece? The U.S. Marshal's airline will pick her up and return her to Athens before your government knows she is being removed from American soil."

"*Special rendition* is illegal. And so is aggressive interrogation."

"Compare the legal rights and suffering of one young woman with the lives of possibly a hundred thousand dead Americans. Which would you choose?"

"You're putting me between a rock and a hard place."

She smiled. "Exactly what Jason and the Argonauts faced when they had to sail between the Clashing Rocks."

"And you're going to tell me the connection?"

"Legend reveals that the blind prophet Phineus told Jason to send a bird between the Clashing Rocks before attempting to sail through. The bird survived, losing only a few tail feathers, and the Argo sailed safely through the passage. The rocks never clashed again."

He blinked. "But Raven has already flown ahead of us."

"Let us see if we can find some of her tail feathers."

CHAPTER FORTY-EIGHT

Waybridge, Ohio

Not Marsha Woods? Then who was the unconscious young woman in his car? Did his hypnotizing her make her legally his patient? No matter. His Good Samaritan act made him ethically responsible. He had to be careful while he figured out what to do.

If the doorman reported him to the police, he would explain what happened during the flight from Athens. The attendants would back him up. His medical credentials at the college would ensure his credibility. He'd check her into the University Motel and look in on her in the morning.

Ten miles from Waybridge University, as he crossed the bridge, he heard her voice behind him.

"Who are you?"

"Dr. Martin Kyle."

"Oh, yeah. I, like, saw you with the tour group when that woman bucked the ticket line to Columbus. I remembered you from a long time ago when you passed my hospital bed in the Athens Asylum without even looking at me. That pointy beard of yours wasn't so grayish back then."

"I must have been covering someone else's rounds. I would remember if I had been your physician."

"Why am I with you now?"

"You became hysterical on the flight from Athens. I'm a psychiatrist and I treated you. Why were you traveling with a passport and driver's license belonging to Marsha Woods?"

"I don't know what you're talking about."

He told her what happened on the plane.

"I don't remember any of it. Am I crazy?"

"Let me ask you something," he said. "Have you been in a mental hospital before?"

She nodded. "At the Waybridge Asylum."

"How do you feel now?"

"That I'm not real. Like I'm outside my body looking at myself and hearing as if I'm someone else."

Oh, Jesus. Dissociation might indicate any of several mental disorders. But he wasn't her psychiatrist, and he had no intention of getting involved.

"Anything else?"

"Sometimes I feel the world isn't real and I'm living in a dream, or a movie."

He groaned. Derealization made things even more complicated. He'd get her to a safe place and wash his hands of her.

"Where are you taking me?"

"To the Waybridge University Motel."

She sat up straight. "Why?"

"I'm on the faculty of the university medical college. I have my practice there."

As they crossed the bridge over the Ohio River, she gripped his hand. "There it is!"

He jammed the brakes. She was staring at the tower of a High Victorian Gothic building. He'd often driven past the boarded-up old Waybridge Asylum. "Until a few years ago, that was a mental hospital."

"I know," she said.

"How do you know?"

"I was once committed there."

He decided not to probe any deeper. He said nothing until they pulled into the University Motel parking lot. "I'll see that you're checked in."

"Don't leave me here. I can't be alone!"

"You've got to sleep somewhere."

"Stay with me!"

"Here's my card. I live nearby. Call if you need me."

"You're my doctor! Don't desert me!"

"I'm not your doctor. I cared for you in an emergency."

"My emergency isn't over."

"Look, I often put up patients who come from a long distance. They know me here. There won't be a problem. But it'll have to be under your real name. What is it?"

She hesitated. "I think it's Nikki . . . Apteros."

He groaned at the reference to Athena's Nike, but he helped her into the lobby and registered her under that name.

"Come with me into the room," she said.

"Not a good idea."

"Just to check it out. I'm not going to drag you into bed, if that's what you're worried about?"

That's exactly what he *was* worried about, but he shook it off. "All right. A quick look around." He led the way into the room and switched on the light. "See? No ghosts."

As he turned to leave, she threw her arms around him and kissed him. He pushed her away.

"Don't reject me. There's something you have to know. Someone's following me to kill me."

"Who?"

"17N is trying to kill me."

He recalled Captain Eliade questioning him after the lecture in Athens. The repeated references to 17N. "They've been caught."

"Not Alexi and the Second Generation. Oh, my God! I let the cat out of the bag."

"Well, it's out. I'm curious."

"I talked with Mr. Tedescu before he was killed."

"Jason Tedescu? He taught here at the university. How did you know him?"

"I was his student. He was my drama coach. I saw him shot in the Athens Asylum. He was talking about 17N."

"According to the news report on TV during our flight, 17N has been defeated."

Her eyes opened wide.

"What's wrong?"

"People have been trying to get me to remember. Now the Second Generation 17N and MEK are going to attack the United States. They're hunting for me."

"Why would they be after you?"

"I was one of them. You've got to believe me. Now that I'm in the United States, I'm a threat to their terrorist operation."

"All right. Get a night's sleep. We'll report it to the authorities in the morning."

"You don't believe me. If Alexi follows me here, he'll kill me too." She pressed her body against his. "Spend the night with me."

He backed away. "That's not possible. After I leave, lock the door and fasten the security chain. I'll look in on you tomorrow after my lecture."

As he left, he heard the lock click and the door chain slide into place. At least, he'd made a clean getaway. Driving home, he told himself, don't let her get to you. A woman whose disorder includes delusions of being stalked by Greek and Islamic terrorists could be dangerous to a therapist's health. What a legendary seduction scenario! *Beauty-in-clutches-of-terrorists-rescued-by-hero.*

Driving home, he laughed at the thought that she considered him her savior. He knew most people saw him as mild-mannered and withdrawn. After all, that was how he'd always seen himself. A sickly boy protected by a mother and father who isolated him from the outside world, schooled at home. His father taught him chemistry and physics and helped him set up a lab in the basement. His psychologist mother shared her own psych texts and notes.

They divorced when he was fourteen.

His mother had left behind two of Carl Gustav Jung's books: *Psychology and Alchemy* and *The Archetypes and the Collective Unconscious*. He could still visualize her penciled-in marginal comments: *Hogwash!* and *mystical madness*. Inside the back cover, she'd written, *Jung betrayed his teacher Freud and psychoanalysis.*

He remembered writing with a black marker beneath her words, *And you, my Freudian mother-teacher, betrayed me.*

That set him on his course. After medical school, he studied Jungian analytical psychology.

Now, what to make of this young woman who adopted the sobriquet Nikki Apteros? Freud would have diagnosed her as paranoid with psychogenic amnesia. Jung, searching deeper, would probably have identified her as an archetypal femme fatale. Both were right—in a way. But to him her behavior and symptoms suggested borderline and histrionic personality disorders. Maddening patients to deal with.

He unlocked the door and went inside his house. The red-blinking answering machine registered three messages. His secretary reminded him of his morning lecture. A colleague confirmed lunch afterward. He erased both messages. The last was her panic-filled voice. *"Dr. Kyle. I need you. Don't push me away. Help me remember Mr. Tedescu's prophecies. You won't regret it."*

He started to erase her message, but decided to save it in case some day he needed it to cover his ass.

He went to his bar, made a double vodka martini and settled in his recliner to enjoy the icy drink. How to help her without endangering himself—morally and professionally? She was beautiful. He had to admit her body against his had aroused him. Who cut off your wings, Nikki Apteros?

He finished his drink. Then went into the bathroom, stripped and took a cold shower.

CHAPTER FORTY-NINE

Columbus, Ohio

Alexi drove within the speed limit from Kent, Ohio, to the neighborhood in Columbus called Bexley. That's where Nikki was most likely hiding out under the name Marsha Woods.

As he pulled up to the apartment building, he saw a uniformed doorman out front. He lowered his window. "I need your help."

The doorman looked unsure. "Yeah?"

"My cousin Marsha Woods was robbed of her purse in Greece. Someone stole her identification and money. I'm trying to find out if she caught another flight and made it back home."

The doorman punched his fist into his palm. "I knew something was wrong. A guy had an unconscious woman in his car. Said she was Marsha Woods, but I knew better. I sent them on their way."

"Did you to notice the license number?"

"Damned well did." He reached into his jacket pocket and pulled out a notebook. "KD-3579. White Lexus with a parking sticker from Waybridge University Medical College."

"What did he look like?"

"Average height. Salt-and-pepper goatee. Said he was

Dr. Kyle. The beard made him look distinguished, but I got wise to the bastard's scam."

"Alert of you not to let them in. Marsha has valuable possessions from her travels. Art, sculpture and other treasures. That's probably what they were after."

"I was going to call the police."

"No need for that now." He pressed a twenty-dollar bill into the doorman's palm. "I'll deal with it."

The man touched his cap in a salute. "Thank you, sir."

He was closing in on her.

He unfolded the road map and traced the route between Bexley and Waybridge. About half an hour later, he passed a huge mansion with a high tower on a cliff. Route 33 on the map led beyond it to the university.

Where did this Dr. Kyle take her? Home? He might be married. To the university hospital? Possibly. But if he had something else in mind, it would be to a motel.

He drove to the Mayflower Motel and searched the parking lot for a white Lexus. Not there. At the Oakland Motel, he saw a black Lexus. No help. In the parking lot of the University Motel, he saw a white Lexus with a Waybridge University Medical College parking sticker. License number KD-3579. He pulled alongside and turned off the ignition. He sat in the parking lot with his lights out.

A short while later, a man with a goatee came through the revolving door. He got into the white Lexus and drove away. Well, now he knew where Nikki was. But he had to know where to find the doctor in case she'd revealed anything to him. He followed beyond a student housing complex to the driveway of a small house. He waited as the doctor checked his mailbox, and let himself in. A light went on downstairs. Okay, he knew where Dr. Kyle lived.

Now to silence Nikki before they extradited her to Greece. He drove back to the University Motel.

The night clerk put down the *Playboy* magazine and jumped to the check-in counter. "Yes, sir."

"I got a call on my cell phone that my sister was going to leave a message for me. Her physician Dr. Kyle checked her in."

The clerk turned to the boxes behind him. All but the one labeled C-06 had envelopes or papers. "Nothing yet."

"Thanks. She must have phoned from outside."

He walked around the back until found section C. Room 6. Better not use his lock pick. She'd surely have fastened the chain and inside bolt. He went to the window. Easy to jimmy. Quiet now, not to alert her. He wanted to see Nikki in bed and throw off the covers before she knew he was there.

Never had the pleasure of making love to a woman while breaking her neck. Better for her to die quickly in passion than slowly under torture.

He raised the window quietly.

CHAPTER FIFTY

Waybridge, Ohio

Dr. Martin Kyle wound up the question-and-answer portion of his morning lecture about the breakup of Freud and Jung. As his graduate and postdoctoral students were leaving, he was pleased to hear snatches of heated arguments about the differences between psychoanalysis and analytic therapy.

He was gathering his notes when a man and a dark-haired woman approached his desk. "Professor Kyle, I'm Frank Dugan, special agent with ICE."

"ICE?"

"Immigration and Customs Enforcement." He pointed to the woman. "This is Agent Tia Eliade with the Athens police antiterrorist force."

"Eliade? Captain Eliade already questioned me in Athens. What do you want with me now?"

Dugan said, "The Greek ambassador, through their consulate, has issued a formal request to our national central board calling on the United States to assist in locating the fugitive you helped enter this country illegally the day before yesterday."

"I don't know what you're talking about."

The woman agent said, "We need you to answer a few questions."

"I have to teach a seminar in half an hour."

She said, "Were you on Hellas Airlines flight 241 yesterday from Athens, Greece, to Port Columbus?"

"Yes."

Dugan was studying him closely. "We need details about your reentering the U.S."

"Who wants that information?"

"LESCID."

"Translation?"

Dugan said, "*Law Enforcement Support Center Investigations Division.*"

"When I left Athens, I converted all my euros into less than five hundred U.S. dollars, and I declared everything I bought in Greece."

"This is not about you," the woman said. "An attendant reported that you deplaned with an unconscious blonde woman in a wheelchair."

"She was hysterical, hallucinating. I'm a psychiatrist and, at the attendant's request, I calmed her. The attendant witnessed the woman giving me permission."

Dugan said, "And you escorted her, while she was still unconscious, through U.S. Customs and Passport Control."

"That's right. She was in my care at the time."

"The passport and driver's license she entered the country with she stole from Marsha Woods."

"I had no idea."

Agent Eliade said, "Dr. Kyle, this concerns a possible terrorist threat in the U.S."

"I can't believe what I'm hearing."

"Believe it," Dugan said. "Under section 53.1(b) of the Homeland Security Act, it's unlawful for any U.S. citizen to depart from, enter, or attempt to enter, the U.S. without a valid passport."

"I told you, I didn't know her passport was stolen."

The woman said, "We have learned that she used a code name while in Greece."

"Code name? Sounds like cloak-and-dagger stuff."

"In a way it is," Dugan said. "You must have learned either her cover name or real name during the time you were with her. What can you tell us?"

"Well, doctor-patient confidentiality prevents me from identifying someone under my care without a release."

"National security supersedes medical confidentiality."

"I don't know what's involved. I could be sued, lose my license to practice. I'd need a judge's ruling."

"We prepared," Dugan said. "Before we came to pick you up, we arranged for an ex parte rendition hearing."

"I'm no lawyer. What do *ex parte* and *rendition* mean?"

"You'll find out when we're in front of a federal judge at the U.S. courthouse in Columbus. As soon as we read the flight attendant's report, we phoned the state attorney's office and arranged for an emergency extradition hearing. Judge Carmen Rodriguez is expecting us in an hour."

"I can't miss my seminar."

"*NSSS.*"

"Which means . . . ?"

"National Security Supersedes Seminars."

"Agent Dugan, may I use the lavatory before we leave?"

"Go ahead. Wouldn't want to have to make a stop along the way."

Inside the men's room he went into a stall. His hand shook as he punched numbers into his cell phone.

A voice intoned, "American Civil Liberties Union. How may I direct your call?"

"Bruce Coleman," he whispered. "Urgent."

Moments later, "Coleman here."

"Bruce, this is Marty Kyle. I need a lawyer. I'm being

taken by an FBI agent and a Greek counterterrorist agent to Columbus for an ex parte hearing. What's *ex parte?*"

"A judicial proceeding brought by one side without giving notice or challenge to the other party. They wouldn't need you there."

"I'm not the other party."

"Then who—?"

"A woman I hypnotized therapeutically on the plane during my flight home from Greece. They're taking me before Judge Carmen Rodriguez in Columbus."

"She's a federal judge. Sounds serious."

"Is rendition the same as extradition?"

"Not exactly. Rendition means transfer to a country where—unofficially—*aggressive interrogation* is often done in a way we can't do here in the States."

"Bruce, can you help me?"

"My office is near the courthouse. I'll be there."

As he heard the door to the men's room open, he quickly shoved the cell phone into his pocket. He flushed the toilet and stepped out, making a big show of scrubbing his hands and wiping them with paper towels.

"We've got to get moving, Dr. Kyle. Don't want to keep Judge Rodriguez waiting."

He followed both agents to a black Mercedes. As they got into the car, the Greek agent said, "By the way, Dr. Kyle, as a Jungian scholar, you deal with various myths and legends, correct?"

"That's right."

"Have you ever heard of a goddess with no face?"

"What does that have to do with this so-called fugitive?"

"It is a peripheral matter," Agent Eliade said.

He searched his memory. "Well, there's Leinth who predates both Greek and Roman mythology. All we know about

Leinth is that she was an Etruscan goddess who waited with the Etruscan god Aita at the gates of the Underworld. Aita, like Pluto, was an archetype of the figures that—"

"Never mind," Agent Dugan said. "We can leave the lecture for another time."

He stared at the hills as they drove west to Columbus. Who would have thought that he had to explain to a judge why he assisted a mentally ill person, wanted by the Greek antiterrorist task force, to enter the U.S. illegally? A woman—the FBI or CIA or whoever—intended to send back to Greece to be tortured.

And what could the seductive young woman who had identified herself as Nike, goddess with no wings, have to do with a goddess with no face?

CHAPTER FIFTY-ONE

Alexi raised the motel window, grateful that it didn't squeak. He padded silently to the bed. Empty. Wait, it was a twin. She must be in the other one. He tiptoed over and checked it. Nothing. She was probably soaking in the tub.

He opened the bathroom door slowly. Dark. He switched on the light. No one. Back in the room he turned on the overhead lights. The damn place was empty! Neither bed slept in—not even rumpled. No clothing lying around.

Was this the right room? He checked the door. C-06.

So his wingless Nikki had flown away.

He would hunt her down, but right now he was exhausted. As long as this rented room was unoccupied, he'd crash for the night. He stretched out on the bed and dozed.

His cell phone's ring woke him. He could see through the window blinds that it was still dark. Who the hell would be calling him at this ungodly hour?

He grumbled, "Yeah?"

"Listen carefully. I am Mr. Tedescu's executrix. I am in the hospital in Athens, and now is the time for me to give you the third quatrain—*HOW.*"

"How did you get my number?"

"He gave me all 17N numbers before he left for Athens."

"What do you want of me?"

"Write these lines. Memorize, then destroy the paper."

He grabbed the motel notepad. "Okay."

She recited in a singsong voice:

> *"His labor-five sweeps dirt from dung-filled stall,*
> *As three-dog's collars break each death-filled glass.*
> *Aeolus hot-cold breath spews every mass,*
> *And reaps the dragon's seed each spring and fall."*

"What does it mean?"

"I don't know. As his high priestess, I just deliver his prophecies." She hung up.

So these were the clues to Tedescu's third prophecy. He stared at the words, trying to recall Greek myths.

His labor-five might be Heracles' fifth labor of sweeping out the crap-filled cattle stall.

Three-dog's collars must refer to Cerberus, the three-headed dog that drooled poisonous foam. That tied in with the anthrax. But what was the reason for leather strips on *each death-filled glass?* Even knowing that *Aeolus* was the ancient god of the winds led him nowhere.

He went to the bathroom and splashed cold water on his face. He had the weapon and—except for the *Unfaced Goddess*—the targets. But no point in distributing anthrax tubes to the 17N sleeper cells, until he could solve the riddle of HOW to use it.

Okay, Jason Tedescu, riddle me this . . .

CHAPTER FIFTY-TWO

Columbus, Ohio

Kyle was familiar with the U.S. courthouse. He'd been called several times to testify in criminal cases.

The car turned into the parking lot. Agents Dugan and Tia Eliade led him through the main entrance up the elevator, past the attorney general's office. They stopped at courtroom B-6. A plaque bore the name: U.S. DISTRICT JUDGE CARMEN V. RODRIQUEZ.

Inside, the bailiff gestured for him to sit at the empty defense table. Moments later, the bailiff called, "All rise! Her Honor, Carmen V. Rodriguez presiding."

At first, he couldn't see her. When she climbed onto the chair behind the judicial bench, he realized how short she was. Long black hair slicked tight. Dark eyes. She glanced around. "Before we proceed with this preliminary extradition hearing, who is representing the State Department?"

A woman in a gray suit stood. "Deputy Attorney General Nelda Taylor, Your Honor."

He stared at Taylor's hard face. Jutting jaw. Muscles rippling under her clothes suggested the body of a wrestler.

Judge Rodriguez asked, "And who are the man and woman at the table with you?"

"FBI Special Agent Frank Dugan and Agent Tia Eliade with the Greek antiterrorist task force."

"And the Vandyked gentleman at the defendant's table?"

Taylor's taut lips barely moved. "Psychiatrist Dr. Martin Kyle, Your Honor, who may have crucial information to support our request for extradition."

"Dr. Kyle," the judge asked, "do you have an attorney?"

"I understand he's on his way, Your Honor."

"The court cannot be kept waiting, Dr. Kyle. We will proceed without him."

The courtroom door swung open. Coleman, lugging a bulging briefcase, dropped it on the defense table. Unruly copper-colored bangs nearly covered his green eyes. He pulled out a handkerchief and wiped sweat from his pale face.

Judge Rodriguez asked, "And you are . . . ?"

"Bruce Coleman, Your Honor, on behalf of Dr. Martin Kyle and Ms. Jane Doe."

"With whom are you affiliated?"

"The American Civil Liberties Union, Your Honor."

She smiled. "Ah, yes. So you've had experience with extradition proceedings."

"Only concerning issues of asylum requested by fugitives who escaped from countries that use torture, Your Honor."

"I'm advised that this is not quite the same, Mr. Coleman, since it includes charges against your client."

"Dr. Kyle hasn't been informed why his presence is required at this proceeding, Your Honor."

"According to information provided by the attorney general, he allegedly aided said Jane Doe to enter this country illegally. The State Department believes she is affiliated with a Greek terrorist group known as 17N. Also, she spent time in Iraq with the radical Iranian *Mujihadeen-e Kalq*, known as MEK. There she converted to Islam."

Kyle remembered how he'd scoffed when she spoke in the motel room about a terrorist tracking her to kill her.

Coleman said, "Since this appears to be an issue of rendition, it comes under the purview of asylum. The A.C.L.U. has represented many asylum seekers."

The little judge scowled. "How is that pertinent now?"

"According to Amnesty International, this proceeding should be dealt with according to the Geneva conventions and CAT—the international *Convention Against Torture*."

Judge Rodriguez said to the court stenographer, "Enter Bruce Coleman, esquire as attorney of record for Dr. Martin Kyle and Ms. Jane Doe."

She turned back to him. "The court wishes to know if the A.C.L.U. is contesting Dr. Kyle's culpability?"

"Well, I haven't had enough time. The defense requests a delay."

"Ms. Taylor, does the attorney general's office agree?"

"No, Your Honor. This proceeding is not concerned solely with her illegal entry. I have been advised by the NSID that this woman may have entered the United States to commit—or assist in the commission of, or has knowledge of—imminent terrorist acts against our country."

Judge Rodriguez half stood and looked at Coleman sternly. "On what basis does Dr. Kyle refuse to cooperate with the National Security Investigation Division?"

"Your Honor, my client wishes to cooperate. However, he is constrained by the doctor-patient confidentiality shield."

Rodriguez turned to Taylor. "Why should this court allow you to pierce the doctor-patient shield?"

"Because, in addition to aiding terrorists, this woman is a fugitive wanted in Greece for bank robbery. Both our countries have extradition treaties for such crimes."

"Were any crimes committed on American soil?"

"Not yet, Your Honor. It was committed against the

Greek-American Athens Bank. Not only was she the get-away driver, she is also accused of participating in firebombing the Piraeus international passenger terminal, with the intention of killing tourists and American sailors."

Rodriguez looked at Coleman. "Your response?"

"Your Honor, the physician-patient confidentiality shield may be pierced to *prevent future crimes*, not to help law enforcement retrieve information about *past* crimes."

Agent Tia glared at him. "You don't understand! Our sources in Athens have information from a captured 17N member that this woman and Alexi Costa, the leader of the Second Generation 17N, are involved in a conspiracy with MEK to commit an assault that will kill more Americans than the Twin Towers bombings."

He slunk back and prayed for the judge to force him to break confidentiality.

Judge Rodriguez studied him. "Dr. Kyle, it is the opinion of this court that, under the Homeland Security Act of 2002, Section 215(b), it is unlawful for any U.S. citizen to depart from or enter this country without a valid passport. In helping this fugitive from Greek authorities, you have assisted her in breaking the law."

"I didn't know it was a stolen passport, Your Honor. I helped her as a Good Samaritan."

Judge Rodriguez pursed her tiny lips. "Dr. Kyle, if you provide the information these agents require, I'll hold off charging you with aiding-and-abetting."

"Yes, Your Honor. Of course."

"Go ahead, Agent Dugan."

Dugan looked at him. "We've learned her nom de guerre is *Nikki*. What's her full name?"

"I'm not sure. She said her last name is *Apteros*. Claims she doesn't know her real name. I assume she has dissociated. The passport identified her as Marsha Woods."

"We believe she's an American named Raven Slade. Her father, clinical director of the Athens Asylum, an under-cover CIA informant, took his own life when confronted by 17N. She was taken hostage."

The judge turned to Tia Eliade. "Are you suggesting an American taken hostage by Greek terrorists would commit a crime against her own country?"

"We know Ms. Slade is highly suggestible, and she may have been subjected to mind control by both 17N and MEK when she was their prisoner. It has been called the Stockholm syndrome which—"

"I know what the Stockholm syndrome is, Agent Eliade. Are you suggesting this young woman may have joined both terror groups?"

"Your Honor, we believe she has memorized a secret code in the form of Nostradamus-like prophecies that—when decrypted—reveals command instructions for *Operation Dragon's Teeth*. Attacks on targets in three U.S. cities."

Judge Rodriguez ran her fingers through her shiny black hair. "The standards regarding competency for extradition deal with only three issues. First: proof of the individual's identity. Second: positive evidence that the individual was physically present at the scene of the crime. Third: here in the state of Ohio—that the person so identified is capable of assisting an attorney in affirming or denying those issues."

Taylor said, "The State Department petitions this court to order an emergency hearing to rule on those matters so that she may be extradited to Greece for interrogation."

Rodriguez twirled the gavel. "Dr. Kyle, do you know where she is now?"

"I registered her at the University Motel last night under the name Nikki Apteros."

Rodriguez turned to the bailiff. "Arrange for the Way-bridge police to take her into custody for an emergency hearing at once. We stand adjourned for a two-hour lunch break." She slammed the gavel.

Dugan whispered to someone behind him. The man took out a cell phone and went to the rear of the courtroom. Everyone stood as the judge climbed down from her seat and headed toward her chambers. The man with the cell phone whispered to Dugan who whispered to Taylor.

"Your Honor," Taylor said, "I'm informed that when officers entered the fugitive's room, they found it slept in, but empty. With the manager's assistance, they checked other locations. Apparently, she switched to an unoccupied room during the night. When sheriff's deputies attempted to enter, she held a broken mirror to her throat and threatened to kill herself unless she could speak to Dr. Kyle."

Rodriguez looked at him. "Do you think she means it?"

"If, as I suspect, she suffers from borderline personality disorder, she is probably suicidal."

"Your Honor," Agent Eliade said, "we need her alive. Only she can lead us to 17N and MEK sleeper cells."

Rodriquez banged her gavel. "Agent Dugan, instruct the deputies to assure Jane Doe that Dr. Kyle is on his way."

Kyle stood. "Your Honor, I need clarification. I have been referred to as *her doctor.* Is she my patient?"

Rodriguez thought a moment. "She is *not* your patient. You are now hired by this court to evaluate her competency for extradition."

"She may refuse to communicate with me. It's my impression that she really is mentally ill."

"In light of this national danger, I'm going to hold you to a full-expert statement. Either the woman is competent for rendition or she is not. Is that clear, Dr. Kyle?"

"Your Honor, she's under the illusion that I'm her physician. As Agent Eliade pointed out, if she kills herself, she'll be of no use to them. I believe she'll react violently if she thinks I'm abandoning her, and she might be a danger to herself and others."

"Can you deal with that, Dr. Kyle?"

He stared at the judge who was impatiently twirling the gavel. How to deal with it . . . ? "I propose the officers allow me to enter the motel room alone. She'll continue to view me as trying to help her. I'll take her to the Waybridge University Hospital where I'll attempt to evaluate her competency."

"If you find her incompetent, how long might you need to treat her and restore competency?"

"I can't predict. Analytical therapy takes time."

"Dr. Kyle, because of Homeland Security concerns, I'm amending this court's order. If you find her incompetent for extradition, you are instructed also to be her treating therapist for the purpose of restoring her to competency."

Taylor stood. "Your Honor, we *don't have time*. Homeland Security has intel that this is a ticking bomb."

"Dr. Kyle," Rodriguez asked, "is there any way to speed up the process? Hypnosis? Electric shock? Any way to counteract such brainwashing?"

He scratched his Vandyke. Drummed his fingernails on the defense table. Brainwashing. Washing. The image of Noah's ark. Forty days and forty nights. The flood . . .

"Your Honor, there is a controversial therapeutic technique called *image flooding* sometimes used with patients who suffer from post-traumatic stress and react with flashbacks, nightmares and memory problems."

"Like war veterans?"

"And rape victims. Desensitization is an effective form of counterconditioning therapy for treating patients also suffering from phobias. The patient is repeatedly exposed to images of the trauma until they cease to cause symptoms of shock."

"How long would such treatment take?"

"Each situation is unique. Weeks, maybe months."

Taylor shook her head. "Your Honor, MEK's anthrax may already be in the United States."

"Dr. Kyle," Rodriguez said, "can you do any better?"

Shifting from one foot to another. Thinking fast. "There is a form of desensitization known as *rapid implosion therapy*. The patient is flooded with real or imagined scenarios that cause intense anxiety. If she doesn't resist the fantasies caused by those images, treatment can progress rapidly. Used with rape victims, rapid implosion has produced improvement almost immediately."

Rodriguez looked at Taylor. "What do you say?"

Taylor whispered to Dugan and Tia, then turned to the judge. "We ask the court to set a time limit."

"The court agrees. Dr. Kyle, we will adjourn for two weeks. That should give you the opportunity to evaluate and treat Jane Doe, AKA Raven Slade, AKA Nikki Apteros with this rapid implosion therapy. You are to report progress, or the lack thereof, to the court at that time."

"Your Honor, there is one significant danger. Not everyone can tolerate such intense anxiety-producing treatment. She would have to possess strong self-esteem and self-confidence. But, as was pointed out, she was a patient in the Athens Asylum and subsequently converted to Islam. Since my preliminary diagnosis is borderline-histrionic personality disorder, implosion therapy might cause a schizophrenic relapse."

"Considering what's at stake, Dr. Kyle, we'll have to take that risk."

Rodriguez left the courtroom.

Taylor, Dugan and Tia went out the main door. Coleman stayed behind to stuff papers into his briefcase. "Kyle, that was great."

"I'm not sure. I haven't the slightest idea what traumas Raven Slade has suffered. What her captors did to her. What phobias may be masking her borderline disorder. I've used regular implosion therapy, but never rapid implosion therapy."

"Well, you made a great impression on the judge. You sure landed on your feet."

"I wouldn't say that. Rodriguez is ordering me to lead a mentally unstable, suicidal woman, possibly brainwashed into an Islamic suicide-martyr complex, across a therapeutic high wire—"

"*That* bad, huh?"

"—without a safety net."

CHAPTER FIFTY-THREE

Raven shrieked at the officers, "Get away, or I'll cut my throat!"

"Put down the broken mirror. Dr. Kyle is on his way."

"You're lying. You were sent to kill me." She dug the point into the left side of her neck. Blood dripped down her blouse.

"Holy shit! Stop! We'll wait outside. Dr. Kyle can come in alone. Is that all right?"

"Okay, but I'm locking the door."

"That's fine with us, lady."

They left the motel room. She slammed the door behind them and fastened the chain. She wedged a chair under the knob and dragged the dresser against it.

Lights flashed through the motel window as a police car pulled to the curb outside her room. To hell with them. She'd never let herself be taken hostage again.

A white Lexus pulled up alongside the cruiser. She saw Dr. Kyle talk to the officers outside her door. She knew he could see her looking at him through the window. He waved and she waved back. Then he was out of sight and she heard a knock. She pressed a pillow against her bleeding neck.

"It's Dr. Kyle, Raven. Please let me in."

"First, tell me why the police are here."

"To help me protect you from the people you said want to kill you."

"Just a minute." She dragged the dresser away and moved the chair from under the doorknob. "Don't let the cops come in with you. Tell them to move to where I can see them."

She heard talk outside; then through the window she saw the officers move away.

"You can open the door now, Raven. I'm alone."

She unhooked the chain, and he stepped into the room.

"You're bleeding. Let me treat you." He opened his bag, pulled out gauze, adhesive tape and antiseptic. As he bandaged her he said, "I'm taking you to University Hospital."

She dropped the shard of mirror on the dresser and threw her arms around him. "I knew you'd save me."

A knock at the door. *"You okay, Dr. Kyle?"*

"We'll be out in a few seconds."

She clung to him. He pushed her away. Grumbling, she raised her hands. "I surrender, Doc."

He opened the door. She walked out, head high. Then she froze. "Smoke!"

"Must be a cookout."

"Where there's smoke there's fire!"

"Probably just lighter fluid to ignite the charcoal."

"Not fire! Can't stand fire!"

"It's coming from the patio on the left, near the pool. We'll go in the other direction."

She felt his strong arm around her, leading her away from the flames. "I knew I could depend on you."

As they rounded the corner, one of the officers opened the rear door of his cruiser.

"No! Only with Dr. Kyle."

She saw them exchange glances. Kyle nodded and opened the passenger door to his Lexus. He helped her in. When he got behind the wheel, she snuggled against him.

He pushed her aside gently. "Fasten your seat belt."

"Do it for me. Don't want to get my blood all over your expensive car."

He reached across her and fastened her seat belt. She rested her head on his shoulder.

It took about ten minutes to drive from the motel to University Hospital. He parked and came around and opened the passenger door for her. As she stepped out, she tripped into his arms. "See? You're my protector."

In the admissions office, a grumpy-faced nurse smiled at them. Name tag J. NATHENSON.

"Raven Slade accidentally cut her neck," he said. "Register her. She'll be staying with us."

"Hello, Raven."

"*. . . i'm not raven . . .*"

"Well, my name is Janette Nathenson."

"*. . . that's your problem. i'll call you whatever i please . . .*"

Nathenson pressed the button on the intercom. "*New patient arrival. Have an attendant report to Admissions to take her to the infirmary.*"

Kyle said, "Janette, please set up a consultation with Ms. Slade at three tomorrow afternoon."

"You have a staff evaluation meeting at three."

"Reschedule the meeting for the following day."

The nurse's eyebrows went up.

He said, "It's important that I get started with her right away."

So, she was more to him than just a patient if she came before a lousy staff meeting. She looked up as a young man in a white jacket came down the corridor.

Kyle said, "Harry, take Raven Slade to the infirmary to change her bandage. Then to ward six. Introduce her to the nursing staff and show her to her room."

"*. . . don't leave me, marty . . .*"

"I'll see you tomorrow. And please call me Dr. Kyle."

She pouted.

"Don't worry. You're in good hands."

As they entered the elevator, she heard Kyle whisper, "Janette, inform the nursing staff to put her on around-the-clock suicide watch."

She turned and faced them. ". . . *don't worry, marty. i promise not to kill myself . . .*"

As the elevator door closed, she uncrossed her fingers.

CHAPTER FIFTY-FOUR

Ashraf, Iraq

Colonel Rashid Omar—code name *Tentmaker*—knew this would be his most dangerous mission since he first penetrated MEK. He had already explained the Pentagon's position to Hassan. She expressed her interest, but he had no idea how the other officers would react. She motioned for him to sit in the rear of the conference room.

When Fatima entered and saw him, she froze. "General, why is that traitor here?"

"Sit, Fatima. It will soon be made clear."

The three other officers entering the conference room also reacted with surprise. He knew they were all thinking the same thing. What was the deserter who helped Raven Slade escape doing back in Ashraf?

All faces turned to the general for an explanation.

Her beefy-faced frozen expression revealed nothing of her thoughts or feelings. "You all know this man as MEK Private Rashid *Ammar*. Actually, he is *Colonel Rashid Omar of U.S. Army Intelligence*, who has been investigating us for many years."

Gasps of surprise filled the room.

"*Omar* is a Sunni name."

"He's a spy!"

"A mole!"

The general held her hand up for silence. "Allow Colonel Omar to explain his reason for being here." She nodded at him. "Colonel . . ."

He rose and faced their hard stares. "I won't start with an apology for being a spy. As fellow Muslims, you all know from our Old Testament that Caleb was sent by God to spy on the land of Canaan. Spies have served the military ever since wars began. My orders were to penetrate MEK and report on your activities."

Lieutenant-Colonel Shahadi smirked at him. "Are you saying you, as a Muslim, were sent to spy on us by the Hebrew God as ordered in the Pentateuch?"

"No, as ordered by the Pentagon."

"I do not think we should develop any relationship with the American military."

"It is no secret," he said, "that the U.S. intends a preemptive strike against Iraq. President Bush has authorized the Pentagon to explore various options that may come into play after the start of hostilities. The chiefs of staff foresee an inevitable conflict with Iran and its Hezbollah puppets in Lebanon."

Major Alieah called out, "How does that affect us?"

"Although you all know that the State Department has labelled *Mujihadeen-e Kalq* a terrorist organization, the Pentagon is now taking the opposite position. Their strategists acknowledge that you participated in the Iranian revolution and led the attack on the American embassy. You fought for a secular Marxist Iran. But they also know that you have been at war with the ayatollah who betrayed your cause by creating a fascistic theocratic Iran."

Cold silence.

"Now they, as well as many senators," he continued, "are currently pressuring State to remove *Mujihadeen-e Kalq* from the terrorist list if—and this is the big *if*—MEK agrees to support America in a potential war against Iran."

Major Alieah asked, "Support in what way?"

"At present, some in Congress have taken sides for or against the State and the Pentagon agendas. But we have intel from Israel's Mossad that Iran and Syria are already supplying Hezbollah with money and arms to control Lebanon."

"Old news, Colonel," Alieah said. "Your point?"

"The chiefs of staff foresee a confrontation between Israel and Iran's puppet Hezbollah. Your pledge to join forces against the ayatollah's Revolutionary Guard will enable the Pentagon to make State reconsider its position."

Murmurs of disapproval from all but Samira. "What part does the Pentagon expect us to play?"

"In the event of a possible Israeli aerial bombing to take out Iran's nuclear facilities, your militia would be expected to spearhead a second front against Teheran."

The general asked, "Colonel Omar, what gesture of goodwill does America require on our part?"

"I know that Saddam hid many of his weapons of mass destruction in Ashraf's tunnels on the border between Iraq and Iran. I know, also, of your alliance with 17N for *Operation Dragon's Teeth*. As evidence of good faith, we ask you to repudiate that alliance. In return, Ashraf will be spared an air attack."

Major Alieah stood and addressed the others. "This spy is asking us to switch sides. Does he think MEK turns in political winds like a weathercock?"

Lieutenant-Colonel Shahadi shook her head. "We are now trapped between Iraq and Iran. I feel we should consider Colonel Omar's offer seriously and distance ourselves from 17N's terror operation. Remember how the Trojans were destroyed when they ignored the warning about the wooden horse.

Seer Laoccon had told them, 'Whatever it is, I fear Greeks even when they bring gifts.'"

Her comments pleased him, but the other officers immediately began arguing. The general held up her hand for silence. "Major Fatima, state your position."

He saw Fatima look slowly at the other officers around the table and then directly at him. "It may be too late."

"What do you mean?" he asked.

"The anthrax is already en route to 17N in America."

The general's frozen face thawed into a frown. "You should have informed me before you consummated the deal."

"You put me in charge, General. I agree with the positions of Lieutenant-Colonel Shahadi and Major Alieah. We should make no deal with the American military."

"Fatima, I order you to take whatever action is necessary to prevent the anthrax from falling into Alexi Costa's hands."

"What if it is too late?"

"We will deal with that eventuality when it arises."

Fatima insisted, "We know that Tedescu's message revealed the cities to be attacked. I feel certain Tedescu tried to kill Raven Slade because she had memorized his prophecies. He failed and was killed. Only she knows the rest of his message."

"You think you can extract that information from her?"

"Raven does not know she has it, General. I tried to break through, but the prophecies are locked away behind her phobias. It would take time."

General Hassan looked at Omar. "You helped Raven escape, Colonel. Do you know to where she has fled?"

He shook his head. "Perhaps Major Fatima does."

Fatima said, "I suspect Raven's nest is in the Waybridge Asylum where—according to her medical records—her father committed her as a young girl."

General Hassan said, "Fatima, you will accompany Colonel Omar to America. First, intercept the anthrax before it is delivered to Alexi Costa. Then, find Raven and break through her mental block."

"I could do this alone," she said. "I would prefer to have no connection with this spy."

"You have my orders, Fatima. You and Colonel Omar will proceed as a team."

It was more than he'd hoped for.

Fatima asked, "What is our plan if I am able to intercept the anthrax?"

General Hassan mused. "That depends."

He knew what that meant. If the Pentagon convinced the State Department to remove MEK from the terrorist list, they would become allies. If State continued to refuse, MEK's weathercock would turn from the West back to the Middle East.

If he and Fatima could not intercept the anthrax, the only solution was for Dugan to extradite Raven back to Athens for interrogation.

As they left the meeting room, he watched Fatima. Her slender and undulating body moving ahead of him. They would be alone together in the States.

Would the rule of women's chastity, he wondered, be binding after they were outside the borders of Ashraf?

CHAPTER FIFTY-FIVE

Lancaster, Ohio

Kyle was halfway through his second martini that evening when Bruce Coleman phoned.

"How did it go with you-know-who?"

"I've committed her, but it's more bizarre than I expected. She's had a paranoid schizophrenic relapse."

"What paranoid symptoms?"

"She believes Greek and Islamic terrorists are hunting for her to kill her."

He heard Coleman's nervous breathing. "You know the saying: it's not paranoia if it's true."

"Are you telling me that—?"

"Not over the phone. Let's meet away from our offices. Breakfast tomorrow at Saleski's Diner in Lancaster."

Next morning, walking from his house to the car, he found himself studying strangers on the street. As he drove, he kept glancing into his rearview mirror to check if someone was tailing him. What the hell was Bruce hinting at?

In Lancaster, he pulled into a curbside parking space in front of the diner. Although there were open spaces close to the restaurant, Coleman parked across the street.

He waited, and they went inside together. "So what's this about someone really out to kill her?"

"I checked with a partner in my law firm who represents Greek shipping interests. One tanker owner has hired extra bodyguards and purchased an armor-plated Mercedes. His friend, owner of several oil tankers was assassinated by Second Generation 17N. That offshoot of the original group is even more ultranationalistic, Marxist-Leninist and anti-American than the first generation."

"Terror groups have been around for years."

"Not a lethal combination like 17N and MEK."

"So she's a highly suggestible young woman subjected to double-cult brainwashing? How can I counteract that kind of psychological damage?"

"You agreed to use rapid implosion therapy, so you're legally treating her to restore her to competency. It's a tug-of-war between Homeland Security's battle against terrorism and our concern for human rights."

"You think she is really in danger of being killed?"

"The fundamentalist mullahs have issued a fatwa against Raven as an apostate. The actual purpose is to prevent her being extradited to Greece and interrogated to expose the leaders of both groups."

"Maybe Rodriguez will decide *against* legal extradition."

"Then our own counterterrorist agency might resort to *extraordinary rendition* and spirit her back to Greece."

"Isn't that illegal? She's an American citizen. Can our government ship her to Greece against her will?"

"According to an A.C.L.U. source—who doesn't want to be identified—the CIA's *extraordinary rendition* program is now one of our major counterterrorism tools. Several attacks have been prevented ever since we began transferring suspects abroad for questioning."

"That implies torture. Do our intelligence agencies have any way to monitor the interrogations?"

"The European CPT—sorry, *Committee for the Prevention of Torture*—made three visits to Greece in recent years. They published their most recent findings in 2001. So it all depends where Raven is sent. Probably a detention center under the Ministry of Public Order in Athens or Thessaloniki. Either the Korydallos Prison Complex Psychiatric Unit under the Ministry of Justice, or the Athens mental hospital run by the Ministry of Health."

"What's the point of torture if a captive dies as a result?"

Coleman shrugged. "A noted Harvard law professor has taken the position that interrogators can stop short of that. They can do something like insert sterile needles beneath the nails to cause excruciating pain without endangering life."

"Torture won't work on her. One hallmark of BPD is self-cutting, even to the point of suicide. Interrogators causing her physical pain will be doing for her what she would usually do to herself. But she'll die rather than tolerate *emotional* turmoil."

Coleman said, "A catch-22! Where does that leave us?"

"If I can make an end run around her phobias with rapid implosion therapy, I might—just might—be able to break through her dissociative states."

"What about her paranoid schizophrenia?"

"In her histrionic phases, she is usually an actress on the stage or being filmed on a set. What she says or does is performance."

"Can you bring her out of it for court?"

"In some of my other cases, I've learned that when patients are hallucinating or delusional, any attempt to reason them out of it often makes them hostile—sometimes violent."

"So how do you prepare her for court?"

"Instead of confronting such patients, I temporarily enter the worlds into which they've retreated. I'll be Raven's prompter, her cameraman, her director. Then, when the time is propitious, if she believes she's acting in a movie, I'll call, 'Cut! Great take! Print!' If she's reliving her drama school theatrical performance days, I'll join the audience's applause, let her take her bows, tell her the curtain is down and lead her offstage."

"Will that work?"

"There are no guarantees, either in psychiatry or show business."

"Remember, since we're facing a ticking-bomb situation, our own agencies' black ops may choose to take matters into their own hands."

"Understood. But speaking of clocks, it's almost show-time."

"What do you mean?"

"I have a session with her in an hour and a half. If I'm late getting back and the performance is delayed, she'll think she's been replaced by her understudy."

"So what?"

"Like most prima donnas, all hell will break loose in her mind."

CHAPTER FIFTY-SIX

Waybridge, Ohio

Crazy bumper-to-bumper traffic back to Waybridge. Kyle slowed through a couple of STOP signs praying no state trooper would pull him over. Raven wouldn't accept a traffic ticket as an excuse for his being late.

To begin rapid implosion therapy, he needed a clearer insight into her phobias. What images could he use to flood her mind until the flashbacks and false memories no longer terrified her?

He pulled into the hospital parking lot with thirty seconds to spare and made it into his office as the attendant knocked and led Raven in. Thank Jung for synchronicity.

"I'll take her from here," he told the attendant.

When they were alone, she whispered, "You can take me anywhere."

He gestured to the chair facing his desk. "Sit please."

"Don't you want me to lie on the couch?"

He hesitated. She liked puns. Hers were mostly erotic-wordplay foreplay, but it was the histrionic playfulness that put her at ease. Not the sexuality.

He took a chance. "You can *recline* on the couch, if you wish. But I'd rather you didn't *lie*."

She took the chair. "Then I'll sit here where I can make sure you don't use sleight of mind."

"Clever."

She giggled. "Well, you're a card."

"Tell me about cards."

"My mother used to tell fortunes with tarot cards. Those pictures of good and evil reveal the unknown."

"Did you enjoy looking at those symbolic pictures?"

"Yes. I think I remember . . ."

"What?"

She shook her head. "It's vague . . . hazy . . . probably something from a dream."

"Dreams are important. If you free-associate to those images, I can try to help you make the connections."

"What do you mean?"

He decided to explain. "In Freudian psychoanalysis, the patient does the free-associating. In Jungian analytical analysis, the therapist often participates, especially to clarify connections to universal images."

"It's a relief to know I don't have to do it by myself. I worried about that all night."

"Would you like to look at some slides?"

"Porn?"

"I collect pictures of architecture, sculpture and paintings. It's a hobby."

"Okay, whatever turns you on."

He turned off the lights and pulled down the shades.

"Aha! So, you're a Jungian sex therapist."

He slid open a wall panel and switched on the slide projector. "No, I'm a Jungian analyst. You and I will explore your dreams and probe your unconscious, but we'll go deeper, and dig beneath your *personal unconscious* to find the roots in the *universal unconscious*."

"Roots, like in the Garden of Eden?"

"That's one image from the Old Testament, but we're considering sacred gardens as archetypes."

"What are archetypes?"

"Images or actions deeply rooted in the human mind and repeated in different cultures over the centuries."

"So, like, what sacred gardens do you have?"

"The *Hanging Gardens* of Babylon, Japanese *karesansui* dry gardens, Buddhist *vihara* pleasure gardens, India's *Perfect Gardens* mentioned in the *sutras*."

"*Kama Sutra*? I looked through that Hindu sex book in my father's personal library. Are we going to try different positions?"

He had to divert her from the sexual allusions. "Let's concentrate on the archetypes that concern you."

"Got any examples of tragic lovers? Like me and Alexi?"

"The star-crossed lovers archetype goes back beyond Romeo and Juliet, beyond Tristan and Isolde, beyond Pyramus and Thisbe. Back to the Tangled Skein forest at Mount Fugi, where ancient Japanese star-crossed lovers committed *shinju*."

"That's it. Alexi and I are star-crossed lovers. Is *shinju* committing double suicide?"

"Yes, Raven, but you have to understand that while you were held hostage, Alexi used mind control to turn you against your own country. The *Mujihadeen-e Kalq* did the same by converting you to Islam. For you, that could mean becoming a martyr."

"I agree about MEK, but not about Alexi. He opened my eyes to reality."

"Let's distinguish between reality and propaganda."

"You're manipulating me."

"Look, I didn't volunteer for this. The court ordered it because you said you wouldn't cooperate with anyone else."

"You won't turn against me?"

"No, but I have to resort to an extreme treatment known as rapid implosion therapy. I want you to keep looking at the screen while I change from one to picture to another."

"All right."

He switched slides quickly. First ancient Greek locations: *Apollo's Temple at Delphi. The Amphitheater of Dionysus. The Forum.*

No reaction. Biblical images: *Creation of Adam* from Michelangelo's Sistene Chapel. *Joseph's Coat* from the Safad Bible. Nothing. But when he switched to *Moses and the Burning Bush,* she screamed. "No fire!"

Then he remembered her reaction to the cookout at the motel. He switched slides to *The Fiery Horsemen* from *Revelations.* She turned away.

"Look at it."

"I can't!"

"Visualize yourself staring into the flames."

"Stop it."

"Imagine fire singeing your skirt but not burning you."

"Oh, God . . ."

He clicked to a slide of the Turner's *Shadrach. Meshach and Abednego in the Burning Fiery Furnace.* "Think of yourself, like them, surrounded by fire."

"I'm going to vomit."

"No you won't. These are just pictures. If you look at them again and again they'll stop bothering you."

"Why are you torturing me?"

"To save you from worse than torture."

"No more! Stop now!"

He turned off the projector and pulled up the shade. "What was going through your mind?"

"I don't remember."

"Let's free-associate to images of fire."

"No."

"Famous images from the Bible. 'Then the Lord rained upon Sodom and Gomorrah brimstone and fire . . .'"

"I remember our minister's sermon," she said. "Lot's wife looked back at the burning city. God turned her into a pillar of salt."

"Is that what frightens you about fire?"

"I don't want to look back like her. Stop rubbing salt into my mind."

"Let's continue."

"No more pictures of burning bushes or fiery horsemen or any other burning shit!"

"We'll take it from there. I want *you* to *visualize* images of fire. Try to see flames in your own mind."

"How the hell do you expect me to do that?"

He thought about it. "Have you ever helped yourself fall asleep by counting sheep?"

"Sure."

"Close your eyes as if you're ready to fall asleep. Then imagine each sheep carrying a burning torch in its mouth. Count them."

She pyramided her fingers. Her lips moved and she whispered, "Okay. One. Two." Jaws clenched. "Oh, God! Th-three . . . F-four . . ." Shoulders relaxed. "Five. Six. Seven." At twenty-five, she opened her eyes. "I can't believe it."

"What?"

"I was sure I'd go out of my skull. Then it got easier. Seeing fire still makes my hair stand on end, but I think I can bear it."

"That's the way it works. Now, for a test. Real fire."

She gripped the arms of her chair. "Like hell!"

He opened his desk drawer, took out a candle and holder

and placed them on the desk. She squirmed. He picked up a Zippo lighter. "I want you to know in advance that I'm going to light the candle. Stare at it. Then lean forward and blow out the flame."

"I can't—"

"We don't have time to unravel the past cause or causes of your pyrophobia. But we can blunt its effect by repetition. Ready?"

She hesitated. He flicked the wheel on the lighter. Sparks. She winced. Flicked a second time. It flamed. She drew back. He touched the flame to the candle wick. It sputtered, leaped up. She closed her eyes.

"Look at it. Stare at the flame. Exhale. Breathe slowly, again."

If this didn't work, rapid implosion therapy was out the window. Maybe she'd be better off not knowing who she was or what was real. He could tell Judge Rodriguez he couldn't make her competent for extradition.

Her body relaxed. She blew out the candle.

"Bravo, Raven! That was great."

She smiled. "No, you are."

He looked at the clock on the wall behind her. "Our time is up."

"What do you mean?"

"Our session is over. We'll meet day after tomorrow."

"You can't arouse me and then send me away."

He went to the door. "We have to set time limits."

". . . the hell with limits. you can't fuck with my mind and then dump me! i need you . . . !"

Her voice had suddenly become mezzo-soprano. Her body language and facial expression changed as well.

"Raven, be reasonable."

Her eyes glazed. She looked around suspiciously.

". . . i'm not raven. i'm nikki and this is my fucking universal *unconscious talking. you said, be reasonable, but you're dumping her . . ."*

"I'm not leaving you, Raven. It's a temporary pause in this phase of your therapy."

". . . i told you, i'm not raven! she's sitting in that chair! pay attention to what i say, you bastard . . . !"

"Control yourself."

". . . i am! first you set her mind on fire, and now you want to leave her . . . !"

"You have to understand."

". . . understand this . . . !" She grabbed a letter opener from his desk and threw it at him. He ducked but it bounced off the wall and grazed his forehead. He pressed an alarm button. The office door flew open. An attendant rushed in and grabbed her. She twisted around and elbowed him in the eye. Two more attendants rushed in. It took all three to restrain her.

". . . that bastard shrink set me on fire . . ."

While they held her down, he went to his medication cabinet, took out a hypo and an ampoule of sedative. As he inserted the needle into her arm, she glared at him.

". . . more of your date-rape shit . . . ?"

"I'm trying to help you."

Tears filled her eyes. Her voice softened. "What's happening to me, Marty? Don't leave me."

"I'm not leaving you. We'll continue during our next session." After she was gone, he took a tape recorder from his desk drawer and switched it on. He paused, then finally got the words out.

"Raven Slade. Borderline personality disorder. DSM Code 301.83. Dissociation with symptoms of depersonalization. Anecdotal history of splitting and derealization. Also, sexual flirtation symptoms of histrionic personality disorder, 301.50, with indications of high suggestibility.

"First image-flooding trial indicates pyrophobia. I suspect other phobias may surface as well.

"Problem: the literature suggests that, since rapid implosion therapy is a very assaultive treatment, it is not usually recommended for borderline or histrionic personality patients. However, given the urgency of the situation, I have no alternative."

He sighed and turned off the tape recorder. If rapid image-flooding worked, he might be able to prevent rendition. But it sickened him to realize that he had to torture her to save her from being tortured.

CHAPTER FIFTY-SEVEN

Ashraf, Iraq, to Giebelstadt, Germany

Fatima told Rashid to wait outside her quarters while she changed. Her only nonmilitary garments were the black skirt and white blouse she'd worn the day she fled the Athens Asylum. White blouse, black stockings and black pumps. Clothes decadent American women used to arouse men.

She smoothed her olive-drab uniform and hung it in the wardrobe. She looked forward to wearing it again after this mission. Plan A: if they intercepted the anthrax before Alexi picked it up in Kent, Ohio, MEK would look favorably on the Pentagon's offer. If Alexi already had it, then Plan B: Cooperate with 17N's homegrown sleepers to launch *Operation Dragon's Teeth*.

Unlike General Hassan, she didn't trust Colonel Rashid Omar. Had little confidence in the Pentagon's offer to protect *Mujihadeen-e Kalq* after the U.S. reinvaded Iraq. Not only because Rashid was Sunni, but because she didn't trust Western capitalists and politicians. Middle East oil greased America's wheels, and oil barons would betray anyone to keep them from squeaking.

She opened her footlocker and reached beneath the spare blanket for the metal box. Pushing aside her medals, she withdrew a container of powder. She slipped it into her purse. Rashid was MEK's direct link to the Pentagon. She might be able to use arsenic to break that link.

She went out to where he was sitting behind the wheel and entered on the passenger's side—as far from him as possible. He stopped at the sentry post and showed the guard his safe-conduct pass.

"You entered Ashraf alone. Who is this woman?"

"A senior MEK officer in disguise for a covert mission."

The guard saluted and pulled a lever. The gate opened.

"Thank you for not identifying me," she said as they passed through the checkpoint.

He stared straight ahead. "It wasn't necessary to arouse curiosity."

"I appreciate your caution."

He dug into his pocket and pulled out a pack of cigarettes. He offered her one, but she shook her head. He lit it with a gold lighter and inhaled deeply.

"Those things kill people," she said.

"So does weaponized anthrax."

She stared. "You know our weapon?"

"I solved the second riddle. The WHAT quatrain of Tedescu's prophecies."

"I do not believe you. It is too cryptic."

"I decrypted it. Listen.

> *"Seeds of Slow Death wait in our tunnels far.*
> *To punish all Crusaders, Inshallah.*
> *And Holy Fighters join our comrades now,*
> *To spread the shearers' dander I avow.*

"Mujihadeen-e Kalq are the Holy Fighters joining Marxist comrades of 17N. *Seeds of Death in tunnels far*, is the biological weapon in MEK's tunnels, to use—not against Iran, but to punish American Christians."

"How did you figure out it is anthrax?"

"Shearers of sheep and wool-sorters are often in contact with natural anthrax from the dander and have to be inoculated. It is often called wool-sorter's disease."

Oh he's clever. But do not boost his ego with praise. "That was easy for you because you were hiding among us—as the saying goes—in plain sight."

He shrugged. "I said it wasn't difficult."

"Have your people been equally successful in deciphering the first and third quatrains—WHERE and HOW?"

"Part of the WHERE. The three cities, but not the precise target of the third. The last prophetic puzzle, HOW, remains—as Winston Churchill said—'a riddle wrapped in a mystery inside an enigma.'"

It was becoming more difficult to despise him. He was not only handsome, but intelligent. She could hardly believe he was arousing her long-dormant feelings.

She retreated into silence, not trusting herself to speak. Suddenly, she glanced around. "This is Kurd territory! Why are we here? If the Peshmerga catch us, we are dead."

"Relax," he said. "They're now friends of America. Kurdistan, Iran and Israel are the only Middle East nations that actively use female soldiers. If the Pentagon convinces the State Department to remove MEK from the terrorist list, the Kurds will be your allies too."

"*Inshallah.*"

"Yes, God willing."

As they pulled up to a short landing strip, she saw the Learjet. "Is this how you extracted Raven?"

"I can't discuss that."

Two men wearing face masks approached the car.

"Don't be startled when they hood you," he said.

She winced as she felt a hood pulled over her head. "You are messing my hair."

A laugh from behind the mask. "We don't have a hairdresser aboard, but if you like I'll redo your braids." He reached over to help her out of the jeep.

She pushed his hand away. "Do not touch me."

"Okay. Just don't blame me if you trip."

She hesitated, then took his hand. "Forgive me. It is a deep-rooted aversion in our culture to being touched by strange men."

He not only held her hand but also put an arm around her waist. As he helped her up the steps into the plane, his hand pressed against her breasts. No point making a scene. This must be what American women expect. They deserve whatever happens to them.

The hatch slammed shut. Rashid removed her hood. "Would you like to sit near the window?"

"I prefer the aisle."

She let him slide in first so his legs wouldn't brush against hers. Then she sat, knees pressed together.

Looking at her legs, he said, "Remember, I am a Muslim. I would never offend you."

"It is my understanding that unlike Shia men, Sunni males are not very considerate of women's feelings. Like Americans, they consider women chattel, good only for sex and making babies."

He smiled. "Well, since I hold dual citizenship, American and Iranian, I must be a double sex fiend."

His mocking style amused her. Not only was he handsome. He was Muslim. "So where is your loyalty?"

"To both country and sex. What about you?"

She felt heat in her cheeks. Roar of the Learjet's engines saved her from having to answer. It sped along the runway. Then airborne. Wheels thumped underneath. Her knees relaxed, legs separated. That startled her. Was her unconscious leading her? Change the subject. "Were you born in the United States?"

"My parents emigrated from Iran after your student group led the attack on the U.S. embassy. My pregnant mother gave birth to me in New York."

"Thus dual citizenship."

"Officially. Yet, as much as I resent hyphenated identity, I consider myself Muslim-American."

"I too had American citizenship. My husband was Iranian-American. But, since we *Mujihadeen-e Kalq* are not permitted divided fidelity, we were required to divorce."

"Is he with the Ashraf men's cadre?"

"He was so bitter about our forced separation that he defected. Since he could not reenter Iran, he went to Syria and joined the Party of God."

"Hezbollah? Is he still with them?"

Her jaw clenched. "When his battalion bombed the American marine barracks in Beirut, he was martyred."

"So he's earned his seventy-two virgins in heaven."

She turned away.

"Sorry. Forgive my stupid humor. Any children?"

It was becoming hard for her to breathe. Do not think of your daughter. Do not speak of her. It is stupid to feel sorry for the past. But the words came out before she could hold her tongue. "A baby girl. In addition to divorce, MEK required us to give away our children. She is with my parents in America. By now she must be in college."

"I'm very—"

"Do not feel sorry for me. I have dedicated my life to our leader and our cause. To what is your life dedicated?"

"I'm army intelligence. What do you think?"

"You might be a double agent. Setting a trap for the *mujihadeen* and reporting to Saddam."

He laughed. "I might also be the Muslim Man-in-the-Moon, awaiting an eclipse that will precede the arrival of the twelfth imam who comes to reestablish the caliphate."

"Do you mock everything?"

"Only the absurd."

"No more talk. I am weary. I must sleep."

She dreamed of her daughter, Nahid.

The grinding Learjet's wheels jolted her awake. "Where are we?"

"In German airspace."

"*Germany?*"

"We'll land at the Giebelstadt Army Airfield, and from there hitch a ride on a C-5 Galaxy to the States."

"Where will it take us?"

"Hunter Army Airfield near Savannah, Georgia. There I'll rent a car and we make the long drive to Columbus, Ohio. In the morning, we'll drive to Kent State University to intercept the anthrax shipment."

"What if Alexi Costa has already picked it up?"

"Then we follow his trail to catch him."

"And if we cannot stop him?"

"I'll notify Homeland Security, and they'll raise the national alert warning to red."

"Will I have time to buy clothes in Giebelstadt?"

"Of course. You'll be able to shop at the PX. We don't depart for Savannah until 0700. Once there, I'll rent a car for the drive north."

The post exchange was stocked with clothes for army wives. Rashid sat outside the changing room while she tried on dresses. She selected four, groaning with disgust at American women's tastes. Only when a three-way mirror reflected her in a black sheath did she pause to admire herself. She undid her black braids and let her hair down. Military activity had kept her body slender and firm. Too bad she couldn't take these clothes back to Ashraf. She stepped out of the dressing room wearing the black dress and high heels.

Rashid's eyes opened wide. Nostrils flared. "You're so lovely." Then he turned away. "Forgive me. I shouldn't speak to you that way."

As she expected, he lusted for her. She felt her heart pounding. When he had mentioned leaving Columbus in the morning for the drive to Kent State, that meant spending the night in a hotel. One room or two? For the first time since joining the *Mujihadeen-e Kalq*, she resented their leader-in-exile in Paris, happily married, yet proclaiming that the women in Ashraf must remain chaste.

Well, she wasn't in Ashraf now.

CHAPTER FIFTY-EIGHT

Waybridge, Ohio

Raven ran her tongue across sandpaper lips. Opened her eyes. Struggled to get out of bed, but the sheet was stretched tight around her. Why did attendants in asylums always strap her down? What did she do wrong this time?

Only one way to get real. Under the sheet, she raked her fingernails across her stomach. Deeper. Harder. Tearing her skin. The smell of blood seeped through the sheet. It felt good to be back.

She heard the door creak. Saw Nathenson staring at her.

"Harry, get in here! The psycho is at it again!"

She said, "Good morning, Nurse. When's my next session with Marty?"

"You can see Dr. Kyle when you're calm and in control."

"I'm okay now."

Nathenson looked her up and down. "I'll see when Dr. Kyle has time to schedule you."

"Call him. I'm sure he'll see me right away."

"Really?" Nathenson gripped her cell phone. "If you stop tearing your skin, I'll see what he has to say."

She stuck out her tongue.

"Bite it off for all I care," Nathenson said. "Maybe that'll shut you up."

Nathenson made the call and frowned. "He'll see you now. He's skipping his lunch hour."

"I told you so."

Nathenson's face reddened. She pressed the button on the intercom and called, "Attendant Harry Newton to the nurses' station!"

Moments later the attendant entered and helped Nathenson unwrap the sheet. "After she cleans herself and gets dressed, take her to Dr. Kyle's office. Make sure she doesn't wander off."

As Harry Newton led her down the corridor, she saw him give her the once-over and lick his lips. Maybe he was a vampire attendant turned on by the smell of her blood.

"I don't think it's right for Nurse Nathenson to say you're stupid, Harry. You're obviously very intelligent. I heard her tell one of the other nurses that all you're good for is to lead crazies around. She shouldn't talk about you behind your back. Just don't let on you heard it from me."

"Thanks. My lips are sealed." When he smiled, she knew she'd made her first ally at University Hospital.

He led her to Kyle's office. Stay calm now and in control. Don't alienate the shrink. "Sorry to interfere with your meal, Doc. It's good of you to work me in."

"It's okay. I had a light lunch." He leaned back. "I understand how difficult this is for you."

"Just so you know, I don't think it's right for Nurse Nathenson to say that since Jung was a pro-Nazi racist, you must be too."

"Well, some anti-Jungians said those things, but it wasn't Jung's fault that Hitler used the concept of racial consciousness to justify the so-called Aryan race."

"I knew Nathenson was wrong. You wouldn't be the kind of psychiatrist who believed in those things."

"Do you know who you are today?"

She put her hand over her eyes. "I'm not sure. Does that mean I'm crazy?"

He sighed. "It's something I have to understand—for the court."

"Well, sometimes I hear two names. Nikki Apteros and someone called Raven Slade."

He hunched forward, elbows on the desk. "Who is talking to me now?"

"Raven. I-I think."

"What makes you think that?"

"Nikki is the one who wants you to sleep with her."

"Before we go any further, Raven, we have to clarify something. Boundaries are important. We cannot cross them."

She nodded. "Between countries, right?"

"Between patient and therapist."

"Oh . . ."

"What are you feeling right now?" he asked.

"Sad. Mother was upset when my twin sister died and I was born. She knew my father wanted a boy. Maybe that's why I get so depressed. Is depression inherited?"

"Some researchers say a predisposition may be genetic."

"You're a sexist, like my father."

"I'm not your father."

"Male shrinks stick together," she said. "Are you going to betray me in court?"

"I have to tell the judge what I think. If I can convince her you need psychiatric help, she may not approve your extradition to Greece."

"She'll take your word for it?"

"She ordered me to use rapid implosion therapy."

"What's that?"

"Remember when I showed you those pictures of fire? That's part of the therapy."

"Oh, sure. I bet that's what all sadists tell their victims."

"I'm not a sadist, Raven. It's the only treatment we have time for. It used to be called *flooding therapy*. Flooding the patient with images that confront his or her worst fears. Over and over, until those things lose their power to dominate the mind."

"Like the flames that burned Toothpick to death."

"What do you mean?"

She described the Piraeus bombing. "I think I was meant to die in that fire."

"But *who* was there? Was it really you?"

"I don't know."

"That helps our case. As long as you don't know *who* you are, the judge isn't likely to find you competent for extradition."

"Thanks for telling me. So there's no rush."

"The judge put a time limit on the treatment before she decides."

"I know that in America trials are public. If Alexi shows up, he'll think I betrayed him."

"This isn't a trial. It's a hearing. Because of national security, it'll be closed to the public."

"He'll find me anyway and torture me to tell things I can't remember."

"I've requested more guards to protect you."

"You did? Let me hug you."

"Boundaries!"

". . . *shit on boundaries* . . ."

"We'll talk about it next time."

". . . *talk wait* . . . *talk wait. always the same thing. i'm sick and tired of talk. how about some action* . . . *?*"

"Well, this interview is over, so we can stop talking."

". . . *no! it's my turn. don't send me away* . . ."

"We've been through this before. There are rules and boundaries." Kyle pressed a button on his phone. "Harry, escort the patient back to the ward. We're finished today."

"I hate you, Marty. Don't send me away."

Harry took her to her room. She asked him to come in with her, but he shook his head and locked her inside. When he was gone, she pulled the sheet off her bed and tore it into strips. Tied them together and wrapped one end around her neck. Where could she fasten the other end? Except for the sink and toilet, the room was bare. No pipes or rods. Should have checked things ahead of time.

Then she thought of the air-conditioning vent. Tie it to the grille. Double-tie the sheet strips short enough to strangle herself. She stood on her bed and threaded the loose end through one of the openings.

Someone told her men had powerful orgasms while they were hanged. Did women have them too? ". . . *ready or not, here i come . . .*"

The door burst open and Harry and another attendant rushed into the room and cut her down.

"*. . . it's my body, my life. you have no business interfering. i have a right to end my misery . . .*"

They took away her sheet-rope and left. She backed away from the door and looked around. Nothing.

. . . all right, i'll drown us . . .

She dropped to her knees. Stuck her face into the toilet bowl. But as the water went into her nose, her head pulled up of its own accord.

. . . can't do anything right. worthless, useless . . . if only i could fly away. but they clipped my wings . . . it's not fair. the goddess of victory belongs to all the people . . . victory to the people. for the people, by the people, up the people, into the peephole.

. . . is peephole a freudian slip? does freud wear a slip? who's a-froid of the big bad wolf? grandma, what big head you give! give me head. who's that standing naked at the door . . . ?

. . . how can i see myself without a mirror? it can only mean i have to destroy raven so alexi will love me . . .

. . . if bitch nathenson takes me to the showers again. i'll bash my head against the tile wall and be free to spend the rest of my life with him . . .

The thought made her so happy she smiled at Nathenson. "Thanks for being good to me. I do need a shower."

"Well, so we're little Ms. Perky now?"

"You too? I won't tell anyone."

Nathenson shook her head. "Let's get you cleaned up."

She cringed. "Nobody touches me!"

"You know, instead of a shower I think you need a bath."

"A nice hot bath will soothe my nerves."

"This way to the bathhouse."

Nathenson led her into a room with a tub that had a plastic cover with a hole in the center. "The lady needs her nerves soothed, fellows. Into the tub she goes."

Harry said, "Is this really necessary?"

"It's not for you to decide."

"I'm not as stupid as you think. She's mentally ill. Why are you punishing her?"

Nathenson's voice hardened. "Harry, if I write up a lousy recommendation, you'll never find another job like this."

He looked sad. He and another attendant grabbed her and lifted her into the tub.

"You don't have to shove me. I *want* a bath."

Nathenson said, "See? She's asking for it."

They put her head through the hole in the plastic cover.

Harry whispered, "Brace yourself, Raven."

The other attendant turned on the spigot. *Ice water!* Like

when Alexi took her out of the closet and gave her a cold shower.

Nathenson laughed, lifted the plastic lid and dumped in a tub of crushed ice.

"H-Harry, she's f-freezing me to death. Save me!"

Harry's shoulders sagged and he shook his head.

She clenched her chattering teeth. Closed her eyes. Pressed her lips tight. And then she was gone.

CHAPTER FIFTY-NINE

Kyle stormed onto the ward. "Nathenson, I never authorized cold-shock therapy."

"As head nurse on this ward, I take my instructions from Clinical Director Harold Unger, not from you."

"You should have informed me."

"I left a message on your desk. Dr. Unger said Raven is scheduled to appear in court on Monday and shouldn't be sedated. Electroconvulsive shock or ice bath was the only way to bring her around. Since no ECS specialist was available on such short notice, I decided on the ice bath."

"Couldn't it have waited?"

"Dr. Unger said Homeland Security is putting pressure on the judge to speed things up."

"All right," Kyle said. "Sorry to be so testy. Have you worked with borderlines before?"

"Yes and, God willing, I pray she's my last one."

"It might help you to understand that her mental disorder includes dissociation."

Nathenson's gaze was cold and unwavering. "Well, the ice-bath shock may have helped pull herself together."

Her look told him Raven had succeeded in pitting the nurse against him. Divide and conquer, a litmus test of BPD.

Back in his office, his secretary handed him a legal document. "People have been looking for you."

He glanced at it. A notice to appear Monday at 9:00 A.M. in court. He closed the door and phoned Bruce Coleman. "I just got the subpoena."

"Are you ready to testify?"

"I have another session with her this afternoon, and I'll need this evening to organize my thoughts."

"With Judge Rodriguez, you'd better have your ducks lined up in a row."

"You mean ravens, don't you?"

"Yeah, her too."

At three o'clock, Harry brought Raven to the office. She looked alert but calm.

He asked, "How do you feel?"

"Okay, I guess."

"I'd like to try something different this afternoon. You said your mother used to tell fortunes with tarot cards."

"I remember telling you, but I don't remember her doing it."

He reached into his desk drawer. "I have a tarot deck."

"You're like a magician pulling lots of interesting things out of your drawers."

He hesitated. Another sexual pun? Don't react. He spread the cards faceup. "There are different brands of tarot decks. This old one has unusual illustrations." He shuffled them like a dealer mucking a gambling deck. "The Keys are the most interesting. *Magician. Fool. Hermit. Wheel of Fortune. Hanged Man.*"

She put her hand to her throat, then picked up a card half hidden by others. Her hand trembled.

"Let me see it."

She shook her head.

"It's important that I know which card is upsetting you. Give it to me."

She crushed it and flung it, nearly hitting his eye.

He picked up the card. On a cliff, *The Tower*, struck by lightning. Flames bursting from the top floor. People falling through windows. Some jumping off the tower.

He sighed. "I thought we reached the point where you could handle images of fire."

"It's not the fire." Tears brimmed. "I can't look."

"The lightning flash?"

She shook her head.

"Help me help you. The figures jumping?"

She pressed her lips tight.

"Talk to me."

She pointed to the center of the card. "*The Tower.*"

"All right, associate to the tower."

"It's on a high cliff."

"And what does the cliff remind you of?"

"I was Faye Dunaway's understudy in *The Towering Inferno*. I collapsed on the set. I can't stand heights."

"Free-associate."

"I'm blank."

"What real tower on a great height frightened you?"

She closed her eyes. "The Waybridge Asylum where my father first committed me."

"Yes, there is a tower. What do you remember?"

"Something from a riddle. *The windswept tower.*"

"Do you know what *windswept tower* refers to?"

Her eyes rolled upward showing only the whites. "It makes me think of my mother."

He hadn't expected that. "Go on."

"I think I told her something about my father. She went ballistic. Took my hand and dragged me with her up to the parapet. Oh, God! She's leading me to the edge. She's saying, 'This world is an evil place. Let us join your twin sister in heaven.' She grabs my waist. Starts to make me jump with her. I pull away. She reaches for me, loses her footing. I see her fly off the tower. Land on the cliffside. Her body rolls to the bottom."

"That trauma led to your fear of heights."

"I-I guess so."

"Do you know the technical term for fear of heights?"

She shook her head.

"It's the first part of the name of the cliff on which the Parthenon stands. Acropolis. Acro——"

She stared at him. "Like in *acrobat?*"

He smiled at the image of himself swaying on the high wire. "Yes, *acro,* from the Greek *akros* meaning top or summit. Fear of heights is called *acrophobia.* Your mother's suicide, and your near-death experience, was so traumatic that you buried it behind the image of a windswept tower. Creating a fear of heights."

"You're not going to treat me with heights."

"First images. The Eiffel Tower. The Leaning Tower of Pisa. A view of looking down from the top of the Empire State Building. You'll reenact a scene from *The Towering Inferno.* Then you'll go with me to the roof of this hospital."

". . . *like hell i will . . . !*"

She swept everything—papers, files, pens and pencils— off his desk onto the floor.

". . . *if I want to get high, i'll take dope . . .*"

He pressed the buzzer. Harry led her out of the room.

When she was gone, he took out his tape recorder. Start. Stopped it. Started again.

"*Raven's second phobia has surfaced. Acrophobia. Connected to her mother's attempt to kill them both in a double suicide by jumping off the Waybridge Asylum parapet. In her delusion, she is on the set of the film* The Towering Inferno. *It will be difficult—if not impossible—to desensitize her with rapid implosion*" *therapy using pictures or visualization. I'll have to find another way."*

He looked at the tarot cards on his desk for a long time. Then he swept them all back into the drawer.

Except the crushed card she'd thrown at him. *The Tower.*

CHAPTER SIXTY

Savannah, Georgia, to Columbus, Ohio

Fatima studied Rashid's profile during the long drive in the rented red Jaguar. He was behaving like a perfect gentleman, but his sidelong glances from time to time made his interest obvious. She realized she was pressing both feet on the passenger's floorboard against nonexistent brakes.

Above all, she must steel herself against her own desires. She was impressed by the intel Rashid received at the Hunter army base. They tracked the package across the Mexican border to Texas. From Brownsville by train to Columbus, then to Kent. She had suspected that's where Alexi would have gone, but for now she would keep it to herself. If Alexi already had the anthrax, he would search for Raven to learn the rest of Tedescu's prophecy.

"We've got to take a break before we drive to Kent," Rashid said. "Nothing more we can do this evening. Let's get a hotel room and have a night's rest."

"It was a mistake for me to have sent the anthrax so soon."

"*The Moving Finger writes,*" Rashid recited, "*and, having writ, Moves on. Not all your Piety nor Wit—*"

She finished, "*—Shall lure it back to cancel half a Line, nor all your Tears wash out a Word of it.*"

"So, you know the *Rubáivát?*"

"Of course," she said. "I too am Persian."

He pulled off the highway to a Westin Hotel. "Let's check in. Get a couple of rooms."

She put her hand on his arm. "No need to waste money. One room will be fine." She felt his arm muscle tighten.

Inside the hotel, she stayed out of sight while he registered. Once in the room she turned to look out the window as the bellboy showed Rashid the amenities.

"Should you need anything, our room service is superb."

He tipped the bellboy. "Send up bottle of your best champagne."

When the young man was gone, she said, "A Muslim drinking alcohol?"

"Only for this special occasion."

"Such extravagance, but I guess it will go on your expense account."

"I have carte blanche." He put his hand on hers. "For you, anything."

She pulled away. "Not so impetuous, Colonel Rashid."

"Why not? We're in the West now."

"Give me time to think."

"All right, Major Fatima. Whenever you decide."

"I must use the washroom and get ready," she said.

There was a knock at the door. She called out, "That is probably your champagne."

"*Our* champagne."

She slipped into a nightgown. A negligee would have been more alluring, but she hadn't bought one at the PX. When she came out, he was already in bed. As she approached, he pulled back the covers and motioned for her to get in beside him.

She sat on the edge of the bed. "There will be no sex, Colonel Rashid."

He leaned forward and nuzzled her shoulder.

"Ohhhh . . ." He knew how to arouse a woman. There must have been many.

He kissed the nape of her neck.

"Ohhhh."

"I've just begun my mission." One hand stroked her left breast while the other moved down between her legs.

"No," she whispered. His tongue slide between her lips. She pulled back. "No . . . no . . . no . . ."

She had never felt this way before, not even with her late husband. Now, she felt wet. Do not pass out. He pulled her closer. Her hand between his thighs gripped his firm erection. Stop? Not yet. She could stop him anytime. Western women said if she cried "no," it was rape. How could she be responsible for breaking her oath of chastity if he raped her?

Then he was inside her.

"I said no . . . no . . . no . . ." But when he reached the spot she had never known, she quivered. "Do not . . . *stop*," she said, tonguing his ear. "Do not . . . *stop!* Oh, no . . . Do not . . . stop."

When he was done she felt her body still vibrating.

He went into the washroom.

She staggered to her feet and went to the table. Poured champagne for both of them. Then she dug into her purse for the vial. Emptied half the arsenic into his glass. The rest she would save for Raven.

When he returned, she handed him the champagne and lifted hers in a toast. "To a successful mission."

He clinked his glass against hers. "Sex makes me thirsty." He sipped the champagne until he had drained it.

She put hers, untasted, on the table.

"Aren't you drinking?"

"I am a Muslim woman. I do not drink alcohol."

His eyes opened wide. The glass trembled in his hand.

"Also," she said, "I have taken an oath of chastity."

"So what the hell do you call what we were doing . . . ?"
He dropped the glass. Coughed. Choked. Face reddened.
His naked body thrashed.

She waited until he stopped moving. "We finish," she
said, "as the beloved tentmaker-poet ended his *Rubáiyát:*

"And in Thy joyous Errand reach the Spot
Where I made One, Turn down an empty Glass."

She rinsed his glass and replaced it on the tray—upside
down.

She went back into the bathroom and soaped herself from
head to foot. She let the steaming water flow down her face,
her back, her breasts, then stepped out of the stall and tow-
eled herself vigorously. She dressed and turned toward
Mecca. Cupped her hands, dropped to her knees, stretched
out, hands facing the holy place. *"In the name of Allah, the
compassionate, the merciful . . ."*

After she finished the eighty-seventh sura of the Quran,
she packed her bag and took the rented car keys from his
trouser pocket. His naked body now offended her. She
covered him, turned off the lights and put the DO NOT
DISTURB sign outside the door.

She had said *no,* several times. When he persisted, that
made it rape. She killed a Sunni rapist in self-defense. According to the strict interpretation of sharia, even though
raped, she should be stoned and buried alive. But it was no
violation of her chastity oath to *Mujihadeen-e Kalq.*

She had done it to cut MEK's link to the Pentagon. Since
he was a spy, turnabout was fair play. She'd used Mata Hari's
technique to lure Rashid into the honeypot.

Now she would drive to Kent State to see if Alexi had obtained the weaponized anthrax. She and Nahid had kept in touch by e-mail, but she had not seen her since MEK's leaders ordered all children sent away. She looked forward to hugging her daughter.

CHAPTER SIXTY-ONE

Columbus, Ohio

Kyle led Raven out of the hospital exit to his Lexus.

He whispered to the deputy, "Follow us." He opened the passenger door for her and, once behind the wheel, locked both doors. No sense taking a chance she might jump.

"You're good to me, Marty." She rested her head on his shoulder.

"Raven, lift your head please."

"Damn you!" She looked out the window, and as they crossed the bridge over the Ohio River, she gripped his arm.

He jammed the brakes. "What now?"

"There's the windswept tower where my mother tried to kill us both."

He saw her staring up at the parapet of the High Victorian Gothic building. She had seemed disturbed when they first passed it heading east to the university. Now it was time to test her. "They locked the asylum and boarded it up long ago."

"Why?"

"It was closed during the last two years of legal battles over the property it stands on. The university wants to tear it down and build a research facility. A corporation wants to put up an apartment complex, with a golf course on the land below."

"No! They musn't destroy it! Mother is there!"

Kyle crossed the overpass. "That's impossible. It'll stay boarded up until it's demolished."

"It's wrong to do that while the dead are still there."

"You talking about ghosts?"

"I'm talking about her body in the asylum cemetery, at the bottom of the ravine. Most graves have numbers instead of names. They mustn't become the numbers of golf fairways and putting greens."

"Ahhhh."

"Yes. Elementary, Dr. Kyle. She's buried there."

Maybe it was a good place for flooding. Have her revisit the place where her trauma had led to acrophobia. "We've got time. Let's stop and take a look."

"I can't. The tower. The cliff."

"I don't mean to the top. You said your mother is buried in the cemetery below. Now that we've established the reason you're afraid of heights, we'll stay below and visit the cemetery."

"Promise?"

"You have my word."

He turned into a narrow road that changed to gravel and then dirt.

She said, "The cemetery is behind the asylum."

He stopped the car. She followed him, hesitating, staring at the ground. Each tombstone was marked with a number. She pointed. "There."

Among the numbered graves, he saw one with a name. ANN SLADE—1951 TO 1992—BELOVED WIFE AND MOTHER.

Raven's eyes misted. "Beloved bullshit!" She picked up a handful of dirt and threw it at the gravestone, then backed away. "No. That's evil. She loved me even though she tried to take me with her to hell."

She still avoided looking at the tower. An opportunity for rapid flooding? Tricky. If she panicked, she'd be unpredictable in court. Maybe that would help her avoid extradition. She didn't have to be psychotic. As Judge Rodriguez said, it depended on: *identity, presence, and the capacity to help her attorney deal with those issues.* What was there to lose?

"Look up at the tower. It's important."

"Are you trying to drive me crazy?"

"How about if we just walk up the path a little ways to the entrance?"

"It's on the edge of the cliff. I can't."

"Partway?"

"You want me to jump off?"

"Of course not. Why would you think that?"

"Because that's where my mother tried to take me with her." She glanced up furtively. "Sometimes I think it was because I told her I saw my father do something bad. Maybe it was just a dream." She took his hand and pulled him back to the car. "Let's get away from here."

As he drove to Columbus, he wondered about the risk associated with desensitizing her acrophobia. Can't hurry it. Yet, too many lives were at stake. Judge Rodriguez wouldn't give him more time to attempt the impossible.

At the courthouse, he parked and led Raven into the building. She pulled back when they reached the escalator.

"What's wrong?"

She looked at the tile floor. "I never go up those things."

"Of course. Sorry. We'll take the elevator."

He led her to the bank of elevators. A door slid open. She clung to his arm and faced the far wall as they entered. She relaxed when the door shut. He punched the number for the third floor, thankful she wasn't also claustrophobic.

She sighed when the door slid open and they stepped out into the crowded corridor. Some people were carrying briefcases, others clutched documents. As he headed toward Judge Rodriguez's courtroom, he felt a hand tap his shoulder. It was Coleman.

"Kyle, I'll take her. You'll have to wait out here until you're called to testify."

Raven hung back. "I want to stay with Marty."

"I'll join you shortly. Go on. You'll be all right." He watched Coleman lead her through the entrance to the courtroom. Then he sat on a nearby bench to wait.

FBI agent Dugan and Greek agent Tia Eliade passed him chatting with each other. Then Dugan left her and entered the courtroom. So she was going to testify too.

The courtroom door opened and the bailiff called, "Dr. Martin Kyle!"

He entered and strode down the aisle. Raven, alongside Coleman at the defense table, blew him a kiss.

Judge Rodriguez said, "Dr. Kyle, take the stand."

He walked slowly to the witness box, put his hand on the Bible, and swore to tell the truth, the whole truth, and nothing but the truth, so help him God. Who but God, he wondered, knows the *whole* truth? And where did he hide it?

Taylor approached, holding a yellow pad, her arm muscles bulging. Would she wrestle him to the mat this round? He should have done more weight lifting.

"Dr. Kyle, at our last meeting, the court assigned you to use a desensitizing procedure known as rapid implosion therapy. Please tell the court if you were able to establish the defendant's identity using that method."

Right off, she caught him in a hammerlock. "Not exactly."

"Please explain to the court."

"As I pointed out, that kind of flooding imagery is so powerful, it creates intense anxiety. I explained that it was impossible to predict how a borderline-histrionic patient would react. I've identified two phobias that prevent me from breaking through her posthypnotic suggestion blocking memories. Pyrophobia and acrophobia." He looked at the judge. "Fear of fire and fear of heights."

Rodriguez scowled. "I know what those terms mean."

"Sorry, Your Honor."

Taylor tossed the legal pad on the table. "How does that affect the court's ability to determine her true identity?"

"*True identity?* The traumas that led her mind to lose itself in the fog of depersonalization haven't surfaced. I haven't yet been able to establish her *true identity*."

The harder she came at him, the easier it was to slip out of her grip. "I must proceed with caution. It's been well established that one hallmark of borderline personality disorder is self-mutilation and threats of suicide."

"How reliable are the suicide threats?"

"Nationwide, 8 percent of hospitalized BPD's attempt suicide. Five percent succeed."

Taylor said, "So 95 percent don't succeed."

Coleman jumped up. "Objection!"

"Sustained," Rodriguez said. "But relax, Mr. Coleman. This isn't a trial. There's no jury to be prejudiced."

Coleman slunk back into his seat.

Kyle said, "She started to cut her throat when the police tried to pick her up at the motel."

Taylor backed away quickly. "No further questions of Dr. Kyle—for now."

He relaxed. She hadn't pinned him to the mat.

Rodriguez nodded at Coleman. "You may cross-examine."

Coleman approached. "Dr. Kyle, are you familiar with what is known as the Stockholm syndrome?"

"Objection!" Taylor snapped.

"On what grounds?" Rodriguez asked.

"Past experience of having been taken hostage has no relevance to the Athens bank robbery nor to her complicity in a terrorist conspiracy."

Rodriguez turned to Coleman. "Your argument?"

"We feel it is definitely relevant. Being abused, tortured and made to feel you'll be killed, leads to identification with your kidnappers, and—"

"Objection!"

"On what grounds, Ms. Taylor?"

"Your Honor, no expert in these matters has testified."

"Sustained. Mr. Coleman, let the witness explain."

Coleman turned back to Kyle. "Please tell the court how the Stockholm syndrome might affect a borderline patient during episodes of dissociation."

He focused intently on Coleman to avoid Raven's stare. "We learned from earlier cases—such as the Patty Hearst kidnapping—that torture, starvation, rape or fear of being raped and killed, can overwhelm even the most stable individual. Constant indoctrination into the kidnapper's social and political beliefs—such as the Greek Marxist-Leninist propaganda of 17N, and forced conversion to Islam by the Marxist *Mujihadeen-e Kalq* may cause her to doubt what she has believed all her life. Or even who she really is.

"When this is compounded by repeated statements that only these groups care what happens to her, she accepts that point of view. Her kidnappers assure her they'll save her and let her join them, and her relief becomes overwhelming. These hostages often fall in love with their captors."

"During your sessions with her," Coleman asked, "was there anything that might make a borderline-histrionic, like Raven, susceptible to the Stockholm syndrome?"

"The histrionic personality aspect makes her not only sexually provocative, but also highly suggestible."

"How might Ms. Slade react to aggressive interrogation by the Greek police?"

"Research shows that females in terrorist groups such as MEK are motivated to be tougher than men. I believe Raven would see herself as a martyr to the cause into which she's being indoctrinated. If officials waterboard her, she'll let herself drown before they can bring her up. Any torment they induce will be surrogate pain taking the place of self-injury. Pain to a borderline often serves as evidence that she is real and reinforces belief that the terrorists are her friends, and those fighting terrorism are her enemies."

As he testified, he saw Raven's expression change from an approving smile to anger. She jumped up. "You manipulated me, Marty. You're my doctor. You're not supposed to reveal what I told you."

"No further questions of this witness," Coleman said.

Rodriguez gazed at Raven. "In that case, since bank robbery is a crime in both countries, I will retire to consider whether or not to extradite Raven Slade to Greece for interrogation. The court will stand in recess until Monday morning." She slammed the gavel so hard the handle broke.

CHAPTER SIXTY-TWO

On Monday morning, outside the courtroom, Dugan watched Raven huddle with Dr. Kyle in the corridor. No telling how she would react if the judge ordered her rendered back to Greece for aggressive interrogation. He felt sorry for her. Not her fault she'd been kidnapped. Not her fault she'd been brainwashed. In the courtroom, her face changed expressions frequently. Focused. Distant. Angry. Confused. Still, mentally ill or not, her mind held the keys to cataclysmic prophecies.

He saw Raven kiss Kyle on the cheek. As she headed for the ladies' room, he signaled for the female deputy to follow her. Maybe this would be his last chance to reason with Kyle.

"There is something you should know," he said.

Kyle backed away. "We shouldn't be talking."

"Look, I know Greece isn't listed among nations that use *aggressive interrogation*, but I've seen firsthand how their Theater of Torture works."

"What do you mean?"

"We both know that, behind her hypnotic amnesia, Raven has the clues to Tedescu's riddles. I've solved two of the three targets. We know they intend to use weaponized anthrax, but we need to know the third target and how they plan to release the stuff."

"I've used rapid implosive therapy, but she's blocked."

"Maybe if you tell her what the weapon is, explain the terrible effect anthrax will have on women and children, she might be horrified enough for you to break through."

"You think Judge Rodriguez will give me more time?"

"If she doesn't, I will."

"I don't understand. How is it possible?"

Before he could explain, Raven came out of the lavatory. The bailiff opened the door to the courtroom and called, "Court is now in session."

He and Tia followed Coleman, Kyle and Raven inside. They stood as Judge Rodriguez entered and motioned for everyone to be seated. She looked directly at Raven.

"This court's decision, in the face of a ticking-bomb terrorist threat, is based on diplomatic assurances by the Greek embassy that there will be no aggressive interrogation. It is ordered that the Jane Doe, AKA Raven Slade, AKA Nikki Apteros, be rendered to Greece. This court hereby certifies the record to the secretary of state."

"*. . . go to hell, bitch . . . !*"

He'd heard that high-pitched voice before.

Rodriguez shouted, "Restrain her!"

He watched the female officer pull her back into her seat.

"*. . . take your fucking hands off me . . . !*"

Rodriguez said, "She's to be remanded until—"

"Objection," Coleman said.

"Overruled, Mr. Coleman! We cannot take the chance she might abscond before she reveals what she knows. I'm sure you know my order regarding extradition is not appealable."

"Then we petition for a writ of habeas *corpus*."

"Denied."

"Your Honor, denying such a writ *is* appealable."

"True, but such an appeal will take time. She'll be interrogated in Greece by then."

He saw Raven looking around the courtroom wildly. She struggled with the female officer who was cuffing her.

Coleman persisted. "Your Honor—"

"The secretary of state will forward my order to the Criminal Division's Office of International Affairs. They will notify the Greek embassy that we are arranging for Raven Slade's transfer to their counterterrorism task force."

As Rodriguez left the courtroom, Dugan noticed the female deputy was having difficulty leading Raven through the side door to a holding cell. Suddenly, Raven spun around and wrapped her manacled hands around the deputy's throat.

". . . *i can break your neck with one twist . . . !*"

The deputy gagged, eyes bulged.

Raven forced her out into the corridor. Hesitated at the down escalator. She looked around wildly.

Was she going to force the deputy into the elevator instead and risk having guards stop it between floors?

She pulled the deputy's automatic out of her holster. ". . . *stay in front of me as we go down. if you try to break loose, you're dead . . .*"

He realized she was using the deputy not only as a hostage, but also as a shield. Kyle had mentioned her fear of heights. For a moment, he thought he saw her close her eyes. She stumbled, but caught herself. When they reached the lobby, she pushed the deputy ahead out the front doors.

He was startled to see reporters and photographers crowding the courthouse steps. Two TV vans parked at the curb were flanked by police cruisers. Spotlights blinded him. TV cameras were recording. So much for a closed special extradition hearing.

". . . *unlock the cuffs, or i'll shoot . . . !*"

The deputy reached around with the key and uncuffed her.

Kyle shouted, "Raven, you're not going to kill her. She's just doing her job."

Hands free now, she screamed, waving the gun. ". . . *everyone, back off . . . !*"

Reporters and cameramen hid behind cars and vans. Three other deputies pulled their weapons.

He called out to her, "This is Agent Dugan. You can't shoot all of us at once, Raven! Listen to Dr. Kyle. Put down the gun!"

She shoved the deputy aside, and stuck the barrel against her own temple. "Go ahead, Mr. FBI. You can render *my corpse* to Greece where they can torture Raven to their heart's content."

Kyle shouted at him, "She's no use to you dead."

". . . *listen to my shrink, or you'll never solve the rest of the riddles . . .*"

With the gun still aimed at herself, she strode to a police cruiser and ordered the officer out. He looked uncertain.

The police chief shouted, "Do what she says!"

She took a second weapon from the officer and forced him out of the cruiser. She slid behind the wheel and shouted, ". . . *if any of you follow me, i'll blow out her brains . . .*"

Over the sound of screeching tires, he heard her call out, ". . . *mother, here we come! ready or not . . .*"

He watched her drive erratically down the middle of the street with one hand on the wheel. The other hand aimed the gun at her head.

CHAPTER SIXTY-THREE

She drove around Columbus for almost fifteen minutes with the police radio on, until she heard the dispatcher:

"Raven Slade, AKA Nikki Apteros, escaped from the U.S. district courthouse by overpowering a deputy and stealing a police cruiser. She is armed and should be considered dangerous to herself and others. Anyone sighting cruiser 726 report to the dispatcher. Follow at a distance, but under no circumstance attempt to apprehend the fugitive."

She had to get rid of the cruiser. Crossed the Franklin County line into Fairfield County, she saw a blue Mercedes go through a red light. She turned on the siren. When the sedan pulled onto the berm, she parked behind it and approached, waving the gun.

The driver opened the window. She called to him, *". . . turn off the engine and step outside . . ."*

"The light just changed, Officer! I'm late for a doctor's appointment."

". . . i said, get out of the goddamn car . . . !"

He opened the door. "Officer, please . . ."

She aimed the gun at him. He mumbled, "You're not wearing a uniform. You're not a policeman. What's going on?"

". . . you're being carjacked . . ."

"What the hell!"

". . . *that's where you'll end up if you don't move your ass,
get out and gimme me your goddamned cell phone . . .*"

He handed it to her. She shoved him aside and floored
the gas pedal.

Why was she heading east? As she crossed the bridge, she
saw the Waybridge Asylum on her left, outlined against the
sky. Marty Kyle said it was boarded up. Probably the last place
anyone would search for her. But it was a tower on the cliff.
That tarot card lightning-struck, windswept tower.

. . . *a place to crash. we don't climb to the top, just hole up
until you get your head together . . .*

"That's crazy."

. . . *where better to hide than our old crazy house . . . ?*

"Okay."

. . . *that's settled. but first, shop for supplies . . .*

She passed the asylum, drove through Waybridge into West
Virginia. It was dark when she stopped at an all-night con-
venience store in Parkersburg. She loaded a shopping cart
with cans of soup, sardines, tuna and a manual can opener.
Boxes of crackers. Hesitated at the counter displaying a
Sterno stove and canned heat. Could she bring herself to
ignite it?

She backed away and picked up soap, toothbrush and
toothpaste. Flashlights. Lots of batteries. She'd set up housekeeping, and weather the coming storm. She knew she
needed sleep, but she was too excited. She picked up a package of sleeping powder. Back at the counter, she stared at the
Sterno stove.

What was it Kyle said? Visualize. Force yourself to face the
image of fire. She grabbed the Sterno stove, the canned
heat, and a box of matches. She paused at the pet section
and picked up a dog collar.

The clerk rang up $143.26. "What kind of dog you got?"

". . . *i don't have a dog* . . ."

"Then why do you need a dog collar?"

She pulled the gun out of her handbag. ". . . *shut up and empty the register* . . ."

"Okay, lady. Don't shoot." His hands trembled as he handed her the bills.

She held out a paper bag. ". . . *large bills too* . . ." He lifted the tray, and she scooped out twenties and fifties. She reached over and yanked the phone cord out of the wall. ". . . *don't think of doing anything foolish. it's the capitalist owner's money, not yours* . . ."

"Yes, ma'am."

She backed out of the store and slipped the gun back into her purse. She tossed her loot into the backseat of her commandeered blue Mercedes and drove out of the parking lot.

. . . *now for clothes* . . .

No other stores open at this hour. She remembered this was a rough neighborhood. Streets were deserted. When she finally saw a USED CLOTHING sign, she pulled around back.

She smashed a window and unlocked the door. No time to try things on. Moving among the racks, she grabbed denims and slacks. Shirts, an Ohio State baseball cap and a jacket for chilly nights. All sizes. Whatever didn't fit she'd donate to charities.

As she came out of the store, she saw three rough-looking young men leaning against the Mercedes.

"Nice car, lady."

"Kinda late for shopping."

"Wanna party?"

She dug into her purse. ". . . *outta my way, or you'll be sorry* . . ."

They came toward her. The tall one reached for her.

She pulled out the gun. ". . . *i warned you* . . ." She fired at the leg of the closest one. He yelped, fell. She aimed the barrel at his head.

". . . *wanna stick around for more, you assholes . . . ?*"

The other two ran. The one she'd shot struggled to his feet and lurched away crying, "Don't shoot no more, lady. I'm goin' fast as I can."

When they were out of sight, she tossed the clothes into the backseat of the car. She slid behind the wheel and turned on the ignition.

She drove past the university medical school, crossed the bridge over the Ohio River and turned up a narrow road. It changed to gravel and then dirt. A deep breath. Then up to the sealed main entrance.

The whoosh of wings startled her. She'd disturbed a flock of blackbirds flying out of the trees. Eerie, outlined against the moon. Probably descendants of the ones who lived here when she was a patient. Mother must have named her after them.

. . . mother reading bedtime stories and poems of eddie allen poe. "the black cat," "the fall of the house of usher." oh, "the raven" scared her most. "quoth the raven. 'Nevermore!'" a memory kyle would call association . . .

She's nine or ten. An attendant is telling her these blackbirds are spirits of the departed insane buried in the numbered cemetery. What was his name? Lukus. Black with missing front teeth that whistled when he talked.

"Late nights and early mornin's," he said, "a visitor spooks 'em and they fly. Don' ever feed 'em, like the guards do at the Tower a' London, or they'll spread the word and thousands a blackbird ghosts'll come an' haunt you."

Then Lukus showed her the hidden passageway.

"How come there's a secret tunnel into a crazy house?"

"This was the las' undagroun' railway station in southeast Ohio for slaves escapin' north. When slave hunters was a comin', blackbirds flyin' give my ancestors time to git inta the cave 'n through the tunnel to hide . . ."

Now, she remembered the cave opening was on the west side of the asylum. She searched until she found it partially covered with earth, behind tall weeds.

Using her new flashlight, she crawled into the cave and followed the dirt path. A few yards along, it ended at a gate with a rusty lock. She hacked away with a rock until it broke off. She creaked the gate open. A brick-lined passageway sloped upward another twenty yards to the asylum basement. Inside, cell doors hung open—some off hinges— where they used to lock up the violent sickos.

She pressed the light switch. No power. Of course not. Could she go up? Just a few worn steps? She closed her eyes and hugged the wall as she struggled up into the lobby. No higher. The linoleum floor—once polished like a mirror— was covered with dust.

Offices lined both sides of the corridor inside the boarded-up main entrance. On the right, she passed Admissions. With her toe, she traced *Raven* in the dust. Across the lobby was Information. She did the same for *Nikki*. Farther along, she peered through the window of Ye Gift Shoppe. Empty shelves.

She hesitated, then looked up at the curved staircase that led to the second floor. Admissions and Intensive Treatment. That's where new patients awaited diagnosis. And doctors' offices. She remembered the third floor housed long-term *chronic* patients who mumbled and waved their arms. Some, without underwear, just faced the walls and shit down their legs. At the nurses' station, she'd made a few friends and lots of enemies.

Fourth floor housed the clinical director's office from where her father ruled his kingdom of lunatics—herself included. On the fifth floor, he spent nights in his private suite when he did twenty-four-hour duty.

She wouldn't go upstairs. Not yet. Maybe, eventually, she'd teach herself to do it the way Kyle helped her overcome her fear of fire.

She found the room at the end of the lobby where orderlies took their coffee breaks. It had a small kitchenette. The door was stuck. She kicked it open. Inside, she set down the groceries and her loot on a rickety table. She turned on the sink spigot. It spat water, first rusty, then cold but lousy-tasting.

She tried the old electric toaster oven. Silly, not without power. She forced herself to light a match for the Sterno. She quickly blew it out. Lit it again. Then again. Kyle's therapy was working for Raven.

This is where she'd set up housekeeping. Reminded her of the ice storm when power went out all over Waybridge County. They weathered the electrical outage because her scout leader father taught *his boys* always to "Be Prepared." Sorry to disappoint you, Daddy, for not being born a boy.

Here's where she was housed during her third year at Waybridge University. She had broken down during her rehearsal of *Lysistrata*. When she spoke the heroine's lines to convince the women to stop the war by withholding sex from their men, she collapsed.

That was when Daddy put her away again in his asylum.

For the . . . for the . . . She fingered the scars on her right hip. Third time? Fourth? Anyway, a long time ago.

She needed sleep. Too wide-awake now. Well, Daddy, I prepared. She opened one of the packets of sleeping powder and poured it into a glass of brackish water. She heated it on the Sterno and forced herself to drink.

But how could she sleep alone? The thought scared the hell out of her. She'd force herself. She couldn't trust people. Safest by herself. Visualize it the way Kyle taught her. Maybe she wouldn't be alone. Maybe the ghosts of crazies past would visit. She could talk to them. Would they answer? Maybe with sign language.

Face it, she'd escaped from the court, stolen a cruiser, carjacked an unsuspecting driver, robbed a store and shot a would-be attacker. Oh, she'd changed all right. Now she had to be strong enough to face the world alone in her asylum on the cliff.

She sat on a folding chair. The sleeping powder started working. Out of her head. Then out of herself. . . . *i can't believe this was once our furshlugginer home* . . .

As her eyes closed, she saw Raven staring down at her with a disgusted look on her face.

CHAPTER SIXTY-FOUR

Fatima pulled the rented red Jaguar into a gas station north of Columbus and filled the tank. She bought an Ohio road map, and had the clerk highlight the direction to Kent. He said it would be an easy drive to the university campus.

It had been so long since she'd seen her daughter. All she'd had to go by, until now, was the photograph Nahid had e-mailed during their last communication.

First stop, the Muslim Student Association. She found it easily in the student union. As she opened the door, a dozen heads turned to look at her. Young women in hijab head coverings on one side of the room. The young men in kufi skullcaps on the other.

"I am looking for my daughter, Nahid."

A pimple-faced young man said, "She has not been to our meetings recently."

She glanced around the room. "When was the last time any of you saw her?"

"Three days ago. Nahid said she was going to pick up a package."

"Did she bring it back to her room?"

Pimple-face said, "She hasn't returned yet. Probably camping out."

She turned to leave.

"*Ma'assalama*," pimple-face said.

Without looking back, she said, "Yes, good-bye."

Outside the student union, she braced herself. Be calm. Nahid had gone to pick up the package. Had she passed it on to Alexi? Did she get the money? Where was she now?

She followed directions to campus security. A stocky officer with the name tag FITZGERALD asked if he could help her.

"I am trying to learn the whereabouts of Nahid Sawyer, the daughter of a friend."

He frowned. "Been trying to locate her relatives. Can you put us in touch with them?"

"They are in Iran. It would be difficult."

"Would you mind delivering the bad news?"

"Bad . . . ?"

"A sheriff's deputy found her in a pond not far from campus. It's still under investigation, but there was something strange. The medical examiner says someone strangled her and broke her neck, but her head scarf was still on, neatly tied."

Be calm. Show no emotion. "Where is her body?"

"In the mortuary. Do you want to identify it?"

"I did not know her personally. But I will pass along the horrible news to her family."

"That'll save us the trouble."

"One more thing, Officer Fitzgerald. When her body was discovered, did she have things with her? Her family might like to know if they can have them shipped back to Iran."

"Just a backpack, stretched like it once held a large package."

"Anything in it?"

"Just clothes and paper wrapping with traces of a peanut butter and jelly sandwich."

"Thank you, Officer Fitzgerald," she said as she left the office.

So, Nahid had already given Alexi the anthrax. But why kill her? She would ask him before she cut his throat.

It occurred to her that Alexi would figure Raven had gone to the asylum where she spent so much time while growing up. He would seek her out in a last attempt to solve the puzzles of Tedescu's prophecies. If Alexi hadn't found Raven yet, she would get to her first. She turned off the bridge onto the road leading to the asylum.

What was left of the arsenic would assure Raven's quick and painful death.

CHAPTER SIXTY-FIVE

As Raven awoke, the last few days seeped into her mind. People were trying to send her to Greece to be tortured.

But Alexi would save her.

She ran through the rooms off the lobby, searching—for what? In the library, she saw dust-covered books scattered on tables, flung down from shelves, some open, others with covers torn like masks from their faces. In the dayroom, dominoes and checkerboard games abandoned in midplay.

She stopped when she saw the tarot cards. Her mother used to tell her fortune. *Mysterious Horseman* carrying the mystic rose on a black banner, the sun shining between two towers. Her mother said it didn't refer to physical death, but casting off fleshly desires. And the card that always thrilled her. *Lovers.* She knew it meant her and Alexi.

She turned the next card and trembled. A woman, bound and blindfolded, standing in water surrounded by eight swords. In the distance, on a high hill, a castle. The card was the *Eight of Swords.*

Before her father locked her away, bullies at middle school used to touch her. She started carrying a pocket-knife. She told the leader, "Touch me again, I'll cut you." He grabbed her from behind, fingers inside her panties, so she cut him.

He went off screaming, "Raven stabbed me! I'm dying!"

Dumb bastard. It was just a scratch. But the principal called Daddy who took her out of school and locked her away in the asylum. That was the first time. She should kill that part of herself as mother tried to do.

. . . *hell no! i'm not ready to die with you* . . .

Could she go upstairs to A.I.T. on the second floor? To be saved, she needed *Admission and Intensive Treatment.* Maybe, if she didn't look down.

Kyle taught her to imagine a scene. Visualize. She closed her eyes. To save her, a knight in shining armor replaces the *Black Knight.* He makes her feel happy. But when he takes her hand and leads her out of the lobby to the upward curving stairway, she's afraid. He lifts her in his arms and carries her safely to the second floor.

Oh, God! Can she? One step up. Then another. And another. Don't look down. She drops to her knees and crawls the rest of the way to the second landing. Don't look down. She's doing it. She forces herself to look up the curving stairs to the third floor where they kept the really sick ones. Not yet.

Alexi should have killed me, Father, instead of taking your place and teaching me about good and evil. I believed him when he said you and other agents of Western capitalism are brainwashing the people. He said oil is the *dope*-iate of Americans. Alexi talked in his sleep so often about the oil-stained *Dragon's Teeth.*

She understood now that when she pulled the face-guard mask over her face while they robbed the bank, it wasn't to hide from the guards. It was to hide from herself.

Suddenly, she heard blackbirds swooping out of the trees. She looked through the crack of a boarded-up window. Who was coming? The only way into the tunnel was through the mouth of the cave. No one but her knew about the secret passageway. Was Lukus returning from the past?

She stopped at the curved second-floor banister. Looked down to the lobby. Too high. Can't go down.

. . . *whatever goes up can come down* . . .

So Nikki was ready to try. She gripped the banister so tight her fingers hurt. She closed her eyes. One step down. Another. Another. Don't faint. Don't fall. At the bottom she dropped to the floor. All right. She did it. Maybe some day she'll be able to climb higher.

. . . *whatever comes down can go back up* . . .

She dug into her purse and pulled out the officer's gun. Now, slowly, through the basement to the brick passageway. She retraced her steps to the rusty iron gate. Out the dirt tunnel and into the cave. She moved the bushes aside and cocked the gun.

What insane spirit was coming to see her in the asylum after visiting hours?

CHAPTER SIXTY-SIX

Fatima looked up at the sprawling mansion on a cliff. The Waybridge Mental Health Center. That euphemism always annoyed her. An asylum was an asylum. The word surely didn't bother the insane. It merely made politicians and professors feel guilty.

She turned the Jaguar off Route 33 onto the road leading to the building. A blue Mercedes in the parking lot suggested someone was in the building. But when she approached she found the entrance and windows boarded.

She walked up the footpath, stepping carefully to avoid rocks and holes. A twisted ankle would be disastrous. Suddenly, the whoosh of flapping wings startled her. Dozens of blackbirds swooped out of the trees, flying around the bell tower into the sky.

"Raven!" she called, "I know you are here! No need to hide from me! Come out, come out, wherever you are!"

A voice from the bushes. "Here I am Major Fatima."

"Raven, did your blackbirds warn you I was coming?"

"Not particularly you. Only that someone was approaching these dangerous grounds."

"I see you are carrying your handbag. Are you going out somewhere?"

"I keep it with me, in case I have to leave in a hurry. What brings you to my humble mad abode?"

"I have come to help you. Let us go inside. There must be a nurses' lounge where we can sit and talk."

Raven turned and led the way. "I'll put up water for tea or coffee."

"We Persians prefer strong coffee."

In the kitchenette, she saw Raven open a can of Sterno. The girl's hand trembled as she took a wooden match from the box. Dropped it, but carefully removed another one. She struck it against the side of the box. The match broke. She took out a third match, scratched it against the box, and stared at the flame. She lit the Sterno, put a kettle on and blew out the match.

Very different from her behavior during Red Wednesday. No longer terrified of fire? "Have you been seeing a therapist? Your pyrophobia appears to be under control."

"The court ordered Dr. Kyle to help me overcome my fears."

"That is wonderful, Raven. Perhaps it will help you find your way back to our true faith."

"Islam? I don't think so. I'm back in my own country."

"There are many Muslims in America."

"Sure, many good ones. But I suspect you're referring to the militant jihadists who want to convert us or kill us."

"You swore allegiance to Islam willingly."

"If you call conversion during brainwashing, willing."

"How about your acrophobia? Has your therapist helped you conquer fear of heights?"

"He started. I'm progressing on my own."

"You have changed, Raven. You appear stronger."

"Thank you. So, is there still a death order—what do you call it?—a fatwa for any Muslim to kill me? Is that why you're here?"

"That depends on you. You have information MEK needs. I have authority to revoke the fatwa."

"What information?"

"The last quatrain of Jason Tedescu's prophecy you memorized."

"Dr. Kyle and I worked out part of it." She hesitated. "I'm not supposed to tell anyone."

"MEK and 17N are now allies. Tedescu wanted you to share it with us. Did the third part describe the method for spreading the weapon?"

"I remember some of it, but I don't know what it means."

"Tell me the lines. I'll help you interpret them."

"What about the fatwa? Are you canceling it?"

"Not until all the prophecies are revealed."

"That's blackmail."

"Call it what you want."

"Then to hell with you and your *Mujihadeen-e Kalq*."

Obviously, a petulant Raven was of no further use. Time to get rid of her. "All right, do not get excited. Let us think about this." The kettle whistled. "Join me in a coffee."

"I'll just have warm milk."

"While you are preparing it, I will use the washroom."

"It's right around the corner."

Once inside, she took the vial with the rest of the arsenic and palmed it. Then she returned to the kitchenette.

Raven put the glass of milk and the cup on the table. "Here. As you said, Persians like strong coffee."

"Also very sweet. Like you. Do you have more sugar?"

She waited until Raven went to the cupboard. Then she quickly emptied the arsenic into Raven's milk.

After the stupid girl drank it, she would watch her die in agony as she had watched Rashid. Then, for the second time in two days, she would *turn down an empty glass*.

Chapter Sixty-seven

As Raven turned back with the sugar bowl, she noticed Fatima's hand jerk away from the glass of milk. The clenched jaw and intense gaze changed to a forced smile as she stirred the sugar in her coffee. "You need no longer be concerned about the fatwa."

. . . a poker player's tell if I ever saw one . . .

"How come?" she asked. "You said the Quran demands that an apostate be executed."

"There are different interpretations of the sharia."

She leaned her elbows on the table. "What's *sharia?*"

"Islamic law."

"Jesus! American law about special extradition. Islamic law about execution. I'm getting sick of the whole thing." As she rose and turned quickly, her elbow knocked over her milk, shattering the glass. "Boy, I'm getting clumsier every day."

No mistaking Fatima's changed expression, from being startled at what looked like an accident, to fury. "Here, Raven, let me help you pick up the pieces."

"That's all right. I can handle it."

Fatima bent down and came up with a shard of glass. She raised it like a dagger. "But can you handle this?"

Backing away, she pulled the chair between herself and Fatima. She grabbed her purse hanging from the armrest and fled from the lounge. Fatima blocked her way to the tunnel. "Today, your blood will be sacrificed to Allah."

Only one way to go.

"You cannot escape up the stairs, Raven. Heights terrify you."

Hesitated. Then grabbed the banister and pulled herself up the steps. She swung her handbag and hit the side of Fatima's head.

"For that I will cut you slowly, Raven."

Up to the first landing. Then yanked herself around the curved banister to the second flight of stairs. As Fatima reached for her, she spun around and kicked. Fatima fell. "Oh, you will beg me to kill you quickly, but there is no mercy for an apostate."

Up to the third landing. Fatima closing the distance. Then the fourth. Don't look down. Past Daddy's quarters on the fifth floor. Up. Up. She burst through the door to the parapet. Slammed it.

But Fatima came through behind her. "No escape, Raven or Nikki or whoever you are. You can jump from the parapet, but you cannot run. Death by stabbing or hurtling down the mountain. Choose."

"Like hell." She dug into her handbag and pulled out the deputy's revolver. Cocked it. "Now you choose, Fatima. Toppling down the mountain like my mother, or taking a bullet between your eyes."

Fatima lunged at the gun barrel. Grabbed to wrench it away. Then, twisting. Both of them falling against the tower. The gun went off. Once. Twice. Three times. Spatter of blood. Smell of blood. Slickess of blood. Whose? She fell back.

When she came to, she saw Fatima crumpled against the bell tower. The gold crescent necklace lay twisted on the parapet. She picked it up and started to throw it down the cliff. She stopped herself. What the hell. She had reversed the fatwa. She went to Fatima and refastened the crescent around her neck. She stood the body on the tower facing Mecca. Would Allah recognize Fatima without a face?

The whoosh of wings and swooping blackbirds scared the shit out of her.

Who else was coming?

Must get back down to find out. She opened the tower door and started forward. But looking down through the curved stairwell made her dizzy. Don't look. Only one way. Like when she was a baby. She dropped to her knees and crawled backward, one step at a time, down to the lobby.

Once again, blackbirds darkening the sky had come to warn her.

But who the hell was coming to kill her now?

CHAPTER SIXTY-EIGHT

Kyle trudged up the path toward the asylum's main entrance. As he passed a stand of sycamores, a flock of cawing crows swooped out—a dark cloud in the morning sky.

"Stop right there, whoever you are!"

He recognized Raven's voice but kept walking.

"Take another step and I'll shoot!"

He looked around. "Where are you?"

"You deaf, mister, or you want to die?"

He stopped. "I'm looking for Raven!"

She emerged from a tangle of bushes. "Put your hands up where I can see them."

"Raven, it's me. Dr. Kyle—you know—Marty."

She ran to him. "Oh, Marty, I'm so sorry. Didn't mean to scare you. How did you know where to find me?"

"You said you were committed here during your childhood. I figured you for a homing pigeon."

"You're still so cute," she said.

"Can we talk?"

"Depends on whether it's shrink to patient, or if you're gonna let the court send me back to Greece to be tortured."

"Shrink to patient."

"Okay." She waved for him to approach.

"So you *did* move into this deserted asylum."

"Sure. Before my father took me to Greece, it was my home on and off for nearly ten years."

"I can hardly believe you're conquering your acrophobia. Last time we were here you wouldn't even look up."

"Nikki fought against her fear of heights the way you taught me to overcome my fear of fire."

"I'd like to see the inside of the asylum."

She slipped the gun back into her purse. "Then enter my nest, quoth the Raven to her shrink."

He followed, unsure of his footing on the dirt path.

She switched on a flashlight, illuminating a dead end. Then an unexpected right turn, through a rusty gate, into a brick-lined tunnel.

"How did you know about this cave and tunnel?"

"An old caretaker—Lukus—showed me. After that I used to explore when I was locked up here."

He could hardly breathe the fetid air.

"Hold your nose, Marty. Air is better inside."

He followed her up stone steps grooved over the ages by boots and unshod feet.

When she led him out of the cellar into the lobby, he saw her look up at the curved staircase. She gripped the banister with her left hand and took his with her right. One step up. Then another. He hadn't used rapid implosion therapy for acrophobia. She was really doing it to herself.

She pointed to a doorway. "Second floor!" she sang out, "Admissions! Intensive Treatment! Dispensary! Commissary!"

"It must be painful being here by yourself. You once told me you couldn't tolerate being alone. Yet, here you are with no one—"

"Oh, I'm not alone. My lunatic ghosts keep me company. Don't worry. They won't bother you, as long as you don't harm me." She curled up on a settee and motioned for him to join her.

He took a chair across from her. "Do you know why your father locked you up here before he transferred to Athens?"

"Whenever I had what he called a *schizophrenic episode*, he treated me like any other hallucinating patient."

"Now, can you tell me what happened when you were held hostage by 17N and MEK?"

Her eyes widened. "Those weren't real. They were scenes in a movie."

Back off. Don't confront her. Enter the world of her theatrical delusions. "Did you like the part you performed?"

"I-I'm not sure."

"Do you recall the major scenes?"

She put her hands to her face and spoke between her fingers. "I've done so many. Everything is out of focus. In one act, I was locked in a closet for a long time. Then I helped rob a bank. I was almost killed in a firebombing at the Piraeus air terminal. Then in act two I was on a train trip to a place where women wear military uniforms."

He had to lead her from delusions to actual memories. "As with most fine actors, you must have drawn on real life experiences. It's called *method acting*."

"You're right."

Slowly, bring her into reality. "How much did you draw on your real hostage period of sensory deprivation in the closet for that scene?"

She looked into space. Then she described her agony during those first days as a hostage. "At first, Alexi's father was going to rape me. Then Alexi called me the spawn of American oil-hungry oppressors. He said he was tempted to cut me to pieces and throw me to the wolves."

"They must have had a purpose for brainwashing you and keeping you alive. Do you have any idea why?"

"Things come to me but then vanish. I hear frightening things I can't believe I'll forget. When I awake, they're like fade-outs."

He tried to evaluate the stress in her voice. Disassociation? Depersonalization? Derealization? Still, he had to press her. "17N members who were finally captured told the Greek antiterrorist task force that you became one of them. You drove the getaway motorcycle during the bank robbery, and the van during the Piraeus terminal bombing."

"I told you they were movie scenes in which I was held prisoner."

"According to those who were arrested and interrogated, you had chances to escape."

"Help me remember, Marty."

"Let's try. Close your eyes. Imagine yourself in that scene, back in the dark closet."

"No!"

"You're now able to control your fear of fire and of heights by flooding your mind with those images. If you want to get through this, you'll have work with me."

Her eyes closed, fluttering under the lids.

"The dark closet," he said. "You hear conversations through the closed door."

A trembling silence. "Someone is saying, 'Operation Dragon's Teeth.'"

"Go on."

"Sowing teeth like seeds. Seeds of death."

"What else?"

"Sleeping warriors."

"Did whoever it was mention the targets?"

She opened her eyes. "That's all I hear."

"Are you sure?"

". . . damn it! of course . . . !"

He backed off at the sound of Nikki's higher voice. Risky to keep pressing hard, but many lives were at stake.

"You don't have to worry any longer about hiding Tedescu's message. Most of 17N members were captured after the Piraeus firebombing. 17N and MEK are defeated."

She stared trancelike. Her voice dropped to a Raven whisper. "Did you say, *17N and MEK are defeated?*"

"Does that mean something to you?"

She squeezed her fists. "I can talk only to the person who says, *17N and MEK are defeated.* I don't understand."

"Your clinical director father, who was directing your performance, must have implanted posthypnotic cues behind your phobias. It has been preventing you from reciting Tedescu's prophecies. But you must tell the FBI."

"How can I tell them what I don't know?"

"Maybe you know more than you're aware of. Do you remember the lines you performed for Tedescu before he died?"

"No. Wait! Yes. The script called for him to choke me to death. But the curtain came down suddenly."

"That was surely a great performance. Did you reenact the scene for anyone else?"

"I tried to tell my father, but he said it wasn't safe for him to know. Oh my God! Then he killed himself."

"He hypnotized you to protect you, but—now that you've broken through the phobias—you can recall the quatrains."

She closed her eyes. "I remember the lines."

"Go ahead. The curtain is rising. You're on."

" '*Unfaced goddess guards future from the windswept tower. And in serious hate she butchers flesh of all.*' "

"Does a goddess without a face suggest anything to you?"
She hesitated. Lips pressed tight. Eyes flicked upward for

an instant. Something on a higher floor? Something on the parapet? Better still not probe too hard.

"Set that aside for now, Raven. The next lines?"

" 'Escaped Bull-man stops 'neath the sunken wall.
DEATH PENALTY EXPLODES FIVE-PETALED
    FLOWER.' "

"Excellent, Raven. The agents figured out the third line means the New York Stock Exchange, and the fourth means the Pentagon. They know the first city is Chicago, but they haven't been able to solve the target. The windswept tower."

She rubbed her eyes. "Wait! Now that you mention it, once—when Mr. Tedescu was giving the cast notes—he spoke about the year a forty-five-story building was completed. He said it was the highest one in Chicago."

"Did he ever mention the *Unfaced Goddess?*"

"His words were actually *Faceless Goddess*. He boasted that he discovered her."

"Why *faceless?* Why *serious hate?*"

"He liked puns. Serious . . . serious. Wait . . . I remember. *Serious* stands for *Ceres*."

"The Roman goddess of the harvest. On the tower? Of course, guarding the future because that's where people invest in *futures:* wheat, corn, and hogs and cows to be butchered. The target is the hub of capitalist futures trading. *The Chicago Board of Trade*."

She threw her arms around him. "We're a duo. We solved it together."

"But why is Ceres *faceless* on the *windswept tower?*"

"Tedescu said the building was the tallest in Chicago at the time. The sculptor, who was commissioned on the cheap, figured no one would be able to actually see the face. So he left it blank."

"One last scene to interpret. *HOW* are the sleepers to spread the weapon at those targets. Anything come to mind?"

She rubbed her eyes. "I'm tired, Marty."

"All right. Get some rest. I'll be back tomorrow."

"What? You can't leave, Marty. Spend the night here with me."

"That's not possible, Raven. You've got to get used to the idea that when people have to go somewhere, they're not abandoning you. I'll be back tomorrow, and then—"

"*You're* not making an exit!"

Her hand dug into her handbag. When it came out she was holding the gun. He tried to turn. Felt a sharp blow to the back of his head. Mustn't die. Have to tell Dugan what he learned. But nothing to hold on to while he was falling . . . falling . . . falling . . . pushed by the faceless goddess off the windswept tower.

CHAPTER SIXTY-NINE

Kyle awoke with his head throbbing. "Where . . . ? What . . . ?"

Light blinded him as the door opened. "You'll be all right, Marty. I didn't mean to hit you so hard. You mustn't leave me."

He stood. "Never mind. I'll be okay."

"It was wrong to put you in a dark room. That's what they did to me in the safe house."

"This isn't a safe house, Raven."

"Oh, you're wrong. I can defend my castle against all invaders."

"Raven, listen. There's very little time. I have to show the court you've overcome the brainwashing—"

"What brainwashing?"

"—or Judge Rodriguez will order you rendered back to Greece to be interrogated."

"Tell me! What brainwashing?"

"What Alexi did to you when he kept you locked in the dark, then turned lights on and off to keep you awake."

"He didn't brainwash me!"

"Then how do you explain your transformation, from a young actress, to a terrorist?"

"I'm not a terrorist."

"You worked with them."

"It's not the same thing."

"Helped rob a bank? The bombing at Piraeus?"

She ran her fingers through her hair, twisting a blonde lock. "I told you, those were scenes from a movie."

He staggered out of the small room into the kitchen. She followed. He washed his face with rusty water, and she handed him a towel.

"Raven, have you ever heard of the Stockholm syndrome?"

"Like Patty Hearst? I read about her when I was young. What's that got to do with me?"

"Like you, after she was taken hostage, she came to identify with her captors. Like you, she helped rob a bank. She was convicted and spent time in prison. Eventually she was paroled and finally pardoned."

"I can't go to prison."

"You might not be convicted."

"Will they really extradite me to Athens?"

"Probably, since that's where you committed the crimes."

"I couldn't survive in Greece. At least here I have my guardians."

"What guardians?"

"I told you. My ghosts."

Another psychotic episode? "Tell me about them."

"Those who die in this madhouse can never leave. I'll be with them for eternity."

"So why did you come back here?"

"To atone for my evil side. The evil me they created when they cut off my wings and named me Nikki."

Now he understood her identification with the name *Apteros* was *Wingless Nike*. "But we just established that you were brainwashed."

"You established it. I didn't."

"Raven, how else could they have turned you into an anti-American terrorist in such a short time?"

"Alexi showed me America didn't care about me. Not a word in the papers about me being kidnapped."

"Your captor-lover betrayed you, just as your father did. Raven, you're suffering from betrayal trauma."

"Bullshit trauma! I don't want to hear any more! *You're* doing the brainwashing!"

She had a point. Maybe rapid implosion therapy was a form of brainwashing. But he was doing this to save her, not to dominate her. "What are you feeling now, Raven?"

"I betrayed my comrades. Because of me, most of them were caught and thrown into prison."

"In a way, that's your atonement. You're free now."

"You still don't understand. I said, *most of them*. Myron wasn't captured. Alexi is trying to find me to save or kill me . . . or Nikki."

"The reality is that he needs to kill you so you won't be extradited to Greece where you might expose *Operation Dragon's Teeth* under torture."

"Alexi wouldn't do that. He loves me. We'll defend ourselves here in Camelot."

Another histrionic delusion? He had to break through. "Raven, have you had any dreams since you've been back here?"

"Yes, day and night. Asleep and awake. A strange one— over and over." Suddenly, her eyes opened wide. She clamped her hand over her mouth.

"You're having an association, Raven. Aren't you?"

"Oh, my God!"

"Go on."

"Something I overheard about terrorist cells planted in America by Mr. Tedescu for Second Generation 17N and MEK."

"Don't try to analyze it. Let it come into awareness."

"When Alexi has nightmares, he talks in his sleep."

"He talks about *sleepers* in his sleep?"

"He never said *sleepers*. He called them something else—more like *cleaners*."

"Do you know what he meant?"

"That they're essential to *Operation Dragon's Teeth*."

"Did he ever talk about what the sleepers or cleaners were there to do?"

She put her hand to her mouth and shook her head.

"Raven, it's urgent. Thousands of innocent people could suffer a horrible death."

"Alexi wouldn't do that."

"What would you say if I told you MEK smuggled a deadly strain of weaponized anthrax into the States for 17N's home-grown sleepers to use."

"I don't believe you. Alexi wouldn't be part of that."

"Do you know what the spread of anthrax could do to thousands—millions—of innocent men, women and children?"

"I've heard of anthrax, but I don't know what it is."

His last chance at rapid image-flooding. It would either desensitize her or drive her over the edge. "As a doctor, I've read reports issued by the World Health Organization. Victims who inhale anthrax spores won't know they've been affected. All they'll feel are stuffed noses, joint pain, dry coughing and exhaustion. Visualize it. At the first symptoms, their doctors might diagnose flu. If discovered right away, it can be treated with antibiotics. But they won't know."

"I don't want to hear any more."

"A few days later, anthrax *eclipse* sets in. People will assume they're getting better—"

"That's enough!"

"Listen! It's important that you know what will happen unless you help us stop them. After the eclipse, bacteria penetrate the lymph nodes. In just a few hours they engulf the entire lymphatic system and release a toxin that attacks all the organs—especially the lungs. It cuts off the oxygen supply."

"You're cruel. Are you trying to drive me crazy?"

"I want to help you wipe out the lies Alexi planted in your mind. He made you believe your own people are evil."

"We are. We are."

"17N and MEK enlisted you in their terrorist plot to kill innocent children who'll die in school yards and playgrounds if you don't see the light. Dying babies being wheeled in strollers by their mothers."

"I'm as guilty as the others. I helped rob the bank so they'd have money to pay for that horrible stuff."

"You can atone by helping stop him."

"I still don't think Alexi would do anything like that."

"In twenty-four hours the anthrax victim's skin begins to turn blue. Breathing becomes incredibly painful. Visualize it. Choking fits, convulsions, then, suddenly—"

"Stop!

"—death."

"I said stop!"

"Only you can stop it, Raven."

He saw her holding back tears.

"You're manipulating me, turning me against the man I love."

"MEK and 17N sleepers are going to spread this plague in the three targets. But we don't know *how*. Time is running out. I need you to help figure out how."

Her voice hardened. "Are you going to tell all this to the judge?"

"Judge Rodriguez ordered me to treat you and report back to her."

She looked dead calm. "Do what you have to do. And I'll do what I have to do."

"Can't we talk this over?"

"Enough talk! You should be able to find your way out through the tunnel."

She left the room and slammed the door behind her.

He stood there for a long time, then went down to the basement, through the tunnel, out of the gate, into the cave.

When he reached his car he phoned Dugan. "This is Kyle. Call off JPATS. There's no need to render her to Athens. I've had a breakthrough."

"I'm listening."

"*The Faceless Goddess* is a statue of *Ceres* with an unfinished face at the top of the Chicago Board of Trade."

"Are you sure what she told you is credible?"

"You're FBI. It's for you to determine."

"All the more reason for *extraordinary rendition*."

"Why? You've got what you need."

"Not all of it. Alexi and Myron are still at large. MEK is still in play, and time is running out. If she was able to retrieve the rest of *where*, and knows *what*, then she probably knows *how* the sleepers are going to spread the anthrax."

"You don't need her to find them."

"That's for the antiterrorist task force to verify. I'm ordering the marshals to pick her up."

"Give me a little more time. I'll try to find out *how* the anthrax will be spread."

"We can't wait any longer."

"Just twenty-four hours. I'll go back inside and flood her mind with more images."

"Not possible."

"Otherwise, she might kill herself."

"We have to take that gamble."

He heard Tia's voice in the background. "Twenty-four more hours won't make that much difference."

Dugan hesitated. "Okay, Kyle, twenty-four and your job is

done. Then Justice and Prisoner Transport System flies her back to Greece."

"You won't be sorry, I'll do my—"

But Dugan's phone went dead.

He turned off his own cell phone and looked up at the asylum. In the ancient legend, the Athenians cut off the wings of their goddess to prevent Wingless Victory from ever flying away from the Athens Acropolis.

He had the feeling that Raven-Nikki—like Nike Apteros—would never fly away from her mountain asylum.

CHAPTER SEVENTY

Alexi pulled into the road leading to the Waybridge Asylum. A blue Mercedes and a red Jaguar in the parking lot. So Raven was here, but who else? He removed the package with the attaché case from the van. No sense risking it being stolen.

As he passed the rusted fountain in the dead garden, a flock of blackbirds swooped out of the trees. Why were they called a *murder* of crows?

At the main entrance, the door and windows were boarded up. He shouted, "Hello! Anybody here?"

No answer.

He shouted again. "Anyone inside?"

Rustling branches. *"Stop shouting! You'll wake the dead!"* Raven's voice from the bushes off to his left. *"I have a gun! Tell me who you are, or I'll shoot!"*

A bluff? No sense taking chances. "It's me. Alexi."

"Walk slowly to the west side of the building, but keep your hands in the air where I can see them."

"Is it you, Nikki? I've been searching for you."

He saw her rise from a clump of bushes. If she had a gun, he would be an easy target. "How did you know someone was here?"

"If birds gather on any spot," she said, "it is unoccupied. Clamor by night betokens nervousness."

"Ah, you remember me quoting from Sun Tzu's *Art of War*. You were never the fool you pretended to be."

"In the tarot, *Fool* is the zero key." She laughed. "But this is not the *Lightning-Struck Tower*. You see, my windswept tower still stands, and I'm the *High Priestess*."

So she recalled Tedescu's quatrains. Proceed carefully not to spook her. "May I approach, Your Holiness?"

"Why are you here, Alexi?"

He reached the path close to her. "To find my soul mate."

She pointed to the package. "What are you carrying?"

"A present for you, sweetheart."

"Let me see it."

"Later, darling. It's a reunion surprise."

"Come inside the secret place of my childhood."

"The entrance is sealed. How do we get in?"

She led him through the cave and passageway. He was surprised when they came out into the cellar, then up to the lobby.

"Where are you taking me?"

"To the room behind the nurses' station."

When they reached the second landing, she led him past a counter to a small room. "This is where the nurses took their rest breaks. Now, I come here often."

He felt his hand twitch in hers. Careful, don't let her suspect. If she'd remembered all the prophetic riddles, he couldn't take the chance she'd tell the FBI.

He felt sorry, then wiped sorrow from his mind. He wanted to treasure the memory of their last time together.

CHAPTER SEVENTY-ONE

She knew Kyle was mistaken. Alexi loved her. They could make a life together.

"It must have been painful," Alexi said, "to be here alone reliving your past horrors."

She wanted to say she was never alone in this place, but was he ready to hear about her guardian spirits? She clung to his arm. "Now that you're here to protect me, I'll never again be alone."

"That sounds like a prophecy."

When his forehead creased in a frown, she felt something was wrong.

He was looking around the nurses' room. "All the comforts of home. Only one problem. That cot is too narrow for both of us."

"My father's suite has a double bed on the fifth floor." She saw his surprise. "You can go up—?"

"I've been working to conquer my fear of heights."

She led him up to the fifth floor. So long since they'd been together. Then, outside herself for a moment, she felt death was close by.

. . . stop being morbid. don't spoil it . . .

Her hand trembled as she reached for the doorknob. "I once saw something in this room too terrible to remember."

"Get it off your chest. You don't want to carry a horrible vision to your—"

"Is it right to betray my father's memory? He wouldn't want anyone to know."

"Was he unfaithful to your mother?"

"Worse."

"Was it with one of the nurses?"

"Much worse."

"You and I are kindred souls, Nikki. Did he abuse you?"

She paused when he called her Nikki. Then she looked at the hand on the knob. Hers? She couldn't open the door. "He never touched me. It was a patient. A boy I cared for. My father called it puppy love. I saw him rape my puppy."

"That's sick."

"He was on top, and the boy cried out, 'No more, Dr. Slade! You're hurting me! I'll tell!'"

"Your father deserved to die."

"There's more," she said. She went to the bed and pulled off the spread. "If I see it again, maybe it'll wipe the stain from my mind."

The sheet beneath was dirty brown.

"He must have fouled himself," Alexi said.

"No. It's my puppy love's dried blood. He didn't commit suicide as my father wrote in the report. I saw him cut the boy's throat. That was the second time he committed me to the asylum—"

"Why didn't he throw away the sheet?"

"I don't think he ever came back to this room."

She slipped out of her jeans and panties, took off her shirt, undid her bra.

"What are you doing?"

"Getting ready to make love."

She undid his belt, pulled down his trousers.

"In this bed? That's sick."

"That's what I am. *Sick*. Dr. Kyle says I've got to flood my mind with images. If we do it on the spot where my father raped and killed him, maybe I can exorcise the evil. If only I'd been born a boy."

"I can't make love to you on this bed, Nikki."

"I know you, Alexi. You can." She pulled down his briefs. "See, of course you can."

"I want to, Nikki, but I won't profane our last—"

"Why last?"

"I love you, Nikki."

"If you did, you wouldn't have cut off my wings. Are you going to kill me afterwards?"

"That doesn't make sense, Nikki."

"Then show me." She pulled him on top of her.

She trembled when he kissed her throat, her breasts, her navel. Ran his hands down her waist, between her legs and stroked until her body vibrated.

"Inside," she moaned. "I need you now more than ever."

He slid in. Gently. Faster and faster until she cried.

The movie screen moved in slow motion; then the camera panned away to clouds drifting in the sky.

He rolled off her and clasped his hands under his head. "Usually fall asleep after sex, but I'm wide-awake."

"I'll get you a glass of warm milk. That'll help."

He nodded. "It's been a long day. I need sleep."

Without putting on a robe, she made her way to the nurses' rest area and checked her supplies. Powdered milk would do. She put the kettle on the Sterno can, and lit it quickly. Good. She was in control. As she put milk into a glass, she remembered the sleeping powder. It would give him a good night's rest. She added the powder and took it back to the bedroom.

"This will relax you."

He downed it. "I appreciate you taking care of me."

"I'll take good care of you from now on."

His eyelids flickered, then closed. Soon he began to snore. She covered him with the blanket and lay beside him.

She expected to fall asleep quickly, but Alexi moaned and rolled over, away from her. Murmuring in his sleep, "*Sweepers . . . Tubes . . . Air conditioners blowing . . . A blow against our enemy . . .*"

He mumbled the words again, and again. What was he saying in his sleep? *Sweepers? Tubes? Air conditioners?*

She recalled Kyle's words about anthrax death. How it killed children, even babies. Slowly. Horribly.

She was curious about the gift he'd brought her. She slipped out of the bedroom into her father's adjoining office. Why couldn't she bear to have clothes touch her body? Maybe she wanted to be Eve in the Garden. Before the tree, before the apple, before the fall.

She stripped the brown wrapping off the package and stared. An aluminum attaché case. What kind of present was that? She tried to open it, but there was a combination lock.

. . . try seventeen . . .

She counted. 1–7. *N* was the twenty-fourth letter of the alphabet. 1–7–2–4. She spun the dial. The lock clicked open. Inside, embedded in cotton, she saw dozens of thin glass tubes. Each had a strip of leather with pointed metal studs like dogs' collars fastened around the middle.

Alexi intended to spread anthrax in the three target buildings. Kyle had made her see the consequences. People choking, turning blue. Men, women, innocent children.

She saw something green protruding from under the cotton padding. She moved it carefully and stared at bundles of hundred-dollar bills.

Was it the money she'd helped him rob from the Athens Bank? Money to pay for terrible deaths?

But why were the metal studs in the leather facing *inward* against the glass tubes?

Then . . . remembering . . . a boy in school who, in exchange for an openmouthed kiss, gives her a leather wristband. It's raining. They run into a barn. Kissing, hugging. After a while, her wrist hurts as the drying leather shrinks, the buckle digging into her skin.

. . . *as three-Dog's collars break each death-filled glass* . . .

She remembered from one of Tedescu's lectures that Heracles' twelfth labor was to capture the three-headed dog.

But the studs of *these* leather collars were wrapped *inward against the tubes.* If they were wet and shrank, the studs would break the glass. But how would that spread the anthrax?

. . . *aeolus hot-cold breath each spring and fall* . . .

Air conditioners!

She checked Alexi's cell phone menu and found programmed listings. Names and numbers with the word, *Sweepers.*

. . . *not sleepers. the sweepers who clean the buildings at night* . . .

She had to tell Marty. She dialed Kyle's number with trembling fingers.

A groggy voice. "What?"

"Don't come back to the asylum," she whispered. "Alexi is here. Talked in his sleep. When he wakes I'm sure he plans to kill me. He brought anthrax-filled tubes. He's going to distribute them to *sweepers—not sleepers—* in the three targets. They're not suicide bombers. They'll have time to get away. As they're cleaning the buildings at night, I figured out they'll wet the studded leather bands and put each tube into an air-conditioning ventilator. When the leather dries and shrinks, the metal spikes will crack the glass tubes. *Aeolus hot-cold breath* in the air conditioners will blow the anthrax powder through each building."

She heard his gasp. "Thousands will die."

"What should I do?"

"Run."

"Where to? I hate him but I can't leave."

"I'm calling SWAT and the marshals."

"No time. I'll deal with it myself."

"How?"

. . . break the damned tubes . . .

"Don't you or anyone else enter the building," she said. "This stuff will contaminate the whole asylum."

"Wait, Raven—!"

She clicked off.

She felt Alexi come up behind her. *"Who are you talking to?"*

She dropped his cell phone and grabbed the tubes from the attaché case.

"What's wrong, Nikki? Why did you get out of bed?"

She faced him. "You manipulated me. I know you're going to leave me."

"Not true. I'll take you with me to a hideaway. I have lots of money. We can be together for a long time."

She held one tube over her head. "According to what I've been told about anthrax, if I break this, it will give us about a week to live."

"I swear, I planned to take you with me."

"Tell me you love me."

"I love you."

She held out her arms. "One final caress? Our bodies touching."

He took her into his arms.

She clenched a tube in her left hand. "I see you still want me," she whispered. "Kiss me." Her hand went to her mouth.

Slipped the tube between her teeth. Before he could stop her, she forced his lips open with her tongue and bit the tube. Glass broke inside both their mouths. She ignored the splintering pain.

Saving thousands with a murder-suicide kiss.

"No!"

She whispered through bleeding lips, "You can never leave me, Alexi."

"You're insane again. I'm getting out of here."

"Too late, Alexi. That was the anthrax kiss of death."

"Then I'll die a martyr. I still have time to sow the dragon's seed with the rest of the tubes."

She pulled away and ran to the banister. Stopped. Looked down the stairwell. Closed her eyes. Sucked a deep breath. What the hell. She was dying anyway.

Stumbling down the curving staircase, she smashed a few tubes against the wall. Struggled to her feet and ran down again. He was behind her. Flung more tubes.

Fourth floor. Third. Second. First.

All gone.

He grabbed her. "You don't know what you've done."

"You said we were soul mates. I've saved thousands of souls as well as our own."

"You're mad."

She laughed. "Of course. They won't be able to demolish our contaminated asylum for years. We can make love here until we turn blue, Alexi. Let's not waste the last days we have flesh on our bodies."

He pulled away. "I'm leaving."

"Where can you run, carrying death inside you? The death you brought here has infected this madhouse. We have about a week of lovemaking together in our asylum tomb."

"You fool! What are you saying? We *don't* have time."

"Do you believe in an afterlife, Alexi?"

"Yes, but I prefer *this* life."

"We'll have each other for a long time, Alexi."

"What do you mean? How long can it be?"

She whispered in his ear, ". . . *as quoth the raven, forevermore* . . ."

POSTSCRIPT

Actual Events

After the Piraeus bombing, Greek police found an arms caché in the safe house. Most 17N terrorists were captured and tried. On December 7, 2003, fifteen were found guilty and sentenced to life imprisonment. Four were acquitted.

Shortly afterward, a message was sent to the media: *"We are still alive."*

At 6:00 A.M., on January 12, 2007, the United States embassy in Athens was attacked with a shoulder-fired missile. A Second Generation terrorist group calling itself "Revolutionary Struggle," claimed responsibility.

According to the *New York Times*, in June 2007, two men and a woman in Athens were caught rigging a police car with homemade bombs. These were the first new arrests in months of nighttime bombings of banks and tax offices. Ten terrorists were spotted throwing Molotov cocktails at a Eurobank branch. The fire was extinguished, but the bombers escaped.

The original 17N leader (here called Myron Costa) has never been found. It is assumed he is hiding on one of the more than 1,400 Greek Islands in the Aegean and Ionian seas.

In Ashraf, *Mujihadeen-e Kalq* leaders are still waiting for the State Department and Pentagon to resolve their differences about removing MEK from the list of terrorists. They hope the Pentagon will prevail and allow them to participate in what they foresee as the inevitable war against Iran. Several senators, Republicans and Democrats, support them. Others oppose that action.

Sergeant William Sutherland is quoted in the *Washington Post* of November 9, 2003, as saying "they're not terrorists— rather they're patriots." Former secretary of state Colin L. Powell, on the other hand, suggested to former defense secretary Donald H. Rumsfeld that *Mujihadeen-e Kalq* forces are not U.S. allies, but captives.

According to the *New York Times* of July 27, 2004, the U.S. military designated the *Mujihadeen-e Kalq* as "protected persons" covered by the fourth Geneva convention immunity against expulsion. The *Christian Science Monitor* wrote on July 29, ". . . protected persons status is a victory for the hawks who favor using MEK against Iran."

According to February 14, 2005, *Newsweek*, the Bush administration intended to use MEK operatives against Iran, and the Pentagon hoped to give some MEK prisoners ". . . training as spies . . ."

A member of Iraq's parliament was convicted and sentenced to death in absentia in Kuwait for planning attacks on American and French embassies during which five Americans were killed. According to the *New York Times* February 7, 2007, he was identified as a terrorist ". . . by Strategic Policy Consulting, an Iranian dissident group in Washington . . . that gets much of its information from the People's *Mujahedeen* (sic), the largest and most militant group opposed to Teheran."

Teheran's leaders still demand that MEK members be returned to Iran, where—it has been alleged—death sentences await them. Other Muslim countries have denied them sanctuary. The controversy between the State Department and the Pentagon has not, as of this date, been resolved.

U.S. military intelligence has been concerned with the possibility of mass suicides inside Ashraf should the United States attempt to dismantle the camp.

In January 2006, the Bulgarian Ministry of Defense assigned 154 soldiers, including thirty-four staff officers (armed with electroshock truncheons and other crowd-control equipment) to control resistance inside the camp in the event the leaders organize resistance against removal of the rank-and-file members. Their major purpose, to prevent mass suicides.

Although the Bulgarians have assumed control over life inside the camp, U.S. forces remain in place outside Ashraf to maintain security in the face of gradual dispersal of the MEK military population.

As of this writing, the fate of MEK, the "Holy Jihadists of the People" in Ashraf, remains in doubt.

Daniel Keyes
Florida—September 1, 2007

INTERACT WITH DORCHESTER ONLINE!

Want to learn more about your favorite books and authors?
Want to talk with other readers that like to read the same books as you?
Want to see up-to-the-minute Dorchester news?

VISIT DORCHESTER AT:
DorchesterPub.com
Twitter.com/DorchesterPub
Facebook.com (Search Pages)

DISCUSS DORCHESTER'S NOVELS AT:
Dorchester Forums at DorchesterPub.com
GoodReads.com
LibraryThing.com
Myspace.com/books
Shelfari.com
WeRead.com

✂ ☐ **YES!**

Sign me up for the Leisure Thriller Book Club and send my FREE BOOKS! If I choose to stay in the club, I will pay only $4.25* each month, a savings of $3.74!

NAME: _____

ADDRESS: _____

TELEPHONE: _____

EMAIL: _____

☐ I want to pay by credit card.

☐ **VISA** ☐ **MasterCard** ☐ **DISCOVER**

ACCOUNT #: _____

EXPIRATION DATE: _____

SIGNATURE: _____

Mail this page along with $2.00 shipping and handling to:
Leisure Thriller Book Club
PO Box 6640
Wayne, PA 19087
Or fax (must include credit card information) to:
610-995-9274

You can also sign up online at **www.dorchesterpub.com**.
*Plus $2.00 for shipping. Offer open to residents of the U.S. and Canada only.
Canadian residents please call 1-800-481-9191 for pricing information.
If under 18, a parent or guardian must sign. Terms, prices and conditions subject to change. Subscription subject to acceptance. Dorchester Publishing reserves the right to reject any order or cancel any subscription.